HONEYMOON WITH THE RANCHER

BY
DONNA ALWARD

AND

NANNY NEXT DOOR

BY
MICHELLE CELMER

MILLS
BOON

Dear Reader,

I love to travel, and I don't do it nearly as often as I like. So when I had the opportunity to include an exotic location in a book, I was in heaven!

Even better was writing about two people falling in love in a great new setting, and watching my heroine move out of her comfort zone as she tried new things— sometimes succeeding, sometimes failing, and most of all learning some important lessons along the way—like trust. Love. And acceptance.

Welcome to Argentina—home of spectacular rainforests, the wide open pampas, and one reclusive gaucho named Tomas, who manages to capture Sophia's heart beneath an ombu tree.

With love,

Donna

HONEYMOON WITH THE RANCHER

BY
DONNA ALWARD

All the characters in this book have no existence outside the imagination of the author, and have no relation whatsoever to anyone bearing the same name or names. They are not even distantly inspired by any individual known or unknown to the author, and all the incidents are pure invention.

First published in Great Britain 2011
Harlequin Mills & Boon Limited,
Eton House, 18-24 Paradise Road, Richmond, Surrey TW9 1SR

© Donna Alward 2011

ISBN: 978 0 263 88867 6

23-0311

Harlequin Mills & Boon policy is to use papers that are natural, renewable and recyclable products and made from wood grown in sustainable forests. The logging and manufacturing processes conform to the legal environmental regulations of the country of origin.

Printed and bound in Spain
by Litografia Rosés S.A., Barcelona

A busy wife and mother of three (two daughters and the family dog), **Donna Alward** believes hers is the best job in the world: a combination of stay-at-home mum and romance novelist. An avid reader since childhood, Donna always made up her own stories. She completed her Arts Degree in English Literature in 1994, but it wasn't until 2001 that she penned her first full-length novel and found herself hooked on writing romance. In 2006 she sold her first manuscript, and now writes warm, emotional stories for the Mills & Boon® Cherish™ line.

In her new home office in Nova Scotia, Donna loves being back on the east coast of Canada after nearly twelve years in Alberta, where her career began, writing about cowboys and the west. Donna's debut Romance, *Hired by the Cowboy*, was awarded the Booksellers Best Award in 2008 for Best Traditional Romance.

With the Atlantic Ocean only minutes from her doorstep, Donna has found a fresh take on life and promises even more great romances in the near future!

Donna loves to hear from readers. You can contact her through her website at www.donnaalward.com, visit her myspace page at www.myspace.com/dalward, or through her publisher.

To Liz Fielding: inspiration, mentor, and friend.
Thank you, Liz, for just being you, and for taking
me under your wise and witty wing.

CHAPTER ONE

"*¿SEÑORITA?* We are here."

Sophia straightened in the seat and peered out the window at the vast plain, her eyebrows snapping together in confusion. Antoine had told her that *Vista del Cielo* translated into View of Heaven. She liked that idea. It conjured up images of wide blue skies dotted with puffy clouds, perhaps seen from a comfortable deck chair with a mimosa in hand. The sky was right, but looking out, Sophia saw nothing but waving grass and a dirt drive flanked by a row of trees. "This can't be it. There must be a mistake."

"No, *señorita*." The driver's accent was thick. "*Esta* Vista del Cielo." He took his hand off the steering wheel and pointed at a small white sign at the end of the long drive.

A sickening, crawling feeling began in Sophia's stomach. The pampas spread out before her, flat and brownish-green. She slid across the back seat and looked out of the other side of the car. It was exactly the same view. On either side the fields spread, endless and dull. Off to her right, one huge gnarled tree looked out of place standing alone, a leafy green sentinel. And ahead, a house. A nice house, but definitely not a hotel. The building was large, a sprawling one story that turned two corners. A low roof over a stone patio added cozy atmosphere and contrasted with white stucco. Flowers in colourful pots stood here and there all along the front patio and another twisted tree formed a soft canopy over one side. It was beautiful, but clearly a family home, not the four or even five-star accommodations Antoine usually insisted upon when booking his travel.

The driver pulled to a stop in front of a shed and put the car into Park. "Don't leave," Sophia commanded. "This is a mistake." She fumbled for the Spanish words. *"Por error,"* she tried. *"No...vayas."* She knew the grammar was incorrect but hoped he'd catch her meaning. Perhaps she should have spent longer learning some important Spanish phrases. She flashed him a smile. She had to find out exactly where she was supposed to be and then get the cab driver to take her there.

"Si, señorita," he replied, and at last got out to open the door for her. This had to be wrong, all wrong. Where were the luxury rooms? The spa and gym? The dining area with a chef and wait staff?

For a moment her bravado failed her. She'd shored it up to make the trip alone, wanting—no, needing—to do this for herself. She'd wanted to find a way to stick it to Antoine for humiliating her so much. What could make a better statement than going on their honeymoon without him?

But that had all been based on things going smoothly and exactly to plan. She finally admitted to herself that she should actually have studied the plan a little more closely. She should have known the route. Especially traveling solo. What would she do now?

Then she remembered what had driven her to this point in her life and she steeled her spine. It had been wrong to accept Antoine's proposal in the first place and discovering his indiscretion had been a disaster. Still, if she had to be thankful for anything it was that she'd found out before the wedding and not after. She had given him three years of her best work, all the while falling for his kind words and sexy smiles. She'd thought herself the luckiest woman ever when he'd asked her out the first time. Marriage had seemed like the next logical step. Everyone had said it was meant to be, and she'd believed them.

But now she knew that Antoine had wanted nothing more than a trophy wife, the proper person on his arm to look good for the public. It wasn't enough for her. She hadn't realized until that moment—walking in on him making love to his mistress—that she wanted more. She didn't want the country club existence that was so important to her mother. She wanted more than appearances. She wanted respect, not betrayal. Love, not suitability.

Acceptance.

And in that defining moment, as her future had crumbled away, she'd found the courage to say no. And to walk away.

Which had led her here. Still, she was sure there had to be a mistake. She took a few steps forward, trying to make out the plaque on the front of the house. It was old and in Spanish, but she made out the words *Vista del Cielo* and the year—1935.

A roar and a cloud of dust had her swinging her head back towards the taxi, only to find the cabbie had dumped her luggage and was now driving back down the lane, tires churning up the dry earth like a dusty vapour trail.

"Wait!" She called after the taxi, running forward as fast as she could in her heels. But he didn't pause or even slow down. In moments he was gone, leaving her stranded with her bags in the middle of Nowhere, Argentina.

Her heart pounded. No one had come from the house to greet her. The place looked abandoned. She took a breath. Told herself to calm down. She would find a way out of this.

What she knew for sure was that she would not panic. She would not cry or indulge in hysterics. She reached for her purse and the cell phone inside, but paused. No. She most definitely would not make a phone call home for her mother to bail her out of trouble. She could handle this on her own.

Her mother had barely spoken to Sophia since she had cancelled the wedding. There was no question of asking Antoine, either. It would be a cold day in hell before she'd ask him for anything ever again.

She took a step forward, feeling the heel of one of her favourite Manolos sink into the soft earth. She gritted her teeth. Why was it that the first time in her life she did anything impulsive, it turned out like this? If it had happened to anyone else, she'd have had a good laugh at the comedy in the situation. But it wasn't happening to someone else, it was happening to her. And the truth was, behind the designer shoes and the skirt and the French manicure, she was scared to death.

She'd been running on righteous indignation for weeks now, and, if she let it, being alone in a strange country could be the straw that broke her back.

"Hola," a voice called out, and she turned her head towards the sound, her shoulders dropping with relief. At least someone was here who could explain the mix-up. Antoine had told her that they were staying at an estancia—a guest ranch—with all the amenities. It had sounded lovely and serene. But she knew Antoine. He never settled for anything except the best. She'd prepared for the trip based on that assumption, and now she wasn't prepared at all. Sometimes it felt as though everything she thought she knew had been turned upside down, and it was hard to find her feet again.

A man stepped out of the shadows by the barn door and Sophia swallowed.

Whatever she had expected to find here in the middle of nowhere, it wasn't this. The man approaching with long, lazy strides was perhaps the best looking male creature she'd ever clapped eyes on. He wore faded jeans and boots and a T-shirt that had seen better days. What was surprising was his face. He had a crown of thick, slightly wavy black hair and gorgeous brown eyes fringed with thick black lashes that most women would die for. The golden tone of the skin over his high cheekbones set his dark looks off to exotic perfection.

What was a man like that doing in a place like this?

"Hello," she called out, attempting to calm her suddenly increased heart rate. She shrugged it off, telling herself that just because she'd sworn off men she wasn't *dead*. She pasted on a smile, fighting to quell the anxiety swirling through her veins. "Perhaps you can help me." After the incident with the cabbie, she felt compelled to add, "Do you speak English? *¿Hablas inglés?*"

"Of course. What is the problem?" His black gaze looked at her suitcases, then her, and then slid down to her feet, to the peacock-blue pumps, one with a now very dirty heel. He raised an eyebrow as he examined the four-inch stilettos and a smile flirted with his lips before he looked back up. She schooled her features into a bland mask. She needed his help, and it didn't matter a bit if he approved of her shoes or not. They would have been perfectly appropriate for the upscale accommodation she'd expected.

"I'm afraid I've been delivered here in error, and the taxi driver didn't speak English. He simply dropped my bags and left. I was hoping you could help me sort this out?"

"Of course."

She smiled, feeling much better knowing she had an ally. "I was supposed to arrive at the Vista del Cielo this afternoon. He claimed this is it, but I am sure he was wrong."

"This is the Vista del Cielo, but you were not expected."

Her smile faltered as alarm jolted through her body. "Perhaps there is another Vista del Cielo?" she suggested, trying desperately to sound pleasant and not panicked. "I am booked there for the next week."

The man's scowl deepened. "No, we are the only one. But we have no bookings for this week. We did, but it was cancelled last month."

"This *is* a hotel, then."

"An estancia, yes. A guest ranch."

A guest ranch. This was no mistake, she realized with a sinking heart. She remembered Antoine's voice as he'd teased her. *It will be different,* he'd boasted. *Lots of privacy for a newly married couple.*

Looking back now, the idea made her blush. The thought of being here alone with Antoine made her suddenly self-conscious in front of the man before her. Thank goodness she'd at least been spared that.

Still, it seemed inconceivable that Antoine, with his lavish tastes, would have booked them here. It looked quiet and peaceful—a definite bonus to her—but it still didn't seem to compute with what she'd expected. "Where is the spa? The pool?" After her long dusty trip, the idea of dipping into the pool for a refreshing swim sounded heavenly. Perhaps a hot tub to soothe the muscles that had been cramped up in an airplane and then the taxi. She could nearly feel the bubbles on her skin already. Maybe this place was more rustic than she'd anticipated, but she knew Antoine would have demanded a certain standard.

"That's why we had to cancel the reservations. There was a fire. I'm afraid the spa building as well as others were destroyed. Thankfully the house was spared."

Everything in Sophia went cold and the polite smile slid from her face. "Fire?"

"Yes…we've cancelled everything until the repairs are made and things rebuilt. The pool made it through, but we've had to have it drained because of the ash and debris."

Sophia felt a growing sense of despair. She stared around her, wondering how things could have gone so perfectly pear-shaped. Her gaze caught on the odd looking tree, standing like a solitary sentinel in the middle of the plain. It looked exactly as she felt. Alone. And lonely. She was beginning to understand that they were two completely separate things.

"Perhaps if you told me your name, we could sort it out," he said, a little impatiently.

"The reservation was under Antoine Doucette."

The man's face changed as understanding dawned. "The honeymoon." Then he looked confused again, looked at her cases, and back again. "And the other half of the happy couple?"

Sophia lifted her chin. She could do this. She could. She could get past the embarrassment and the hurt and explain dispassionately. She had faced worse in the last months. She'd faced Antoine, her family and friends, even the chokehold of the press closing in around her. She could handle one annoying Argentinian…whatever he was. Farmer? Gaucho? Who was he to judge her?

"I came alone. I'm afraid the marriage did not take place."

"I see. I am sorry, *señorita*."

His words said apology but his tone certainly did not. It was strictly polite and almost…cold. "Don't be," she replied, putting her hand on her hip. "I'm not." It was only a half lie. She wasn't sorry she had called off the wedding. Under the circumstances it had been the right thing to do.

But it had been far from easy. She'd bear the scars from it for a long, long time.

A huff of surprise erupted from his mouth, followed by mutterings in Spanish that she couldn't understand. That made her angry. It made her feel inadequate and even more of an outsider, and she was tired of that feeling.

"Why were we not notified of the cancellation, then?" She pressed on, annoyed.

"I don't know." His brow furrowed. "Maria handles all the reservations and business. I can't imagine her making a mistake."

"Someone did. I'm here, aren't I?"

And so she was. She had to convince him to let her stay.

Antoine had thrown in her face how he'd not bought travel insurance and her breaking their engagement would cost him thousands of dollars. She'd told herself she had nothing to feel guilty about—after all, he was the one who'd been caught red-handed. She'd also spent money on a wedding that had never happened. The dress. The deposits for the printer, the reception, flowers, cake—all the trappings of a society wedding. His protests about the honeymoon money had fallen on deaf ears. It was only money. It would take a long time to replace it, but it would take longer to erase the pain of his betrayal. It was the betrayal that had hit her deep in her soul. She had been blind, had not recognized the signs. She had been left wondering if she could ever trust her own judgment again.

And now she was in Argentina with no place to stay.

She could go back to Buenos Aires. She could try to change her ticket and go home with her tail between her legs. Or she could book herself in somewhere and stay for the duration. It would mean taking most of her savings to pay for the hotel and food, but she'd have her dignity.

Wouldn't Antoine have a laugh about that? And she could already hear her mother chiding, *I told you it was a mistake to take that trip alone.*

That hurt. At a time when she'd most wanted her mother's support, it hadn't been there. Margaret Hollingsworth had thought she was crazy to call off the wedding and a life of security. Sometimes Sophia wondered why she kept trying to gain her mother's approval. Once, as a child, sad and missing her dad, she'd hidden in a cellar, not wanting her mother to see her tears. But she'd ended up locked in by accident, unable to get back out again. It had been hours before she'd been found, crying and terrified. Even now, she could still feel the dark, damp chill and hear her mother's furious words when what she'd wanted was a hug and reassurance. It was a hurt that had scarred her heart that day, and she'd never forgotten it.

But she couldn't spend her whole life seeking approval from

someone else. She knew that now. It was time for her to stand up for herself. To make her own happiness. She straightened her shoulders. She'd make the best of it and move forward.

"I insist on staying the week," she said clearly. "I did not receive notification that our booking was cancelled, and I have flown all the way from Ottawa. I have no intention of going back." She leveled a gaze at him, hoping that she appeared to mean business when inside she was trembling. He had to let her stay. The savings she had put aside were what she had been planning to use as a security deposit for a new, cheaper apartment, necessary now that she no longer had her well-paid job with Antoine. But there was pride at stake here and she relaxed her shoulders, determined to see it through.

The man's jaw hardened and his dark eyes glittered at her sharp command. "I am sorry, but we simply are not prepared for guests. I can arrange for you to go back to San Antonio de Areco. There is a hotel there. Or perhaps back to Buenos Aires."

Which sounded lovely, she supposed. Her gaze caught the strange tree again. It gave her a strong yet peaceful feeling. This place wouldn't be so bad. She would have time to relax and recharge. Besides, there was something in his dismissive tone that put her on edge. He was telling her what to do, and at some point she had to take charge of her own life. She'd been a people pleaser for years, always trying to do the right thing, not to create waves. This time it was up to her.

"But I want to stay here," she insisted firmly.

"No, you don't," he replied, calling her bluff. "I could see it on your face from the first moment. It is fine. Estancia life is not for everyone." He cast a disdainful look at her handbag and shoes. "Obviously."

Sophia gritted her teeth. He didn't think she could handle it? Obviously he hadn't ever been mobbed by the press at Parliament Hill or been surprised by a photographer shoving a camera in her face outside a downtown club and taunting her about political scandal.

"I insist," she replied. She looked around her at the plain surroundings. "Unless you can provide proof of the refund. In which case I am happy to pay the going rate if I am wrong."

Consternation showed on the man's face. She couldn't bring herself to back down an inch even though the prospect of spending her savings made her blanch. She was doing all she could just to keep it together. She wanted him to let her stay. Not just to prove something to Antoine, who probably couldn't care less. No, to prove something to herself. And most of all at this moment she wanted to be shown to her room, so she could close the door and decompress. Her legs suddenly felt weary—was it jet lag? And she had the oddest urge to cry. She was so tired. Tired of everything. Something had to give sooner or later and she really hoped that when it did, it would be in private. The past months seemed to catch up to her all at once, and she refused to cry in public.

The man stared at her for a moment, making her squirm inside. "I will try to get to the bottom of this. In the meantime, you'd better come in."

It wasn't exactly gracious, but Sophia felt weak with relief. Surely there was someone inside who could help her with her bags while this…man went back to work. If they were running an estancia, someone must be here to cook and clean and make sure the amenities were looked after. It didn't have to be fancy. A simple glass of wine and a hot meal would be most welcome.

Sophia held out her hand. "I'm Sophia Hollingsworth."

"Tomas Mendoza."

He took her hand in his and something twisted inside her, something delicious and unexpected. His hand was indeed firm, with slight calluses along the pads of his fingers. It was also warm and strong, and it enveloped her smaller, perfectly manicured one completely. It was a working man's hand, she realized. Honest. Capable.

"Miss Hollingsworth, I do not know if you realize what you're asking. Since we are shut down for another few weeks, the regular hosts of the estancia are away."

She waited, not exactly sure what he meant.

He pulled his hand away from hers. "Maria and Carlos Rodriguez normally run the place," he explained. "While I finish overseeing the repairs, they've gone to Córdoba to visit their son, Miguel. I will have to check the paperwork in the office for your reservation. At the same time, I need to make it clear that while they are away the full amenities are not available."

Dear Lord. So she was stuck here with a handyman? And who was to blame? Herself. Why hadn't she followed up before coming all this way? Another mistake to add to the list.

"And your job?"

He nodded at her. "I do what needs doing. I work with Carlos with the stock. Fix things. Do the trail rides."

Trail rides? Would he expect her to do that?

"One of our selling points is an authentic estancia experience. Our guests are encouraged to work alongside us."

She swallowed. If she backed out now she'd be giving in. Moreover, he'd know it. From deep inside came a need to rise to the challenge. But, for right now, the afternoon sun beat down on Sophia's head and she grew more tired by the moment. "Could you just show me to a room for now? I'm feeling quite hot. The air conditioning was broken in the taxi, and I'm really just trying to make sense of what's happened today."

"Certainly."

Tomas picked up two of her large cases, leaving the third, smaller carry-on, for Sophia. She put the strap over her shoulder and followed him along the gravel to the patio. He opened the front door and stepped inside, tugging her luggage in behind him.

For better or for worse, this was where she would be for the next week.

It could only get better from here, right? It would be what she made of it. She reminded herself of that fact as she followed Tomas down a hall and around a corner to her bedroom. His earlier polite smile had been replaced by a cool, emotionless expression. "You should be comfortable here," he said stiffly, opening the door to a room and then stepping back to let her pass. She stepped inside and instantly felt the stress of the last few months drain away.

"It's beautiful, thank you." It was simple and certainly no luxury suite. But it was brilliantly clean, meticulously cared for and suited her perfectly. The walls were pristine white, looking as though they'd been newly painted, and she immediately went to the open window that looked out over the grassy plain, stretching endlessly to the south. The air was clean, free of pollution and smog, and it refreshed her. More than that, the place was private, and privacy was something she craved quite desperately.

The bed was gorgeous, an intricately patterned iron bedstead adorned with linens the soothing colour of a summer sky. A basket of towels and toiletries sat on a low dresser, the plush cotton the same blue as the bedspread. Right now all she wanted was to sink into the bed's softness and let the stress of the day drain away.

She turned back to Tomas, suddenly aware that they were standing in what was now her bedroom. The silence stretched out awkwardly. There was nothing inappropriate about being in here with him. He was filling the role of concierge and apparently so much more. So why did she suddenly feel so self-conscious?

"What a lovely room."

"I am pleased you like it." The hard gleam in his eyes softened just a bit, as if her approval validated her in some way. As soon as she glimpsed it, the gleam disappeared.

What would it take to win him over? It was going to be a very long week if this was the extent of their conversation.

"It's so peaceful. Listen." She went to the window again, trying to escape his keen gaze. She pushed aside the curtain with a hand, looking out, leaning her head back so that the warm breeze caressed her throat. "Do you hear that?"

He came closer behind her, so close she could feel his presence by her shoulder even though he had to be several inches away. "Hear what?"

She laughed then, a carefree, feel-good laugh that she felt clear to her toes. The sound was unfamiliar to her ears, but very, very welcome. Suddenly the situation didn't seem so catastrophic. She had no one to please but herself this week. "That's just it. Nothing. I hear nothing, and it's wonderful." She closed her eyes and let the sunshine and wind bathe her face.

When she turned back around, the severe look on his face had disappeared. He understood, she realized. That took away the self-conscious part of being alone with him but left in its wake the flicker of attraction she'd felt when holding his hand. A flicker she wasn't sure what to do with.

She needed to escape his gaze and the nearness of him, so she moved to the dresser to touch the towels and trail her fingers over the wood. It was slightly scarred and Sophia loved how the markings added character to the piece. This was no sterile hotel room without a wrinkle or scratch. It wasn't about perfection. It had a level of familiarity and comfort that simply said *home*. The kind of home she'd secretly always wished for and had never had.

"That's the idea," he replied. "The city has its charms. But sometimes a person needs to get away to where things are…" he broke off the sentence, and Sophia wondered what he had been going to say. The impression she got was that big problems became small ones here. She found herself curious about him. Who was Tomas Mendoza? Why did this simple life hold such allure to him?

"Less complicated?"

Tomas stared out of the window as the moment drew on. "Yes, less complicated," he confirmed, but Sophia didn't feel reassured. Had his life been complicated once? For all his good looks, there was a wall around him, as though no matter what, he would keep people at arms' length. He was impossible to read.

"Just leave the bags," Sophia suggested. "I think I would like to freshen up and have a nap."

Sophia shouldered her tote bag and was just reaching for one of her suitcases when the tote slipped off her shoulder, catching on her elbow and knocking her off balance. Her heel caught as her right toe snubbed the edge of her biggest case and she lurched forward.

Straight into Tomas's arms.

He caught her effortlessly, his strong arms cinched around her as he righted her on her feet. Without thinking, she looked up. It was a mistake. Her cheeks flamed as she realized his hand was pressed firmly against her lower back. It was tempting, having her body pressed close to his, but the real trouble was the way their gazes clashed. She had not been held in such an intimate embrace for a long time, and never with the nerve-tingling effect she was suffering now. A muscle in Tomas's jaw tightened and Sophia's breathing was so shallow her chest cramped. For a breath of a moment she wondered what it would be like to be kissed by him. Really, truly kissed.

And behind that thought came the intimate realization that for the next several days, it was just the two of them here.

The thought tempted but also made her draw back. There was making a statement of independence by taking this trip alone, and then there was just being foolish. This was not why she had come. A holiday fling was not what she was looking for. She pushed away and out of his arms and straightened her blouse.

"In addition to poor fact checking, I think we can safely add klutz to my list of faults today," she joked, but the quip fell flat as she saw the wrinkle between his brows form once more.

"I hope not," he answered, pushing her suitcase into place at the end of the bed and straightening into that damnable rigid posture once more. "This is a working ranch, Miss Hollingsworth." He'd reverted to her formal English name again, backing away. "The Vista del Cielo was established to give guests an authentic gaucho experience. Our guests live like the locals for the duration of their stay. In the absence of our other facilities, I do hope you take advantage of all the estancia has to offer." Once again he looked at her shoes, then up at her tidy skirt and linen blouse, which was now wrinkled beyond recognition. "I hope you've brought other more... appropriate clothing."

Sophia felt like an idiot. She'd been so sure and so blindly determined to soak up every entitled minute that she'd thrown her best things in her luggage and jetted off. Now this gaucho was issuing a challenge. She hated the indulgent way he looked at her clothes. She'd show him. She'd do everything on his damned list of activities!

She sniffed. It wasn't as if she made a habit of falling down all the time, or worse, falling into men. She wasn't incapable. But he had hit on yet another obstacle—her suitcases were packed with totally inappropriate clothing. Bathing suits for lounging around a pool, a selection of skirts and dresses, all with matching shoes for Michelin-starred dinners with a view.

This wasn't Tomas's fault. It was hers, for not being more thorough. If she'd known what sort of establishment this was, she would have packed the proper things. Sometimes she felt as if she could do nothing right. She trusted in all the wrong things instead of relying on herself.

If she were determined to change, why not start now? She could fake it until she made it, right? She would show this Tomas that she could take on anything he dished out.

"I'm looking forward to it," she replied, desperate to save face. Did helping out also mean horseback-riding? She felt herself go pale at the thought. She'd ridden a horse exactly twice in her life. The first time the mare had been led by her halter. The second time had been a few years later when a friend at school had asked her to an afternoon at a local stables where she took lessons. That time Sophia had held the reins. She'd managed a very choppy trot but had nearly panicked when the horse had broken into a canter. She thought she was probably twelve when that had happened.

But she wasn't twelve any longer. She could handle herself better this time. She didn't want to look like a fool in front of him. Not when he looked so very perfect.

"First I think I would like to rest," she suggested, putting reality off a little while longer. When the time came, she'd go with him and she'd do just fine. "It has been a long flight and drive."

"Very well. While you are resting, I'll see what I can find out about this mistaken reservation."

His insistence that she was wrong grated. "Mr. Mendoza…"

He paused by the door and looked back at her. "Yes?"

She gave him her sweetest smile. "I appreciate you accommodating me during an inconvenient time for you. I do apologize for the disruption."

She tried a smile, an olive branch to smooth the way for the next few days. She knew that aggravating one's host—

especially a host who was already less than cordial—wasn't the way to get the best service.

"Dinner is at seven," he replied, unsmiling, and shut the door behind him.

In a fit of juvenile satisfaction, Sophia stuck her tongue out at the door before collapsing on the bed.

CHAPTER TWO

TOMAS had planned on a quick meal for one tonight but instead found himself making *locro*—a stew of beans, meat, corn and pumpkin. It was simple enough to make and something typically Argentinian for his guest.

Guest. He snorted, stirring the stew. What a mix-up. The first thing he'd done was check the books, but no notation had been made next to the name *Antoine Doucette*. Then he'd called Miguel's number in Córdoba. Maria remembered the reservation, but couldn't remember if she'd cancelled it. Tomas hadn't pushed; Maria was still traumatized by the fire. When Miguel had suggested they visit, Tomas and Carlos had agreed it would be good for Maria to get away for a few days. Tomas wanted her to see things nearly as good as new when she came back. The spa building had to be reconstructed, but the other outbuildings were nearly repaired. If things went well, they could even have the pool refilled and working in another week.

But it was Maria's words to him today that had caused him the most trouble. He'd explained the situation and Maria had instantly been sympathetic to Sophia's plight. "Take care of that girl, Tomas," she said firmly. Then she'd laughed. "She must be a real firecracker to take her honeymoon alone. She's your responsibility now. You will see to things until we return."

As if he needed reminding. He chopped into the pumpkin, scowling. Maria had been mothering him for so long that she sometimes forgot he was a grown man. He knew what his responsibilities were. They were impossible to forget.

"We'll sort the rest out when Carlos and I come back. Maybe we'll come Wednesday now."

"There's no need…"

But Maria had laughed. "She will be tired of your cooking by then. Wednesday. Just be nice, Tomas."

"I would never…"

"Yes, you would." Maria had laughed, but he knew she meant it. Maria and her family knew Tomas better than anyone else on earth. Too well.

Wednesday. That meant he had three days after today in which he not only had to do his work, but had to entertain Sophia as well. She'd put on a brave face, but he knew she had been expecting something totally different from what she was getting. He indulged in a half smile, but then remembered the look on her face when she'd thought he was going to send her away. She had been afraid behind all the lipstick and talk. And he had been just stupid enough to see it and go soft.

He turned down the heat and put the cover on to let the *locro* simmer. Going soft wasn't an option for him right now. The estancia wasn't due to reopen for another few weeks. There was still work to do—and lots of it. The boutique had to be restocked now that it was painted. The horses and the small beef herd Carlos raised still needed to be cared for. The storage shed behind the barn had been rebuilt since the fire, but the paint for the exterior was sitting in the barn, waiting for Tomas to have a few spare moments. As if. And the builders had had another job lined up, which was why it was taking longer for the pool house to be rebuilt.

With Carlos here, they could have muddled through just fine. But they'd agreed that getting Maria away for a few days—letting her visit her son—was a better course of action.

Tomas simply hadn't counted on babysitting a spoiled princess and playing cook and maid. That was normally Maria's area of expertise, and he and Carlos stuck to the outdoors. The estancia was a business that ran smoothly, just the way they'd planned, with everyone playing to their strengths. He could stay in the background, exactly where he liked it. He was polite and friendly to guests. They were only strangers passing through, asking nothing more from him than a trail ride and some local history. They made the same mistake Sophia had made today—assuming he was the jack-of-all-trades around the place. That was fine, too. He stayed a silent partner in Vista del Cielo and got the peace and isolation he craved. Carlos and Maria had their livelihood. Everyone was taken care of.

He heard a noise from down the hall and guessed that the princess was waking from her slumbers. He imagined briefly what she would look like asleep on the blue coverlet, her hair spread out in a great auburn curtain around her. He shook his head and reached for a pair of bowls from the cupboard. There was no denying she was beautiful. Stunning, actually, with her dark red curls and roses-and-cream complexion. Maybe she had a sense of entitlement about her and was used to getting her own way, but he could see why. She'd turned her dark eyes on him and said she was tired and he'd left her to nap without a word. Now he was finishing dinner and setting the table when the whole purpose of this place was for everyone to work together. It was one of their biggest selling points. A feeling of family.

And that was something he had no desire to feel with Sophia Hollingsworth.

"Something smells delicious."

He nearly dropped the bowls when she appeared in the doorway behind him.

Her hair was down but slightly tousled from sleep, the curls falling softly over one shoulder. Heavy lidded eyes blinked at him and she was several inches shorter, thanks to the fact that she'd left her shoes in her room and appeared in bare feet. That was why he hadn't heard her approach. His gaze stuck on ten perfectly painted coral toenails. She had extraordinarily pretty feet, and even without the shoes he could tell she had a great set of legs hiding beneath her straight skirt.

It was the princess, unwrapped, and he swallowed, realizing he found her very appealing indeed. At least physically.

That was the last thing he needed.

"Did you sleep well?" He turned away from her, putting the bowls on the table.

"Yes, thank you. I feel very refreshed."

Her voice was soft and Tomas felt it sneak into him, down low.

"I didn't mean to sleep so late," she apologized, and he swallowed as the husky tone teased his ears. "Whatever you've cooked smells wonderful."

"It's nothing fancy." He turned back to her and steeled his features. He would not be swayed by a pretty face and a soft voice. Damn Carlos and Maria. If they were here, they could handle Miss Princess and he would be in the barn where he liked it. "I do not usually do the cooking."

"I'm not used to a man cooking for me at all, so that in itself is a treat." She blessed him with a shy smile.

His pulse leapt and he scowled. His physical response to her was aggravating. "I expect you're more accustomed to five-course meals and staff to wait upon you, right?"

A look of hurt flashed across her face and he felt guilty for being snide. He was just about to apologize when the look disappeared and she furrowed her brow. "What makes you say that?"

"Oh, *querida.*" The apology he'd toyed with died on his lips and he reached into a drawer for cutlery. "You practically scream high maintenance. It is clear you are used to the best. Which makes your presence here alone all the more intriguing."

"High maintenance?" A pretty blush infused her cheeks. She really was good, he thought. An intriguing combination of innocent ingénue and diva. Maybe a few days mucking around a ranch would be good for her. It had certainly done wonders for him.

She stepped forward, the soft, injured look gone. "I see," she said. "You think I'm some sort of pampered creature who lives to be waited upon."

"Aren't you?"

"Not even close."

"Oh, come on." He finished setting the table and turned to face her. "Designer clothes, perfect hair… You expected to arrive at some retreat or spa, didn't you? Not a working estancia. Admit it."

Her cheeks blazed now, not with embarrassment but with temper. "Okay, fine. Yes, this is not what I expected. You are not what I expected."

He smiled with satisfaction. "No, I am not. If you're not up to it, say so now. I'll arrange for you to return to Buenos Aires tomorrow." There, he decided, he'd given her a perfectly legitimate out. The few hours it would take to drive her back to the city would be worth it to have the rest of the week free to work. Better yet, she'd be gone before Maria and Carlos got back. Maria would get ideas into her head. She'd been prodding lately about Tomas getting away more. That he needed to stop hiding. That he should find a nice girl.

Not that a woman like Sophia, on her solo honeymoon would qualify in Maria's eyes, but it would be better all around if the potential were erased altogether. Tomas didn't want a nice girl. He didn't want to get away more. He wanted the life he'd chosen here on the pampas. Simple and uncomplicated. He'd chosen it to help him forget.

His insides twisted. Some days now he tried to remember. Forgetting seemed so very wrong. Disloyal.

"And you'd like that, wouldn't you."

Her saucy tone turned his head. *"¿Perdón?"*

"Are you trying to get rid of me, Mr. Mendoza? Get me out from under your feet? This wasn't my mix-up. You think by threatening me with some honest work I'll run and hide away somewhere where staff will wait on me hand and foot?"

"Isn't that what you want?"

She paused for a moment, then leveled him with a definitive glare. "No."

"No?" He raised an eyebrow.

"No. I want to stay."

"I checked the books and spoke to Maria, by the way."

"And?"

"And the refund isn't notated in the regular spot and Maria doesn't remember. She said she will straighten everything out when she comes back on Wednesday."

"And then Wednesday you will see," Sophia replied confidently.

"You realize what I'm saying, right? People who stay at the estancia participate in all kinds of activities. Working with the animals, in the barns. Even in the house. They become one of the family. With the hard work and the benefits, too."

"You don't think I can do it?"

He looked at her, all hairdo and perfect makeup and pedicured feet. "No, I don't."

"Then perhaps we're in for a week of surprises." She flashed him a superior smile. "Maybe now you can surprise me with what's cooking in that pot. I'm starving."

He'd expected her to heave a sigh of relief and take him up on his offer, not challenge him. He wasn't sure whether he admired her spunk or was frustrated by it.

But time would tell. Let her enjoy her home-cooked meal and scented bath tonight. Tomorrow would be a different story.

What to wear was definitely a quandary.

Sophia went through the open suitcase one more time, looking for something suitable. Clothing lay scattered on the bed like seaweed on a sea of blue linen. She checked her watch. Tomas had said breakfast at seven sharp, and it was already quarter past. Being late gave him even more ammunition. There had to be something here she could wear!

She held up a pair of trousers the shade of dark caramel and frowned. The only shoes she had that would match were the Jimmy Choo sandals she'd bought on sale during her last trip across the border. Why hadn't she thought to bring something more casual? A pair of sneakers. Yoga pants. But no, the only exercise wardrobe she'd packed was her swimsuits, thinking she'd be spending time beside the pool. Perhaps relaxing in a sauna. She looked in despair at the flotsam of clothes on the bedspread. How could she have been so stupid?

Seven twenty-five. She was so late. She remembered the way Tomas had looked at her last night and felt anger flow through her veins as she sifted through her suitcase again. He'd been patronizing. Granted, she hadn't made the best impression, and yes, she'd been shocked. She grabbed a sundress out of her second open case and pulled it over her head, out of time for further deliberation. For the last three years she'd been treated that way. She hadn't realized it then, but looking back now it was so very clear. She'd been more of a decoration than someone useful. That kind of treatment stopped today. It stopped with Tomas Mendoza and his superior attitude. If it took eating a little humble pie for breakfast, she'd do it.

She hurried down the hall to the kitchen. The smell in the room was to die for. A covered basket sat on the table and she lifted the towel. The rolls were still warm, soft and fragrant. Bread? He'd made bread?

She paused, her hand on the plate left at the place where she'd sat last night. She tried to picture Antoine making bread in the morning. The very idea was preposterous. He wouldn't even have made pastry out of one of those cans in the refrigerated section of the grocery store. Heck, Sophia had never made bread from scratch in her life.

The breakfast was completed with a bowl of fresh fruit and coffee waiting in the pot, hot and rich.

She'd missed mealtime, and the thought stole the smile from her face. She'd have to eat quickly and then find Tomas. Showing up late was not the way to get off on the right foot. Hurriedly she buttered a roll and poured a half cup of coffee. When she was done she put her plate in the sink and the platter of fruit back in the fridge. She went outside, feeling the warmth of the morning soak into her skin as she searched for Tomas. She nearly ran into him turning a corner towards the outbuildings at the back.

"Oh!" she gasped, stopping short and nearly staggering backwards. She would have if he hadn't steadied her with a quick hand on her arm. His warm grip sent a shaft of pure pleasure down to her fingertips. He let her go as soon as she was stable and dropped his hand.

"I see you're up."

"Yes, I'm sorry I'm late. I slept so well…" She would sweeten him up. She would let him know his garrulousness didn't get to her. "My bed is very comfortable."

"Apparently."

The pleasure went out of Sophia like air from a balloon. But she wouldn't give up yet. She'd kill him with kindness if that's what it took. "The rolls were still warm. Did you make them?"

He stood back, looking at her as if he were measuring and finding her wanting. "Yes, I did. Maria showed me how long ago. When she returns you'll have real cooking, not my second-rate impression of it."

"I wouldn't call your cooking second-rate. The stew last night was delicious."

"I'm glad you liked it."

The politeness was a cold veneer, meaning little when she felt it wasn't sincere.

"So what did I miss?"

"Today's activity," he remarked dryly, and swept out an arm.

Behind them was a utility shed. Beside it were supplies for painting—a large bucket of paint, two smaller cans and brushes.

"Painting?" This was a vacation. Shouldn't there be guided tours? Even without the pool and other amenities, shed painting was hardly a unique Argentinian experience.

He shrugged. "You did say you were prepared to surprise me. So here we are. It needs to be done."

He was trying to get the best of her. She was sure of it. He was planning on pushing her until she quit. But she would not be dismissed. She smiled, quite enjoying the liberating feeling of making up her own mind. If Tomas said paint, she'd paint.

Just not in a sundress and heels.

"I'll need a change of clothes. I'm afraid I came unprepared for painting."

He shrugged again and headed towards the paint supplies.

"Señor Mendoza!"

To her credit, she did a brilliant job of rolling out the ñ in *señor*. He turned around, surprise flattening his face. She reveled in that expression for a fleeting second before continuing. "If you will please find me something to wear, it would be greatly appreciated."

"Do I look like a clothing store, Miss Hollingsworth?"

He put the emphasis on the *miss* just as she had with *señor* and it had her eyebrows lifting in challenge.

"There were brochures in my room." Oh, if she'd only thought to look at them at home before packing! Seeing them last night had made her cheeks flush with embarrassment, but there was nothing to be done about it now. "I know you have a boutique on site. Perhaps I might find something there?"

He scowled and she felt victory within her grasp.

"If you have any trousers at all, put them on. And meet me back here in five minutes." With a put-upon sigh, he disappeared.

She had gotten the better of him, and while it was a small victory, it felt good. He had to know she was not a meek little sheep that needed caring for. She was discovering she had a daring, adventurous side she'd never known existed. Oh, perhaps painting a shed wasn't very adventurous. But after being the girl who'd done as she was told, too afraid to do otherwise, all this felt absolutely liberating.

She skipped to the house and came back moments later wearing the caramel trousers and a white linen blouse. It was as casual as she had in her cases, but she'd remedy that somehow. Tomas came back holding a navy bundle in his hands and she drew her eyebrows together, puzzled. It didn't look like something from a boutique.

"Put these over your clothes," he said, handing her a pair of paint-splattered coveralls.

"You're kidding."

"You don't want paint on those clothes, do you?"

"No, but…"

"Anything from the boutique is brand new—you don't want paint on those things, either, do you?"

Why did he have to be right?

She put on the coveralls, hating the baggy fit but zipping them up anyway. The sleeves were too long and she rolled them up. And felt ridiculous standing there in her sandals.

She caught a glimpse of a smile flirting with the corners of his mouth. "Sure, go ahead, laugh. I know I look silly."

"Put these on," he said, handing her a pair of shoes.

"What are these?"

"*Alpargatas.*"

She put on the canvas and rope shoes that looked like slip-on sneakers. They were surprisingly comfortable.

"I believe I am ready."

"I hope so. The morning is moving along."

Like she needed another reminder that she was late.

She followed him to the shed, admiring the rear view despite herself. Today he was wearing faded brown cotton pants and a red T-shirt that showed off the golden hue of his skin, not to mention the breadth of his back and shoulders. He was unapologetically physical and she found herself responding as any woman would—with admiration. Seeing how capable he was made her want to succeed, too, even if it was just at the most menial task.

"Don't you have horses to feed or something?"

He shook his head. "I did most of the chores while the bread was rising."

"You didn't need to make bread on my account." She pictured his hands kneading the dough and wet her lips. He really was a jack-of-all-trades. It wasn't fair that he was so capable and, well, *gorgeous*. A total package. It made her feel very plain and not very accomplished at all.

"I was up. In Maria's absence, it is up to me to make sure you're looked after."

Great. He didn't need to say the words *obligation* and *burden* for her to hear them loud and clear.

"Is there nothing you can't do?"

"When the gaucho is out on the pampas, he is completely self-sufficient. Food, shelter, care of his animals…he does it all."

"And have you always been so capable?"

A strange look passed over his features, but then he cleared his expression and smiled. The warmth didn't quite meet his eyes. "Oh, not at all. It was Carlos who taught me. And I'll be forever in his debt."

Sophia wanted to ask him what that meant, but he reached down and grabbed a stick to stir the paint.

"Tomas?"

"Hmm?" He didn't look up from his paint. He kept stirring while Sophia's heart hammered. Getting the best of Tomas was one thing. But dealing with this relentless…stoicism was another. There was no sound here. Nothing familiar. All that she might have was conversation. It was the only thing to connect her to anything. And the only person she could connect to was Tomas.

"Could we call a truce?"

His hand stilled and he looked up.

"I know this is not what either of us planned. Can't we make the best of it rather than butting heads?"

His gaze clung to hers and in it she saw the glimmerings of respect and acceptance and something that looked like regret. That made no sense. But it was all there just the same.

"I am not generally very good company."

Sophia laughed a little. "Shocker."

Even Tomas had to grin at that. She saw the turn of his lips as he bent to his work again.

He handed her a can and a brush. "I thought you could start on the trim. You probably have a steadier hand than I do."

The shed wasn't big, but it did have two doors that opened out and a window on each of the north and south sides. Sophia held the can in her hand and wondered where to start. The door and windows had been taped to protect against errant brush strokes. She stuck the brush into the can and drew it out, heavy with the white paint.

"You've never painted before, have you?"

She shook her head.

Tomas sighed. Not a big sigh, but she heard it just the same and felt a flicker of impatience both at him and at herself for not being more capable. "It was never…" She didn't know how to explain her upbringing. Or her mother's philosophy on what was done and what wasn't. You hired people to do things like painting and repairs. They were the help. It had been made especially clear after Sophia's father had moved out. It was then that Sophia's mother had put her foot on the first rung of the social climbing ladder.

"We weren't much for do-it-yourselfing," was all she could bring herself to say.

He came over and put his hand on top of hers. "You've got too much paint on the brush. It will just glop and run. This way."

Sophia bit down on her lip. His hand was strong and sure over hers, his body close. Her shoulder was near his chest as he guided her hand, wiping excess paint off the bristles. "There. Now, if you angle your brush this way…" He showed her how to lay the brush so the paint went on smoothly and evenly. "See?"

"Mmm hmm." She couldn't bring herself to say more. She was reacting to his nearness like a schoolgirl. His body formed a hard, immovable wall behind her and she wondered for a moment what it would be like to be held within the circle of his arms.

She pulled away from his hand and applied the paint to the trim, chiding herself for being silly. The purpose of the trip was to do something for herself, to show her independence. It was not to get besotted over some grouchy gaucho.

Tomas cleared his throat and went back to pick up his own brush.

As they put their efforts into painting the shed, Sophia stole a few moments to look around. The morning was bright, the air clear and fresh. The area around the barn was neat and trimmed and beyond it she saw a half-dozen horses or so seeking shade at one end of a corral, their hides flat and gleaming. Birds flitted between bits of pampas grass, singing a jaunty tune.

No traffic. No horns honking or elbows pushing. Also no shops, no conveniences, no restaurants.

It was stunning, but it was very, very isolated.

"How long have you been at Vista del Cielo?

"Three years."

"You've worked for the Rodriguezes all that time?" She slid excess paint off her brush against the lip of the can, but looked around the corner when Tomas paused in answering.

"Pretty much."

Hmm. Having him answer questions about the estancia wasn't much easier than their previous conversations.

"It is quite beautiful here," she persisted. "You can see for miles. And the air is so clear."

"I'm glad it meets with your approval in some way," Tomas replied.

She defiantly re-wet her brush and worked on the trim of the window as Tomas moved to the main section around the corner. If this was a working ranch, then she'd work. Just like anyone else. Just because she'd never had to didn't mean she couldn't. She continued swiping the paint on the wood. What would Antoine say if he could see his very perfect fiancée now? The idea made her smile. She might hate the baggy coveralls, but knowing Antoine would drop his jaw at the sight of her gave her perverse satisfaction. And the work was surprisingly pleasant. Simple and rewarding.

"Is the morning meal something the female guests would do with Maria?" she asked, more determined than ever to get Tomas talking.

"Sure," he answered, filling his can once more with the white paint. "But not just the female guests. Everyone helps where they can. Before the fire, we had one guest who made cornbread every morning for a week. It melted in your mouth, even without butter. He said he got the recipe from his grandmother. But his wife, she was hopeless in the kitchen. She was terrific at rounding up cattle, though. Once she got started."

Sophia grinned. "Well, well. A regular speech at last. I must make a note—cornbread makes Tomas talk."

He sent her what she supposed was a withering look, but there was little venom behind it this time, and she laughed.

"What are you good at, Sophia?" He efficiently turned the verbal tables.

She swallowed. The question took her by surprise. The lack of an answer was even more shocking. Was she really so lacking in self-assurance she couldn't recognize her own strengths? "I don't know."

"You don't know?"

Her pride was stung. She had worked as Antoine's assistant and had done a good job. She doubted Tomas would see it that way. "I'm good at answering phones and taking messages and keeping a schedule. I can type seventy-five words a minute."

Resentment bubbled up once more at how Antoine had used her capabilities for his own purposes, with complete disregard for any true feelings she might have. She stabbed the brush back into the can. "I'm good at showing up on time in the appropriate outfit, and saying the right things." She realized how empty and foolish that sounded. "I'm not good at much, it seems."

"Those things have their place," he said graciously, and she began to feel a bit better. "But not at an estancia."

The bubble burst. "I'm beginning to see that."

"Giving in?" he asked mildly.

She took out her brush and gave the window trim an extra swipe. "You wish. Maybe it's time I learned a new skill set. How'm I doing?"

It felt wonderful to let some of the old resentment go, to look forward. When she got back to Ottawa, she'd make some changes. She'd already resigned her job and this time she'd do something she enjoyed. Truth be told, she hated politics. She frowned, her brush strokes slowing. She thought about all the private meetings she'd set up, the hand shaking and air kissing. It was all so fake. There wasn't a man or woman among that crowd who wouldn't stab you in the back if it suited them. Then she thought of the wardrobe sitting in her suitcases. Yes, she loved those pretty things. They had made her feel feminine and, in her own way, important.

But maybe, just maybe, she'd sold her soul a bit to get them. Maybe Antoine hadn't been the only one to lie. Maybe she'd been lying to herself, too. Maybe she'd made up for the lack of the right things in her life by filling it up with *stuff*. Was she more like her mother than she thought? For years her mother had insisted Sophia participate in one thing or another, when all she had wanted was to curl up in her room with a good book. When had that shifted? When had status become so important to her, too?

How many other lies had she told herself?

She bit down on her lip and dipped her brush in the can. It was something to think about.

CHAPTER THREE

SHE was so lost in her ponderings that she didn't notice a long drip of paint trickling down the side of the building. "Watch what you're doing," Tomas called. "You'll want to swipe that drip."

It annoyed her to be under his supervision and she gritted her teeth, taking the brush and swiping it down the side of the shed. She was nearly to the bottom when a movement caught her eye. She jumped backwards, sending the paint can flying. At the clatter, Tomas came running around the corner while Sophia stared at the grass, shuddering. "Kill it! Kill it, Tomas!"

Tomas held his paint brush aloft as he stepped ahead to see what the trouble was. When he saw it, he scowled.

"It's a little wolf spider, that's all."

"Little?" she gasped. She shuddered and took another step back. Anything with a body bigger than a dime lost the right to be called "little" when it came to spiders, and this one was substantially larger than that. "You call that thing little?"

"It won't bite you. Even if it did, it wouldn't kill you."

Wouldn't kill her. There was a sense of relief knowing it wasn't poisonous, but Sophia's skin still crawled at the thought of the hairy eight-legged monster getting anywhere near her. She hated spiders. Hated them! The look of them. The thought of their legs on her skin. And the one at the base of the shed was the biggest she'd ever seen.

Tomas went forward and merely touched the spider with the end of his brush. The contact made it scuttle away to parts unknown. He picked up the paint can. Half the contents were on the grass, and wide white splashes went up the side of the shed, spatters on the glass of the window. He sighed, the sound impatient and aggravated.

He patiently took his brush and, with no concern for spiders whatsoever, moved it back and forth over the wall to blend in the spilled paint.

It made Sophia feel completely and utterly foolish. "I'm sorry," she murmured. "I have a thing about spiders." A huge thing. She knew she looked silly and the words to exonerate herself sat on her tongue. But she could not tell him why. It was too personal. Too hurtful.

"Maybe you'd like to work on the other side," he suggested. "I can finish here."

She would be a wreck trying to paint and watch for spiders at the same time. Maybe she looked like a diva, but even the thought of one crawling up her leg made her weak. Spiders and dark places were the two things she simply could not handle. "Will you check it for spiders first?"

He had to think her the most vapid female on the planet. But she could never tell him the real reason why she was afraid. The hours spent in the cellar had shaped her more than she could express. There'd been spiders there, too. Just small ones, but they'd crawled over her arms and she'd brushed them away, unable to see them. She'd held on to her tears that day until one had crept through her hair. It had completely undone her.

This was bad enough. She didn't need to let Tomas see any more of her faults.

Tomas accommodated her indulgence and checked the wall, foundation and grass surrounding the area. "Satisfied?"

"Yes, thank you." Sophia was embarrassed now. No wonder Tomas looked at her as though she was more trouble than she was worth. She dipped her brush and continued where Tomas had left off, determined to overcome the panic that still threaded through her veins. Not that she didn't watch. She did. Her eyes were peeled for any sign of foreign creatures. But if another spider came by, she would not scream or throw her paint can. She would shoo it away, just as Tomas had done.

The sun climbed higher in the sky and the air held a touch of humidity. Sweat formed on Sophia's brow as they worked on into the morning. She was beginning to appreciate all that went into a place like this. It wasn't just meals and fresh linen and saddling a horse or two. It was upkeep, making sure things were well-kept and neat. The plain shed was starting to look quite nice, matching all the other buildings with their fresh white paint, and there was a sense of pride in knowing it was partly to do with her efforts. There was pleasure to be found in the simplicity of the task. It was just painting, with no other purpose to serve, no ulterior motives or strategies. The sound of the bristles on the wood. The whisper of the breeze in the pampas grass, the mellow heat of the late summer sun.

She sneaked glances around the side of the building at Tomas. He had mentioned that Carlos had taught him the ways of the gaucho, but he had said nothing about himself, about where he came from. He could dress in work clothes but there was something about him, a bearing, perhaps, that made her think he wasn't from here. That perhaps he was better educated than he first appeared.

It was nearly noon when they finished the first coat, and Tomas poured what was left in their paint cans into the bucket, sealing the lid for another day and a second coat. "It's going to look good," he said, tapping the lid in place. He picked up the bucket and she watched the muscles in his arm flex as he carried it to the barn. She followed him, carrying the brushes, feeling indignation begin to burn. That was it? She'd worked her tail off all morning, and his only praise was *It's going to look good?* She sniffed. Perhaps what Tomas needed was a lesson in positive reinforcement. Or just being plain old nice!

She trailed behind him as they entered the barn. It was as neat as everything else on the estancia. The concrete floor was cool, the rooms and stalls sturdy and clean, the scents those of horses, fresh hay and aging wood. Tomas took the brushes from her and put them in a large sink. He started the water and began washing them out.

"You were a big help this morning."

Finally, some praise.

"Except when I threw paint everywhere."

"It is probably a good thing you didn't see him jump," Tomas commented.

She paled. "Jump?"

"*Si.* Wolf spiders—they don't really spin webs. They jump, and they're fast on the ground. Usually we don't come across them in the daytime. He scooted away, but when they jump…"

"Do we have to talk about this?"

"I find it very interesting."

He scrubbed at the brushes with a renewed energy. What he enjoyed was teasing her, she realized. There really was no need. She was already feeling quite foolish. She had no business being here. It was not her scene. The inside of her thumb was already blistered from holding the paint brush all morning.

Face it, Soph, she thought. *He was right. You're pampered and spoiled.*

She wished Tomas didn't see her flaws. The problem wasn't with the estancia or Tomas. It was her. She was the one lacking. She didn't want to be spoiled. What she wanted was validation. And somehow she wanted it from Tomas. She got the feeling that if she could earn *his* respect, she could earn just about anyone's.

Tomas finished with the brushes and laid them to dry. He was enjoying teasing her too much, and it unsettled him. It felt strange, like putting on old clothes that were the right size but somehow didn't fit just right anymore. He had left that teasing part of himself behind long ago. It disturbed him to realize it was harder and harder to remember those days. But seeing Sophia's huge eyes as he spoke of the spider, and then the adorable determined set she got to her chin when she was mad…

He should not be reacting this way. And it wasn't as if he was going to catch a break. Until Maria and Carlos came back, Sophia was his responsibility. Even his subconscious knew it. The bread making was not an attempt at being a good host. It was simply the result of waking far too early and needing to be busy to keep from thinking about her.

Which reminded him that it had been hours since they'd eaten.

"Come on," he said, leading the way out of the barn. "Let's get some lunch." Surely a meal was a good, safe activity. If he couldn't escape her, keeping occupied was the next best thing. And he was starving.

While Tomas got out the food, Sophia crawled out of the overalls and hung them on a peg. The meal was simple: a lettuce and tomato salad and cold empanadas that Tomas took out of the refrigerator. "Normally best when they are fresh and hot, but Maria made a batch before she left. It makes a quick lunch. I'll cook a proper dinner tonight."

He thought of the two of them sitting down to a meal together and frowned as an image of gazing at Sophia over candlelight flitted through his mind. It was too easy to stare at Sophia, admiring her heart-shaped face and the way her flame-tossed curls danced in the light. He hadn't missed the way her trousers cupped her backside, or that with her shirt button undone at her throat he could see the hollows of her collarbone. He wished for some interference to keep him distracted, but there would be none. And he would not let on that she got to him in any way, shape or form.

"Maybe I can help you. Cooking is one thing I can manage. Usually."

"Ah, so the princess has a skill."

He was baiting her again, but it was the easiest way to keep her at arm's length.

"Everyone has skills. Just because they're not like yours doesn't mean they don't exist."

She was right and he felt small for belittling her. What was getting into him? She was, he acknowledged. He'd been hiding behind his estancia duties for too long. With all the reconstruction after the fire, he was aware that things around the Vista del Cielo were changing. It wasn't the same place he remembered from when he'd first come here. Back then it had been simpler. Full of life and possibility. And Rosa. Her dancing eyes, her laugh had been in every corner. Now there were times he could barely recall her face; the memory seemed like a shadow of her real self, like a reflection in the water that could disappear with the drop of a pebble on the surface. Rosa was slipping further and further away, and damned if he didn't feel guilty about it.

And he was taking it out on Sophia.

"I'd appreciate the help," he offered as a conciliation.

As they sat down to the meal, Sophia looked at him curiously. "You're not from here, are you?"

Tomas looked up at her briefly, and then turned his attention to the platter of empanadas. "No."

"Where are you from, then? Where did you learn English? It's practically perfect. A hint of an accent, but otherwise…"

"Why do you need to know?"

Sophia huffed and toyed with her empanada. "I was just making conversation, Tomas. You do know what that is, right?"

Si, he'd been right. His social graces were so rusty they were almost nonexistent. Small talk. One didn't make small talk out here. But it had been part of his life once. He should remember how.

"I grew up in Buenos Aires, and went to private school in the U.S. for a few years. Then I came back and studied Engineering."

"Studying in the States?" Sophia's fingers dropped the pastry pocket as she gaped at him. "You have a degree in Engineering?"

He nodded, reminding himself to be very careful. He didn't like talking about himself, or the man he'd once been. Keeping it to plain old facts was plenty. "Yes, Mechanical Engineering. You're surprised."

"I am. How does a Mechanical Engineer end up working as a hired hand at an estancia?"

The explanation was long and unpleasant for the most part, and Tomas definitely wasn't sharing. It was better that she thought him simply the help. She'd look at him differently if she knew he was part owner of Vista del Cielo. And it would open up a lot more questions he had no desire to answer.

"This was where I wanted to be," he replied simply.

"It is quite a leap from engineering to the Vista del Cielo," she commented, biting into the pocket of spicy beef.

"Right."

Tomas went on eating, silent again. This hadn't always been his life. He'd let obligation and duty dictate until one day the price was too high. He'd let so many people down. His mother and father, who had such hopes for him and the family business. His brother, who was supposed to work by his side. And most of all, Rosa.

Carlos and Maria had offered him a place. He'd ended up making it his home. When he thought of his other life, it was like thinking about a stranger. Everything seemed so very far away.

"Tomas…"

"No, no," he said, pushing his plate away and leaning back in his chair. He forced a smile when he felt none, knowing that he had to change the subject. He ran his hand through his hair. "My turn. How does a pretty, pampered woman like yourself end up with a broken engagement? Who broke it off? You or him?"

As soon as he asked the question, he was surprised to find he wanted her to admit she'd been the one to call it off. It should have made no difference to him. He wasn't interested, so why did it matter if she was on the rebound or not? She hadn't sounded particularly sorry when she'd explained arriving alone yesterday, but then pain manifested itself in many ways.

"I did," she replied. She put down her last empanada and dusted off her fingers.

She looked so serious he felt compelled to tease her again, just to bring that light back to her eyes—even if it was anger. "What happened? Would he not keep you in the lifestyle to which you were accustomed?"

She raised her dark gaze to his, and he saw bleak acceptance. "Do you really think this is about lifestyle?" She smiled sadly. "If by lifestyle you mean affection and loyalty…" She looked down and cleared her throat before raising her head again. "Let's just say he was enjoying marital benefits—without the benefit of the marriage." She paused. "Or the wife."

Understanding dawned. The dog had gone elsewhere, all the while planning a wedding with Sophia. "He was cheating?"

"We never should have gotten engaged," she replied.

"Both of us were settling for what looked good, I suppose. I'm ashamed of that. I should have seen…"

He recognized self-blame when he saw it and for the first time he felt sorry for Sophia Hollingsworth.

But she surprised him by squaring her shoulders and pinning him with a direct, confident look. "At least I had the gumption to kick him to the curb when I found him with his…"

Tomas rattled off a few words in Spanish. The words were similar enough to English that Sophia puzzled them out and she burst out laughing. "Oh, thank you for that. That's perfect!"

Dios, she was beautiful, especially when she forgot herself and laughed like that. Her eyes lit up and her cheeks flushed rosy pink. How could her fiancé cheat on her? *Why* would he? She was a stunning, sensual woman, and he'd bet she had no clue of her own allure. He'd thought she was spoiled but now he was wondering if she'd just been sheltered. Either way, she hadn't deserved to be treated in such a fashion.

"For a man to do such a thing—he has no honour. Why would he stray? You're a beautiful woman."

Her gaze struck his, and he felt the impact clear to his toes. For a long moment a rich silence enveloped the kitchen as his gaze dropped to her full lips.

This was exactly what he needed to avoid. He cleared his throat, searching for words to break the spell. "A bit spoiled, perhaps, but not unkind, I don't think."

"Gee, thanks," she muttered, looking away. For a few seconds she studied her fingers and then she asked, without looking up, "You would never cheat on a woman, would you, Tomas?"

It was as if a cold breeze blew through the room and he froze. Cheat? No. But cheating was not the only way to wrong a woman. He'd failed Rosa in other ways. He rose from his chair and began gathering the dishes.

"Did I say something wrong?"

"It is nothing." He ran some water in the sink for dishes. This conversation had to end now. And he had to stop looking at her as if she were his favourite sweet. "This afternoon we need to ride. I will do these if you will go to the closet and find some boots that fit. And a hat. You may borrow one of Maria's, I think. The sun is already making itself known on your cheeks. You will also need some *bombachas*. They're in a box in the office. First door on your right."

"Some what?"

"*Bombachas*. Gaucho pants. You were right about the onsite boutique restocking—it is also on the agenda for this week."

"Where are we going?"

"I need to check the cattle this afternoon. We will ride out along the pasture. It is not a hard ride, Sophia. You will be fine."

Sophia looked down at her hands, torn between wanting to know about what had caused Tomas's abrupt change of subject and knowing she should probably let well enough alone. And that moment when she'd told him about Antoine...there had been something in his eyes that had taken her breath away. She wasn't used to a man having such a physical effect on her. There was a part of her that wondered if she could make it happen again, to feel that queer lifting in her chest when he settled his dark gaze upon her, or the shiver on her flesh the few times he'd touched her. She'd never felt anything quite like it before.

Not even with her fiancé. She looked down at her manicured nails, marred and slightly chipped from the morning's work. She was beginning to understand that the spa days and shopping sprees were only ways to cover what had been wrong from the start. Antoine had never loved her, and perhaps she'd never truly loved him, either. She'd only fancied herself in love.

It had hurt her incredibly that he'd taken a... No. She wouldn't even think the word *mistress*. It was too lofty a title for the tawdry piece he was...well, doing what ever he was doing on the side. She'd even blamed herself for a while, thinking that if Antoine had been satisfied at home he wouldn't have strayed. She had harsh memories of the things Antoine had said about her at the end. Like that she'd driven him to it. That she was an ice queen. Those words still hurt. Because on some level, she was afraid they were true.

But a man who loved her would have waited. He wouldn't have resorted to an affair. Tomas's words helped more than he could ever know. It hadn't been her fault. It had been Antoine's lack of character. And the way Tomas made her feel when he looked at her was anything but icy.

Sophia sat, nonplussed at the abrupt change as Tomas banged dishes around in the sink. Only moments ago they'd been talking about her and even laughing a little about her situation. And in a flash, the curtains were drawn again and Tomas was locked away.

She didn't feel it was the time to push. She stared at Tomas's back at the sink, so straight and rigid and unwelcoming. Perhaps he would relax during their ride. She guessed he was the type that would feel most at home out riding the pampas with the wind and wide open space for company.

Unlike her. Her heart quailed. She had known since arriving that she would end up on horseback. But she hadn't thought it would be today. For a second she considered confessing her inexperience to Tomas. But when she looked at him, his jaw was set in a tight line. He was shutting her out.

That was his right, after all. They were strangers, really, simply in the same place at the same time due to circumstance. He didn't owe her anything and she didn't owe him anything, either. And yet she was so tired of being shut out.

Of being in the background, patted on the head. She was sick and tired of her role as 'behaving appropriately' because she was too afraid to do anything else. Wear the right clothes, meet the right people, say the right things. And for whose benefit? Certainly not for hers. For her mother's ambition that Sophia would raise them above their station—and mostly for Antoine's political aspirations. He'd insisted that his success was hers as well, but she knew now that was a bunch of claptrap.

She wanted a success of her own. Even if meant riding a stupid horse across the pampas to impress a stubborn Argentinian. She wanted the disdain in his eyes to turn to admiration.

She found the box in the office and took out a pair of gray trousers, crestfallen at the pleating and narrow bottoms. They certainly weren't in vogue, but beggars couldn't be choosers. Then it was on to the closet for black boots and a hat with a rounded brim to shade her eyes. "If you'll excuse me for a moment, I'd like to freshen up. Put on some sunscreen before we go out."

"Take your time," Tomas replied. "I will have to saddle the horses anyway."

Sophia detected a note of satisfaction in his voice, as though he was pleased he'd diverted her questions. It only made her more curious and determined to find out what secrets he was hiding. He'd skilfully changed the subject, but she wanted to know what had led him to leave his life in the city for one of isolation in the pampas. A loner like the gaucho, relying on no one but himself.

She stood in the kitchen minutes later, feeling a bit conspicuous as she looked up at a framed picture on the wall. The woman in it was relaxed and happy, astride a black horse and beautiful in full gaucho gear. Sophia wondered what it would be like to be that comfortable in her own skin. And she wondered who it was. Maria, perhaps? Whoever, the picture made her feel somewhat foolish as she left the house and walked across the yard in her outfit. The boots were new and stiff and she felt ridiculous in the black hat that shaded her eyes, as though she was dressed up for Halloween. All she needed now was a poncho and a donkey, she thought.

And then she saw Tomas, waiting beside two horses. She blinked, looking at him with new eyes. He looked so different, so exotically handsome. He too had proper boots and a hat and a bandana tied around his neck. He looked the part of a romantic gaucho, while she felt like a complete imposter.

She inhaled and stepped forward. She could do this. It was simply a matter of faking it until it was true. She'd had lots of practice growing up.

"You look very authentic," he commented. So the ice man thawed a little, Sophia thought irritably.

"I feel sort of silly."

"Don't—you look the part. And you will appreciate the gear when you have been in the saddle beneath the sun." He smiled from beneath his hat. "Perhaps tomorrow if there's time, we can go into San Antonio de Areco and you can purchase a few things there to get you through the week. I don't expect your designer clothes will hold up well otherwise."

She knew he was right. She couldn't swan about in Chanel and Prada all week, and to be truthful the idea of a pair of plain old comfortable jeans was heavenly. How long had it been since she'd lounged around in comfortable clothes, enjoying the sunshine as she had this morning? The thought perked her up.

"Are you ready?"

She swallowed, remembering there was still the issue of her riding skills to conquer.

She approached the mare and tried to appear confident. It seemed to her this horse was slightly shorter than the others she'd ridden—or perhaps she was just taller now. Either way, it helped alleviate some of her anxiety. With a bright smile she took the reins and then stopped short at the sight of the saddle.

"Problem, Sophia?"

It was unlike any saddle she'd ever seen. There was no saddle horn, and the whole thing was covered with an unusual padded skin and then cinched again. "This is different."

"We keep to a gaucho saddle. It's not too difficult. I think you'll find it quite comfortable."

She resolutely put her toes in the stirrup and gripped the top of the saddle where she'd been hoping to find a saddle horn. On the second bounce she got it, and settled into the seat.

It felt different than the western saddles she remembered, but Tomas was right. It was fairly comfortable. The blanket cushioned her bottom.

With ease Tomas mounted up and flashed her a smile. "Neck rein, like in western riding," he instructed. "You do know how, right?"

Sophia resisted the impulse to bite down on her lip. It would be like learning all over again, but she would do it. After the spider incident of the morning, she would not let him see another weakness. This time she'd conquer her fear.

She put her right foot in the stirrup—somehow he'd managed to get the length just right—and with a nudge of her heels to the horse's side, followed him out of the corral and towards the sweeping plain surrounding the estancia.

For the first few minutes they kept to a nice, sedate walk. Sophia felt the breeze on her face and the sun on her back as they took the path through the maze of green pasture and pampas grass. Once the trail opened up, though, Tomas spurred his mount to a smooth canter and without any urging, Sophia's horse followed their lead.

The jolt of the motion and the unusual saddle nearly unseated her, but she gripped with her knees and after a few tense moments she settled into the rhythm of the stride. Not comfortably—she was too inexperienced for that—but she thought she might just manage to stay on top and not end up on her bottom in the dirt. Tomas slowed and eventually she caught up to him, fighting to control her breath and her heartbeat and act as though she did this every day of her life.

She envied Tomas. In comparison to her clumsiness and insecurity, he seemed as if he could do anything with ease. His hands held the reins loosely, unlike the death grip she seemed to have on the leather. His back was straight, his bearing almost regal. He looked like a god of the pampas up there, and the idea did funny things to her insides. For a woman so newly determined to be independent, the idea of having someone like Tomas as a protector was dizzying.

Oh, this was crazy. She was being romanced by the idea of some reticent cowboy and a South American version of the lawless West. She gave a small frown as she came back to earth. The distance she'd put between herself and her life back in Ottawa gave her perspective, and she knew she'd let herself be guided—pushed, molded, nudged—through life for too long. Did she even know who she was anymore? Wouldn't this week be a good time to find out?

"What do you think?"

Tomas reined in and swept his arm out in introduction to the wide, grassy plains below them. Cattle dotted the landscape, peacefully grazing. To their left, the stream the taxi had followed to the estancia twisted and wound like a silvery snake.

It reminded her of the rolling land she'd seen once when she had gone to Alberta for a student conference. As the bus had driven them from Calgary to Banff National Park, they'd passed rolling land like this, dotted with round bales of hay, horses and cattle. The estancia was a taste of that cowboy culture with a twist. There were no Stetsons and spurs here, but when Sophia looked over at Tomas, his brown eyes gleaming beneath his gaucho *campero*, she realized that some allures translated through language and location.

"It's gorgeous," she admitted, always aware of the animal beneath her, ready to adjust the tension of the reins if she needed to. "It's so open and free. Wild and a little intimidating."

Tomas got a little wrinkle in his brow. "You surprise me, Sophia. I expected more of a city-girl perspective from you."

"There are many things you don't know about me, Tomas," she remarked, pleased when the wrinkle got a little deeper. It was encouraging, knowing she had the ability to throw him a little off balance too. "You can be anything you want to be out here, can't you? There are no limits."

She saw him swallow and look away. "That's how I feel about it too. It is not so much frightening, but that there is a vastness to respect, *si?* I never knew what I was missing until I made friends with Miguel and he invited me to visit. The pampas…it is in my soul." He looked back at her, his gaze sharp and assessing. "Maybe being here all the time has made me forget that. It is good to see it through your eyes again."

"Then why don't you look happy?"

Sophia kept a firm grip on the reins as she watched Tomas's face. For a moment she thought he was going to say something, and then a muscle ticked in his jaw and she knew the moment had passed.

"This Miguel—he is Carlos and Maria's son?"

He nodded. "We became friends in university. An unlikely pair. Me from the city and him from the pampas."

Tomas laughed, but Sophia heard sadness behind it. "You weren't happy?"

"Maria and Carlos welcomed me like I was family. They were determined that Miguel have a better life. They might have been bitter about being poor, but instead they were just happy."

"And it isn't like that in your family?"

He laughed, but it sounded a bit forced. "No."

Sophia relaxed more in the saddle now, getting used to the shape and feel of it. "After she divorced my father, my mother was always very aware of the distinction of money... and the importance of opportunity. Hence my engagement to Antoine. A lawyer turned politician, full of money and ambition and the promise of power. He was everything she wanted in a son-in-law." In a flash of clarity, Sophia realized that her mother had wanted for her what she'd never quite had for herself. Sophia blinked, staring over the waving pampas grass, feeling some of her resentment fade as understanding dawned. "Mother just wanted security for me. When we announced our engagement, she was in heaven."

"And were you? In heaven?"

She thought back to the day she'd started working on Antoine's campaign staff. "I was dazzled for about thirty seconds. And then I was just practical. Antoine had a lot to offer. And he was charming and connected. He treated me well and I fancied myself in love with him, I suppose. We skated along and after a suitable amount of time he proposed. I would have a good life and he'd have a good wife for the campaign trail."

"Sounds passionate," he remarked dryly.

It hadn't been, and Sophia hoped she wasn't blushing. In this day and age it seemed unbelievable that in two years of dating and being engaged, she and Antoine had never slept together. Something had always held Sophia back. At the time she'd thought it sensible and cautious, considering how stories exploded through the news about the private lives of public people. Looking back now, though, she wondered if there hadn't been more to her decision she hadn't considered, if she hadn't put Antoine off for a bigger reason that even she hadn't understood. Looking at Tomas, feeling the thrill that zapped through her at the mere sight of him, she was beginning to see a glimmer of her reason. She'd overlooked an important ingredient—chemistry.

"Not exactly," she replied, staring out at the waving grasses. She'd blush again if she looked at Tomas. She was twenty-five years old and still a virgin. There was no way on earth she could say *that*.

"So, he was someone to keep you in shoes and handbags?" He tipped the brim of his hat back a little, his mischievous gaze settling on her face.

"Absolutely. More than that, it was stability." Something had changed between them. There was no malice in his accusation. She knew he was teasing, and she welcomed it. A teasing Tomas was far preferable to a grouchy one, even if his teasing did hit rather close to home at times. It was easier to take than the stares of disapproval. "Like Carlos and Maria, my mother was poor. My grandmother was a war bride from England and life on a Canadian farm wasn't all she'd dreamt it would be. She eventually divorced my grandfather. My mother fell into what she called the same trap, and she and my father split up when I was eight. Mom didn't handle poverty with the grace and humour of your friends, Tomas. She was alone. She was the one who made sure I had the opportunities and schooling and met all the right people."

Tomas nudged his mount forward, keeping the pace at a steady walk. "So you came here to throw it in your ex's face."

Had she? Perhaps in a way, but the trip had been far more about her than it had been about Antoine. "If I had wanted to throw it in his face, I would have gone to the media and given them all the details. It wasn't necessary. Calling off the wedding was damaging enough. Even without making an official statement, I had reporters in my face. It is big news when a high-profile party member is embroiled in a scandal—even if it's not quite clear what the scandal is." She angled him a wry smile and he smiled back.

"You're tougher than I thought," Tomas admitted. "Maybe I underestimated you, Sophia Hollingsworth."

"Maybe you did. But the real reason I came was because I was looking for someone."

He turned his head towards her again. "Who?"

A lump formed in Sophia's throat as she gripped the reins. The horse perked up at the feel of her hands through the leather.

"Me," she replied, and nudged the mare along and down the path leading to the creek.

CHAPTER FOUR

TOMAS followed her, his eyes trained on her back as it swayed gently with the motion of the horse. She had taken the initiative and started down the path before him, rather than follow behind. There was definitely more to Sophia than he thought. More than the designer shoes and air of supremacy she'd put on yesterday, or the panic she'd exhibited this morning during the spider episode. She was not experienced with horses. He'd known it from the start and had wanted to push her, test her. Not in a dangerous sort of way, after all he'd given her Neva, the gentlest mare in the stable. It was his job to gauge someone's experience and give them a proper mount. But he'd wanted to shake her up a bit. He'd nearly expected protests when she'd seen the gaucho saddle. But she hadn't said a single word. Just mounted and followed him.

She'd shown some pluck, and he liked that.

Maybe they had more in common than he'd thought. The thought niggled. He didn't want to find common ground. Maybe they had both felt pushed into a life of appearances. Tomas had lived that way once. For his father, money and status were everything. The biggest mistake of his life was going along with it as long as he had. He was far happier here, at Vista del Cielo.

Sophia just hadn't found her place yet, but it wasn't his job to show her. The words of assurance sat on his tongue but he remained silent, knowing that if he offered them to her, it would open him up to more questions. He wasn't sure where life was going to lead him and he didn't want to get into it with Sophia. Too many people offered their opinions as it was. As much as he loved it here on the estancia, his family kept asking when he was coming back. It was a question he could not answer. The idea of going back to Buenos Aires and taking his place at Motores Mendoza held little appeal. Lately he'd been feeling disconnected, and it unsettled him. Going back to Buenos Aires and the family business would sever that connection completely, and he couldn't do it.

"It is beautiful here," Sophia called from ahead of him. "So open and free." She reined in a bit so his horse's head was at her flank. "The big things melt away, don't they."

He exhaled slowly. Perhaps she was faking her riding experience, but there was no faking the approval he heard in her voice. "It does tend to put things in perspective," he replied carefully, pleased that she understood but still on his guard. Somehow the words tethered the two of them together, and that made him uncomfortable. "I have done a lot of thinking riding along this path." And he had, ever since the first visit when Miguel had brought him home to meet his family.

He'd walked in the door and everything in his world had changed. Everything. He had been greeted warmly. And he had laid eyes on Rosa and it was as though the world stopped turning.

The path grew steeper as they descended to the creek bed. She was being cautious, he noticed, knowing the *criollo* horses' nimble feet could more than handle the narrow path. At the bottom the mare gave a little hop and he heard a squeak come from ahead.

He watched the curve of Sophia's bottom as it swayed with the lazy stride of the mare. This morning he'd been sorely tempted to reach out and pull her into his arms when she'd seen the spider. Her alarm had been real, not put on, and he'd felt oddly protective of her. He shook his head. They would keep the pace slow, that was all.

A little further down the bed was a lee, sheltered from the wind. Tomas and Miguel had come here often to build a fire and share *mate*. He urged his horse forward and past Sophia, leading the way. If she didn't take a break, she would be sore in the morning from sitting in the saddle too long. This was the perfect place to rest. He had been here many times since coming to the estancia.

He dismounted and waited for her to follow, then tethered both horses to a low bush. "Come," he said, and held out a hand to help her over the scrabbly rocks. "I want to show you something."

She put her hand in his and his body tightened.

It was a trusting move and he hadn't expected the sweetness of it. The sharp-tongued cobra of yesterday had disappeared... when? When she'd come to the kitchen in her bare feet? This morning, when she'd blinked up at him in the baggy coveralls?

Her hand was small and soft and a lump formed in his throat. When was the last time someone had put their hand in his so trustingly? A long time. It bothered him that he couldn't remember. So many things he'd taken for granted and brushed off, not realizing how important they would become later. Things like the last time he had held Rosa's hand, kissed her lips. The last time he'd said "I love you" and heard her say his name. Those moments were gone forever, leaving a vacuum in their place.

They went to the curve in the hill where two flat rocks waited. "Oh!" she exclaimed, letting go of his hand and moving forward delightedly. Sophia went to the first stone and perched upon it, her hands on her knees.

She looked about eighteen years old. Where was the high fashion barracuda in stilettos demanding he make good on the reservation? It had been false bravado. He understood that now. The woman before him was an enchanting sprite with flaming curls and bright eyes. This was the real Sophia. Her excitement was fresh and genuine and far more difficult to resist.

"This is so neat! You can't even see it from above!"

"Which made it perfect for staying hidden." He followed her, moving towards the twin boulders, his boots crunching on the gravel.

"Who were you hiding from?"

"Mostly Carlos and Maria. Miguel and I would grab a couple of horses and come out. He was in a hurry to finish school and go to the city. I was dying to get out of the fast pace and expectations and this became my second home. He still loves it—I don't think you can take the pampas out of the boy. But he is working in Córdoba now, teaching at one of the universities."

He sat on the other stone and stared at the bubbling creek.

"Do you normally bring guests here on the trail rides? It's lovely."

"No, not usually." He suddenly knew this was a bad idea. The last thing he needed to do was start doing special things with her. She was no different than any other guest. She couldn't be.

"And so you have made your home with Maria and Carlos, working the estancia with them."

Tomas smiled. She made it sound so simple, when it wasn't. Not at all. He could tell her that he was joint owner, but for some reason he didn't want to.

"I prefer it to being with my own family. I know, that sounds awful, as if I don't love them. And I know in my way I do. But what you said before, about looking for someone…I understand that. It is when I am here that I feel most myself. If somehow a trip here is managing to give that to you, too, I'm glad. Sometimes…" He thought about what she'd told him only minutes before. "Sometimes being here I remember I don't have to try so hard."

They were quiet for a few moments. He looked over at Sophia. She was gazing out over the creek and the waving grasses, her expression utterly relaxed, her hands resting on her knees.

"I know what you mean about trying hard out here. It's beautiful, isn't it? I didn't think so when I first drove up. It wasn't what I was expecting. But now I think perhaps the estancia is well named. View of Heaven...yes. I think your pampas might have a way of winding itself around a person's heart."

And just like that, Sophia started winding herself around *him*. She understood what it was he felt about the pampas, about Vista del Cielo. It was the last thing he expected and the sensation was pleasant and disturbing all at once.

"I think I've been trying hard for a long time," she continued. "To please people. To be what they wanted me to be. I don't even really know what I want."

He nodded. "But you have time. You're what, twenty-four, twenty-five?" He traced a fingernail over the rock's surface. "This is a whole new beginning for you. You get to decide who you want to be."

Her smile was wide. "Thank you, Tomas." She tipped her *campero* back further on her head. "I sometimes worry that I've taken this trip for revenge. It's not a very attractive quality. After what you just said...I hope that instead I use it as a springboard for doing things better." He saw a glimmer of moisture in her eyes. "Living honestly, if that makes sense."

Oh, it made sense all right. And at least her catastrophe was only a cancelled wedding. She had no need of the remorse that Tomas still felt about his own personal wake-up call.

"Anyway," she changed the subject lightly, "I am looking forward to meeting Maria and Carlos." She stretched out her legs and tilted her face up to the sun.

"You will like them," he answered quietly.

"Do you suppose their son will ever have children? Is he married? My grandmother always joked that grandchildren were the bane of her existence. She didn't like kids any more than she liked farm life." Sophia chuckled.

Tomas did not know how to answer. She was just making simple chatter, but the subject of grandchildren was a painful one. As the silence stretched out, he searched for a safe topic of conversation. He thought about giving her a spiel on the history of the gaucho but suspected she'd see clear through his motive to deflect the conversation away from himself. "Or maybe you." She kept on, oblivious to the sickening churning he was feeling in his gut. "Maybe you will have children and will bring them out here to visit."

The innocently spoken words were like a knife in his heart.

He and Rosa had sneaked out to this spot on occasion too. If he had been any other boy, Carlos and Maria would have had a fit. But not with Tomas. They had trusted him to take care of Rosa. To keep her safe and cherish her. Sophia's words were nothing that he had not thought of a million times since Rosa's death. Time, and yes, even healing, could not erase the awful responsibility he felt.

"Tomas?"

He hadn't noticed her rising from her rock and coming to his side. Her small hand lay on his forearm and when he turned his head she was watching him, her dark eyes wide and worried. Her skin was creamy and her hair was a mass of flaming waves. But it was the concern, the gentle way she touched him and his reaction to it that caused pain and resentment to rip through his insides.

"Did I say something wrong?"

He shook his head, knowing she was not to blame. It was him, all him. *Take a breath,* he commanded himself. Sophia was a guest. That was all. He should still be grieving. He shouldn't be thinking of her this way.

"I think it is time we got back. I wanted to get the boxes moved into the boutique this afternoon."

She bit down on her lip and his gaze was drawn to it, unerringly, inevitably. Soft and pink, it regained its shape as her teeth released it.

He got up from the rock and straightened, staring unseeingly at the creek. He would not touch her. He would not kiss her or take her in his arms.

"Why do you shut people out all the time, Tomas? Or is it just me? For a few moments I think you're going to relax and then you wrap yourself in layers again."

She was right, and he refused to respond. What could he possibly say that would be appropriate? That he was contemplating how soft her skin might be beneath her blouse? The only thing he could do was remain silent.

"Did she hurt you that badly?" Sophia pressed him. "I asked about you before, but maybe it was the other way around. Did someone cheat on you the way that Antoine cheated on me?"

"What?" He swung his head around. "No. Never!"

But the question had revealed a chink in his armor. "So there was someone else," Sophia prodded.

She would not let this go, and what had begun as a relaxing afternoon changed into something painful and raw. Why was he finding it so hard to treat her like a guest? He should be pointing out landforms and local history and instead they were talking about failed relationships. How had he lost control so easily? How had she managed to get under his skin?

She thought he was some romantic gaucho figure, someone honorable and upright. But he wasn't. She had to stop looking at him this way—with a soft understanding, as if she knew… She didn't know.

He'd made peace with what had happened. He'd accepted

the blame. And he'd moved on to the kind of life he'd wanted, throwing himself into developing the estancia. Good, honest, put-your-back-into-it work. So why did Sophia have to show up now and make him want things he had no right wanting?

Two days. Two days and Maria and Carlos would be back. His duty would be discharged and he could be back behind the scenes where he belonged.

He retrieved Sophia's horse and brought the mare to her, holding the reins while she used the height of the rock to get her feet in the stirrups. "Hold her steady," he commanded, going to get his gelding and swinging up into the saddle.

Even with her own set of troubles, he still saw Sophia as naive. She'd had a rude awakening with this Antoine, but he knew deep down she still believed in a forever kind of love. In happily-ever-afters. Tomas had known for a long time how the world worked. Those who succeeded at love and marriage and happiness…they were just lucky. The majority of people wandered through life trying to figure out how they'd gotten so lost.

"Let's get back," he said tersely, nudging his horse forward and up the hardened slope. They needed to move on before he said something he'd really regret.

Like the truth.

Sophia gripped the reins in fingers slippery from the afternoon heat. Her thighs already ached from exercising unused muscles. She nudged the mare with her heels and followed Tomas up the slope and on to the level table of the pampas. He was already a bit ahead, and Sophia gritted her teeth.

She had done just fine during the first part of the ride, so she nudged the mare into a trot and hoped for the best. First he had clammed up when she'd asked a simple question. Now he had deliberately gone ahead and he hadn't looked back to check on her once. That particular fact agitated her. His bossiness was just another way of keeping that stoic, annoying distance. If he thought he could shake her that easily, that he could just ride off without another word, he had another think coming.

Her thighs burned as she tried to hold on to the saddle. *Don't let me fall off,* she prayed as she jounced along at a trot. Finally she caught up with Tomas.

"You might have waited."

Tomas looked over, his dark eyes shaded by his *campero*. Sophia felt a momentary flash of annoyance and attraction together, which only served to irritate her further. She should not find him attractive at all. He was a closed-mouthed, stubborn man who kept setting her up to fail. She was just about to tell him so when a puff of wind stirred up a dust devil in front of them.

Tomas's gelding shied and Tomas quickly settled him, but Sophia's mare took a scare and bolted, Sophia clinging helplessly to saddle and reins. Hooves pounded against the earth. She tried to keep her posture, but her feet bounced in the stirrups, bumping against the mare's side, unintentionally prodding her to go faster. Then Sophia heard Tomas shout in Spanish as the mare leapt forward, heading straight for the estancia at breakneck speed.

Sweat poured down her spine now and she could see the gate in front of her. If they didn't slow down soon…

Tomas shouted again. Desperately she pulled on the reins but their length was uneven in her damp palms and the mare shifted abruptly to her right. Everything seemed to slow as she felt the horse plant its feet, throwing her from the saddle. There was a sense of weightlessness as she flew through the air and a fear in knowing she was likely to be hurt.

When Sophia hit the ground, every last breath of air was forced from her lungs and she felt several seconds of panic as they refused to work. Finally new oxygen rushed in, painful and a blessed relief all in one.

Tomas reined in beside her and jumped off his horse, leaving the reins dangling from the bridle.

"Sophia!" Tomas knelt beside her and she felt his hands behind her shoulders as she tried to sit. "No, lie down," he commanded, gently placing her on the grass. "Catch your breath, and tell me you're all right."

His face swam before her eyes as she inhaled and exhaled, trying to steady her breathing to somewhat near normal even though her chest felt as though someone was stepping on it. Lying down helped. Tomas's hat was on the grass beside them and she saw a slight ring around his scalp where the band and sweat had flattened his short dark curls. He was beautiful, she realized. In an unreal sort of way—dark and mysterious and perfect. She felt horribly dirty, provincial and awkward. She'd tried to fake knowing what she was doing, but she'd been unequal to the task, just as she'd been at painting this morning. She'd failed yet again. All she'd had to do was stay in the saddle for another fifteen minutes and she would have been home free.

Now she looked like a prize idiot next to Tomas's stunning looks, self assurance and...

Oh Lord. The way he was looking at her right now. Like he *cared*. His lips were unsmiling, his eyes dark with anxiety. How long had she wished for someone to look at her in just this way? As though if something happened to her it would be a catastrophe? Antoine certainly never had. He'd acted as if her feelings, her needs, counted for nothing.

And counting for nothing hurt, dammit. She finally acknowledged to herself that Antoine's betrayal of her had hurt most because she had felt inconsequential. Had felt that she didn't matter.

Tomas's hand reached behind her head and cradled it in his hand, cushioning it from the hard earth. "Sophia, please," he said roughly. "Tell me where it hurts."

His plea broke through every defence she'd erected since

walking into the hotel room and seeing Antoine with his mistress. Her whole life hurt right now. She had never felt so alone. And the worst part of it was that she knew she couldn't make sense of any of it until she figured out who she was. It was a horrible, horrible feeling to realize that she'd lost herself along the way. She was like a boat bobbing aimlessly on the sea with no direction. And it had taken this rough-and-ready gaucho to make her see it. Maybe she'd looked like a fool just now, but there was no mistaking the genuine concern in his eyes. She held on to that, letting it be a beacon in the darkness.

I hurt everywhere, she thought, and she felt the telltale sting of tears behind her eyes. And the last thing she wanted was for him to see that. She'd lost enough face today.

She gripped his forearm with her hand and pulled herself up to sit.

"It's my fault," Tomas berated himself sharply. "I never should have gone off ahead. I knew you were inexperienced." He brushed a piece of hair off her cheek and tucked it behind her ear. "You were doing wonderfully. You have more pluck than I gave you credit for."

Sophia's face softened. Did Tomas blame himself? That was ridiculous. He couldn't have known the mare would run off.

"I'm fine," she insisted, knowing that nothing was broken, only bruised. There was an ache in her hip from landing on the hard ground, and she suspected she would be stiff later, but the greatest harm had been done to her pride. And yet his words stirred something warm inside. Had he actually said she'd been doing wonderfully? She had been faking the whole way, trying to remember what she'd learned about riding in those two childhood rides. So she hadn't fooled him. But she hadn't made a disaster of it, either. At least not until the end.

"At least you know I never do things halfway," she replied.

She looked around. Both horses were standing a few metres away, looking utterly unconcerned about Sophia's welfare. Her *campero* had flown off and was lying in the dust.

"Don't move," he ordered, and he went to the horses, gathering the reins and tethering them to the fence. He snagged her hat and came back, sliding an arm under her knees and picking her up while the *campero* dangled from his fingers. Her breath hitched as he stood and gave a little bounce, adjusting her weight in his arms.

"What are you doing?"

"Carrying you inside, what do you think?"

It was heavenly being in his arms, the primitive physicality of it thrilling. She was held closely against the wall of his chest, so close that she could see a single bead of sweat gather at the hollow of his throat. She wanted to reach out and touch it with the tip of her finger, but didn't have the courage to take such initiative.

He began carrying her towards the house. No man had ever done such a gallant thing for her before, and it would be very easy to get swept away. But this was definitely not standing on her own two feet and the last thing she wanted was to look like some helpless female. She'd done that enough today. "Please, put me down. I can walk."

"You took quite a fall, Sophia." His chocolatey eyes were still heavy with concern and a tiny wrinkle marred his brow.

Her arms had gone around his neck by instinct and her body bobbed with every long stride of his legs. "Then let me walk it off. Nothing is broken, Tomas. This is silly."

They reached the gate and she stuck out a hand, grabbing on to the metal bar and pulling them to a halt. "Let me down. You can walk me to the house if you want." His gaze caught hers for long seconds. "The fault is mine. I felt I had something to prove, but I was wrong. I should have asked for help. I didn't mean to scare you," she apologized.

He gave in and gently put her down. "Are you sure you're not hurt?"

She did hurt. She missed the feeling of being held in his arms already, and she ached all over. Her left hip pained when she put her weight on it. But it was just bruising. "Nothing serious. I'm more humiliated than anything."

They took slow steps to the house. Tomas remained right by her side, slowing his strides to match hers, his right arm always near in case she needed support. "I'm the one who should apologize, Sophia. You are inexperienced with horses, and I knew that. This is all my fault. I should not have ridden ahead."

"Why did you?" She hobbled along, looking up at him from beneath her *campero,* the hat resting crookedly atop her head.

"I…"

"You're going to put that wall around yourself again, aren't you? Fine. I get it. You are allowed to ask questions. I'm not. Loud and clear, Tomas."

"*Dios,* your tongue is sharp!" He bristled beside her. "You might have been killed, do you understand? What if Neva had gone down? What if she'd rolled on you?"

He turned on her, anger darkening his face now. "I should have stayed with you. You might have broken your neck."

"Oh, what would you care? You'll be glad to be rid of me, admit it!" she shot back. She instantly felt bad for saying it. "Tomas, I'm…"

But he never gave her a chance.

"*¡Maldita idiota!* I cannot figure you out. You panic at the sight of a spider, but when the danger is real…"

"Perhaps you should have thought of that before giving me a skittish horse that runs at the least little thing!"

"I gave you the calmest horse in the stable!" They were standing in the middle of the yard now, shouting.

"Do you treat all your clients this way?" She scoffed, her

voice ripe with derision. Her blood was up now and it felt marvelous! All the righteous anger she'd channeled into cancelling the wedding and reorganizing her life came bubbling to the surface. "Oh wait…I'm the only one. Remind me why that is again?"

"¡Cállate!" He shouted. "Enough!"

And then he gripped her arms in his strong hands and kissed her.

The pain in her hip disappeared as his lips covered hers. Passion, a passion she hadn't known she even possessed, exploded within her and she reached out to hang on to his shirt. He braced his feet, forming a solid wall for her to lean against, and in return she twined her arms around his ribs and over his shoulder blades, craving the feel of his body against hers.

This was what had been missing, she realized with a shock. Pure, unadulterated physicality. The kind of force that rushed in like a hurricane and frightened the hell out of her.

She shuddered and the fingers gripping her arms eased. His mouth gentled over hers until his lips played, teased, seduced.

It made her want to weep. How was it that even in anger this stranger seemed to know exactly what she needed? How did he know that she needed gentleness?

"Are you still angry at me?" she whispered as their lips parted. She couldn't make herself meet his gaze; instead she stared at his mouth as though she hadn't seen it before. Full lips, crisp in their perfection, soft when they needed to be soft, firm when they needed to be commanding…

"Yes," he admitted, letting out a ragged breath. "Are you still angry at me?"

"No."

"Why?"

She sighed. "Because I'm tired of being angry."

"I shouldn't have shouted. You scared me, Sophia."

"I scared myself."

She risked a look up at him then. His eyes were dark with concern again and she marveled at it—why should he care about her? Who was she to him? But she wasn't about to argue. At the moment, sad as it was, he was all she had.

He turned from her and they began walking towards the house again. Sophia's legs felt like jelly after the kiss, but she forced one foot ahead of the other.

"Why didn't you say anything earlier when I mentioned going riding?"

"I didn't want you to know." She raised her chin. "After the way I showed up yesterday, and then my overreaction this morning...I didn't want you to think I was some vapid female who couldn't handle as much as a broken nail. I didn't expect to be racing across the pampas, either."

She wouldn't look at him, but to her right, she heard a soft chuckle. "You are very stubborn, Sophia Hollingsworth."

"Thank you. I'll take that as a compliment."

This time he really did laugh, and the sound reached in and expanded inside her. She knew it was ridiculous. She had made a miscalculation and now she was limping back to the house, dirty and with dented pride claiming that stubbornness was an attribute and not a fault.

"I didn't foresee that happening. I was a very poor tour guide today. If nothing else, I should have asked you about your experience instead of assuming."

"And what would you have done differently? Stop blaming yourself." She stopped and put a hand on his arm. His solicitousness was lovely, but it wasn't required. "It was the wind, that's all." Her body warmed as their kiss was still foremost in her mind. "And...about what happened before...I don't want you to fix things, Tomas. I came on this holiday to be my *own* solution. Please don't take this as an insult. I'm coming to understand I have spent far too long being at the mercy of other people. I need to prove to myself that I am capable, too."

"And just what did this afternoon prove?" He raised an eyebrow, challenging.

They were at the house now and Sophia paused with her hand on the door.

What did it prove? Perhaps that the appreciation she had for Tomas had blossomed into full-blown attraction. And it had proved that the feeling was mutual. The potential in that stopped her in her tracks. It was an exhilarating, terrifying thought.

She took a careful breath. "It proved I am in dire need of a hot bath. And perhaps a glass of wine."

"I think the Vista del Cielo can handle that."

But Tomas waited a moment before backing away. "Are you sure you're okay? I can call a doctor." His hand rested on her shoulder and she tried not to like the heat of it there— but she did anyway. She could protest all she wanted, but it felt good to be cared for, taken care of, even just a little. The simple touch made her wonder what it would be like if he came inside with her, maybe kissed her again. Would it be as good the second time? Better?

"Truly, I'm fine, thank you." She didn't want him to leave. She wanted to see him smile, and feel the way his gaze fell on her, warm and approving in the Argentine sun. She wanted him to touch her cheeks with his lips again and maybe slide that small distance to her mouth. Her gaze fell unerringly on his lips too and then back up to his eyes. She'd give up her soak in the bath for that.

"I will see you later. I must look after the horses if you are all right."

"I'm not going anywhere."

She wasn't going anywhere, not yet. But in another week she would be on a plane headed back to Canada. That much would not change no matter how enamored she became of her surroundings. She took one last approving look at his retreating figure. *All* of her surroundings.

CHAPTER FIVE

"WHAT are you doing?" Tomas asked, stepping into the kitchen. He'd spent a long time in the barns, avoiding Sophia after their kiss. Needing to clear his mind. It hadn't worked. The taste and feel of her stayed with him until there was no more tack left to polish. He'd put things off a little longer by having a quick shower. Now he'd come to the kitchen to scrounge something to eat, never expecting to find Sophia there. He'd figured she'd be exhausted from her eventful day.

"Making dinner. You were busy in the barn, and I was cleaned up, so…" she broke off the sentence, turning around to face him as she wiped her hands on a towel. "I didn't know what sort of food you were used to, so I put together a cold meal. I hope that's okay."

Tomas stepped forward, just enough to catch the perfumed scent of her skin. She should have been dead on her feet after the extraordinary day they'd had. Instead he found her here looking like an ad in a magazine. She wore a dress that managed to hug her figure yet appear elegant, drawing his gaze to the soft curve of her hips. Her hair was up in some sort of twist that looked simple and casual and that he expected took a great deal of talent to arrange. Silver and amethyst earrings dangled at her ears. And the shoes were back. Lower heels this time, but he raised his eyebrows at the sandals that blended shades of pink, lime green and turquoise. They should have been garish. Instead, they complemented everything, making her look young and stylish.

Like the woman who had arrived yesterday. Tomas knew he should be relieved. It was easier to distance himself from her when she looked like this—foreign and out of his league.

But he missed how her eyes had glittered up at him from beneath her *campero* and how cuddly she'd appeared in his coveralls. "You didn't have to make dinner."

"But you said everyone pitches in. I ditched you earlier— literally. And my bath was very refreshing. I fear today's activities have left me starving."

She smiled up at him and he felt his breath catch. This was wrong. It was purely physical. But it was just attraction. Nothing more. He could handle it. Another few days and she'd be gone. Just a blip on the libido radar until things got back to normal.

"How is your hip?" he enquired politely, ignoring the way his pulse had quickened and moving to help with the preparations. She'd already laid out a selection of cold meats from the fridge, as well as cheese and sliced vegetables. The food was placed strategically on a platter, in sections and precise layers that made it a work of art.

"Sore, but the bath helped, and the scented salts, too. They are a lovely addition to the room, Tomas. It should be mentioned to Maria. A nice touch." She put the last few slices of tomato in place and stood back. "There. All that is missing is slicing the bread."

"I can do that. You should get off your feet." Tomas felt off balance at the change in their conversation. In some ways it felt polite and distant, and yet there was a comfortableness to it that made it seem that they'd known each other far longer than a couple of days. And then there was the kiss that neither of them had mentioned. It stood between them, a lump of something that was hard to ignore. They had both retreated to their respective corners since then, looking for solid footing. Had it affected her as strongly as it had him?

He sliced the bread and Sophia laid it on a plate around a small bowl of herbed butter. "Let's eat outside," Tomas suggested. He wouldn't feel so closed in if they ate in the backyard. "I can light a fire. We often do in the evenings."

"That would be lovely." Again she smiled, warm and polite, and Tomas got the sneaky suspicion that it was her friendly meet-the-politician smile.

It was no more than he deserved, and he should be glad she'd taken a step back. But he hated it.

They carried the food outdoors, and while Sophia went back into the kitchen to retrieve a bottle of wine and glasses, Tomas began laying a fire.

This formality was exactly what he'd wanted. So why did it feel so awkward?

After the meal he insisted on doing the cleaning up and sent Sophia to rest her hip. When the last dish was dry and back in the cupboard, he found her in the living room, curled into a corner of the sofa, sleeping.

She looked so innocent with her lashes on her cheeks and her lips relaxed in slumber. Her shoes were on the floor and her dress had slid up her thigh, revealing the soft skin to his gaze. Gently, so as not to wake her, he ran his finger up the smooth length, stopping at the hem and drawing back. He didn't know what to make of her. One moment fragile, the next stubborn as a mule. Today he'd felt he'd let her down. He knew she could have been seriously injured, and he'd expected her to retreat to spoiled form. But instead she'd risen above it and had proved her mettle.

He reached out and touched her shoulder, and as her eyes opened and focused on his he felt the burning start, deep in his gut.

"It's time for bed," he said quietly.

For a few moments something hummed between them.

The memory of the afternoon's kiss seemed to sizzle in the air. Her eyes had the same hooded, dazed look now as they'd had then, and he swallowed, resisting the urge to reach out and run his thumb over her cheekbone.

He had the most irrational thought of taking her down the hall to the family quarters and tucking her beneath his sheets before crawling in beside her and holding her close. Her dark eyes showed the slightest hint of alarm as if she understood the direction of his thoughts even though no words had been spoken.

But that was wrong, and crazy, and definitely not what Maria had meant when she'd ordered him to look after their guest. He stepped back and cleared his throat.

"Sleep well, Sophia," he said, and gathering all his willpower, walked down the hallway alone.

Sophia dug in her pitchfork, wrinkled her nose and, holding her breath, deposited the soiled straw in the wheelbarrow.

When she'd heard Tomas rise this morning, she'd hurriedly hopped out of bed and pulled on the *bombachas* of yesterday. She would not be late. She was determined not to lag. She put her hand on her still-aching hip. She'd show Tomas she was made of sterner stuff. Last night she'd been exhausted and still reeling from Tomas's kiss. Putting on the dress and shoes and making dinner was the best way to keep her guard up, to show him a tumble from a horse would not defeat her. And neither would a most heavenly kiss from her sexy gaucho. What she wanted and how far she was prepared to go were two very different things.

The kiss had nearly been repeated before bed last night. She had seen it in his eyes, and for a few seconds she had leaned the slightest bit towards him, her nerve endings on high alert. In the end he'd backed away. She should have been relieved. Would he expect her to be a woman of the world? She knew she was an anomaly—a virgin at her age. The pull to him was undeniable, but her hesitancy was equally strong.

She'd lain awake a long time thinking about it, and this morning she'd awakened tired but more determined than ever to pull her weight. To prove that she was up to any challenge he could throw at her.

But that was before she'd realized that the first chores of the morning were mucking out stalls and feeding the horses. Now Tomas had turned the stock out into a nearby pasture to graze while they shoveled manure. There was no other polite way to put it. She put another forkful in the barrow as Tomas strode up the corridor whistling. It was obscenely early to sound so cheerful. When she saw his boots stop beside her, she turned with a scoop of dirty straw and was deliberately careless so that a bit fell on his boots with a plop.

Then, calm as you please, she deposited the rest in the wheelbarrow.

"Thank you for your help this morning," Tomas said, shaking off his foot, unconcerned. "You're really getting into the swing of things now, aren't you?"

The sun was barely up and Sophia was dying for a first cup of coffee, and the sooner they finished the sooner she could have it. But despite the unpalatable chore, the dew on the grass and the early morning birdsong somehow made everything rosier. "It's not so bad."

He took the pitchfork from her hand. "I'll get rid of this. There's fresh straw over there to put in the stalls."

Sophia spent the next fifteen minutes putting down the layer of straw, all the while listening to Tomas's cheerful whistling. After the hours she'd spent puzzling out what exactly their kiss had meant, Tomas was acting as if nothing had happened at all. She shook out the last of the straw and dusted off her hands.

"Are you ready for breakfast?" Tomas came back around the corner and Sophia straightened, bracing her lower back with both hands. There had been a communion to working with him this morning. A satisfaction of working together, much like that she'd felt yesterday as they'd painted the shed. Her stomach grumbled and Tomas smiled at her. "I'll take that as a yes."

She followed him back to the house as the sun peeked over the rolling hills, colouring the pampas with a fresh, warm glow. She inhaled deeply, enjoying the open space that was at once youthful and timeless. Each day started anew, with the flaws of yesterday behind it. As they reached the door she closed her eyes and let out a breath. Antoine, her mom, her friends—they would be appalled at the fact that she'd spent her first daylight hours cleaning a dirty horse barn. And yes, it had been an unusual experience. But not a bad one.

As she and Tomas pulled off their boots, Sophia realized she was perhaps made of more than she was given credit for. Perhaps she simply hadn't tried because it had been safer that way. Secure. No risk, no loss.

"What's so funny?" Tomas's voice broke through her thoughts as he went to the sink to wash up. She joined him there, sharing the soap as they washed their hands beneath the running water.

"Two days ago when I arrived, I didn't plan on shoveling… well, you know."

"You did a fine job for a beginner."

She dried her hands and gave him the towel. "Thank you, but now I want to know what's to eat. All that fresh air has given me an appetite." She would kill for bacon and eggs, the sort of breakfast that never passed her lips anymore. Perhaps it was the combination of hard work and fresh air. Perhaps it was knowing that she need not hold to the conventions of the past at Vista del Cielo. Either way, she was famished.

As if he read her mind, Tomas took eggs from the fridge. "I will fry some eggs and there is the bread from yesterday."

Her mouth watered at the thought of a fried-egg sandwich. "That sounds perfect."

They worked together to prepare the meal, and once they sat at the table Tomas asked, "How's the hip?"

Sophia chewed and swallowed. It still pained, but she didn't want it to keep her from whatever Tomas had planned for the day. Now that she had made a success of something, she wanted to build on the momentum. The sense of accomplishment was addictive. "It's a little sore, but I'm no worse for the wear."

"Since the chores are done, I thought you might like a trip into town. You can find some clothes there, perhaps some souvenirs to take back home with you."

"What about the shed? We still have to put on another coat of paint." But Tomas shook his head.

"I decided it can wait. We should be back later this afternoon and I can paint it then."

"Are you sure?"

Tomas swiped his bread across his plate. "Yes, I'm sure. You helped this morning. It is your vacation after all. If Maria were here, she would take you on a day trip to town. In her absence, it's my job."

Sophia felt her excitement deflate. This was nothing more than Tomas living up to his responsibilities once again. Making up for yesterday, too, she supposed. It had nothing to do with actually *wanting* to spend time with her. It was his duty. His job.

Still, a day in town sounded fun. She didn't want to spend her whole trip on the estancia. She wanted to see new things. And perhaps she could purchase some comfortable clothes. But first she'd have to have a shower to get rid of the barn smell.

"Just give me twenty minutes to clean up."

Back in Canada, it would have taken her three times that

long to be ready for a day out. Sophia smiled as she took her plate to the sink.

In Argentina, nothing was the same.

"Me, too," Tomas replied. As Sophia went back to her room to gather fresh clothing, she told herself she would not think about Tomas's dark, lean body beneath the shower spray.

Sophia's feet were beginning to ache from all the walking, but it had been worth it. She wiped her lips with a paper napkin and then crumpled it, tossing it into a nearby garbage bin. They'd stopped at a sausage cart for lunch, grabbing a snack to tide them over before heading back to the estancia for the afternoon. The chorizo had been suitably spicy and the bread chewy and fresh. Beside her, Tomas gave a satisfied sigh and she smiled.

"That was delicious."

"Not fancy, but one of my favourites." He too wiped his mouth and disposed of the napkin.

The afternoon was hot and Sophia soaked in the heat, enjoying the feel of it on her skin. Tomas had proven a better tour guide than she'd expected. They'd spent the morning visiting the Gaucho Museum and browsing the silver shops, admiring the craftsmanship. She'd bought two casual outfits and a pair of silver earrings for her mother as a gift. Meanwhile, Tomas had taken her to a local *bodega* where he'd picked up several bottles of Malbec, claiming it was Maria's particular favourite. Once they'd stowed their packages in the estancia's SUV, he'd suggested a quick lunch of grilled sausage wrapped in a bun. It had been perfect. They had munched while walking along the river. Now, with the shops closing for the afternoon, they ambled along the pathway.

A group of boys were playing soccer ahead, their shouts a happy sound in the peaceful quiet. "This is such a lovely town," Sophia said. "Honestly, Tomas, the more I see you here the more I understand. I'm a city girl, where things are vibrant and rush, rush, rush. But here, it's…" She broke off, confused. "It's hard to explain."

But Tomas nodded. "That's what staying at the Vista del Cielo is all about, remember? Maybe sometimes I take the quiet and slower pace for granted."

He paused and faced her, taking her hands in his. "Sophia…"

He stopped and his jaw tightened. His fingers clasped hers tightly as she looked up into his face, falling under the spell of his dark gaze as her heart began to pound. Did he possibly know how attractive he was, how magnetic? They didn't even have to be close to one another for her to feel the pull. It had been there yesterday, too, even as they'd shouted at each other.

But now, as he held her hands in his, she couldn't help but wonder what it would be like to throw caution to the wind and take things a step further. A holiday romance had been the very last thing on her mind when she'd left Canada. But faced with Tomas… The trouble was that he wasn't just a sexy, enigmatic gaucho anymore. She knew what it was like to see him smile. Her heart still caught when she remembered the look in his eyes as he'd cradled her head in his hand yesterday, asking if she was all right.

And her body practically sang at the memory of feeling his lips on hers. She couldn't deny the possibility of a brief romance held a certain allure. But as soon as she thought it, she dismissed it. What if she flirted? Tried to get him to kiss her again? Then what? What would he expect? Maybe nothing. But maybe a whole lot more than she was comfortable with. In some ways, she'd already bitten off more than she could chew with this trip. Tempting Tomas might definitely turn into more than she could handle, and if she were honest with herself, she just wasn't ready.

"Is there something you want to say?" She gave his fingers a gentle squeeze.

For a long moment his gaze plumbed hers, but then he released her hands. "Just…it seems strange to be saying this, but seeing your view of the town, the pampas…" He paused, then offered a small smile, just a faint curving of his lips that reached out and held her in its grasp. "I had forgotten how to appreciate it," he said. "Thank you."

"Me? I've done nothing. I know I came across as a bit of a princess, Tomas…"

His warm chuckle sent tingles down her arms.

"I'm really not. Not deep down."

He looked as if he wanted to say something, but instead merely inclined his head towards the path. "Let's walk."

And there he went again, poking his head out of his shell just a little bit before turtling in again. It frustrated her even though she knew it was probably for the best.

They resumed walking along the path. "I'm afraid I haven't been very good company. I hope Carlos and Maria don't plan on using me as a tour guide very often."

"Don't be silly. I arrived unexpectedly and threw a monkey wrench into your week."

"You're our guest, Sophia."

He'd said *our* and not *my* and Sophia felt the difference. She watched the boys kick the ball around, one rushing in to score a victorious goal. Another boy, smaller, scuffed his toe on the ground in frustration. Sophia knew how that felt. It was like trying to gain Tomas's approval. It was a rare commodity, and somehow she felt it was worth striving for. A romance was out of the question. There was so much potential for things to go wrong. But she somehow wanted to think that they were friends of a sort. Someone who was a friend to the new and improved Sophia.

"I…I'd like to think maybe we're friends," she said quietly.

"Friends?" he asked, and she heard the surprise in his voice. Didn't he have friends? Was it so incomprehensible?

"Sure," she smiled as their steps slowed even further.

"*Amigos.* I mean, you know more about me than you normally would about a guest, right? Far more than 'where are you from, what do you do?'"

"I suppose."

But did friends get that twirling of anticipation from simply knowing they were going to be together? She knew they didn't. There was more between them. The question was, were they going to ignore it or explore it? Which did she really want? This was supposed to be a simple trip, uncomplicated. And Tomas was one big sexy complication.

They kept on until they reached the *Puente Viejo,* a gorgeous salmon-pink bridge spanning the river. They stood at the crest of it and rested their arms on the ledge, looking down at the smooth water.

"Sophia," Tomas began, and she looked up at him, surprised to see his brows pulled together in a pensive frown when they were in one of the most beautiful, relaxing places she could remember.

"What is it?"

"As friends, I feel I should apologize for kissing you yesterday."

"It has bothered you," she acknowledged. Was this why he'd spent hours in the barn rather than coming to the house? Was it why he'd brought her to town today? Guilt?

"I was very out of line yesterday, Sophia. You gave me such a scare. I fear my actions made you uncomfortable."

Oh yes. In the most heart-stopping, glorious way, but there was no way she was going to tell him that. Especially when he clearly didn't feel the same. With Tomas it was always duty first. She could resent him for that if it weren't so darned admirable.

"It's okay, Tomas." Sophia forced a smile when she felt none. "I know it was just a reaction. The fall scared us both. I know it wasn't real."

Tomas didn't respond and the silence was more awkward

than any words might have been. Was there any clearer confirmation? She needed to say something, something to dispel the tense atmosphere. Was Tomas thinking about it as she was? Clearly he regretted it. He was not interested in her. She, on the other hand, was remembering the kiss quite differently. She was feeling quite giddy about it, which wouldn't do at all.

"I'm afraid I'm not a great host," Tomas said, relaxing just a little. Sophia supposed clearing the air about the kiss was a relief to him. Tomas linked his fingers together over the railing. "Maria is much better at this sort of thing. She knows how to make people at home."

What would Maria say if she knew Tomas had held Sophia in his arms? Or that Sophia had kissed him back as though she was dying of thirst and he was cool, reviving water?

"She'd flay me alive," Tomas continued, almost as if he'd heard Sophia's question. "For letting you take a fall like that."

"It sounds like she cares about you. As a mother would."

He laughed then, quietly, but it was warm and heartfelt, and Sophia loved how it changed his face.

"Maria is the heart and soul that keeps *this* family together," he said easily. "I'm afraid of what she'd say if she saw you. She'd be meddling in the first five minutes."

"Why?"

This time when Tomas met her gaze, he said nothing, but then he didn't have to. The memory of their kiss was suddenly front and centre again, the diversion shattered. "Do you have experience with meddling mothers?" Tomas said it quietly, his magnetic gaze never leaving hers, with tacit acknowledgement that they were attempting to change the subject.

Which made the attraction they were trying to ignore simmer all the stronger.

Sophia forced a laugh. "Are you kidding? My mother is the biggest meddler of them all. She was the one that introduced me to Antoine. And she pushed me into a country club wedding."

"Don't all girls want a fancy wedding?" Tomas stood tall and turned to face her, resting against the bridge.

She shook her head. "Not all girls. I didn't. Not a big production with two hundred guests, a photographer and a champagne fountain. I would have chosen something far simpler."

"I still find it hard to believe this Antoine let you get away."

"Oh, he didn't. He just thought he could have everything," she replied. And he had. Antoine had never considered that he would get caught. And even if he had, the expectation was that she'd fall in line just as she always did.

"It's made me think about my gram a lot," Sophia admitted. "Gram hated her life on the farm. She'd had a very different childhood in England. But I don't think she ever got over leaving her husband. He was the right man in the wrong place, you know? She always sort of regretted leaving him, I think." Sophia touched her finger to one of the amethyst earrings she'd always loved and sighed. "She gave me these when I was a girl. They'd been a gift from him. I think having them caused her more pain that she'd admit. Gram always said she didn't know what was worse—a love that was impossible or one that was practical and suitable. After what happened with Antoine, I think I realized that practical and suitable really isn't love at all. It was hard to understand at the time, but now I know that his infidelity broke my spirit, but it didn't break my heart."

"I'm glad he wasn't the great love of your life. You would have been far more hurt if it had been otherwise."

"Like you were?"

"What makes you say such a thing?" He conjured up a look so innocent Sophia couldn't help but chuckle.

"I get it. You won't talk about it. That's okay."

"I can't, that's all."

What was so awful he couldn't bring himself to talk about it? But then, Tomas wasn't the type to do much talking anyway. What little bits she got from him were too small to let her piece them together to get a complete picture. She traced a finger over the pink stone of the bridge. "Why is it parents—and grandparents, I suppose—think they know best?"

Disappointed by his silence, she pushed away from the bridge. "Well, at least you're not hiding a mistress somewhere." Suddenly her gaze narrowed. "Are you?"

He laughed, and relief flooded through her though she couldn't quite imagine why. "No," he chuckled, "I'm not hiding a mistress of any sort." He folded his arms. "Would it truly matter if I were?"

His soft question shattered the silence and she inhaled, held her breath. And then she turned her gaze up to him again and her chest constricted. "Yes," she murmured. "It would. It would destroy the good opinion I have of you, Tomas."

"Good opinion?" His mouth dropped open in surprise and then he shut it again just as quickly.

She wanted to tell him why but didn't know how without feeling like an idiot. How did she tell him what it meant for him to pay her the smallest compliment? How it restored her confidence when he wondered how Antoine could have let her get away? And the kiss aside, she had seen the worry and fear on his face as he'd leapt off his horse and come rushing to her side after she'd fallen off Neva. Yes, good opinion.

And to elaborate would make her look like a girl with a crush—starstruck by her knight in shining armor.

Sophia noticed a small girl standing on tiptoe a few meters away, her hands on the edge of the bridge. She swung her arm and two coins dropped into the water. When they sank to the bottom, the girl ran off, pigtails bobbing, to clasp her mother's hand and continue across the bridge.

"What's she doing?" Sophia asked, intrigued.

"Many people stand in this very spot and throw coins in the water," he said quietly. "They toss them in and make a wish."

Once again Sophia went to the edge and looked down. She wondered what the little girl had wished for. Tomas came up behind her. She felt his body close to hers, felt as though every place they nearly touched was alive. "What about you?" she asked quietly, trying to still the sensations coursing through her. "Have you made wishes?"

He pulled back, putting space between them and she sighed, shaking her hair back over her neck. Why was it she always seemed to ask the very thing that would break the spell?

She wondered how often he might have stood here in the past. She wondered what he had wished for. Did he believe in wishes at all? Or did he think this was just a tourist trap and a pretty story?

It took a while for him to answer, but when he did, his voice was low and rough from behind her. "I did, a long time ago."

"What did you wish for?"

Tomas sighed, and moved slowly to stand at the edge of the bridge, looking down into the water. "Things that could never be."

Sophia felt the same odd warning slide through her as she'd felt yesterday when he'd been so cryptic during their ride. Tomas was hiding something. He was so reticent, so closed-lipped, she knew it had to be big. She wanted to know, desperately. But what gave her the right to ask? They'd only known each other a few days. It was none of her business.

"Now you're going to chide me for holding out on you. For not baring my soul."

It was as if he read her mind. Sophia shook her head. "I know when I'm beaten. Getting anything out of you is like getting blood from a stone."

"Be careful what you wish for," he answered, dark tension clouding his voice.

"I haven't made a wish yet, so don't worry."

He dug into his pocket and drew out some coins, coming to stand beside her at the edge of the bridge. "Wishes should be happy things. They should be about looking forward." He held out his hand, offering her the change. "Didn't you come on this trip to look forward, Sophia?"

"Yes, I did."

"Then make your wish."

There it was, that swirling again, that anticipation of possibilities. His fingertips touched her palm as he gave her the money.

"I don't know what to wish for. It's been a wonderful day with you." She tilted her head up to look at him. "I've kind of enjoyed living in the moment."

"I've enjoyed it, too," he admitted. He raised an eyebrow. "Maybe you should wish for better riding skills. I'd like to take you out again this week."

"That might be a wise idea." She laughed lightly, but ended it on a soft sigh. "I needed this vacation badly," she murmured, watching a duck bobbing on the surface. "I didn't really know how much. Despite my obvious lack of equestrian prowess, I'm finding I kind of like myself. I haven't for a while."

Tomas leaned closer, putting his free hand on her waist. "You are turning out to be a surprise to me, too. You're not nearly as annoying as I thought you'd be."

Coming from Tomas, that was nearly a declaration. Her heart hammered at his nearness, and she felt herself get swept up in the moment. His lips hovered close and she rose up on her toes, tentatively touching her mouth to his.

The gentle contact blossomed into something more, something deeper, and Sophia clutched the coins tightly in her palm as her other hand gripped his arm. Behind them a group of boys hooted and clapped. She broke off the kiss, lowering her heels to the ground once more, slightly abashed and affected by the kiss just enough that she couldn't meet his gaze.

But that didn't stop Tomas from leaning forward and murmuring in her ear, "Make a wish, Sophia."

She closed her eyes, wished and tossed the coins into the shimmering water.

"Your turn," she said, turning away from the circles spiraling out from the coins she'd thrown.

Tomas shook his head. "No, I've made my wishes before. Today is for you to experience."

He looked so serious her heart stuttered and she smiled, trying to cajole him out of his somber mood. "Come on. What can it hurt? A few *centavos* in the river."

A dark look shadowed his features and Sophia drew back. "Tomas?"

He simply shook his head, stepping back, his face an immutable formation of angles and planes.

What had he wished for that had caused so much pain? She reached out and laid a hand on his arm. It was taut as a band of steel beneath her touch.

"What is it? Please, Tomas, tell me. Let me help you, like you've helped me."

"I should not have brought you here," he murmured. "You and your questions…"

"But you did bring me here, and it is lovely. There is more to you than you want people to see." She squeezed the muscle beneath her fingers. "But I see it. I know you are hurting. Does it have something to do with this bridge? Tell me what you wished for."

His dark gaze seared her for several seconds. "I wished to forget," he finally said, grinding out the words like shards of glass. "I wished to forget and now I wish to God I hadn't."

CHAPTER SIX

TOMAS wished he could bite back the words. What had made him admit such a thing? What was it about Sophia that got around his guard without him expecting it? Her kiss just now had nearly undone him. It had been innocent and sweet and freely given. She'd initiated it, not him. It hadn't been in anger or fear or any other sort of reactionary emotion, either. She had simply lifted her face like a rising sun and touched her lips to his.

He'd liked it—too much. So much that his mind had been wiped clean of anything but her until the boys had shouted and brought him crashing back to earth. He wasn't supposed to like it.

Dammit, she wasn't supposed to be able to see so much.

"Tomas." Her soft voice saying his name seemed to catch him right in the solar plexus, jamming up his breath. "What are you trying to forget? What has hurt you so much?"

He had to tell her. Had to tell someone or it would eat away at him like acid. He couldn't tell Maria or Carlos; he felt guilty enough already. With the changes going on at the estancia, it was as though the past was being erased a little more each day. With every new building and updated amenity he felt Rosa slipping further and further away. He knew Maria would not understand. She would be hurt, knowing he was moving on. And he wouldn't hurt Maria for the world.

"You are not the only one with a failed engagement, Sophia," he said quietly, running his fingers over the edge of the bridge. Sophia's lips dropped open and he clarified, "But it wasn't broken off. My fiancée died."

Sophia's large brown eyes glazed over with tears as she absorbed his words. "Oh, Tomas," she whispered. "That's horrible."

It had been. It had easily been the worst moment of his life, when the police had brought the news of Rosa's death. Like a knife to the heart, only the pain never went away.

"Was she ill?"

He shook his head. "No. She was mugged in Buenos Aires. The autopsy said the cause of death was blunt force to the head."

Sophia's fingers went to her mouth; he saw them trembling there. Her normally rosy cheeks drained of color. Why were the details so easy to repeat now? It was as though he was talking about another person, another lifetime. "It was three years ago," he finished.

"I'm so sorry," she murmured, taking his hands in hers. "And here I was whining over my situation. Oh Tomas," she whispered, her voice breaking, "How did you stand it?"

He spun away, away from the pity in her eyes and the sympathy in her voice. Turned away from the benevolent scene of ducks bobbing away on the water, evidence that the world kept on turning, blithely uninterested in whatever suffering he'd encountered. He had grieved so hard, so completely, that he would have done anything to take away the pain. "Now you know why I came to the bridge. There was a time that all I wanted to do was make the pain go away. To forget all the things that made me hurt."

"And you regret that now?"

He turned back and looked at Sophia, so young and naive. She really had no idea. "I shouldn't forget. I should be able to remember what she looked like, but sometimes I can't.

It's like she's there but blurred, you know? The sound of her voice when she laughed at a joke. The way she moved. Those things are slipping away from me." He scowled. "Especially when I'm with you."

"I make you forget?" Her voice was small.

"Yes, dammit, you do."

Long seconds passed and Tomas realized he'd been breathing fast and hard. He slowed his breaths to normal. He had made it sound as though this was her fault when it wasn't. "I'm sorry, Sophia. It is not your fault. It is mine."

"You don't need to grieve forever, Tomas. It is okay to move on. To have a life." She tried to curve her trembling lips into a smile, but they faltered. "To be happy. It doesn't mean you loved her less."

"Perhaps," he responded, knowing in his head she was right but feeling that heavy, sinking feeling in his heart just the same. "But it feels…"

"Disloyal to her memory?"

He nodded, not sure if he was relieved or not that she seemed to understand.

"Oh, Tomas. You are a good man beneath all your prickles and stings." Sophia took his hand and led him back to the edge of the bridge. He let himself be guided because he didn't know what else to do. "Is that why you hide away at the estancia?"

"At first it was to be close to her…"

Sophia's head whipped around to stare at him. Surprise widened her eyes and he realized that, of course, she didn't know the rest. "Rosa was Maria and Carlos's daughter," he clarified.

He saw the shock ripple across her face, and couldn't blame her. What would she say if she knew opening the estancia as a guest ranch had been his idea? Or if she knew he had been the financial backer behind it? He had already seen her impression of him change before his eyes as he told her about Rosa.

"I didn't see that coming," she admitted, and his eyes focused on her throat as she swallowed thickly. "So, what, you moved to the estancia after her death? To be close to her family?"

"They are *my* family, Sophia. Carlos and Maria are like parents to me. There was nowhere else I wanted to be. But since the fire, with all the changes happening, it doesn't feel the same. It is not the same place I came to when I was younger. I went home with Miguel and there she was. There they all were. I've been trying to hold on to that feeling, but it's slipping away."

"You're not just grieving for Rosa, then," Sophia replied softly. "You're grieving for everything that was and isn't anymore. You're grieving for your grief. And you feel awful for wanting to move on with your life. But Tomas....this is a good thing. Living now doesn't mean you didn't love her."

"It feels that way."

"But it won't bring her back. I know this is going to sound clichéd, but would she want you to go on hiding out at the estancia, never finding happiness again?"

The answer was simple. In theory.

"Why tell me, Tomas? Why now?"

Indeed. Yes, he'd been increasingly unsettled lately and the only people in the world he could really talk to were the last ones he should speak to about his feelings. "Because I can't talk to them. And you're here. And in a few days you'll be gone and it won't matter."

There was also the fact that there was this bizarre attraction to her, always simmering between them no matter what they were doing. She was bringing out all sorts of needs in him that he'd locked away for a long time. He pressed his lips together. That was more than he wanted her to know.

"I'm making it more difficult, aren't I?" Her cheeks

pinkened, a becoming flush of roses beneath her deep eyes. "I kissed you just now…"

How was it that she seemed to keep reading his thoughts? Having her put words to them fanned the flames all the more. "It's not your fault," he repeated. "You just make me…"

"Make you…?" the softly asked question came out with a wobble and he had the insane urge to wrap his arms around her.

"You make me want things," he admitted.

"Want me?" She lifted her chin boldly, but he could see through the gesture to the insecure girl behind it.

"Yes," he said, lifting his hand and placing it on her cheek. "Want you."

She looked down, biting her lip as if he'd flustered her. "I shouldn't have kissed you…"

He wanted to taste her lips so intensely again he knew it had to be a bad thing. "No, you shouldn't have."

"I'm not ready for a fling."

Of course she wasn't. She was on the heels of a broken engagement. He turned away, dropping his hand. "No. Sophia, I would never take advantage of you. Maybe that's why I told you. I don't want you to have any illusions of what is between us. Yesterday's kiss was a mistake."

"Of course."

The words sounded polite, but he detected a note of hurt behind them. "I didn't mean to make the afternoon so depressing," he said, needing to lighten the mood. This was why they needed to keep busy, occupied with other things!

"No, I'm glad you told me. It explains a lot. And I am sorry for your loss, Tomas. No one should have to endure such an ordeal."

"It is over and done," he replied. "I know it. I sometimes just have a problem being okay with it." He straightened his shoulders. "Now, let's shake off this heavy cloud and head back to the estancia."

He'd made some arrangements for while they were absent. The fact that the surprise excited him was a little worrying, but he shook it off. It didn't matter. It wouldn't matter. Sophia would be gone in a few days. Why shouldn't he enjoy her company until then?

Sophia's senses were whirling as she stood in the centre of her room, sorting through her purchases. Dinner was over and the mess tidied. Now the long evening stretched before her, leaving her too much time to think. Tomas had been engaged to Maria and Carlos's daughter. He had mentioned Miguel but not Rosa—a telling omission. And to have her taken in such a way...she suddenly realized there was a depth to Tomas that she hadn't counted on. For a man to close himself away from life as he had at the Vista del Cielo...beneath his tough exterior was a broken heart.

At first she had thought the swirling sensation she felt every time he was near was just physical. But, after today, she knew it was more. She felt a connection. And he felt it, too. He must, to trust her with such a confidence. How he must have grieved for the woman he loved. A woman who had grown up right here in this house, she realized. Of course letting go was hard when he was surrounded by reminders of her every day!

Sophia had just put her purchases away when Tomas showed up at her door. Simply seeing him there made her heart beat a little faster. Something had shifted between them. It had been daring of her to kiss him this afternoon. Maybe a simple kiss was not daring for some women, but it was for her. Taking the initiative was not her style, but there was something about Tomas that tempted her to try new things. She felt safe with him, a feeling she had never anticipated.

"Come with me. I want to show you something."

As his dark eyes watched her, an energy seemed to fill the room and she felt a little thrill. Following the set path had always been comfortable before, but she was beginning to see she'd been hiding behind it, too, the same way Tomas had hidden behind the estancia. Never taking risks. It was time for her to come out of the dark and find out just what Sophia Hollingsworth was made of.

Then there was the delicious tidbit that Tomas had admitted—he wanted her. She'd been honest—she wasn't ready for a fling, even though the thought was incredibly tempting. After this afternoon's shared honesty she felt she could trust him. He would not press her. And he was standing in the doorway looking like a kid on Christmas morning, impossible to resist.

"Okay, I'll play. Where are we going?"

"It's a surprise. Close your eyes."

A surprise? Tomas didn't seem the type for surprises. The heavy mood that had hung over them earlier had completely dissipated as his eyes danced at her. She closed her lids and felt him take her hand in his, leading her from her room and down the hall. With her eyes shut, she felt the intimacy of their connection running from her fingers straight to…well, straight to the part of her that kept insisting on being attracted to Tomas. It didn't help that every now and then this lighter side peeked from behind his rough exterior.

He led her out into the warm air, over prickly grass that tickled her legs and then she felt the dull hardness of patio stones beneath her feet.

"Open your eyes."

She lifted her lashes and squinted against the sun. Suddenly Sophia understood. They were at the pool. There was water in it, the reflection of the sun glimmering off the surface and filling the air with dancing light. "The pool!" she exclaimed, delighted. "You had it filled!"

"I had them come when we were gone. I wish you could enjoy it now, but I'm afraid it is too cold, and it needs time for the chemicals to balance. But I'll test it in the morning and you should be able to cool off and work on your back float tomorrow afternoon."

Sophia didn't know what to say. Of course this was part of the repairs Tomas had talked about but she got the feeling he had put a rush on it just for her. He clearly took pleasure in the surprise and the realization made her heart give a little skip. She took a step forward, could smell the sharp tang of chlorine and could feel the cool water on her skin even though it was just in anticipation. After all his bluster about the fire and repairs and lack of amenities, he had put a rush on the pool. To please her? Or to get her out of his hair? After what he'd told her on the bridge, Sophia wondered.

"Thank you, Tomas. For everything. For the day in town and for this great surprise."

"It had to be filled anyway," he replied. "You can enjoy it while I'm working."

Sophia couldn't help feeling a little deflated. Would it be so difficult for him to say a simple 'you're welcome?' Perhaps they'd broken through some barriers today, but it was clear that he wanted to get on with his work around the estancia now that she had the pool at her disposal.

"Yes, but it didn't need to be filled today. Tomorrow I'll help you with the chores and in the afternoon we'll go for a swim." She smiled her prettiest smile. She sensed that after this afternoon, he was trying to keep her at a distance. He would not get rid of her that easily. Tomas needed a bit of fun as much as she did. "It's no fun alone."

For a moment he hesitated, but she stuck out her hand to seal the bargain. Finally he took it, his big hand encompassing her smaller one until it all but disappeared within his fingers.

Tomas looked down at Sophia's glowing face and felt his heart do a little slide.

She had his number, no doubt about it. She'd seen through

his attempt to pass it off as no big deal. He had done it to please her and for that reason only—the arrangements had been made before this afternoon and what happened in town. "I thought it might help your hip," he said, pulling his hand away. "And any other sore muscles from the torture I'm putting you through."

She smiled up at him. He wished she'd stop doing that. She had a beautiful smile, easy and unaffected and it did funny things to him. Like today, on the bridge. What had he been thinking, kissing her back like that? Baring his soul?

"You are quite a taskmaster, but it's not torture," she teased. "I'm having fun. Truly."

"Right," he answered, and sent her a skeptical look.

She turned to look at the sparkling water. The flickering refraction of the sun on the surface lit her face, a shifting pattern of light and shadow that captivated him. "Whatever the reason, Tomas, it was awfully thoughtful. Thank you."

"Stop thanking me. If you remember correctly, you told me it should have been here waiting for your arrival."

Her cheeks coloured a little and an unfamiliar current seemed to heat him from the inside out. It was getting harder and harder to deflect her warmth and charm.

"Don't remind me, okay? I acted like a spoiled brat."

"I saw through that fairly quickly." Sophia had exhibited a fair bit of heart and willingness over the last few days, meeting each challenge he'd set out for her. He could add *beautiful* and *compassionate* to that list of qualities. It all combined to become a package to be reckoned with.

That he was even considering reckoning with her at all was shocking. He took a step back, a frown puzzling his brows. After hiding away for so long, the thought of consciously making a decision to move on was strange, even if he had been leading up to it for months. Now Sophia was insisting he join her in the pool tomorrow. He shouldn't, there was too much to do. There should not be any repeats of today's kisses or locked gazes, and the thought of her in a bathing suit, the cool water smooth against her skin…

He swallowed, trying to erase the image but failing utterly. Tomorrow night Maria and Carlos would return. The hours that he would have alone with Sophia were numbered, and he was surprised to find he didn't want them to end.

But what was the alternative? It would be wrong to let things go any further. She was a guest, he was the host. And there were things she still didn't know about him. Couldn't know, either. All she'd done since her arrival was stir things up. The more time they spent together, the more she seemed to sneak past his defences, and he had to put a stop to it.

Everything would settle again once Sophia went back to Canada. The estancia would be back in tip-top shape and they would go on as usual. The thought should have alleviated his worry, but it didn't. Because what he really wanted was more time with her.

And that was the most dangerous thing of all. The truth was she was cultivating feelings in him that scared him to death with their intensity.

"You knew I was afraid?" she asked, bending over and trailing her fingers in the water. He imagined the feel of her cool fingertips on his skin and swallowed.

"You covered it well. It was in the little things."

She nodded, making swirls with her fingers, random little shapes that rippled outward from her fingertips. "What things?"

"The look in your eyes. The way you tried to smile but didn't quite succeed."

Her fingers stopped moving. "I didn't realize I was so transparent."

Tomas went to her then, put his hand beneath her elbow and nudged until she stood beside him, the pool water dripping from her fingers. "Not your fault," he said quietly. "And you were right about some things. The estancia does have to hold a certain standard."

She smiled then, not a trace of fear or nervousness in her face. She was beautiful this way—unspoiled, artless. Irresistible.

"The estancia is perfect, Tomas, just as it is."

There it was, that burn that started deep within his belly every time she used that husky voice on him. Her acceptance of the estancia was simply another thread weaving their connection together.

He wanted more. It shocked him how much more. She had plagued his thoughts ever since they'd kissed in the yard. It hadn't just been anger that had driven him to take her in his arms. It had also been fear and need and desire. Emotions he'd locked away long ago, determined not to feel them again.

The banked fire in her eyes only fed the flames of desire burning through him. There was a flush to her cheeks that was caused by more than the sun beating down on them, and her eyes shone up at him. It suddenly seemed like too much work to carry on fighting against the attraction that kept flaring up like a hotspot that refused to go out. Forget what if and the past. It was over and done. What if he took her in his arms right now? What would happen then?

His gaze dropped to her lips. "You need to be careful when you look at me that way."

Her lashes fluttered as he leaned closer. He knew what he wanted. The same thing he'd wanted ever since he'd kissed her on the bridge. He wanted to lose himself in her, just for a little while. To live again, as he hadn't lived in three years. It had been his choice. Always his choice. But Sophia had awakened something in him. Curiosity. And hunger. He wanted more.

She tried to hide it, but he knew she was just as curious about him as he was about her. It was in the sidelong glances, the way she pulled back from the little touches as though his skin was on fire. The way her lips tasted. The little sound she made as their kiss ended. Was she even aware she did that? Did she know how hard it was for him to walk away? He wasn't sure he could any longer.

He watched, fascinated, as her tongue sneaked out to wet her lips. She was nervous. Somehow the thought was comforting. He was glad she wasn't taking this attraction—if that was what it could be called—in stride. He wasn't completely insensitive to what she'd been through. She'd caught her fiancé with another woman, for heaven's sake. She'd come on her honeymoon alone. A deliberate act of defiance, but he could see through it to the insecurity underneath. He adored her for it.

They were only a breath apart. "You, Sophia, are a delightful contradiction."

"What sort of contradiction?"

Her lids fluttered open and he could see the reflection of himself in her pupils. Had he ever needed a woman with such intensity? He cupped her face in his hands, gathering strength from feeling her soft skin against his palms, finally giving in to the insane desire he'd been feeling ever since she'd arrived and making the conscious decision to let it have its way. "One side gutsy and brilliant. The other side fragile as a flower. Both sides equally attractive, you see. *Querida,* there are times I'm not quite sure what to do with you."

"Querida..." she murmured, their lips only inches apart, "What does that mean?"

His heart clubbed, hearing her say the Spanish word, wanting to hear her say it again. "It means *darling,*" he replied, and the simple voicing of the sentiment ratcheted everything up another notch. Darling. Was she his? Or was he hers? Did it matter?

She lifted her hand and put it over top of his, then turned her head to kiss his palm. "*Querida*," she murmured thoughtfully. "Tell me, which side do you like most?"

Her voice was soft, but it shook, and Tomas knew he was sunk.

"This one," he replied, and lowered his mouth.

CHAPTER SEVEN

SOPHIA melted against him. *Finally.* Her body seemed to breathe the sentiment as she returned the kiss, looping her arms around his neck and losing her fingers in his hair. Her heart accelerated as she let herself give in to the moment, realizing where she was and who she was with and just awed enough to be stunned by it all. She felt like a butterfly set free from a cocoon. No longer the Sophia of old, but a reinvented one, seeing new places, trying new things. And one of those things was a very sexy Argentinian willingly in her arms.

The kiss gentled and Tomas pulled his lips away from hers, though they hovered near her ear and his breath sent shivers down her spine. His hands rested on her hips. Suggestion slid through the air and Sophia felt all her nerve endings kick into overdrive. She ran her hands down his shoulder blades, marveling at the taut muscles beneath the cotton of his shirt.

And then he touched his lips to the soft spot behind her ear and whatever else was in her mind fled.

The early evening sun sent a blaze of amber light across the yard as Tomas slid his mouth across her cheek and captured her lips again. He pulled her against him with a new urgency and the air caught in her lungs.

"Tomas, I…" She wanted to find the words but somehow couldn't string them together. How could she explain how much she wanted him? How touched she'd been that he'd confided in her this afternoon, and how awed she was that he wasn't pushing her as she'd expected? How could she resist a man who had loved so deeply? She knew perhaps she should be careful. He was moving on but reluctantly so. It was potentially a red flag, but as his hands spanned her waist she knew that the depth of his feeling for Rosa was part of his allure. He was touching her so gently, so reverently, that she was afraid she'd melt into a pool at his feet.

How could she explain how special he was and then express her own hesitation and fear? Why did she keep holding back? She was twenty-five years old and an independent woman. Why did it have to be so difficult to make the choice to move forward?

She sighed with bliss as his lips touched the underside of her jaw, the curve of her neck. His hand trailed over her hip to cup her bottom.

She knew why she held back. She was smart enough to know that the way they were holding each other—touching each other—created a certain expectation. It was foreplay. It wasn't that she didn't want him. She did. She closed her eyes and knew she shouldn't let her inexperience matter so much. What was she waiting for? Tomas would be gentle and… Her body shivered with pleasure as his fingers played in her hair. And thorough. A gasp erupted from her lips as he licked the column of her neck.

But Tomas wasn't expecting a virgin.

Gently he cupped her jaw with his hand. "Are you sure, Sophia?"

Of course she wasn't. Everything her body was screaming right now was at war with her heart and head. Making love for the first time was important. She wanted it to go right. She didn't want to be awkward or show her inexperience. She wanted it to be with the right person. As she looked up into his eyes, her heart thumped. She knew he was a good man.

His actions had shown it and this afternoon had confirmed it. But she wasn't able to form an answer to his question.

Tomas didn't wait. "Sophia," he murmured, and did what every woman fantasized about at least once in their lives— he scooped her up in his arms. The first time he'd done this, after her fall, had been a surprise. This time it was filled with a darker intention, and it thrilled her right to her toes.

With strong, purposeful strides he carried her to the door of the house and into the cool, shadowed hallway. She looped her arms around his neck and pressed her lips to the side of his throat, tasting his warm and slightly salty skin. She could do this. She could. She *wanted* to. Here, on the wild plains of South America, with the warm, scented wind wafting through the windows, carrying the sweet sound of the finches in the bushes outside. Here nothing else mattered. Just Tomas. And her. Two damaged souls healing each other.

He took her to the room he occupied in the family quarters at the opposite end of the house. It was smaller than her room, and hadn't been through the obvious renovation of the guest wing. But it was warm, with woven mats covering the floor and a homemade blanket stretched out on the bed. The window was open, the draft tingling over her skin as Tomas laid her carefully on top of the blanket.

And, oh, he was so gentle. Instead of using his physicality to dominate, he shattered her with patience, opening up all her nerve endings and making her feel beautiful, desirable beneath his touch.

He took his time, removing the clip from her hair, letting the weight of it fall around her shoulders. He sank his fingers in it and Sophia closed her eyes, luxuriating in the feel of his hands against her scalp.

"I love your hair," he said roughly, tightening his fingers so that he controlled her head. He lifted and brought her face up to his. "The colour of flames," he said. "The colour of sunset on the pampas."

Then he was kissing her again. It was heavenly, and a bit surreal knowing he couldn't seem to help himself. She moved against him, feeling the warmth of his skin through her shirt.

She was in danger of losing herself completely as he disentangled his hands from her curls and made short work of her light blouse. Trepidation vibrated inside her, but she pushed it away. She wanted this. She trusted him. It wasn't until he reached for the button of her jeans that she couldn't breathe and instinctively put a hand down to stop him.

"Tomas…"

"Too fast?" His breath was laboured now and the room seemed full of his heartbeat as she pressed her palm to his chest.

"It's not that, it's…"

But how could she tell him? She felt the heat rush to her face. What would he think of her? She already felt awkward and like a teenager trapped in a woman's body. And Tomas was such a strong force, so much larger than life. He'd suffered so much. She was awestruck by him and felt so completely out of her league.

"What is it, *querida?*"

He was calling her darling again and it made her heart want to weep. He was still holding her, but his brows had drawn together and she now felt utterly silly seeing the concern darkening his eyes. She felt a sting behind her nose and the ridiculous urge to curl up in his embrace to make everything right.

"Sophia?" He put a finger under her chin and lifted it, forcing her to look into his eyes. Why couldn't this be carefree and easy? Why was it so hard to let go of the past and step forward into a new, reinvented Sophia? Instead she felt nothing but mortified. And the caring way he was looking at her now told her he deserved an explanation. No, not just an explanation. The truth. Nothing but the truth would be right for Tomas. Not after today.

"Whatever it is, you can tell me."

"I have never…I mean…"

He chuckled, the lines clearing from his face in relief. "Sophia, I wouldn't think as much of you if you did this all the time. I cannot deny I feel a connection to you that is very unexpected. When you first arrived…" He paused, shook his head. "I have hidden myself away for a long time, Sophia. You know that."

Oh God. He thought her reservations were about having a one-night stand? Once more she felt unbearably young and naive.

If only it were as simple as a one-nighter. If that were her biggest obstacle, she'd not stand a hope of coming through this with her dignity intact. But she had to tell him. It wasn't as if he wouldn't find out… Her breath caught as she realized exactly what would happen.

"No," she stopped his hand, which was reassuringly stroking her shoulder. "Tomas please…" the words came out all strangled and she fought her way through them "…I've never done *this* before."

"This…" There were the wrinkles again as he sat back, clearly confused. "You mean…"

"*This*," she replied meaningfully. "Any of it."

"You're a…"

"Yes," she said, her voice finally coming out strong and clear. "I am." And the little voice inside her had to know. "Does it make a difference?"

He reached out for her hands. "Matter? Of course it matters! Sophia, you must be…"

"Twenty-five," she offered, wincing inside as the words came out a bit primly. She squared her shoulders. "I am twenty-five years old and I have never had sex. There. I said it."

The smile he sent her way was soft and indulgent. "I had been going to say afraid."

She wanted to sink through the floor.

She *was* scared. She had built this moment up in her mind for so long that when suddenly faced with it she turned coward, unable to go through with it. What if she didn't know what to do? Tomas might be patient but how far would his patience extend? It was easier to back away.

"Not even with your fiancé?" he probed gently.

It would have been better if he had been repulsed by her admission. That would have been much easier than the way his gentleness seemed to hold a mirror up to her flaws. She'd put her faith in the wrong things, and now had to admit to herself that she had been played for a fool, convincing herself Antoine had loved her enough to wait.

But that was the problem. He hadn't loved her, and deep down she'd known it. She had struggled for Antoine's approval just as she had from everyone else in her life, too, and she'd never quite gotten it. He'd been remarkably patient about not having sex. But she understood now. It was because he hadn't wanted to. He hadn't wanted *her*. He'd had his mistress for sex.

And now Tomas was here, and he wanted her, and knowing it was beautiful. And yet she was still too afraid.

Afraid that she'd get in too deep and end up hurt in the end. Because Tomas was temporary. It wasn't even a question of *when* he would take his love away. It wasn't hers to begin with. He might be ready to move on and leave his grief behind, but it was a long leap from there to love. And as much as she'd like to think she was modern enough to disassociate sex from love, she just couldn't.

She shook her head in answer to Tomas's question and already she could feel the distance opening up between them. It was clear the moment was over. Being swept away in the magic only went so far, and she had no one to blame but herself. She'd made a calculated risk, overestimated herself and failed. Again.

She pushed herself back on the bed and began rebuttoning her blouse. Once it was fastened she pulled her knees toward her chest and hugged them with her arms. Tomas sat down at the opposite end, his back against the iron foot rail. To her surprise he reached out and put a warm hand on her ankle, tethering them together, reassuring.

"The more you speak of this Antoine, the more I am convinced he's a total fool," Tomas said quietly, his thumb rubbing persistent circles around her ankle bone.

"He didn't love me, and that's the end of it," she replied, but she couldn't help feeling a little empty. "He never did. And I wouldn't want him back now for any reason." She looked up at Tomas, who was watching her patiently. "But it might have been nice to know that maybe he did love me, once."

"Sex isn't always about love, you know."

He gave a small smile, and his eyes twinkled at her just a little bit. She adored the way he was looking at her, appreciated how he was trying to make things right again, but she couldn't quite manage to get there. "But don't you think it should be?"

His thumb paused. "Obviously you do." Then it started circling again. "Sophia Hollingsworth, you are incredibly old-fashioned despite first impressions."

"I'm sorry..."

"It wasn't a criticism."

The whole conversation, rather than putting her off, was making her appreciate Tomas's good qualities all the more and that was a frightening idea. She craved the intimacy, but it terrified her as well.

She was a mess, she realized. And she had been for some time.

"I don't want to be in love," she admitted, and the silence

in the room was momentarily deafening. "And I know you don't, either."

The evening waned and the shadows lengthened in the room. Tomas shifted to the head of the bed and put his arm around her, pulling until she turned into the curve of his arm. She thought of the way he'd picked her up in his arms and a curl went through her tummy. Why did he have to be so damned honorable?

"You're right," he murmured. "I don't want to be in love. But I like you, Sophia. I like you a lot."

"I am afraid of spiders and can't ride a horse."

"Well, there is that."

She rested her cheek on his shoulder.

"I'm not really good at anything."

"You are good at trying. I respect that, Sophia."

She wanted to ask him if he could ever see himself being in love again, but she kept the words buttoned up inside. The night had been embarrassing enough without bringing the topic of Rosa into it. She knew she should push away and go to her own room. The very thought made her so lonely her chest cramped. Tomas on one side of the house, her on the other. She was tired of being alone. She was tired of having to pretend she was strong. She had spent years following the rules, doing what was asked of her because she'd been afraid of being alone. Afraid of having that love taken away should she make a mistake.

Well, here she was, in spite of her best efforts, alone anyway. Except for Tomas. And he was making her see that toeing the line was no guarantee. From now on she wanted to be herself. And those that loved her would love her for that—not because she'd done what they wanted.

But oh, it was hard to let go. The backs of her eyes burned with unshed tears.

"I should go," she whispered, knowing that if she were going to cry it would be better to do it privately.

* * *

Tomas knew he should let her go. He could hear the tears in her voice and he knew he should be running in the other direction. Slaking his need for her was one thing. Taking a virgin was another—especially one who felt that making love actually should have some ingredient of love in it. He closed his eyes, knowing he'd gotten himself in too deep.

The problem was that he knew she was right. When two people shared bodies, hearts got involved, and his relationship with her—could it be called a relationship?—was complicated enough. Making love to her now was out of the question. But sending her off to her own room felt callous and cold. Instead Tomas shifted his weight and lifted the blanket, covering them both as they slid down the bed.

"Don't go yet. I don't want you to leave upset."

"I'm not." And still she held on to his warmth and he felt her soft curves curl against him. He tightened his arm. It felt so natural, so right.

"Let me hold you for a while, then."

She let out a breathy sigh and her head relaxed fully against the curve of his shoulder. Tomas felt something open up inside him. It had been so very long since he'd held a woman this way. Since he'd let someone trust him—since he'd trusted himself. Sophia made him feel good and strong. Protective and invincible.

Which should have been a wonderful, beautiful thing.

But as her breath evened out and she fell asleep, her breath moist on his skin, all he felt was regret, sharp and bittersweet.

The sun filtered in through the window as Sophia woke, the corners of her eyes gritty with sleep. She was curled up next to Tomas's body, her head tucked beneath his chin and her ear pressed against his warm chest. She could just make out his heartbeat and the rise and fall of his steady breathing. She closed her eyes again, indulging in the moment of being held in his arms while he slept. Her cheeks burned as she realized that she had managed to do something she had never done before. She had spent the night in a man's arms. In Tomas's arms. They had slept together in the most literal sense of the term.

For that, she most definitely was not sorry.

She opened her eyes again and very carefully shifted so she could rest on her elbow and examine him. She got a thrill simply looking at him sleeping: his golden skin so much darker than her own pale, slightly freckled complexion, the thick fringe of lashes that lay on his cheeks and the hint of dark stubble on his jaw. For a fleeting moment she let herself believe that he was hers. No one else's. Just hers. It was an unsettling feeling knowing she wanted him to be. Sex or not, her feelings for Tomas were growing and becoming more complicated. Not love, but definitely something.

She counted down days. Only three left, after today. Her time here was drawing short, and she found she didn't want to go home yet, even though she knew she must. It was more than the country working on her heart, she realized. More than the novelty and the exoticism of it, so very different from her own way of life. More than the comfort and peace of the estancia. No, it was Tomas. She knew that months from now when she looked back, it would be Tomas she would remember most. Tomas whose face would still be clear in her mind.

Her hand began to fall asleep and she carefully tried to change position. Tomas's lashes flickered and then raised. When the sleep cleared, his eyes focused on her, and she felt the queer lifting in her chest once again. Tomas tightened his arm around her and pulled her in against him, drawing her close and dropping a light kiss on her forehead.

"Buenos dias," he said softly, and Sophia smiled against him, feeling that any errors of the previous night were forgiven.

"Buenos dias to you, too," she replied. She supposed now

that they were both awake they'd have to get up and out of their cozy cocoon. But Tomas's possessive arm stayed where it was and she held on awhile longer.

"The bed is too comfortable," he grumbled. "I suppose I should get up and tend to the animals." Tomas shifted on to his side so he was facing her. "You could help me today. You can wear your new jeans and you can help me move the cattle."

"You'd trust me to do that?" She rose up on to her elbow. Were they not going to speak of last night then? On one hand she was vastly relieved, and she was pleased he had asked her to help today. But on the other, it showed her nothing had changed for him. It was back to work as usual.

"Of course. It will be fun. It is one of the things Carlos will be doing with tourists, you know. I'll show you what to do. And I would like your company."

"I'd like to go with you," she admitted. What had she expected? Morning declarations and flowery speeches? Of course not. She would show him that nothing had changed for her, either. "It would be lonely here in the house alone."

"Maria and Carlos will be back this evening. It won't be quiet for long."

When she'd first arrived Sophia had wished for the Rodriguezes' presence simply so she wouldn't have to butt heads with Tomas. Now she wanted more time alone with him, and he sounded relieved that Maria and Carlos would be here to run interference. Sophia suddenly felt embarrassed about last night, clinging to him when she should have gone to her own room. He'd only been polite. He'd acted kindly instead of pushing her away. She wanted to bury her face in her hands, but resisted. Now she just wanted to get out of here.

"Sophia…"

"Hmm?" She sat up and began to swing her legs over the edge of the mattress.

"I want to apologize for how I treated you when you arrived."

The apology gave her pause and she carefully put her feet on the floor. She forced a laugh and looked over her shoulder at him. "I deserved it. I might not be very good at this ranch stuff, Tomas, but I think I am done with putting on appearances. It feels liberating, so don't apologize."

She pushed herself up off the bed and ran her hands down her wrinkled blouse. "Now, if we're going to be working today, we need a good breakfast. I'm going to make pancakes."

He raised an eyebrow. "Are you now?"

"Yes, I am. You're not the only one who can cook, you know." He wasn't the only one who could do a lot of things. Like pretend last night never happened.

"Have you been holding out on me, Señorita Hollingsworth?" He pushed himself to a sitting position and she tried not to stare at the bare expanse of his chest, and the warm skin where, up until a few minutes ago, she'd been snuggling.

His teasing was light with innuendo, and she couldn't help the bit of relief that rushed through her as she replied, "Most definitely, Señor Mendoza."

"Then get to it. After lunch, we can try out the pool."

Sophia's cheeks warmed as she scuttled from Tomas's bedroom. So he would come with her after all. She told herself not to get her hopes up, not to read more into things than was there. Last night had been a disaster and this morning there hadn't even been a good morning kiss. No, there was nothing more going on with her and Tomas.

Nevertheless, the thought of basking in the sun with him, dressed only in her two-piece suit gave her a queer feeling in her stomach.

Sophia finished the tidying while Tomas got the horses. She quickly changed, deciding on her new jeans for a morning spent in the saddle, as well as a cotton shirt, boots and the dusty *campero* she'd worn during her first eventful ride. As she passed by the living room, her gaze fell once more on the girl in the photo. She was still smiling, so confident as she sat on her horse. She frowned as a sudden thought occurred. Was this Rosa? Sophia's cheeks flamed. It very well could be. The face was happy and carefree, the picture taken just outside the barn here at the estancia—Sophia could see the door on the edge of the photo. It gave her an odd feeling, knowing she'd been in Rosa's house, sharing a bed with Tomas. As if she were trespassing somehow.

It was better that they hadn't gone through with it last night, she realized. Nothing could come of their relationship. All she could worry about was the here and now. Today, Sophia would help Tomas. Today, she would refuse to let anything else matter.

Tomas had the horses ready and Sophia let the maudlin thoughts flutter away on the dry wind as together they worked their way south. He showed her how to position her mount to urge the cattle in a specific direction, and other than calling his instructions, the distance between them prevented any real conversation. But Sophia didn't mind. She was actually having fun. Moving the cattle and working the horse took all her physical and mental concentration. She'd be tired later, but for now it was invigorating.

She reined to the left and brought several cows back into the group as Tomas shouted his approval. She urged the last one through the gate and took off her hat, swinging it through the air in victory. Tomas dismounted, moving to close the latch.

"I told you you could do it," he said, dusting off his hands and squinting up at her.

"It is not a very large herd," she acknowledged, but inside she was proud of her achievement. If someone had told her even a week ago she'd be herding cattle, she'd have laughed in their face. Now here she was, dusty, dirty, hot and happy. She dusted off the *campero* and put it back on her head.

"It doesn't matter. There were only two of us and it worked."

"I think I stopped needing to prove something," she admitted. "And I just wanted to help."

"Well, you did a fine job for a beginner. Are you sure you don't want a job as a hand here?"

He was joking but the idea temporarily knocked Sophia off her pins. For a split second she thought about leaving her whole life in Canada behind and making a complete change. It was a giddy thought. But she dismissed it as quickly as it had come. It was also silly. She was no ranch hand, and she didn't belong here. He was just teasing.

"You're very funny, Tomas. And you know once Carlos is back you'll have everything handled."

Tomas held up a hand, halting any more discussion.

"What is it?" She looked around, wondering if he'd heard some animal she wasn't aware existed in this part of the world. His eyes were sharp and his cheekbones taut as he scanned the pasture. "Are we in danger?"

"Sophia. For God's sake, hush," he commanded.

He looked at the retreating herd and she saw his lips move as if he were counting. "It is as I thought. We're short one. Are you sure you didn't miss any?"

Great. Had she messed up again?

"You take the far side, and I'll come up this way. If you find our missing cow, call out."

Sophia nudged her mare towards the far side of the pasture. Why had her first thought been that of failure? Of doing something wrong? A fly buzzed around her head and she swatted at it, annoyed. She was far too desperate for his approval. Why did she continue letting him be so important?

Because he was the one person who challenged her, and seemed to think she could meet the challenges he put before her. He wasn't setting her up to fail. He pushed. She was learning to push back. And dammit, she was learning to respect him, too. It would be easier to resent his perfect hide if she didn't.

Tomas called out; Sophia had half hoped she'd be the one to find the stray animal just to prove a point. Instead she slowly made her way across the field to where Tomas was already examining the errant cow.

"She's cut," he said, examining the leg below the knee joint. "I don't have my bag with me…"

Sophia interrupted him with a raised brows. "You mean you're not prepared?"

"Not this time. We'll have to ride back, and I'll come back out with supplies. It's not bad, but there's always concern of infection."

They rode back to the barn, Sophia managing an easy canter behind Tomas. When they rode into the barnyard, Sophia looked over at him. "Do you need help? I can come with you."

"No, I'll be fine. Let's just turn Neva out for some fresh grass."

Sophia helped him remove the saddle and bridle from Neva and she turned the mare out into the paddock by herself, a task she could never have accomplished a few days ago.

"Go enjoy a swim," he said as he began packing things into a leather bag, but he paused to squeeze her hand. "I don't know how long I'll be, and you should enjoy the afternoon. I'm sorry I can't join you, Sophia."

She couldn't quite erase the feeling that he was conveniently out of her path for the afternoon. But the incident was also a clear reminder to Sophia that this was a working ranch, and that Tomas's job also included caring for the stock in addition to interacting with guests. And this week he'd been doing the jobs of four people—cook and host, handyman and gaucho. He looked weary as he mounted his horse again, but she smiled. "I will. I'll see you later."

The pool was gloriously cool, but after a half hour Sophia got out and spent a few moments basking in the sun. It was only early afternoon and she didn't know when Tomas would be back, and even though he could be completely exasperating, the day seemed empty without his company. Carlos and Maria were returning and she knew Tomas had wanted to finish several jobs before their arrival. A new energy filled her as an idea blossomed. She knew Tomas expected her to soak up an afternoon of leisure. It was what he'd *told* her to do. But Sophia was quite enjoying exercising her own mind, and he would be in for a surprise when he returned if she had anything to say about it.

As the golden orb of the sun sank towards the horizon, Sophia made her last swipe with the brush, put it across the top of the can, and braced her hands against her lower back, easing out the ache.

Then a dot appeared on the horizon where the pampas met the sky and Sophia felt her heart thump. For a few moments she watched as it got gradually bigger, until she could see that it was horse and man. He was cantering across the plain, straight and tall in the saddle, and Sophia forgot her aching muscles and jogged to the gate. As she opened it, she heard the hoofbeats match the motion of the stride and she swung the gate wide to let them through.

The look of surprise on Tomas's face as he slowed and trotted through the gap was worth all the hard work she'd put in.

She closed and latched the gate behind him and followed him to the barn. He dismounted, leading the gelding through and cross-tying him to remove the tack. Sophia hung back, simply watching the way Tomas's muscles moved beneath his shirt as he removed saddle and pad.

But when the saddle was put away, the horse watered and turned out, Tomas put his hands on his hips and looked her up and down.

"And what have you been up to? Because that doesn't look like the swimsuit I imagined you'd wear for an afternoon poolside."

First of all, the idea that he'd imagined her in a bathing suit sent a tingle through her body. Then she realized she was in the dirty coveralls again. And that she had yet to clean up the mess from the painting. Brush and can still sat beside the shed door.

"I have a surprise for you," she said, excited to show him her handiwork.

She led him to the shed and watched his face as he saw the fresh paint. "You did this?"

She nodded. "I knew you wanted to have it done for Maria and Carlos's return."

Her excitement turned sour when the smile slipped from his face and his jaw tightened. "What is it? Did I do something wrong? Is the job not good enough?"

"You didn't have to do this," he said sharply. "You should have spent the afternoon by the pool."

All her elation sank into a pit of disappointment. She'd wanted to please him. She'd wanted to help, to pay him back for the things he'd done for her all week. The low feeling was suddenly infused with anger. At him, for taking the pleasure of completing the task away from her and at herself, for letting him. She stalked over to the can and brush and picked both up. She spun back, intending to head to the barn but he shot out a hand, stopping her—and paint splashed up over the lid and down the leg of the coveralls.

Oh-so-coolly, Sophia reached out and removed his hand from her arm.

"I did go for a swim," she informed him. "It was lovely. And I felt absolutely useless. So I decided to finish what we started the other day. You would have, if you'd had time. And I knew you wanted it done for Maria and Carlos's return. So yes, I did it. Not that you're grateful in any way, shape or form."

Tomas pulled off his hat and ran his hand through his hair, leaving the curls lying in rills on his head. A smudge of dirt darkened his cheek and Sophia inhaled, fortifying herself. It was not sexy. It was not.

And perhaps if she told herself that long enough, she might just believe it.

She swept past him, determined to clean the brush and put the lid back on the can before going to the house. She was glad the Rodriguezes would be back tonight! Maybe she'd have someone to talk to who didn't feel the need to move between both ends of an emotional barometer!

"Sophia!" His steps sounded behind her, boots on hard ground. She refused to turn around, just kept walking, bound up in righteousness and feeling vastly unappreciated.

"Sophia! Wait."

She stopped at the imperious command, then with a toss of her head started off again.

He refused to chase after her. "You are so infuriating!" he called.

That had her turning around. "So are you!"

He'd meant it when he'd said he didn't know what to do with her. He'd phrased it all wrong, he knew. But any other words he formed in his head seemed to say way more than he wanted to. If things hadn't halted last night, he knew he would have made love to her. Just the thought of it now was enough to tie him in knots. And it would have been a huge mistake. Now it seemed everything he'd said made her angrier with him. Was it what he said or was it because of last night?

He'd be damned if he'd ask her.

"I just meant…you're a guest, Sophia. This wasn't necessary."

"This is a working estancia, right? Didn't you tell me that one of the big draws is helping out?"

"Well, yes, but…"

"But I didn't do the job well enough? Is that it?"

"No, it looks great, but…"

"But what?"

Tomas took a step forward, his patience wearing thin. It had been a long, hot afternoon and he'd tried putting her out of his mind and could not to his growing irritation. "If you would let me get a word in, I would tell you that I did not expect you to do this. This is above and beyond. It is my responsibility to have things repaired, not yours."

"Is that your version of thank you?"

How he could want to kiss and throttle a woman at the same time was beyond him.

"I do thank you." The shed did look wonderful. And Sophia was riled up and looking as gorgeous as he'd ever seen her, even in the ratty coveralls. "It's not that. I put that expectation on you and I shouldn't have."

"And so the painting on the first day? That wasn't my job, either?"

She had him there. She knew exactly why he'd had her painting the first day. She'd come in with her fancy shoes and the chip on her shoulder and he'd wanted to teach her a lesson. "I was testing you, all right? Pushing you. Which, by the way, I have already apologized for. I thought we'd moved past this."

She lifted a finger and shook it. "And yet today what did you do? Came back issuing edicts on what I should and should not do. I have my own mind, Tomas Mendoza. So you can take your imperatives and…and…"

"Stuff them?"

A smile made its way to her mouth, though she tried not

to show it. Her lips twitched as she admitted, "Those weren't quite the words I was thinking of."

"You shook your finger at me just the way Maria does. There may be hope for you yet."

"Why do we always fight?"

"We don't...always."

He shouldn't have said it. Her mouth opened and closed a few times and he knew they were both thinking about the other thing they seemed to do with disturbing regularity—kiss.

She put her hand in the pocket of her coveralls. "You were busy doing other things today," she said finally. "Your work and Carlos's and Maria's. And getting pools filled and taking me to town. So pardon me for trying to help."

He sighed, so heavily it felt like the weight of the world was on his shoulders. And bit by bit the anger fuelling him drained away.

"It was meant as a gift, Tomas. Nothing more. A chance for me to help you. Don't you think I've noticed how hard you work?"

"And I thank you for the gift, Sophia, I do. But I feel guilty about it just the same."

"Why?"

"Because..." He came forward and took the paint can and brush from her hands. "Because finishing the shed was my job, not yours. You were right. This is your vacation, it's not slave labour. And I would have had it done if..."

"If?"

"If I hadn't been enjoying myself with you."

The boutique wasn't restocked and he'd left the second coat of paint to spend the day in town with Sophia instead. He'd managed to get the pool filled, but with the work crew not coming until the weekend to work on the spa building... He should have had it all done. He knew how Maria felt about the damage, how nervous the fire had made her. That should have been his priority. Not kissing and making wishes on bridges and…

And every other thing that had been on his mind today. Moving on for real, not just in his head.

"Can we stop yelling now?" she asked.

"Yelling is safer," Tomas said, going to the sink and running water for the brush.

"Safer than what?"

His hands paused under the water and Sophia's mouth formed a knowing O.

He gave up and put the brush to soak, turning off the water.

"I do appreciate the work on the shed, more than you know," Tomas offered. "And so will Carlos and Maria. Maria especially. The fire hit her hard, Sophia. It frightened her. She wanted things back the way they were, and I wanted most of the work to be done because of that. The estancia is starting to look even better than it did before. But I feel awful that I made you think you needed to do this."

"You didn't make me do anything. I was sitting by the pool, bored, wondering what you were doing, and I took the idea to do it." She lifted her gaze to his, a challenge but with that bit of shyness that hit him in the gut every single time. "I wanted to do it. For you."

For him? The notion took the starch out of his argument, leaving him floundering. Oh God, the last thing he needed was Sophia getting serious romantic notions about him. They couldn't get in too deep. And yet he couldn't find it in himself to push her away, or be sorry. There was something in her gaze now, something he hadn't seen before, and it changed the air between them. It was like the loosening of a screw, the untying of a knot, and taking off the pressure made him feel more trapped, rather than less.

He'd thought last night was the closest he'd ever be to her, and that was the safest course. But he'd been wrong. Right now they were connected in a way he'd never felt before, and he didn't even know why.

"Maria and Carlos will arrive soon," he said finally. To explore what was going on between them would be a mistake. Sure, maybe Sophia had brought him out of his well-guarded shell, and maybe he was having fun. Was it so wrong to enjoy a few precious days? She'd be gone soon enough and he'd still be here at Vista del Cielo.

"You should go get cleaned up. I'll look after this."

It was all she was going to get from him. As she turned her back on him he knew this was the last time they'd be this alone. Any moment would mark the return of Maria and Carlos. And after that, it was back to Canada for Sophia.

CHAPTER EIGHT

WHEN Sophia emerged from her room in fresh jeans and a T-shirt, Maria and Carlos had arrived. Sophia stepped into the kitchen amid the chatter and stood shyly, not sure how to interrupt. A small, dark-haired woman was shaking a finger at Tomas and Tomas was laughing at her. A man—Carlos— was watching with a smile on his face. He saw Sophia first and smiled at her.

"You must be Sophia. I am Carlos, and this is Maria. Welcome to Vista del Cielo, though our welcome is long overdue."

Maria spun around, a ball of energy that filled the room with light. She rattled off a greeting in enthusiastic Spanish— the words were lost on Sophia but not the meaning. Barely over five feet, she was a firecracker. "We're so glad you could join us, Sophia. And first thing tomorrow we will straighten out your reservation, I promise." Then she came forward and gave Sophia a welcoming hug and beamed.

The reservation. Sophia had forgotten all about it! "Don't worry about it. If it was a mix-up, it's been a most pleasurable one." She looked at Tomas as she said the last, feeling a little challenge build. She knew that Tomas would never want Maria to know how they'd fought—and how they'd made up, too. She smiled, wondering if she'd finally found his weak spot in the woman who would have been his mother-in-law.

"And our Tomas has been a good host." It was a statement from Maria, not a question. Sophia nearly laughed. Yes, it gave her a perverse pleasure speaking to Maria while Tomas waited in the background. She wondered what Maria would say if she knew about falling off the horse. Or that Sophia had painted the shed. Or that she had kissed 'our Tomas' on the *Puente Viejo* just before making a wish.

"The very best," she replied, sobering. This was also Rosa's mother, the woman who had lost her daughter and the hopes and dreams that went along with that. "You have a beautiful home, Señora Rodriguez, and a beautiful estancia. The views are amazing."

"I *am* sorry we were not here for your arrival, Sophia."

Sophia smiled. "Don't worry. Tomas looked after me. He's a fine cook. Did he learn that from you?"

She caught Tomas's gaze briefly and saw approval there. He should not have worried. His secrets were safe with her. And Maria was charming.

"Nothing beats Madre Maria's cooking," Tomas replied, and Carlos nodded.

Maria patted Tomas's arm and then impulsively went up on tiptoe to kiss his cheek. "In case you haven't noticed, Tomas is family." Maria patted Sophia's arm like she had Tomas's and Sophia bit down on her lip, a little overwhelmed and startled at the immediate intimacy of the welcome.

"We treat all our guests as family," Tomas corrected firmly, but Maria glanced between them, unfooled.

"Aha, aha," she replied, nodding, but her sharp eyes seemed to take in everything. "We will see, Tomas. Now come and eat. We brought dinner from the cantina Carlos likes. It has been a long day. Tomorrow will be time enough for *asado*."

During the course of the meal Sophia listened to Maria and Carlos talking with Tomas. It was clear to Sophia that there was much affection between them all. Often they spoke in English in deference to her, but now and again they slipped into their native Spanish, and even though Sophia couldn't make out the words, she could understand the teasing going on through the affectionate tones and smiles. She didn't have to understand the language to know that he was closer to Carlos and Maria than she had ever been with Antoine's family, or even her own. Affection in her house had seemed to hinge on conditions: scholastic achievements, involvement in the right things and with the right people. Margaret had wanted the best for her daughter, but the one thing missing was what Sophia saw now in the faces of Carlos and Maria. It was acceptance, and it was lovely—even if it did leave her feeling a little bereft.

Many things had become clear on this trip, and the one thing Sophia promised herself was that she would respect and accept herself. She didn't always have to seek approval from others to have value. She glanced at Tomas, who was laughing at something Maria said about Miguel. She didn't need Tomas's approval, either. There was a difference however, she realized, between needing and wanting.

Carlos sat back and listened to the exchange, and when Maria slipped into rapid Spanish once more and shook a finger at Tomas, Carlos looked at Sophia and smiled. Something warm spread through her, a feeling of welcome. After a particularly loud burst of laughter, Maria looked over at Sophia. "I'm sorry," she said, still chuckling. "We forget and have put you at a disadvantage, Sophia, by speaking in Spanish."

"Which is a blessing, as I am sure Sophia is not interested in your stories of my bad behaviour, Madre Maria." Tomas sent Maria a most severe look, but Sophia could see the good-natured devilment twinkling there.

"On the contrary," Sophia countered. "I think they would be highly entertaining. I didn't know you had it in you to misbehave."

Carlos laughed then, the rusty sound so unexpected that they all burst out laughing again.

"Another time, Sophia. When Tomas isn't here to add his *centavos*. My children turned my hair gray."

Sophia laughed, since Maria's hair was jet-black without a streak of the offending colour. "I look forward to it," she replied.

After the meal Sophia offered to help clean up, but Maria brushed her away. "You go," she said, waving her away with a hand. "Tomas said you have kept busy. He has done a good job, our Tomas." Maria spoke of him as though he was her own. How blessed Tomas was to have two sets of parents.

"He must have told you about the fire," she continued, her face falling and Sophia finally saw a hint of middle-age wrinkles around the woman's eyes. "And now so much is repaired. The shop and the pool…he told us you helped with the painting, Sophia. That was very generous of you."

Tomas hadn't told Maria that he'd practically forced her into helping that first day, but his secret was safe with Sophia. She remembered what he'd said about Maria being affected by the blaze, and she was doubly glad she had helped. "It was no trouble at all," she replied. "I've enjoyed my time here, Señora Rodriguez. All of it."

She swallowed against a lump of emotion. She had, even the arguing with Tomas. She'd felt more alive here in a handful of days than she ever had before.

"You call me Maria like everyone else." Maria smiled at Sophia. "And get some rest. No rounding up cattle for you tomorrow. Carlos is here now. I am looking forward to getting to know you and treating you to a real *asado*. We will work together. Do you like cooking, Sophia?"

"Yes," Sophia answered. "Yes, I do."

Sophia bade Maria and Carlos goodnight, but after a pause went to say goodnight to Tomas, too. He was standing at a window, looking over the pampas and the big, gnarled tree standing guard on the plain.

When she'd first arrived, she had felt a kinship with the

tree—it too seemed lonely and out of place. But as she looked at Tomas, and then at the sweeping branches, she wondered if maybe it wasn't more like him. Solitary, standing guard, looking after the Rodriguez family. She didn't know why he felt such responsibility to them, but clearly he did. Sophia felt protected, too, but she also felt sadness for a man who had suffered such a loss that he had withdrawn to the pampas.

"Goodnight, Tomas," she said quietly, looking up at him. His jaw was set, his lips a thin line. He turned his head slightly and looked down at her. For a moment their gazes caught and her breath stalled.

"Goodnight, Sophia," he said quietly, so low that she knew it was meant for her ears only. "Sleep well."

Instantly she was transported back to the previous night and sleeping in his arms. Tonight she would be in her own room. It was the way things needed to be.

But as she walked away from him, she couldn't help being a little bit sorry. It looked like anything that was blossoming between them was over. And despite the extra company and chatter in the house, Sophia went to bed feeling lonelier than ever.

As Carlos and Tomas worked outside, Sophia helped Maria in the house.

The large meal today was *asado*, the Argentine version of barbecue, and Tomas had told her over breakfast that it would be unlike anything she'd ever tasted. Maria explained the different dishes as Sophia finished up her coffee and fresh bread and butter.

Already Maria was bustling about the bright kitchen. Once the estancia started taking bookings again, Maria would be cooking for them, too. But for now it was just the two of them in the quiet, comfortable room.

Carlos would start the grill around noon, and the women would make the accompanying dishes. Dessert, Maria explained, was a particular favourite of Tomas's, cookies called *alfajores*. When Sophia asked if she could help, Maria said she would show her how to make them.

Sophia imagined taking the sweets to Tomas later, a way to thank him for all he'd done for her so far—and one that would perhaps go over better than yesterday's painting. She wanted to see the look on his face when he realized she had baked them. She knew she could cook—at least that was one thing she'd accomplished just fine in her old life. Other than the pancakes yesterday, Tomas had done most of the cooking. But the *asado* seemed to be a group affair, and Sophia was determined to have fun.

Maria put milk to heat on the stove while Sophia washed up the breakfast dishes. "These days it is faster to buy *dulce de leche* in the store," Maria explained. "But I like to make my own." She showed Sophia how to whisk in sugar and vanilla and baking soda. "Then I simply let it cook for a few hours."

"It's that simple?" Sophia had eaten the caramel treat from a jar in Canada. She'd had no idea that it took so few ingredients.

"*Dulce de leche* takes time, but the *alfajores* will take more effort," Maria smiled. "Tomas always told Rosa that he would only marry her if she came with my *alfajores* recipe."

The light went out of her face for a moment, and then she brightened again. "I still try to make them on special occasions."

Sophia averted her head, making a show of drying dishes. "Rosa was your daughter, Tomas said."

Maria's youthful face looked weary and Sophia held her breath, waiting. "*Si,* Rosa was our daughter." Maria's hand paused on a cupboard door, but then she opened it and took out a container of flour. "She and Tomas…they were going to be married."

Sophia made herself move, retrieving butter from the fridge

for the cookies, trying to keep things conversational while inside everything seemed to be churning. The picture on the wall seemed to stare at her. "Is that your daughter? The photo of the girl on horseback?"

Maria nodded proudly. "Oh, she knew how to sit a *criollo* like she was born in the saddle." She laughed suddenly. "Tomas was a polo player, but she rode circles around him, our Rosa."

Tomas and polo? It felt like a key to the missing gap in Tomas's life. "Tomas played polo? I thought that was a rich man's sport."

Maria handed Sophia a bowl. "Tomas is sort of the rogue Mendoza. He chose here over the family business. Even after our Rosa…" Maria sighed, and made the sign of the cross before wiping beneath an eye. "I apologize. I'm afraid you don't get over losing a child."

"No, Maria, no," Sophia said, going to the woman's side and putting her hand on her arm. "I shouldn't have pried. It's none of my business, truly."

Maria nodded towards the picture on the wall, the one that had stopped Sophia many times during her stay. "She was beautiful, don't you think?"

Sophia's throat closed over and she tried not to gawp at the picture. This was their daughter and the woman Tomas had loved. The kisses, the night spent in Tomas's arms…it all felt wrong. It felt as though she had intruded. And to think she had looked at the image in the photograph and had wanted to be like her. She had wished for the happiness, the confidence in Rosa's face. It gave her an unsettled feeling; she felt like a thief, when all along her intentions had been innocent.

"I would have thought Tomas had told you about his family," Maria said, greatly recovered as she patted Sophia's fingers and moved to measure out butter, sugar and flour.

But Tomas had told her nothing about his former life.

"We didn't talk about that," Sophia replied numbly, trying

to make sense, trying to apply what she'd just learned to the conversations she'd had with Tomas. Reconciling that with the man who had kissed her, who had said he wanted her…

She closed her eyes, remembering the gentle way he'd touched her, the way he'd thought she was afraid. And she had been. She'd been afraid of Tomas from the moment they'd met. Afraid of the intensity of her own reactions and feelings, too.

"Sophia?"

She turned her attention back to Maria and pasted on a smile. "What are *alfajores?*" she asked dumbly, not sure what else to say without giving herself away. And the last thing she wanted was Maria reading more into the situation than there was. If that were possible. What would the woman say if she knew Sophia had spent the night in his room? She was nice enough now, but it had the potential to be incredibly awkward.

Maria handed her a wooden spoon, adjusting to the change of topic smoothly. "Cookies. We will bake them and when everything is cool, sandwich them together with the *dulce de leche.*"

The earlier excitement about making Tomas's favourite treat was slightly bittersweet now. She'd wanted it to be something from her, but now she knew the sweets would come with a reference to Rosa built in. Had Rosa made him these same cookies in the past? She must have, if what Maria had said about them being Tomas's favourite was correct. There were so many questions Sophia longed to ask and she knew she had no right to the answers. Maria spoke and Sophia pulled herself out of her thoughts and started creaming butter and sugar together, the sweet smell now repulsive to her.

"I worry about him," Maria said, going to a cupboard for a baking pan.

"Who?"

"Tomas, of course. We love having him here. We couldn't

run the estancia without him. But he has closed himself away from the world. He needs to find a good Argentine girl to make him a home. Sometimes I wonder if we made a mistake, going into partnership. It ties him here too much."

Sophia struggled to keep beating the batter. She would say no more, at least not to Maria. Partnerships and dead fiancées. Tomas had told her that only he'd gone to university and that he had chosen the estancia instead. But it looked as though there was much more to him than met the eye. To think he'd let her believe he merely worked here. Heat crept into her cheeks as she realized she'd been played. She could probably find out all she needed from Maria. But she wanted to hear it from him.

"I am very sorry about your daughter, Maria."

Maria sniffed, but then lifted her head and smiled. "Thank you, Sophia. She was taken from us so suddenly, so young. But God works in mysterious ways. We gained another son anyway. I couldn't love Tomas more if he were my own." She patted Sophia's hand and then reached for an egg. "I see a difference in him this week. It is good to see him happy."

Sophia's head came up sharply and Maria laughed. "Don't be so surprised. He is more alive. Carlos noticed it, too. When you are in a room together, the air changes."

"But I'm…I mean…" What did Maria think had happened between them? She'd expected disapproval, not encouragement. "I'm going back to Canada in a few days."

"Of course you are," Maria replied, adding flour to the bowl and taking the spoon from Sophia's motionless hand. "But I am glad you came. He has punished himself long enough."

Sophia could only hold out for so long, and this latest revelation pushed her over the edge. "Punish himself? Whatever for?"

But Maria suddenly became quiet, refusing to elaborate. "If you want to know more, you will have to ask Tomas."

"But she was your daughter."

The *alfajores* dough was a smooth ball now and Maria began to roll it out. "No, I think you should ask Tomas. He should be the one to tell you. It will be good for him."

"And if he won't?"

Maria looked at Sophia, her gaze sharp. "I think he will."

Sophia felt a blush climb her cheeks as Maria turned back to the baking. Maria had mentioned how obvious the attraction between the two of them was, but Sophia thought she was seeing what she wanted to see.

"Maria, I can see you want Tomas to be happy. But that can't be with me. I'm only on vacation, and then I'm going back to Canada and my life there."

Maria gestured for the cookie cutter and Sophia handed it to her. "Oh, Sophia. You young people. You plan everything out and how it is supposed to work. Everything on a schedule. You're on *vacation*. Don't worry about it, let it go. There will be time enough for life to ask its price later."

Maria suddenly seemed weary and Sophia wondered if her words had more to do with Rosa and Tomas, maybe even Miguel. It seemed to Sophia that perhaps life had already exacted its price from Maria, and she still met the day smiling.

She stepped up to the counter and took the spoon from Maria. "Okay then." She smiled brightly, determined to dispel the cloud that had suddenly fallen over the kitchen. Perhaps she'd felt sorry for herself before, but her troubles now seemed minor, distant. Right now the only thing that was supposed to matter was butter and sugar and flour. She looked at Maria and forced a smile. "What's next?"

They moved on to the other preparations, but a cloud hung over Sophia. Did she really want to unlock the rest of the mystery that was Tomas? And how on earth could she find the time and place to ask?

* * *

Sophia sighed, feeling lazy and contented in her chair by the fire. She couldn't remember ever being this full. The fire blazed as the remnants of the *asado* lay about. There had been beef, so many different cuts, so mouthwateringly delicious, and potato salad, fresh vegetables and Maria's crusty fresh bread. There had been bottles of the ruby-red Malbec that Tomas had picked up in town during their trip. And just when Sophia was positive she couldn't eat another bite, Maria brought out the platter of *alfajores*.

"I should have known," Tomas said approvingly, and with a boyish smile he reached out and took two. He grinned up at Maria. "*Madre* Maria never fails when it comes to *alfajores.*"

Sophia took one, unable to resist, but couldn't bring herself to try it yet. She leaned forward in her chair, toying with the sweet as she waited for Tomas to sample his, hoping they would meet his approval.

"You're an easy mark, Tomas, if you can be won with cookies," Maria teased.

Tomas forced the smile to his lips as he looked up at the woman who had mothered him during his rebellious years and beyond. "The cookies did not bring me here," he explained as he bit into one. He felt Sophia's eyes on him and he winked up at Maria, trying to keep things light, though his heart was suddenly heavy. "But they go a long way toward keeping me here."

Maria grinned back and said something in Spanish, then turned to Sophia. "Tomas is one for flattery, isn't he, Sophia? You have passed the test." She laughed at Tomas and ruffled his hair. "Sophia made the *alfajores,* Tomas."

Tomas ran his fingers through his hair, straightening it after Maria messed it. Sophia had made them? It had been impossible to keep her from his thoughts today, knowing she was indoors working side by side with Maria. Something twisted inside him at the thought.

He smiled stiffly at Sophia. "You made these?"

She nodded proudly. "Maria showed me how."

"They are very good," he admitted as the buttery treat melted on his tongue. Sophia nibbled on her cookie as Maria put the plate on the table. Sophia stole a shy look at him and his body tightened unexpectedly in response. Instead he forced a laugh at something Carlos was saying.

This was crazy. It had only been days. How had she wiggled her way into his life so completely? For heaven's sake, he'd held her in his arms all night and now he was complimenting her cooking while thinking about kissing her again. Her innocence did nothing to deter him, except perhaps make him understand he needed to be cautious.

She was watching him and he took a third cookie from the platter, something, anything to keep his hands busy as he tried very hard not to look back at her. He didn't want Maria or Carlos to see what he knew would show in his eyes. Desire. More than that. Caring. He cared about her now. He licked the *dulce de leche* from the side of the cookie before biting into it. Joining the real world again was a bit painful, but perhaps good. For the first time, he felt as if he could leave his past behind him.

He brushed the crumbs from his lap and stood, stretching. Sophia watched him, and he felt his pulse leap beneath her appraisal. Maybe he was feeling the effects of the generous helpings of Malbec. Maybe things were finally waking that had been slumbering too long. And who safer than Sophia? She was only temporary in his life and they both knew it. She would not expect more of him than he was prepared to give. Right now all he wanted was to be alone with her. He had missed her today. He'd missed it just being the two of them.

But first there was another tradition to uphold. He went

over to her and held out his hand. "Sophia. Maria has made *mate*. You must try it. It's practically our national drink."

Maria was at the table pouring hot water into a gourd. "Oh, Sophia. I have made us some *mate*. Have you tried it yet?"

Sophia shook her head, looking curiously down at the gourd. Tomas watched her, amused at her skeptical expression. He'd seen that look before during the *asado* whenever she'd been offered something new and different. She'd pressed to know what some of the selections were and he'd laughed when she'd politely—but definitively—passed. But the *mate* was safe. "It's tea," he explained. "Nothing sinister, I promise."

She looked up at him and wrinkled her nose. "It doesn't look like tea."

He couldn't help it, he smiled. There it was again, the childish innocence that was so refreshing. "It's an acquired taste," he admitted. "But you should try it."

"Come," Maria called, and led the way over to the campfire where they all sat, looking into the flames, relaxing.

"Sophia, I checked my books today. I thought you would want me to get to the bottom of your reservation."

To her left, Tomas accepted the gourd from Maria and drank of the tea. "Yes, of course! I totally forgot to ask you today."

"It does seem we refunded your…*perdón,* Señor Doucette's money when he cancelled."

Sophia's face flamed. "Oh," she said, suddenly embarrassed as she realized she had spent the week here without paying for it. "I see." She tried a smile but it felt false on her lips. "Well, I'm glad to know. Perhaps we can look after the details in the morning, Maria?"

"Of course. And there is no rush, Sophia. Don't give it another thought."

Tomas drank his tea and Sophia couldn't meet his eyes. She'd been wrong all along, and she remembered how bossy and horrid she'd been to Tomas that first day. She'd been wrong about so many things—the reservation was the least of it.

Then he passed the gourd to Sophia. "You drink it from a straw, see?" He said it quietly. "A *bombilla*."

"*Bombilla*," she repeated, staring down at the straw and feeling foolishly adolescent as she realized his lips had been the last on it. She took the gourd and put her lips on the *bombilla*. She sipped the hot brew, slightly bitter but somehow pleasant.

"Now you pass it back to Carlos. And we pass it around until it is gone."

As the *mate* made the rounds no more was said about her unpaid bill; it was as though it didn't even matter. What was important to the Rodriguezes tonight was being together. She saw it in Carlos and Maria as Carlos reached over and took his wife's hand, and in Tomas, who sipped the *mate* and reached for another cookie. She was beginning to see how many things here centered around family and community. It was a far simpler approach to life than she was accustomed to and she found she preferred it to rounds of air kisses and handshakes.

And it was something she didn't dare get used to. Now that she knew her reservation at Vista del Cielo had been cancelled, she knew she needed to leave. She had started to care about Tomas too much. What was left for her here? Nothing. Nothing but getting more accustomed to Tomas, and to Maria's friendliness and Carlos's quiet ways. Used to more sunrises over the pampas and listening to the birds call goodnight through the open window of her room. More pretending that this was her life when it wasn't. Not even close.

When the *mate* was gone Tomas leaned over, his quiet voice warm in her ear. "Would you like to go for a walk?"

She nodded, shivering both from the cool air on her arms

and from the intimate whisper. "Yes, I think I would. I need to walk off some of this food."

More than that, she needed to tell him she was leaving. She was free to do as she pleased—settle up the bill and do what she wanted for the last few days of her trip. It was time for this charade to end and for her to get back to reality.

Tomas informed Maria and Carlos in Spanish and held out his hand. Sophia took it, more affected than she cared to admit by the feel of his warm, rough palm encompassing hers.

But if he had ideas of kissing in his head again, he was sadly mistaken. No more kissing, no long looks, no arguments that served to fuel the passion between them.

No, tonight would be goodbye, and that would be the end of it.

CHAPTER NINE

THE evening was waning as they ambled down the lane, Tomas's stride slow and relaxed while Sophia felt like a bundle of charged nerves beside him. The air held a late summer chill. For several minutes they walked silently, with the sounds of twilight filling the gap of conversation until Sophia understood where they were headed—the gigantic gnarled and twisted tree in the middle of the field.

It stood, a lone sentinel on the pampas, and Sophia reached out and touched the bark, running her fingers over the odd texture. The leaves made a canopy above their heads, cocooning them in semi-privacy. Tomas stood like a shadow behind her, his steady presence making her stomach tumble over itself.

She had wanted privacy to talk to him, but not like this. Not with the whisper of the leaves shushing around them, the single ombu tree a life raft in the grassy sea of the pampas. She had to be strong. Definitive.

"The ombu tree." She looked up at him, wondering why here, and why now. Did he realize he was making it more difficult for her?

"You said you wanted to see it," he said quietly, his hands on the trunk beside hers. "Did you know, some call it the lighthouse of the pampas."

"Lighthouse? To guide lost travelers?" Sophia laughed a

little at the description, but her attempt at lightness seemed false to her ears. "I guess that works. It was the first thing I noticed when I drove up in the taxi. Big and strong but very solitary."

"Like you, Sophia?"

She nodded, watching her fingers make patterns on the rough surface. She wasn't that strong, but she was getting better. "I suppose, maybe a little. But I think perhaps more like you."

Tomas paused, and Sophia waited for him to say something—anything—significant.

But he said nothing. Nothing about the picture in the house—he could have pointed it out a dozen times. Or he could have told her that he wasn't just involved with the estancia but was a full fledged partner. Why hadn't he wanted her to know?

"And what about you? Is the ombu a lighthouse for you, too?" She thought about all that Maria had told her today, even if Tomas was infuriatingly closed-mouthed. Was the estancia the beacon in his life, signifying home? Safety? Was it better for him than what had waited for him in the family business?

"They have shade for when it gets hot." He deliberately put the focus off himself and back on the tree. "And the trunks are full of water, kind of spongy, see? So they will not burn in a wildfire."

Sophia looked up above her at the veil of leaves. "An angel, then, in the middle of the plains?"

"An angel with bite. The sap is poisonous."

Sophia drew her hand away abruptly and Tomas laughed. "Not that poisonous." He came over and rested against part of the trunk, his feet braced on the gnarled roots as he looked into her face. "Like most things in life, Sophia, the ombu has two sides. The pampas is beautiful, but it is also harsh and unforgiving. It is important to learn to respect both sides."

Like Tomas? Perhaps she could, if he'd bothered to reveal his other side. Why hadn't he trusted her? Surely nothing could be worse than Rosa's death. But then, perhaps he wouldn't have said anything if she hadn't put him on the spot.

She looked over at him, his dark form silhouetted in the darkness, and softened. Maybe she was being too hard on him. He'd known Sophia mere days. Was she expecting too much, wishing he'd confided in her the way she had in him?

"The *mate* has made you especially wise this evening," she noted, genuinely wanting to lighten the mood and not argue anymore. She simply wanted to understand. But the sight of him, shadowed by the tree, his dark eyes gleaming nearly black in the growing night, did funny things to her insides. Things she thought maybe she had never felt before, or even imagined. More than chemistry. When she left Argentina, she would be leaving a piece of herself behind.

"You enjoyed the *asado*."

"I have enjoyed everything about being here." She smiled and took a step closer to him, knowing this was the perfect lead-in. "Maria and Carlos welcomed me. Do you know we spent the whole day together and we never once thought to get to the bottom of my reservation?"

"About that…"

"You were right, Tomas, and I was wrong. I'll fix it in the morning, don't worry."

He opened his mouth as if to say something and then shut it again, his brows pulling together. Sophia bit down on her lip, wondering if he'd had the words *I told you so* on his tongue but had held back.

When she'd first arrived she'd despaired of using her savings for the trip. Now she considered it money well spent. She was going back a different woman. A stronger woman. She couldn't put a price on that.

Sophia inhaled, suddenly nervous but needing to say what

was on her mind. "Maria and I talked about things, Tomas. A lot of things."

Ah, there it was. Even in the shadows she could see the flare of recognition in his eyes. But only for a moment. His face cleared and he smiled politely. "She wanted to make you feel at home. It is her way."

Bullheaded man! He knew what she was getting at, and he still deflected. She lifted her chin. "At home in a way you aren't with your real family?"

Sophia knew she was taking a chance. But hadn't he considered she might hear the details from Maria? When he didn't answer, she took a step forward. "Why couldn't you have told me, Tomas?"

He turned away from her so she couldn't see his face, but she heard the frustration in his voice. "Tell you what, Sophia?"

"Tell me about being part-owner of the estancia. And what happened to Rosa. Maria wouldn't tell me. She said I had to ask you."

"Why? So you could pity me instead of wallowing in your own ruined life?"

But she knew that was not true, and what's more he knew it, too. "That is grossly unfair. I did not wallow. I have never wallowed. Was I hurt? Yes. But I came here to start over, Tomas. You of all people know that. Because I told you. And I did every damn thing you asked. And what did you share with me?"

"Sophia," he said, entreating her.

God, she loved it when he said her name that way. She would never tire of the soft tones of his accent. But the gap between them was wider than she'd ever imagined.

"Don't Sophia me. You told me about Rosa, but that was just skimming the surface. You could have told me the rest. When we were out riding, the night that we…"

She couldn't finish the sentence. Humiliation burned its

way up her cheeks. She had confided in him about her virginity. Now she felt foolish.

She blinked back tears. He'd given her understanding and gentleness. But he hadn't given her himself. Not all of himself. Just enough to appease her questions.

"You should have told me," she whispered.

But Sophia wasn't prepared for the way her heart would crack when he admitted softly, "I know."

"Can you tell me now?"

"I don't want your pity," he said sharply, moving away from the trunk of the ombu but staying beneath the protection of its branches.

"Her picture is on the wall, Tomas. We walked by it many times each day and still nothing. You spoke of Miguel, but never of his sister. Not until that day on the bridge. Maria said something about you blaming yourself. Why?"

"It doesn't matter. I've moved on."

She shook her head. His body was as taut as a wire, a wire that would snap at any moment. "No, you haven't."

He turned on her then, his eyes blazing, his body emanating anger and frustration. "Why couldn't we just enjoy the week, hmm? We both knew you were only here for a short time. So what difference can it possibly make now?"

The answer came to Sophia as clearly as the stars hanging in the black Argentine sky. Because she was falling in love with him. That was the strange feeling she kept having, the one she'd never felt with Antoine or with any man before him. It made no sense, but it didn't need to, did it? It was just there, a complicated, tangled ball of emotions for a most inconvenient man at a most inopportune time. The man who had given her coins to make a wish and had understood that she was afraid to make love for the first time.

"Because you want to move on and you're stuck. You've withdrawn from the world, Tomas, and you can't find your way back." She went to him and put her hand on his arm. It was warm, but hard as a band of steel.

"Maybe I have. Maybe I just decided that this was what I wanted. I am happy here."

"I don't believe you."

Sophia was surprised at her temerity in saying that, even if it was true. She was more convinced than ever that his silence was his way of handling his grief.

"You don't have to believe me."

She couldn't help the smile that sneaked on to her lips, turning them up as she conceded the point. "I guess I don't. Perhaps I realize how much being here has helped me move past a lot of things, Tomas. It isn't just being here that has done it, either. It has been being with you. You challenge me, and force me to see things I'd rather ignore. But it is good. I need you to do that. And I have no idea how to show my gratitude."

"When have I needed gratitude?"

She raised her eyebrow at him.

He nodded. "That's right. Never."

"But you have it just the same. And of all the things you've said to me this week—all the difficult things to hear—it has been your silence that has hurt me most."

"Hurt you?" He turned his head to stare at her. "How could I hurt you?"

"When people care about each other, they share things. They don't keep secrets." She swallowed thickly. "I cared about someone once, and he kept secrets from me. Secrets that ended up hurting me very much. He betrayed my trust, and you knew that. Why would you think I would let you do the same?"

"But Antoine was with another woman."

"And you were…"

She let the end of the sentence hang, unsaid, but both of them knew the last two words were *with Rosa*. What she didn't expect was the way Tomas came forward and gripped her fingers in his. The pressure on her knuckles was nearly painful, until he released one hand and reached up to cup her jaw.

"Not with another woman," he denied. "You need to understand. I loved Rosa, and a person never truly gets over losing someone they love. But I wanted to keep Rosa out of it. I was with *you*, Sophia." He sighed, the sound intimate in the dusky night. "Only with you. No one else."

Hope, she realized, was a treacherous thing. It made her heart lift at his words, and she leaned her cheek into the wide palm of his hand. Had he truly not mentioned Rosa because he didn't want it to interfere with them? It seemed impossible.

And if it were true, then what on earth was she to do now?

"Tell me about polo. Tell me about the Mendoza family business."

He turned his head. "I can't. I can't go back. I won't. I'm sorry."

Resignation filled Sophia like a heavy weight. She had given him ample opportunities. Had flat-out asked him and still he refused, ensuring there was always that barrier between them. Leaving was still best, before she got in any deeper. Before she did something she would regret.

"You must be cold," he murmured. "You should have worn a sweater."

"I'm fine," she whispered. If she admitted she was cold, he would suggest they go back, and she wasn't ready to give up her time alone with him yet. These might be their last private moments together.

"But you are shivering."

She couldn't tell him the reason why. She could admit it to herself, but she could not verbalize it. He would think she was silly. He chafed her arms with his hands, the friction sending delicious warmth down to her fingertips.

"It has been a memorable week," Sophia said, knowing she had to tell him of her plans now, get it over with.

"*Si,*" he replied. "More eventful for some of us than others."

"I seem to create chaos wherever I go." Sophia smiled.

"But I didn't take good care of you. Some things…" he paused, frowned. "Some things never should have happened."

It would hurt her desperately if he meant kissing her, or spending the night together. She couldn't bear for him to say it, so she took his hand in hers. "You didn't ask me to go racing across the pampas with my hair on fire, did you? My fall was hardly your fault."

He looked at her head, lifting his hand and twining a curl around his finger. "But, *querida,*" he said softly, "Your hair *is* on fire. Gorgeous flames, like sunrise."

His hand was threaded into her curls now and her body swayed closer to him. She knew he was trying to distract her, and it ceased to matter.

"I bet you sweet-talk all the *señoritas,*" she whispered, desperately trying to keep herself on an even footing with him and failing beautifully. But she regained her balance quickly. "And the other night you said my hair was like sunset, not sunrise."

She couldn't tell if he was blushing in the dark, but the abashed expression on his face was gratifying enough. This was the Tomas she wanted to remember, the one she wanted to hold in her dreams when she returned to Canada.

"That is a bet you would lose," he responded. "I am not in the habit of sweet-talking, as you call it. Not at all. As you can see."

His other hand sank into her hair. "I don't know what to do about you, Sophia. I can't seem to stay away, but on the other hand this seems pointless."

"There's nothing pointless about feeling this way," she

whispered. "It feels wonderful, Tomas." She blinked slowly, opening her eyes again, almost to make sure he was really there holding her. One last chance before leaving. "Don't stop."

Her arms hung by her sides as her breath caught. The rising moon cast shadows on his face that had her heart knocking about like crazy. Was he going to kiss her?

"What am I going to do with you?" He whispered it, his voice silky and with the gorgeous Spanish lilt.

"I don't know," she replied. "But I wish you'd do it soon, Tomas. *Por favor.*"

He didn't need further invitation. As the breeze fluttered through the ombu leaves, he placed his lips on hers, tasting, savouring. The air came out of Sophia's lungs in a soft, breathy sigh. He tasted like all the best things of the day—the rich Malbec, the caramel sweetness of the *alfajores,* even the tang of the *mate*, all combined with a flavour that was Tomas. Gentle and persuasive, he guided her until her body was pressed against his. He was strong and solid, an unmovable wall next to her softness. And she did feel soft and delicate and feminine next to his strength. She tilted her head and slid her hands up over his chest to rest on his shoulders as she kissed him back.

With a groan, Tomas spanned her ribs with his hands and lifted her as if she weighed nothing. His gaze held her captive as he moved them back and to the side, and then braced himself back against part of the ombu tree. Gravity worked to his favour and her body rested against his, feeling all the ridges and planes of his body. She sank into him, losing herself in the kiss, letting everything from her past stay a continent away.

His hands skimmed down her ribs and desire rushed through her as she pressed against him.

A door slammed up at the house, the dull sound echoing through the stillness and Sophia pushed away. This was why she had to go. Another few days with him and leaving would be even more difficult. This could go nowhere. They both knew it. Now they needed to accept it.

"I'm leaving tomorrow," she announced, her voice clear and abrupt in the soft night.

"Tomorrow?" Tomas reached for her, but she stepped back.

"No, please don't." She held up a hand, knowing if he reached for her again she might change her mind. "I can't go on this way, Tomas. There is nothing holding me here—not even a reservation now. What are we doing exactly? Flirting? Kidding ourselves? I'm going to square up with Maria in the morning and go back to Buenos Aires. I've been thinking and I'd like to see Iguazú before I go home. I can do that if I leave tomorrow."

"Iguazú? But that's hours away."

It was, and she knew it. "There are tours that leave all the time. Or I can rent a car and drive. I can read a map, Tomas."

She realized her attitude was quite a change from the frightened, defensive girl who had arrived at Vista del Cielo and she stood tall. "All I will need is a drive back to the city."

"Sophia, this is silly."

"No, it is not," she replied. She wished he'd stop looking at her that way, his dark eyes soft and his hair rumpled and sexy. He couldn't possibly know how hard it was to say no to him. But what other choice did she have? She didn't belong here. She never had. She had only pretended because it had suited her. They were all wonderful, but this was not home. Home was a place she needed to make for herself.

"I care about you," he said. "It's the first time I've cared for someone in a long time. I know it's a passing thing. You have always been going to leave."

Her heart began to crack just a little, knowing this had to be the inevitable let-down. He was speaking nothing but the truth. He couldn't know how deep her own feelings ran, so why did it actually hurt to hear it?

"But I'm not ready for it to be over."

And just like that, her heart leapt. "You see? You say things like that and I don't know what to do with it. We're from two different worlds, Tomas. On borrowed time."

"So we enjoy it while it lasts."

"I don't have any practice with that. I always plan things out, you see. Weigh the pros and cons."

"And how is that working out for you?"

His voice held a trace of smugness, as if he knew the answer.

She ran her fingers over a large curve of the ombu tree. "It's not." She sighed. "For a long time I sat quietly and didn't rock the boat. It was easier to go along with what people told me was best rather than do what I wanted."

"We all have to live with our choices."

"Then respect mine, please, Tomas." Sophia looked up at him, needing him to understand. "Take me to Buenos Aires tomorrow and let me go."

"Sophia…"

"If you don't, I will ask Carlos. And he will say yes."

Tomas didn't answer her, but they both knew she was right. His shoulders relaxed and he sighed, giving in.

He held out his hand and she took it. He led her to a place where the tree root extended, curved and knotted before disappearing into the ground. It was large enough to sit on, and they did, Sophia putting her arms around her knees for added warmth.

"If you are determined to go…I got you something in San Antonio de Areco." He reached into his pocket. "I have been trying to find the right time to give it to you. Now it seems this will be my only chance."

Sophia's mouth dropped open. A gift? It was totally unexpected. "You did?"

"You were admiring the silver jewelry. I had the shop-keeper wrap this up."

Sophia felt a curl of pleasure, bittersweet as it blended with the inevitable knowledge that this was their last night together. The trip to town seemed like ages ago, not two days. He had thought of her, even then? Before the kiss on the bridge? "You didn't have to do that."

"I wanted to. Please, just accept it as a token of your trip. A memento."

He put the small box into her hand. "Open it," he suggested.

Sophia took the simple white box and removed the cover. She gasped at the beautiful necklace inside. "Oh, Tomas."

"It matches your earrings. The amethyst ones."

She reached inside and carefully lifted the chain so that the pendant swung free. The silver pendant was in the shape of an ombu leaf, an echo of the ones that covered them like a veil. There was a marquise-cut amethyst in the middle. "It is stunning. I don't know what to say."

"Don't say anything. When you are back in Canada, you can wear it and remember your time here."

Her smile trembled as she turned the pendant over in her fingers. And now she would have the necklace to remember. Remember learning to love herself again and remember the precious gift he'd given her, even more precious than Argentine silver. The gift of being herself and knowing it was enough.

The thought was beautiful and sad all at once, because it really was starting to feel like goodbye. She held out the chain. "Will you put it on for me please?"

"Of course."

He put the box back in his pocket and took the fine silver chain from her fingers. She could feel his body close behind her and the coolness of the metal pendant against her collarbone. His hand swept her hair away from her collar and a shiver went through her body as she reveled in the simple touch. When the clasp was fastened, he kept his hand against the nape of her neck.

"Don't go," he murmured, touching his lips to the sensitive skin below her hairline. "Stay until the end of the week."

That she wanted to say yes with every molecule in her body was enough warning. "I can't, Tomas." And she couldn't tell him the reason. The last thing he wanted to hear from her was the *L*-word. He did not love her, and she would only be hurt in the end.

CHAPTER TEN

SOPHIA had her bags all packed when Tomas entered the kitchen the next morning. He stood in the doorway for a few moments, listening to her talk with Maria and Carlos. He'd meant to be up early, to talk to her about her plans, but instead he'd tossed and turned late into the night, replaying their conversation beneath the ombu and wondering if she was really right after all. Had he simply been hiding? Running? He thought of his family back in Buenos Aires, and of Motores Mendoza. He had closed the door to them and had been determined never to open it again. He'd flatly refused to talk to Sophia about it. And why?

Because it was easier to forget than to face the truth. He'd said goodbye to his old life and started over at Vista del Cielo.

And what had it fixed? Nothing. And then along had come Sophia.

Did she really have any idea of what she'd done?

She was folding something—was that her receipt?—and tucking it into her purse. She was really leaving, then. Sticking to her guns.

He admired her for it, but he couldn't let her go. Not yet.

He pushed off the door frame and came into the kitchen. "Oh, Tomas," Maria said, giving him a good-morning smile. "Sophia just told us of her plans. I'm sure she'll have a wonderful time. Iguazú is so beautiful."

"So you've straightened out the bill?"

Sophia looked up, met his gaze with her own. Firmly, no shyness or evasion. *Dios,* when had she become so strong? He swallowed as his throat felt dry. Today she was back in one of her tidy designer dresses, bronze shoes on her feet that seemed to be constructed of threads—how could something that flimsy hold someone's weight? And yet he couldn't deny how the criss-cross pattern drew his gaze to her ankles and the smooth calves leading to her hemline.

"I've paid Maria for my time here," Sophia explained. "The mix-up is fixed. Thank you—especially you, Tomas, for a lovely stay."

She was far too composed and Tomas felt annoyance build, tensing his shoulders. Lying awake meant he'd slept longer than he'd expected. He'd intended on speaking to her this morning. The idea of her paying for the week didn't sit well with him. He had expected an argument, but he also wanted her to know that he would look after the costs of her stay.

This way made it seem like she was no more than a guest, and she was. Much more.

"So that's it?"

She gave him a cool look. "What else is there?"

And yet she wore the necklace he'd given her around her throat, and the earrings, too. They'd shared things, personal things. It was wrong to have such a cold goodbye, as though none of it mattered.

"I told Miss Hollingsworth I would take her to the city," Carlos said quietly, and Tomas shook his head.

"No," he said firmly. "I will do that." He stood up straight and met Sophia's gaze. "I will do more than that. I will take you to Iguazú."

He was aware of Maria's mouth dropping open and the smile blooming on Carlos's face. And he was aware of the consternation twisting Sophia's features. This was not part of her plan, and he was damned glad to complicate things for her. She'd certainly done enough complicating of her own. She'd waltzed in here and turned his whole life upside-down.

"I don't recall inviting you," she replied. She kept her expression friendly but he heard the vinegar behind the words.

"You didn't. But you'll waste a lot of time going to Buenos Aires, then finding transportation, then sorting out touring the park on your own...it's just easier if I take you."

Every single word he'd said was true. She would face those difficulties, but his reason for going with her had nothing to do with travel time at all.

He refused to let her go. Even if it meant leaving the estancia and driving across country to the waterfalls that attracted hordes of tourists, he'd do it.

Because he was in love with her.

The knowledge seeped into him like rain into dry ground, making everything expand and grow. What a hell of a situation. He did not know what he was going to do about it, but he knew to say goodbye now would be a mistake.

He stood his ground. For long moments their gazes clashed—his determined, hers resisting. He was vastly relieved when she relented, dropping her gaze to her handbag. "All right, fine," she said irritably. "I'm ready when you are."

"Ten minutes," Tomas replied, disappearing back into his room to throw some clothing in a bag.

When he came back out, Maria and Carlos were waiting with Sophia. Maria gave him a hug and her eyes were suspiciously bright. "You come back to us," she said, and Tomas had to pull away. He knew why. Sophia had been right when she'd accused him of hiding out at the estancia. For him to volunteer to leave for even a few days was unusual behaviour. Maria understood him more than most. She knew that taking Sophia there himself was important. And it was more important than any of them knew.

"Don't worry," he murmured, accepting a bag of *alfajores* for the road. "I'm just taking a few days off."

But it was a few days with a woman—something he'd never done before. Not since Rosa, and they all knew it.

Maria hugged Sophia. "You have the recipe, yes?"

Sophia nodded, and Tomas watched a curl droop over Sophia's cheek as she hugged Maria back. "I sure do. Thank you, Maria."

Carlos shook her hand. "You come back any time," he said, his accent thick, but his smile more easy than Maria's had been, not quivering around the edges like hers.

Tomas's stomach clenched. He knew as well as they did that Sophia would not be back.

"We'd better get going," he stated, moving past the group to load the bags in his truck. "It's a long drive."

They were halfway down the dusty lane when Sophia spoke up.

"You do not have to go with me. Just drop me in the city and I will be fine."

"You don't want me to come?" He kept his eyes on the road, knowing if he looked at her now he might just pull over and kiss that stubborn set of her mouth until it was pliable beneath his.

"I…"

"You what?"

She huffed out a gigantic breath of air. "I didn't want to have to say goodbye twice, all right?"

"Maybe I am not ready for you to leave," he said, turning on to the main road in a cloud of dust.

"But I *am* leaving, Tomas. We both know it."

"Not yet," he replied. "I know what you said last night, but not yet, okay?" He reached over and turned on the stereo. "Let me show you Iguazú." And what else, he wondered. What more did he want? It was all impossible. They were from two very different worlds. If he had to content himself with forty-eight more hours, then that was what he'd do.

He would simply keep his feelings to himself. She never needed to know. Sophia had been so angry with him last night, and as much as he would not admit it, he knew she had a right. He hadn't been totally honest with her. She would never love him, he was sure of it. He'd worked too hard at making himself unloveable.

So he would love her, for the last moments they had left together.

Sophia finished the last of her coffee and put the empty paper cup in the cup holder as Tomas pulled into the parking lot at the Iguazú National Park and killed the ignition. "This is the best time to get started, before all the tour groups come in," Tomas said, sliding out of the driver's side and hefting a day pack on his shoulder. "Later this morning it'll be packed."

Sophia hopped out, clad in jeans and sneakers and a cotton T-shirt. The air was heavier here, rich with moisture and the scent of the rain forest. She followed Tomas to the entrance of the pathways and wondered if it were possible to absorb each detail, cataloguing each sight and scent and sound into her brain so she could recall it perfectly later.

They hadn't arrived in Puerto Iguazú until after dinner last night and Tomas had booked them into a hotel. She'd expected awkwardness, but he'd assumed she wanted separate rooms and had booked them next to each other. He'd handed her the keycard and she had tucked it into her pocket, reaching for her carry-on to avoid looking into his face. She would have insisted on her own room anyway, but it still stung that there hadn't even been a hint of indecision in his eyes. He'd helped her with her bags and without so much as a peck on the cheek or a squeeze of her hand he'd left her to freshen up.

Over dinner he'd given her a little history of the area and

this morning he'd pulled out a park map and they'd planned their day while grabbing a quick breakfast.

Absolutely nothing personal. No talking about Rosa, or his family, or the hour of her departure that was racing towards her faster than she wanted to admit. No words about their kisses or anything remotely intimate.

It was driving her absolutely, completely crazy.

She grabbed his arm as they walked down the pathway, sidestepping to avoid a group of German tourists who, like them, were getting an early start.

"Tomas, please," she whispered, her fingers digging into his arm.

He stopped, looked down at her. Waited.

She had to swallow back the hitch in her breath as she gazed up at him. When had he become everything? Why did this have to happen now, a world away? Even if she did admit her feelings, what good would it do? His life was here. Her family—her life—was in Ottawa. Worlds apart. Tomorrow she'd say goodbye to him forever. The very thought made her feel empty inside, as though a great cavern had opened up, her emotions echoing off the sides. There was no sense fighting her feelings now. The damage was already done.

"What is it?" He reached for her arm, gripping it just below her shoulder, his gaze plumbing hers, searching for answers she didn't have.

"I just can't take this…this impersonal way you are with me. Are you angry with me? Did I do something wrong?"

As soon as the words left her mouth she closed her eyes. She was still afraid, after all the progress she'd made. Tomas had been distant and polite ever since the night under the ombu. Her lip quivered. The very moment she had realized her true feelings, he had locked his away.

"No, *querida*. I am not angry."

"But you…"

He placed a finger over her lips, halting her words, and

then gently touched his mouth to hers, hovering, tasting, their breaths mingling in the humid air of the rain forest.

Tomas felt his heart pound against his ribs as he forced himself to go slowly, gently. Now her lips were parted beneath his and he drank in her flavour, soft and sweet and tasting like strawberry lip gloss.

Reluctantly he pulled away, but he couldn't shift his gaze away from her face. Her dark eyes were dreamy, the pupils dilated and her lips were full and puffy.

"Tomas…" She murmured his name and he watched, mesmerized, as a bright yellow butterfly paused and perched on a burnished curl of her hair.

"Wait," he whispered, releasing her. He let the backpack slide from his shoulder and reached in to take out a small camera. "Smile," he commanded, and he was instantly gratified as her lips curved in a slow, sexy smile.

He snapped the photo and looked at it in the viewfinder, struck by the vivid colours. Her auburn hair, the bloom in her cheeks from being freshly kissed, the depths of her eyes that made her look as if she was sharing a secret with the camera, the shocking yellow hue of the butterfly and the vibrant green of the jungle forming the backdrop. This was how he wanted to remember her—still soft and flushed after his kisses. Full of colour and light and life. The person who had brought such colour back to his own life.

"Come on," he said, uncomfortable at the strength of his reaction to a simple snapshot. Sophia shook her curls and the butterfly flitted off. "We have to catch the train, or we'll miss it and have to wait another half hour."

They caught the train that took them to the *Garganta del Diablo*—the Devil's Throat. Tomas had made this trip before, and knew what to expect, but he loved watching Sophia's face as they went deeper through the rain forest toward the most famous part of the falls. Her eyes danced and she twisted in her seat, looking out of the open window and trying to see everything. His kiss had stopped her questions, but for how long? What if she knew the whole truth? Would she feel the same? Or would that light in her eyes dim just a bit knowing he wasn't the man she thought he was?

Tomas would not let it ruin their day. He pointed out birds as they went along, and cautioned Sophia to put on her poncho unless she favoured getting wet. "The day is clear, but the mist never goes away," he explained. "And Sophia—you will get wet," he promised, as they followed the rest of the throng to the boardwalk.

The roar of the water was deafening as their shoes clunked along the metal structure. They hadn't gone far when Sophia clutched at his hand, her eyes huge as she looked up at him. "The water is moving so fast." The shore was behind them and a thick cloud of mist indicated their destination—the cusp of the Devil's Throat. Right now the only thing standing between them and the rushing water was a metal grate.

"It's safe," Tomas assured her, keeping her hand in his. "And the view is so worth it. Come on, Sophia." He pulled her along, keeping her close as he sensed her unease. The vibration of the water shimmered up through the soles of their shoes. It was impossible to ignore the river's power.

When they reached the end of the boardwalk, the mist hovered, a filmy cloud settling on their clear ponchos. As they approached the rail, Tomas heard her gasp with pleasure, her hesitation temporarily forgotten. "Tomas, look! A rainbow!"

The sun was shining through the mist and an arc of colour decorated the view. "See the birds?" he called to her above the falls' roar as they tumbled and crashed to an invisible bottom. The birds were dark darts, flitting in and out of view.

"It's incredible."

Tomas took out his camera, wanting to capture her this alive, looking so free and vibrant. Did she know how brave, how gutsy she was to come on this trip alone, to gamely take on anything he suggested? Sometimes even foolishly. She was the kind of woman a man would be proud to call his. A woman who would walk beside her man so they could face things together, given the chance. Her ex had to be the biggest fool on earth to throw that away.

She stood on tiptoe, hanging on to the railing and looking down into the cleft in the rock. As the wind tossed her hair over her shoulder, he knew that she was the kind of woman *he* could easily spend his life with.

The realization was so sudden that he felt everything within him drop to his feet, shifting the grate beneath the soles of his shoes. A lifetime? Impossible. Recognizing his feelings as love was different than contemplating forever. He'd felt that longing with Rosa, and he never wanted to go through that pain again. His brain leapt ahead, searching for logic. What kind of life would they have? He could resume his place at Motores Mendoza, he supposed, but he'd be miserable, stuck in the city with no room to breathe. At the mercy of the boardroom and his father's legacy. And the estancia was a fine place for a holiday, but would a woman like Sophia ever be happy out in the middle of the pampas? Living there wasn't the same as a week's vacation.

He took several steps away from the observation platform, back towards where the boardwalk narrowed. Sophia looked back at him and smiled, her curls darker now from the damp, the corkscrews springing up and framing her tanned face. Even if they could agree, it was crazy to think of asking her to stay after only a week of knowing her. The heavy feeling in his chest, the way his words felt as though they were going to stick in his throat when she was around—this was simply a holiday fling, right? A far cry from building a life with someone. That was complete and utter nonsense.

Sophia was mesmerized by the thunder of the water and the spray that settled like a film on her hair. It was majestic, staggering, awesome. She closed her eyes, listening to the crash of the water, feeling the power vibrate through her feet up her body, loving the way the mist moistened her skin.

And then she opened her eyes and looked at Tomas. He was standing back towards the opening of the observation deck, watching her with such a serious expression that her heart stuttered.

She smiled at him, wanting to see him smile back at her, needing the warmth of it. Every time she thought about leaving she felt a little piece of her heart break away. Tomorrow it was back to Buenos Aires and the airport. It was hours on a plane and a life of uncertainty waiting—a life she could choose. It should have felt like a world of excitement and possibility.

Right now it just felt empty. Because there would be no Tomas in it.

She took her hand off the railing and went to him, curling her hand around his arm. "You're looking glum."

"Am I? I didn't mean to." But there was something in his voice. It was too perfect, too cautious. "Let's walk. There are tons of trails. Let's just enjoy the day, okay?"

They made their way to the train and soon they were chugging their way back to the station where they could connect to walking trails. Tomas pointed out coatis scurrying through the grass, searching for discarded snacks from the tourists. "Tomas?" Sophia watched a coati shoving a piece of bread into its mouth, reminding her of the raccoons back home. "If I ask you now, will you answer? Why didn't you tell me you were part owner of the estancia?"

Tomas dropped his hand and sighed. "Maria has a big mouth."

Sophia couldn't help but laugh. "It's like you hung the stars and the moon for her, Tomas. She just loves you. She's proud of you."

Was it pain that suddenly slashed across his face? If it was, it was gone just as quickly. "I have money, Sophia. My family owns Motores Mendoza—an auto parts company."

"Is it a big company?"

He chuckled, the sound tight, no pleasure in it. "Fairly big. My father's empire. I chose the pampas instead. I invested my money in Vista del Cielo."

"Because of Rosa?"

She saw him swallow. She knew it was a tough topic, but it had bothered her that he'd let her believe he was nothing more than a gaucho, a worker.

"Partly. Because I love it there. And because I wanted to help Maria and Carlos. I am the silent partner. In exchange for capital, I have a job, a place to live."

"No," she replied, shaking her hair to let the breeze dry it. She could feel the humidity turning her curls into tight ringlets. "That is a business transaction. What you have, Tomas, is a family who loves you. What about your other family? Your real father and mother?"

He shook his head. "I haven't spoken to them in some time. I should have taken my place at the head of the company when my father retired. He felt betrayed when I resigned and moved to the estancia."

"But they are your family. If they love you…"

The train rolled into the station and they got off. Sophia peeled off her poncho and shook the remaining moisture off. Tomas rolled it and tucked it within the straps of the pack.

"Sophia, I never meant to mislead you. Not about any of it. I'm just a very private person. Talking about my personal life just doesn't happen."

"That explains me having to drag it out of you, then." She started down the path, hearing his footsteps behind her. "But the result is that your silence can make a person feel very insignificant and meaningless."

"Not meaningless!" He jogged to catch her and grabbed her hand. "Sophia…I know how he made you feel. I never meant to do that. Never. There were times I wanted to tell you, but how would I bring up such a topic?"

"The elephant in the room." Sophia sighed, and their steps slowed as they walked the route to the lower falls.

The jungle seemed to close in, sheltering them in a green canopy of privacy as they traveled. A toucan flew in front of them and perched in a nearby tree. Butterflies dotted the foliage. Sophia was thinking about getting on the plane tomorrow and wondering how she was going to make it through that.

"After what happened to you, aren't you afraid to love again?" Tomas asked. "Doesn't it frighten you?"

Sophia nodded. "Of course. Once you've been burned... you grow cautious."

"Then imagine if the person you'd loved had died. Wouldn't it scare you to think of loving someone that much again? Knowing how it had hurt?"

The thought of leaving Tomas tomorrow was ripping through her insides, but he'd still be alive and well and riding the pampas. To think about a world without Tomas in it...

"Yes," she whispered. "That would make me think twice."

"Then perhaps you understand why I had difficulty opening up to you, Sophia. You frighten me."

She stopped in the path. "Me?"

"You didn't realize I care for you? You didn't trust my feelings were real?"

"I thought the feelings were all on my side."

Tomas put down the pack. "After all that happened? The kiss on the bridge? Telling you about Rosa? The night in my room? Did you think it meant nothing to me?"

"I...I..." She stammered, off balance. "Of course not," she replied, but then had to confess. "I mean, you were wonderful, but I thought you were just...being..." She sighed. "Nice," she finished.

"I see," he said quietly. "You told me things, but you didn't trust me. I understand why my silence upsets you. I do, Sophia, and I'm sorry for that. But have you told me everything about yourself?"

Her silence spoke louder than any words could have.

"You did not trust me, either. And what do we have if we don't have trust?"

Sophia had no words. Was he right? Did he have bigger feelings for her than she realized? And had she passed them off as if they were unimportant? She had trusted him, but had she trusted *in* him? He was talking about faith, a completely different thing, and up until now she hadn't separated the two.

"Tomas…"

"Never mind," he said. "Let's take a boat ride before we go back to the hotel. This is your only chance, right? You might as well make the most of it."

He shouldered the pack once more and led the way down the path.

Sophia had felt many things over the past week, but feeling that she'd let Tomas down was suddenly the worst of them all. And with only hours left, how could she ever make it up to him?

CHAPTER ELEVEN

Sophia saw the boat and instantly felt her insides seize. It was really just a Zodiac crammed with people and Sophia had already witnessed the awesome power of the river—how could a Zodiac compete with that? But Tomas was right beside her, and she refused to back out. She could only let her fear dictate for so long and eventually she had to stand up to it. At least this time she had Tomas by her side. She had climbed many mountains this week. This felt like the ultimate test, and she was determined to face it.

She donned the life jacket provided and took her seat next to Tomas.

The tour started with the guide narrating a spiel about the river and falls but Sophia heard nothing other than the rushing water. Tomas pointed out something on the shore, and she dutifully followed the direction of his finger and nodded, but she had no idea what she was supposed to be looking at. Instead, she could only feel everything closing in around her. The side of the boat pressed against her leg and Tomas's body was an immovable wall to her left. The grumble of the motor was nearly drowned out by the crash of the water, and the wall of river and people pushed in on her from both sides until she could hardly breathe.

All around her there were exclamations of excitement and whoops as passengers got in the spirit of the adventure. But as they got closer to the roaring falls, the cloud of mist darkened the sky and Sophia was surrounded by it as the pilot took them closer, closer, closer.

The walls closed in, dark and with no escape.

Sophia began to tremble.

It had been a mistake. It had all been a mistake. She should never have done this. Why had she thought that this was a good idea? Her breaths came in shallow pants as she fought against the panic. She wanted out, *right now*. And there was nowhere to go.

She tried to force deep breaths, to visualize being anywhere else, but all she saw was darkness and all she felt was the claustrophobia of being trapped. Drops of water crawled down her skin and she shuddered, unable to stop the shaking.

Then Tomas was there, saying her name.

His arm went around her shoulder, holding her as close to him as their life jackets would allow while all around them screams of wonder erupted as the boat passed daringly close to the falls. His left hand came across and took hers and she gripped it, a lifeline in the middle of the terror. Tears streamed down her cheeks, mingling with the droplets of river water that soaked them all. Sophia fought for logic. *This is not then. It is not the dark, dingy basement and I am not alone.*

She was with Tomas. The boat turned, heading back toward the docking area and Sophia went limp with relief. It was over. Sunlight reappeared as they drew away from the falls, the warm light of it soaking into the top of her head. Still Tomas kept his arm around her and she kept her fingers within his.

She turned to look up at him. His dark eyes were clouded with concern, his lips unsmiling. She blinked, feeling the tears warm on her lashes as her lower lip quivered. Tomas leaned forward and stopped the trembling with his mouth. The kiss was incredibly tender, and he let his forehead rest against hers for a moment before sitting back.

But he never let go of her hand.

The boat docked and the passengers disembarked. Tomas and Sophia shed their life jackets and Sophia stepped away to the trail. The ground felt as though it was shifting beneath her feet. Without saying a word, Tomas took her hand and they began the hike through the rain forest that would take them back to the parking lot. She followed blindly, one step after the other, going slowly until all the others of their party pulled away and they were left behind.

A side path opened up and Tomas led her down it, until they stood at an outcrop overlooking the falls, the roar now a distant hum. He shed the pack and turned to her, holding out his arms. She went into them, and the numbness that had sustained her through the Zodiac ride and walk fled, making room for the painful pins and needles of recirculation as her feelings came rushing back. She didn't realize she was crying until she heard Tomas say "Shhhh" into her hair, and she took great gulps of air, trying to regain control.

"Sophia, please don't cry." His voice was rough with emotion. "Please, Sophia. You tear me apart when you cry."

He cared about her that much? She closed her eyes, inhaling his scent that was man and water and fresh air and knowing it was a smell she'd always associate with security. She was safe here, in Tomas's arms.

"I'm sorry," she whispered. "I didn't mean to cry."

His hand cupped the back of her head, stroking her hair.

"If I had known about the boat...I never would have suggested it, *querida*. I'm so sorry. Why didn't you say anything?"

She sniffled, and pushed out of his arms just enough that she could look up at him—she didn't want to be out of his embrace completely. "I thought I needed to face it. I wanted to show you I could be brave." Her lip trembled again but she stopped it. "It wasn't the boat, Tomas. It was..."

She took in a great breath and let it out again. "It was the way I've lived my whole life, and I'm so tired of it. I'm tired of being scared. I'm tired of being afraid."

"Afraid of what?" He placed a finger under her chin. "Sophia, I would keep you safe. You must know that. I would do anything to keep you out of harm's way."

Her heart gave a solid thump at the assurance in his voice. "I know, Tomas, I know." She put her hand on the side of his face and looked up into the eyes that seemed to see her so well. "Don't you see? I could only face it because I had you. And because deep down I knew that no matter what I did, you would be there. Because you are Tomas. Because that is what you do."

She thought she saw pain flash through his eyes before he lowered his lashes, but when he lifted them again his gaze was clear. "What is it that frightened you so much? I looked over and your face was white. And you were crying. But Sophia, you never cry. Not when you showed up at the estancia by mistake. Not even when you fell off the horse. Talk to me, Sophia."

She led him to a bench on the side of the viewpoint and they sat down. Sophia kept her leg pressed against his, needing to feel close to him. "I should never have been angry about you keeping secrets. You were right, Tomas. I haven't told you everything, either. I've never talked about this before," she whispered. "But I need to now. I need to because I want to stop feeling this way."

He squeezed her hand, the only encouragement she needed.

"When I was eight, my father and mother separated. My mother had never been really happy, but when Dad was gone she was really bitter. She made a point of sending me to the right schools and she worked long hours to make sure we had a nice house in a good neighbourhood. But she really didn't see me. I never understood how he could have left us like that. But when I asked about seeing my dad she never answered my questions. It all went wrong when he left, and I would go to bed at night just wishing he'd come back."

She took Tomas's hand in hers, ran her fingers over the work-worn fingertips and strong muscles of his wrist. He had reliable hands. She lifted it to her lips and kissed the spot at the base of his thumb before continuing on.

"We were staying at a cottage in Muskoka the next summer. It was beautiful, but I was so lonely. I hadn't seen my dad in months and I didn't know any of the kids there. I didn't want mom to see me cry—she hated when I did—so I hid in the basement. I thought I'd be left alone there to have my cry in private.

"Someone went out and they locked the cellar door before they left. I couldn't get out. I had left the door open a crack for light, but once it was shut, there was nothing but blackness.

"I cried to get out. I banged on the door but no one heard. I heard them calling for me, but then the voices went away." Sophia suppressed a shudder, determined to tell him everything. He needed to understand. Someone needed to understand—she was so tired of being alone. And he had been wrong. She did trust in him.

"I sat in the dark for four hours. Nothing but the sound of my own breathing, and the scratch of insects on the walls. But I lost it completely when the spiders got in my hair. I started crying again, and it was a neighbour who heard me screaming and opened the basement door."

"Oh, Sophia," Tomas said, holding her close. "So the morning you saw the wolf spider…"

"I know it is childish, but I've never gotten over my fear of them. Every time I see one I feel it crawling along my scalp."

He pressed a kiss to her temple and she sighed, sinking into him. "That's not the worst part though, Tomas. My mother was livid. She yelled at me for playing dangerous games, told me how terrible we looked to our hosts now—you have to understand this was a very affluent area with big summer homes. We looked bad. That was her big concern. And then she said…she said…"

Even now it stung. Sophia knew it was a horribly wrong and untruthful thing for her mother to say, and that it had been done in the heat of panic. Margaret had apologized later, but the damage had been done nonetheless. "She said I was so much trouble it was no wonder my father had left."

Tomas said something in Spanish she didn't understand, but his tone was dark and angry.

"Being at Vista del Cielo with you—it showed me that all my life I've been afraid. Scared that if I didn't do what was expected of me, she'd leave, too. She was all I had left. So I went to the right schools and socialized with the right people and did the right job. Antoine was the 'right' sort of man— well positioned, well-liked, with a shining future. And I'd been doing what I was told for so long that I was the perfect wife for him."

"Until you caught him with his mistress." Tomas smiled a little, and Sophia couldn't help it. She found herself smiling back.

"Yes. That was the deal-breaker. That was the beginning of me finding who I was, rather than who everyone else wanted me to be. Looking back, I can see that my mom only wanted security for me. She wanted for me what she didn't have for herself. It's just not what I want."

"And that is why you were so angry that I didn't tell you about the estancia."

"Someone else has been in control of my life for so long, it felt as though you were manipulating me, only letting me see what you wanted to, rather than the real Tomas. And that hurt. Because I was really starting to care for you."

"And I didn't tell you everything because I was starting to care for you, too, and I thought if you knew, it would ruin what time we had together."

"Why would you think that? It's wonderful that you set up the business with them. They adore you. She was your fiancée, Maria and Carlos's daughter. She is a part of you. Knowing about her wouldn't have changed anything, Tomas. It's not like it was your fault."

Tomas let go of her hand, slid down the bench and stared straight ahead. "But it is my fault, Sophia. Rosa died because of me."

Tomas hadn't planned on telling her everything. Especially today, knowing she hadn't truly trusted him. He'd thought they were over. But the boat ride had changed everything. He loved her. There was no question in his mind now. And there could be no more secrets between them, especially now when she had told him the truth.

But oh, it was tearing him apart to say the words.

"I meant what I said earlier, Sophia. I would do anything to protect you. But I didn't protect Rosa. She died because of me. Because of the man I was. I was like Antoine. I was focused on business. We were supposed to have dinner to talk about wedding plans, but I was working late, trying to finish up a final deal before a board meeting the next day. Rosa called to say she would meet me at the restaurant. She walked instead of me picking her up. But she never made it to the restaurant."

He swallowed. Wanted to feel Sophia close to him, but he couldn't bear to look at her face right now. He wasn't the knight in shining armor she seemed to believe him to be. He didn't want to see the disappointment in her eyes. So he folded his hands on his knees and forged forward.

"She was mugged on the way to the restaurant. She must have put up a fight—the Rosa I knew wouldn't have gone along easily. There were scrapes where her engagement ring had been pulled off her finger. The coroner said she hit her head when she fell. By the time she was found and taken to the hospital, it was too late. And it all could have been avoided if I'd picked her up like I'd promised instead of being full of myself and of work."

"Oh, Tomas," Sophia said softly.

"You see?" He jumped to his feet, moved a few steps away. "That's what I didn't want. Pity. I don't deserve pity, Sophia!"

"So you turned your back on the company, on your family, and decided to punish yourself by isolating yourself at the estancia?"

He nodded, knowing he shouldn't be surprised that she understood. This was Sophia. Sophia who seemed to get everything about him.

"Maria and Carlos never blamed me. Being close to them I was close to her. And I could help them. It was more than my duty. I wanted to."

It had been the only way he could think of to help. Maria needed people around, people to mother. There was no more Rosa, Miguel was gone to Córdoba and the grandchildren she yearned for were a distant hope. "I couldn't stand to see the loneliness in Maria's eyes anymore. We built the place together."

"What about your family in Buenos Aires? They must miss you. And the company. Did you resign?"

"My brother took my place. And my father and mother…" He swallowed. Yes, they had their faults but they loved him. He knew that. The Rodriguez family didn't run in the same circles as the Mendozas, but he'd finally admitted to himself that his parents had been good to Rosa. Their concern hadn't been for appearances but for Rosa, and how she would adjust to the kind of life she'd never known.

Finally, finally, he looked at Sophia.

She was sitting on the bench, her jeans dark with water, the wet patches on her shirt with still drying. Any makeup she'd worn had been washed away in the spray and her hair lay in dark, wet curls. She was the most beautiful woman he'd ever seen. And he knew as sure as he was standing here that somehow he couldn't let her go.

"My father told me there is always a place for me at Motores Mendoza. It was me who shut the door."

"And will you open it now?"

Would he? He found himself blinking as he thought of his father's booming laugh and his mother's soft smile. He had tried to stop feeling for so long, but Sophia had changed everything. She had made him feel alive again—with pain but there was also pleasure. Warmth. Hope.

"I still do not think the company is where I will be happy. For me it is still the pampas and the estancia. It is where I belong, Sophia." He realized it was true. He was through with the city and boardrooms and suits and ties. Even if the Vista del Cielo wasn't exactly as he remembered, he knew he wanted the wild freedom of the pampas, the simple evenings by the fire and the sound of the birds at the end of the day. But rejecting the life was different from rejecting the people, and he'd done both for too long. "But I need to mend things with my family. And it is you who has shown me that."

Sophia looked up at him, in awe of the man he was, a man perhaps he did not even see. A man who had carried the heavy load of his burdens and responsibilities and sacrificed his own heart for it.

She stood from the bench, her damp jeans tight and uncomfortable on her legs, but that didn't matter. Not at this moment, with this man. She knew the one thing he needed, because it was the one thing *she'd* needed her whole life long. She went to him, lifted her face to his and said simply, "I love you, Tomas."

For a fleeting second, shock made a blank of his face as he seemed to struggle to understand. So she repeated it, this time in his own language: "*Te amo*, Tomas."

He cupped her head in both hands and kissed her, a kiss full of love and wonder and pain and acceptance all at once. She twined her arms around his neck as his hands slid from her face down to her waist and pulled her close. She melted against him, wanting his kiss, his touch, to go on forever.

But it couldn't, and knowing that added an urgency, a desperation to the way she pressed herself against him. Now she wished she'd made love to him while she'd had the chance. She wished she hadn't been so afraid. It had nothing to do with losing her virginity. It was about wanting to be as close to someone as a person could be. It wasn't about the physical, it was about loving him wholly.

Tomas's hands settled on her hips and pushed her back slightly so that the kiss broke off. She was breathing heavily and Tomas's chest rose and fell with effort, but it was the look in his eyes that undid her. It was yearning. The same yearning she'd been feeling only seconds before. She wasn't afraid of it anymore.

"*Te amo*, Sophia. And I never expected to love anyone ever again."

He took her hand and pressed it to his cheek. "I don't want you to leave. I don't know what the solution is, but I can't bear to lose you. And we have so little time…"

"What are you asking, Tomas?" *Say the words*, she thought desperately. *Say the words so I can say yes.*

"Stay with me."

"At the Vista del Cielo?"

"It is a lot to ask, I know. It doesn't have to be there…"

"But you love it there, Tomas. It is where you belong." She looked into his eyes, feeling love run through every pore. It didn't matter that they'd known each other such a short time. They knew each other better than many did in a lifetime. "It is where I belong, too, if you are there."

"I want you to make your own choice, Sophia. I love you,

and it is not conditional. Nothing you can do or say will make me take it away. I need you to understand that."

She nodded. "And you need to understand that this is me, making my own choice. I believe in you, Tomas. I found myself in your heart." She put her hand on his chest, feeling the solid beat beneath her fingers. "As long as I am there, nothing else matters."

"They will say we're crazy…"

"It doesn't matter what anyone says."

Tomas linked his fingers with hers, and her heart was full when he knelt on one knee before her.

And it overflowed when he bowed his head and pressed his forehead to her hand for just a moment.

But when he looked up, it was with determination and love and hope in his eyes. "Marry me, Sophia. Marry me and I will spend the rest of my days making you happy."

The falls roared, birds called and monkeys chattered in the trees, but Sophia heard nothing but the thunderous beat of her own heart as she flung herself into his arms.

"Yes," she whispered, feeling the world tilt, shift and settle exactly where it was meant to be. "A million times, yes."

CHAPTER TWELVE

THE dancing had already started when Tomas tugged on Sophia's hand, drawing her into a shadowed corner of the patio. Beyond them, over the hill, the ombu tree stood guard, and all around them the air was colored by the sounds of friends and family, enjoying themselves at the celebration.

"Tomas," Sophia insisted with a laugh, "we're ignoring our guests." But the protest was weak and in fun; she had been longing to be alone with him for many long and tedious minutes.

"I am only trying to sneak a private moment with my wife," he persisted, and her resistance melted when he touched his lips to her neck.

"I can't think when you do that."

"Thinking is not required."

That made her laugh. "You're teasing me."

With a groan, he let her go. "Only half. The other half is completely serious, *querida*."

The day had been utterly perfect. It had seemed to take forever to arrive, though. They had spent the week after the trip to Iguazú in Argentina. First they had gone to Vista del Cielo to tell Maria and Carlos the news and ask if they could have the wedding at the estancia. That had been important to both of them, but Tomas especially felt he needed their blessing. Rosa had been their cherished girl. Without saying the words, they knew that the estancia had been refurbished in her memory. Maria had wept a little, but in happiness, because she and Sophia wanted the same thing—Tomas's happiness. Sophia had been overwhelmed at their generosity, and after talking it over, they decided they would stay with Maria and Carlos while their own house was being built close to the creek. The guest ranch was about to turn the page to a new chapter and become a real family business.

Then there had been the trip to Ottawa, making arrangements to move or give away Sophia's things and explaining the latest developments to her mother, Margaret. That meeting had been the most difficult, as Sophia had been honest with her mother for the first time. There had been tears and recriminations on both sides, but now things were beginning to heal. In the end Margaret had insisted that if Sophia were happy, that was all that mattered. Sophia had even convinced her mother to attend today.

Tomas had done some fence-mending of his own, reconciling with his parents. Today they'd taken Argentine tradition and given it a twist as Sophia had proceeded up the aisle escorted by Tomas's father and Tomas had walked with Margaret.

Now the revelry was well in hand as a band played in the backyard and a massive *asado* fed the crowd that had come to celebrate.

"It has been the most beautiful day," Sophia murmured. Tomas's hand slid over her shoulder and down her arm, the contact soft and intimate.

"And you were a most beautiful bride," he replied. "Too beautiful to resist, I think."

He moved in for another kiss but the unstoppable Maria came around the corner and spied them cozying up in the shadows.

"Oh no you don't," she said, shaking a finger at them.

"You haven't even danced yet. And there is the cutting of the cake."

"Madre Maria," Tomas began, but Sophia burst out laughing. Even now, Maria was still the boss, and ever would be.

She went forward to Maria and took the older woman's hands. "If I haven't said it yet, thank you for letting me be part of your family."

"You are our daughter now," Maria said, emotion thickening the words. "Nothing could have made me happier, Sophia. All is as it was meant to be."

Unbelievably touched, Sophia leaned forward and kissed Maria's cheek. "Do I need to call you Madre Maria, too, then?" Sophia smiled tenderly at her, understanding yet again why Tomas loved it here so much. It was the people, the family.

"Of course not. You call me Mama."

Miguel came around the corner carrying a bottle of beer. "I thought I'd find you here in a dark corner." He winked at Sophia and grinned at Tomas. "It's time for the wedding couple's first dance. If you don't want to dance with your new wife, I will."

"Not a chance, Miguel."

Miguel laughed and the foursome made their way into the backyard again.

Lights dotted the scene and a fire burned brightly. Sophia and Tomas had insisted that a regular party at the estancia was what they wanted and it was exactly what they got—food and drink flowing freely, laughter and goodwill and fun. Tomas's father was talking to Carlos and Margaret was chatting to a young professor of economics that Miguel had brought as his guest. It was a blend of old and new, tradition and innovation as the music changed. Tomas's smile was wide as he wiggled his eyebrows and swung Sophia into his arms for a tango.

She put her hand on Tomas's shoulder and admired the ring on her finger. Instead of a traditional band, Tomas had

had one fashioned from platinum and amethyst to match the necklace he'd bought her. She wore both the necklace and earrings today, knowing they connected her past to her future.

"My beautiful bride," Tomas said as they stepped to the music, their feet moving in a one…two…one two three rhythm and their bodies so close together a thread couldn't pass between them. Sophia's long skirt made swishing sounds on the short grass. "You are a princess today, Sophia. My beautiful, Argentine princess."

She saw him looking at the tiara sitting atop her curls. "It was my mother's. And Maria lent me her blue petticoat that she wore under her dress when she and Carlos married. Wasn't that sweet?"

"Not as sweet as you," he replied, gazing down at her with such adoration she felt her pulse give a kick.

"How much longer do we have to stay?" she murmured, and Tomas chuckled as he swung her in a turn and she slid her foot seductively up his leg.

"Impatient?"

Their gazes clashed. "No more than you."

His warm gaze darkened with what she knew now was an edge of desire. The thought no longer frightened her. She welcomed it. She tightened her fingers on the fabric of his jacket.

"You have learned the flavor of the tango well," he murmured, his breath warm in her ear.

"I was well-motivated," she returned, smiling saucily at him—the man whom she now called husband. "How *long*, Tomas?"

"Not long," he said, putting his lips up to her ear. "The party will go on long after we disappear."

When the dance ended, Maria herded them to a table holding the wedding cake with several ribbons cascading over its top. One by one the single women pulled on a ribbon, hoping to pick the one with a ring on its end, foretelling that they'd be the next to marry. When the winner happened to be Miguel's colleague, Tomas burst out laughing and Miguel turned a telling shade of gray.

But then they said their goodbyes, and minutes later were heading back to San Antonio de Areco and the room Tomas had booked there.

The lobby was quiet as they checked in and Tomas held her hand as they made their way to their room. Once inside, Sophia felt nerves slide through her stomach as she took in the turned-down bed. This was her wedding night, and she was completely inexperienced. She wanted everything to be perfect and was entirely unsure how to make it happen.

But then she looked up at Tomas, who had taken off his tuxedo jacket and loosened his tie, and nerves gave way to certainty and then anticipation. This was the man she loved, and who loved her. Nothing else mattered, except wanting to belong to him heart, soul and body. It had been so worth the wait.

She reached behind her and pulled the zipper running down the back of her dress. She stepped out of it, clad in Maria's pale-blue petticoat. Tomas came forward and took her dress from her hands, draping it carefully over a chair. Then he came back and gently removed the tiara from her hair, putting it on the small table.

The nerves started jumping again, clamoring, demanding.

"Señora Mendoza," Tomas said softly, taking her hands and holding them out to the side. "My beautiful wife. You do not need tiaras and fancy dresses. You are so beautiful, just as you are."

"Oh, Tomas," she sighed, still loving how he was able to woo her with his honesty. She stepped into his embrace. "We've waited so long," she whispered hoarsely. "Make me your wife."

With one fluid movement he had her in his arms, and he took her to the bed, laying her gently on the coverlet.

"You *are* my wife," he corrected. "And my life. And I'm going to spend the rest of my days proving it."

NANNY
NEXT DOOR

BY
MICHELLE CELMER

All the characters in this book have no existence outside the imagination of the author, and have no relation whatsoever to anyone bearing the same name or names. They are not even distantly inspired by any individual known or unknown to the author, and all the incidents are pure invention.

First published in Great Britain 2011
Harlequin Mills & Boon Limited,
Eton House, 18-24 Paradise Road, Richmond, Surrey TW9 1SR

© Michelle Celmer 2011

ISBN: 978 0 263 88867 6

23-0311

Harlequin Mills & Boon policy is to use papers that are natural, renewable and recyclable products and made from wood grown in sustainable forests. The logging and manufacturing processes conform to the legal environmental regulations of the country of origin.

Printed and bound in Spain
by Litografia Rosés S.A., Barcelona

Dear Reader,

Words cannot express how thrilled I am to be a new addition to the Cherish™ family. It's given me the opportunity to share the story of two people who have been living in my head for a very long time.

I first "met" Sydney and Daniel in the late 1990s. Their story was one of the first full-length romantic novels I ever finished. I'll admit that the writing left a lot to be desired, but there was something special about the characters. But as is the case with first books, they were filed away, and though I tried to forget them and concentrate on new stories and characters, they would occasionally pop back into my head, demanding revisions. I could never resist giving them once last chance to shine. In a way I felt I owed it to them, and they've taught me a lot over the years.

Their story has changed considerably with every rewrite, and they have developed as people in ways that both surprised and delighted me, but deep down they're still the same two characters who popped into my head and refused to leave me alone until I got their story right!

I always hoped that some day I would have the chance to introduce them to my readers, and here they finally are! I hope you enjoy them as much as I have.

Best,

Michelle Celmer

USA Today bestselling author **Michelle Celmer** lives in southeastern Michigan with her husband, their three children, two dogs and two cats. When she's not writing or busy being a mom, you can find her in the garden or curled up with a romance novel. And if you twist her arm really hard, you can usually persuade her into a day of power shopping. Michelle loves to hear from readers. Visit her website, www.michellecelmer.com, or write her at PO Box 300, Clawson, MI 48017, USA.

To Beppie and Geoff,
for many evenings of good food,
lots of laughs, and tales of ever-shortening skirts.
We love you guys!

CHAPTER ONE

SYDNEY HARRIS ran a finger over the dent in the kitchen wall next to the side door. The dent from the coffee cup she'd lobbed there after she'd spent a miserable night in the local lockup—thanks to her corrupt, narcissistic, creep of an ex-husband. At the time she'd considered that dent a symbol, a reminder that things could only get better, so she'd left it there. Except things hadn't gotten better. In fact, they'd gotten worse, and after today, every time she looked at that dent, she would remember the day her career went down the toilet.

"Sydney, are you still there?"

She tightened her grip on the phone. "You're firing me?" she asked Doreen Catalano, director of Meadow Ridge Early Learning Center. Her now former employer.

Her now former best friend.

"Technically, this isn't a termination. We're simply not renewing your contract. We're within the legal parameters of your employment agreement."

"Legal parameters? What about loyalty? What about the fact that we've been friends for ten years?" She applied pressure to the center of the dent and her finger popped through the drywall. Wonderful. Now there was a hole. Kind of like the rest of her life. One big gaping hole—no husband, no friends, no job. What else could she lose?

No, Syd, don't even go there.

"Call it whatever you want," she told Doreen. "I'm still out of a job."

"Sydney, you're a wonderful teacher, but you know as well as I do that we can't ignore the concerns of the parents. The rumors…"

"Will you at least write me a recommendation?" she asked. "I think you owe me that much."

After several seconds passed and Doreen didn't answer, the last of Sydney's hope sank somewhere south of her toes. "I'll take that as a *no*."

"If we were to write you a recommendation and something were to…happen…we just can't take that kind of risk. You'll receive the rest of your vacation pay and a generous severance."

If something were to *happen?* Sydney's voice shook with anger. "Forgive me if I sound ungrateful, but that hardly softens the blow. You were there, you know how much I had to drink—one lousy glass of wine at dinner. As did you, I might add, and I don't see you losing your job over it."

"I wasn't arrested for a DUI."

"I guess it doesn't count that they dropped the charges. And excuse me, but in ten years have you ever known me to be a raging alcoholic? Did I ever once show up late for work, or hungover—or intoxicated? This is all about Jeff getting revenge."

"He's the mayor. People trust him."

More like people feared him. It was obvious Doreen

did. "Let me guess. Did he threaten to have the school investigated? Maybe he said there would be trumped-up abuse charges if you didn't fire me? Did he say he would have the school's license yanked?"

There was a pregnant pause, and Sydney knew she was right. That manipulative, egotistical *bastard*. She could sue them, but frankly, she'd spent enough time in court this past year. And why would she want to teach at a school where no one trusted her?

"Sydney, maybe...well, maybe you should consider relocating. Getting a fresh start somewhere new."

No way. "I'm not running away. Prospect is my home. I won't let him steal that from me, too."

"I have your personal effects from your desk and your check if you'd like to pick them up today. This is for the best, Sydney."

"Best for whom?"

Doreen didn't answer, but Sydney had heard enough anyway. She punched the disconnect button and tossed the phone down on the counter. Nothing would change Doreen's mind, and begging wasn't an option. Not if she planned to maintain at least a shred of her dignity.

The satisfaction of raking Jeff over the coals in the divorce had been short lived when he'd set out to systematically destroy her reputation—and had now succeeded. If he heard that she'd begged for her job, and failed, he would never let her live it down. She wouldn't give him the pleasure.

She had honestly thought this mess would blow over and everything would go back to normal. She thought people knew her better than this.

Apparently, she thought wrong. Either that or people were just too afraid of her ex to cross him.

Even though Sydney had spent the past sixteen years of her life in Prospect, California, after the divorce she had been deemed an outsider. No more significant than the thousands of tourists who visited every year.

"Legal parameters, my foot," she mumbled, poking at the hole in the wall. Bits of drywall broke off, leaving a dusty white pile on the floor. It was time to patch this up and move on. To stop living in the past.

Rummaging through the kitchen drawers for something—*anything*—to cover it, Sydney settled on a roll of duct tape. It would have to do until she could buy a putty knife and spackling. She pulled off a length, tearing it with her teeth, and smoothed it over the hole. Not great, but better. Now, if she could just use the tape to temporarily repair her life.

"*Gawd,* what are you doing do to the wall?"

Sydney turned to see Lacey, her fifteen-year-old daughter, standing in the kitchen doorway. She should have left for school over an hour ago. "I was fixing a hole."

"With tape? It looks dumb."

She had to admit it did look pretty dumb. She tore the tape off, taking another chunk of drywall along with it. "You're late again."

"I overslept." Lacey shuffled into the kitchen and Sydney cringed when she noticed the latest condition of her hair—pale blond and freshly streaked in varying shades of purple. Her makeup wasn't much better. Thick black eyeliner reduced her eyes to two narrow slits, creating the illusion that she was perpetually pissed off—which, come to think of it, she was. Mauve lipstick added a touch of obstinacy, perfecting that "rebellious teen" look she worked so hard to achieve. Even her school uniform was a wrinkled mess.

It broke Sydney's heart to see the transformation her daughter had gone through. From a somewhat happy, fairly well-adjusted teenager to Wednesday Addams gone emo. Couldn't Jeff see what his behavior was doing to his child? Didn't he care?

Of course he didn't. Jeff cared about one person—*Jeff.*

"You only have a week of school left. Could you at least *try* to get there on time?"

Lacey shrugged. "Who called?"

If she could shelter Lacey from the truth, she would have. The kid had been through so much already. All she could do now was try to minimize the damage. "Doreen Catalano, from the preschool. They'll be replacing me now that my contract is up."

Lacey's mouth dropped open. "They *fired* you?"

Sydney kept her voice even. "No. They just chose not to renew my contract."

Lacey wasn't buying the calm act. "He did this, didn't he? Dad is screwing with you again."

"It's not a big deal." Sydney forced a smile. "Really. I'll find another job." *And won't that be fun without references,* she thought. Ten years of experience down the toilet. But she would manage. God knows she had overcome worse. And on the bright side, Jeff paid so much in alimony and child support, technically she didn't *need* a job. She would just have to tighten the belt a little.

They would be fine.

"I wish he would leave us alone." Lacey poured herself coffee and dumped half a cup of sugar into her mug. "I wish he would marry that bimbo and forget we exist."

Sydney suppressed a rueful smile. "Lacey, honey, please don't call your father's girlfriend a bimbo."

"Mom, she's, like, only a few years older than me. Do you have any idea how embarrassing that is?"

Seven years, actually, but who was counting? And of course Lacey was bitter. Her father's infidelities had hardly been a secret. But the last time, with his "bimbo" assistant, Sydney had had enough. She wished she could have seen his face when he'd been served with the divorce papers. And though he'd put her through hell this past year, she was still glad she did it. She was relieved to finally be free.

She gave Lacey's shoulder a squeeze. "I have to go pick up my final check. I could drop you off at school on the way."

Lacey shrugged out of reach. "No, I'll walk. I'll be home late today. I'm going to Shane's house to study for Spanish finals."

"You don't take Spanish."

She rolled her eyes. "*Duh.* I'm helping *Shane* study."

Sydney forced herself to take a deep breath and count to ten. *She's still adjusting,* that rational inner voice reminded her. *Give her time.*

"I expect you home by six," she said.

"But—"

Sydney held up a hand to shush her. "Don't bother arguing. You know your father is coming to get you for dinner."

Lacey's eyes narrowed until they all but disappeared. "I don't want to see him."

"I know you don't, and I understand why, but no matter how angry you are or how unfair all of this seems, he's still your father and he has a right to see you."

"*Fine*. What do you care if I'm psychologically scarred for the rest of my life!" She yanked her backpack off the kitchen table and stormed out the side door, slamming it behind her.

Sydney sighed, wishing there was something she could do to make this easier on her daughter. She had suggested to Jeff that they take her to see a counselor, but he refused. He didn't want people to put a label on Lacey, or so he claimed, but she was sure it was more about people labeling him a bad father. Either way, without his consent, her hands were tied. She could sue for the right, but another lengthy court battle would only make things worse.

She grabbed her car keys from the crystal candy dish on the counter, shoved her feet into her flip-flops and stepped out the side door into the late morning sun. In the distance a grayish haze ringed the crest of the Scott Bar mountains so she knew it was going to be a warm and sticky afternoon.

A thick wave of heat enveloped her as she opened

the door to her minivan, and as she climbed in she noticed that the new tenants appeared to have settled into the rental house next door. Yesterday there had been a moving van and now there was a red pickup truck in the drive. There was also an unmarked police car parked out front. She hoped that didn't mean there was going to be trouble with the new neighbors.

The previous resident, Mr. Bellevue, had been moved into an assisted living facility last month after he'd forgotten to turn off the stove and almost burned down the house for the fourth time in month.

Sydney made a mental note to stop on her way home and pick up a housewarming gift.

Pulling out of her driveway and around the police car, she started driving toward the preschool, but had barely gone fifty feet when she glanced down at the passenger seat and realized she hadn't brought her purse. No purse, no ID.

Ugh! Could this day get any worse?

She slammed on the brakes, threw the van into reverse and floored it. A blur of black in the rearview mirror made her jerk to a stop, but not before she felt the impact and heard the unmistakable crunch of glass.

And just like that, her day got worse.

Jamming the van into park, she let her head fall against the steering wheel.

Just what she needed. Another run-in with the Prospect County Sheriff's Department. One more reason for them to harass her.

She took one long, shaky breath, and with trembling

hands pushed the door open and climbed out of the van. She circled around back to check the damage.

A dented bumper and obliterated taillight on her van—that wasn't so bad. Besides a broken headlight, the police car didn't have a scratch on it. So why did she feel like throwing herself down on the pavement and sobbing? Maybe she could just leave a note on the windshield and skulk away.

Just as she'd completed the thought, she heard a door creak open and turned to see a man walking toward her from the house next door. He wore faded jeans and a sleeveless T-shirt, but she recognized him as one of Prospect's finest. Deputy Daniel Valenzia, or as she had often heard him called, Deputy Casanova. He was a confirmed bachelor and notorious breaker of female hearts all over town.

There was a time when Sydney had also been seduced by a man with authority. The only problem with authoritative men, she'd learned, was that they abused that power for selfish reasons.

She was guessing by the lack of uniform, rumpled dark hair and several days' worth of dark stubble, Deputy Valenzia wasn't here on business. He wasn't part of Jeff's lynch gang, so Sydney had never actually met him, but cops were cops as far as she was concerned. It was sad, really, because before the divorce she'd had tremendous respect for law enforcement. Now if she saw a patrol car headed her way, she pulled down the nearest side street or into the closest parking lot. A couple dozen tickets—for things as ridiculous as dirt on her license plate, not to mention a baseless arrest for DUI—could make a woman a little paranoid. Being hauled away in handcuffs on Main Street on a busy Friday night in front of half the town and twice that many tourists had been the most humiliating experience in her life by far.

Deputy Valenzia stopped a few feet from her to inspect the damage, his face unreadable. Sydney waited for the explosion, for him to berate her for her stupidity. To call her a careless woman driver. When he finally met her eyes, she was jolted with awareness.

Set over a pair of amazingly high cheekbones—cheekbones any woman would sell her soul for—his eyes were black as tar and so bottomless she felt as if she were swimming in them. And…warm? A little amused even, which made no sense at all.

Why wasn't he screaming at her? Why wasn't he ranting and raving? If it had been Jeff's BMW damaged in a fender bender, he'd have chewed the poor driver to shreds by now with harsh words and legal threats.

"So, what happened here?" he finally asked.

"I'm very sorry," she said. *I'm very sorry?* Lame, Syd, lame.

Valenzia just nodded, his eyes still locked on hers, as if he expected her to say something else. Or maybe he was checking to see if her pupils were dilated.

"I didn't mean to hit it," she said, and the second the words left her mouth, she cringed. *That's a good one,* she thought, realizing how dumb that sounded. People didn't usually *mean* to hit anything, and if they did, they didn't admit it. And what had her lawyer told her? Never give more information than asked for, and when they do ask, only give them the basic facts. Never elaborate.

Police had a way of tripping people up and making them say more than they meant to, or even things they didn't mean.

Deputy Valenzia looked at her van, then back to his car, rubbing a hand across his rough jaw. "I have to ask, how exactly did you hit the front of the car with the back of your van?"

"I was, um, backing up."

One eyebrow quirked up and she could swear she saw another glint of amusement play across his chiseled features. It was unbelievably sexy. And the fact that she thought so was unbelievably *wrong*. Just because he wasn't one of Jeff's men, it didn't mean he wasn't a bad cop.

"You make a habit of driving around the neighborhood in reverse?" he asked, the corner of his mouth twitching.

"I was going home," she said, hitching a thumb over her shoulder to indicate her house. "I forgot something." She didn't mention *what* she'd forgotten, because then he would probably cite her for operating a vehicle without a license. It would never hold up, but having to actually go to traffic court was a huge inconvenience. She'd found that if it wasn't a moving violation that would ultimately affect her driving record, it was easier just to pay the ticket and be done with it.

"You have insurance?" he asked.

"Of course." Did he think she was irresponsible?

He shrugged and pulled out a cell phone. "You never know."

Here it comes, she thought. He was going to call in

his sheriff buddies. She couldn't begin to imagine the rumors this would start. Maybe they would give her a Breathalyzer test and make her recite the alphabet backward, every third letter, just for fun.

He punched a few buttons, frowned, then banged the cell against the heel of his palm, mumbling a curse. "Phone's dead." He stuffed it back in his pocket. "Could I use yours?"

She hesitated. Wouldn't that be like bringing a gun to her own execution?

"Come on," he coaxed, giving her a lazy smile that revealed a neat row of white teeth. "It's the least you can do."

"Umm…"

"If you're worried about your safety, I'm harmless," he assured her. "I'm a cop."

Hence the cop car. If she told him no, would she look like she had something to hide? It's not as if there were no other phones in town. In fact, she was surprised he didn't just call it in on the car radio.

But maybe if she cooperated he would go easy on her. "Sure, you can use my phone."

"I'll need your insurance information, too."

"It's inside."

He gestured to her house. "After you."

She walked up the driveway, acutely aware of him behind her. She could only hope her butt didn't look as huge as it felt. As if he would even be looking at it. When they approached the side door he reached around her to open it. At least he had decent manners.

"Nice place," he said as they stepped through the door.

Not nearly as nice as the family estate she'd lived in with Jeff, but appearances had never mattered much to her. A modest three-bedroom, two-bath Cape Cod, this house suited her and Lacey just fine. And though it was older, like the house she'd grown up in back in Michigan, it had character, not to mention almost half an acre of land. And the best part was that it was all hers.

"The phone is on the counter," she said, and as Deputy Valenzia brushed past, his bare arm grazed hers, making her breath catch. The sheer energy of his presence seemed to somehow shrink the room to the size of a closet. He could have been standing fifty feet away and he would still have been too close.

With sudden alarm she wondered if maybe he wasn't as harmless as he seemed? What if he did work for Jeff and, now that he had her alone, planned to harass her? Or something worse. Who would people believe? A respected officer of the law, or the local lush?

"Proof of insurance?" he asked.

She grabbed her purse and dug through her wallet for her insurance card, aware that her hands were trembling again. She held it out to him, clutching the purse to her chest like a shield. He just stared at her for a moment and she could swear she saw that hint of amusement again in the slight lift of his brow. Did he think this was funny?

"Everything okay?" he asked.

"Of course."

"You look a little…tense."

In her situation, so would he. "I'm fine."

He shrugged, then reached up and took the card from her, his fingers brushing hers. She jerked her hand back, as though she'd touched a hot oven.

He gave her a look that said he might be questioning her mental stability. "Thanks, I'll just be a minute."

He dialed and leaned himself against the edge of her kitchen counter, crossing long muscular legs at the ankles. His jeans were tattered to the point of indecency and his T-shirt, in addition to having had both sleeves torn off, was faded black and emblazoned with the state seal.

And he was *big*. At least six-one, maybe even taller, and at five-three, she felt like a midget.

Sydney stayed close to the door—just in case she had to make a run for it—clutching her purse to her chest. Maybe she was overreacting. Absolutely nothing in his stance suggested he was about to pounce. In fact, he seemed totally relaxed.

But the way he stared at her with those dark, dark eyes, it was as though he could see right through her. Maybe it was a cop thing. Or maybe, playboy that he was, he was checking her out.

Sure he is, Syd. A gorgeous man like him looking at a woman like you.

Not that she didn't consider herself attractive. She was, in an unrefined way. Makeup, though she'd tried every subtle technique known to man, made her look cheap and her wild red hair never cooperated when she attempted the latest sleek, sophisticated style. Most days it ended up in an unruly mass of curls pulled back in a ponytail or wrestled into a clip.

And clothes? That was another disaster. She wore conservative skirts and blouses to work, but otherwise had the fashion sense of a brick. She relied on her daughter for fashion tips and clothes swapping and as a result was the only thirty-four-year-old resident in all of Prospect who dressed as if she were still in high school. But she was comfortable that way. She *liked* herself that way, and all of the complaints and criticisms Jeff had dished out over the course of their marriage—and there had been a lot—hadn't broken her spirit. Though at times he'd come close.

"Hey, Margie," Deputy Valenzia said to the person on the other end of the line. "My car was hit and I have the insurance info." He paused, scowling. "Can't I fill it out the next time I come in?" The answer must have been yes because he read off Sydney's name, insurance company and policy number. Glancing up at the clock over the sink, he scowled again. "Could you just take care of it for me? I have to get back before April wakes up."

April. His latest conquest? Maybe that was her new neighbor. Great. That meant a constant police presence on the block until they broke up, which from what she'd heard, thankfully wouldn't take long. The only thing worse would be if Deputy Valenzia was living there, but her luck couldn't possibly be that lousy.

"No," he continued, sounding irritated. "I'm next door. My cell phone is dead. I think April drooled on it."

Okay, unless his girlfriend had overactive salivary glands, April had to be a dog. One never could tell though…

He rattled off what she figured was probably his badge number, thanked Margie—whoever she was—then hung up the phone and pushed away from the counter, rising to his full, intimidating height. "Thanks."

Wait a minute? That was it?

She frowned. "You're not going to call for reinforcements?"

His dark brows knit together. "For a fender bender?"

"No Breathalyzer?"

"Do you need one?"

"Of course not! I just thought—" She really needed to keep her mouth shut.

He walked toward her, his footsteps heavy on the tile floor, and Sydney stiffened again, even though it was obvious he didn't plan to arrest her. Maybe he didn't work for Jeff after all.

She took a deep breath, forcing herself to relax.

He stopped barely a foot away, towering a good ten inches over her, until she had to crane her neck to meet his eyes. He held out the insurance card for her. "Next time watch where you're going," he said.

She nodded and plucked the card from between his fingers, careful not to make contact again. God, she hoped he was only visiting next door. She didn't think she could handle the stress of knowing there was a deputy living so close, monitoring her every move.

"Thanks for the phone." He stepped past her to the door and as he was walking out he turned back, flashing her a lazy grin. "See you around, neighbor."

CHAPTER TWO

DANIEL VALENZIA managed to contain his amusement until he was out the door and on his way across the lawn to his rental. Sydney Harris needed to take a big fat chill pill. But he couldn't really blame her for being tense, considering all she'd been through the past few months.

Her sleazebag ex-husband must have done quite a number on her. Daniel had overheard a few of the mayor's henchmen bragging about how they'd been harassing her. He'd been half tempted to take his concerns to Sheriff Montgomery, but he knew that as long as Jeff Harris was mayor, no action would be taken.

Call him old-fashioned, but Daniel believed in the law and the principle of innocent until proven guilty. He also believed that what goes around comes around, and eventually the mayor would get exactly what he deserved. And who knows, maybe Mrs. Harris was getting exactly what she deserved for being stupid enough to marry a man like the mayor.

Slipping through the front door, Daniel paused. He'd been sure April would have woken from her nap by now. Rousing every fifteen minutes last night had apparently worn her out. He tiptoed down the hall and paused in front of April's room, pressing his ear to the door.

Silence.

In hindsight, he shouldn't have left her alone in the house, but he was still getting used to taking care of a baby.

He opened the door a crack and peeked into the room. The sounds of her faint, whispery breathing assured him she was still sound asleep. He should have just enough time to hop into the shower and take a long-overdue shave.

He crept down the hall to the bathroom. April, however, had some sort of supersonic baby radar, because the second his foot hit the tile floor she started to wail.

Daniel felt like banging his head against the wall. Something had to be wrong with that kid. She never slept! He just wasn't cut out for this parenting stuff. What if he screwed her up for life? April was so small and helpless and he didn't know the first thing about what an infant needed.

He hurried back down the hall to her room. She was lying on her back, fists balled up tight, legs and arms extended, face purple as she screamed bloody murder. Boy did she have a temper; just like her mother, if memory served. And yet when April wasn't screaming she was a pint-size heartbreaker.

When she looked up at him with her big blue eyes, tears rolling down her rosy cheeks, his first instinct was to do something crazy, like run out and buy her a pony. He'd always been good with kids, but usually when they were old enough to toss a football or swing a bat. Like his nephew, Jordan.

He had no idea what to do with this squirming, demanding bundle of attitude.

He lifted her up out of her crib and cuddled her to his chest, patting her warm, little back. Her lower lip quivered pathetically and her cheeks were damp with tears. She looked up at him with wide, accusing eyes, then let loose again with another round of ear-piercing screams.

"Come on, April," he coaxed, bouncing her gently. "Go back to sleep. Twenty more minutes, kiddo, that's all I'm asking for."

Things would get easier when he found a babysitter, he told himself. Which had better be soon because he'd used up all of his paid leave. The next option would be to take unpaid family leave, but he'd already blown through a chunk of his savings buying baby furniture, diapers, formula and the million other things required to properly care for an infant. She'd been dropped on his doorstep by the social worker with little more than a diaper bag with a dozen or so diapers, a few threadbare sleepers and a couple of bottles.

It was no wonder the dads on the force never seemed to have a nickel to spare.

He'd placed an ad in the paper for a sitter, and even put up a flyer at the local high school to find a kid looking for a summer job, but most high school and college students spent their summers working at the resort up the mountain. He couldn't begin to compete with the hourly rate they paid. So far the ones who had answered the ad either couldn't work the hours he needed, or were so scary he wouldn't let them within ten feet of April.

The only decent, affordable day-care center in town had a waiting list almost four months long—and he'd still need to find someone else to watch her when he worked the occasional evening or weekend shift. In the past few weeks Daniel had developed a healthy respect for the stresses a single parent faced. He'd never considered having kids, much less having one alone.

He still had no idea why April's mother listed him as the father on the birth certificate. A simple blood test would have proven the baby wasn't his. Maybe Reanne didn't know who the father was, and Daniel's name was the first to come to mind. Or maybe because he was a cop she felt he was the only person she could trust. She'd told him horror stories about growing up in foster care, being shuffled from family to family, never feeling she belonged anywhere. He could understand why she wanted better for April. But he couldn't be the one to provide that. He didn't know a damned thing about raising a baby. But when social services had contacted him after Reanne's death and he saw April, looking so tiny and helpless, he hadn't been able to turn her away.

He would take care of her until her real family could be found. He'd hired a buddy of his, a retired cop turned private investigator, to locate a relative willing to adopt her.

Daniel just had to hold on until then, and in the meantime hope he didn't scar the kid for life.

SYDNEY SMOOTHED the putty knife one last time over the newly patched wall. A little sandpaper and paint and it would be good as new.

After returning home she'd taken a long, hot shower, hoping to wash away some of the festering resentment toward her former employer. It hadn't worked. And now, as she sorted through the items lying on the table in front of her—handmade gifts from her students, class photos and keepsakes—she felt pitifully empty as well. Teaching was her life. Nothing filled her with joy like spending her day surrounded by her students.

Through the kitchen window she heard a car door slam. Then the side door flew open and the source of her troubles breezed in like he owned the place. Which he did just to annoy her, despite being warned by her lawyer that it was against the law. Law that he carried conveniently in his pocket.

Jeff's short blond hair—which without the dye would now be mostly gray—was neatly combed and sprayed into place, his dark blue Italian silk suit tailored to an impeccable fit. He never left home looking anything less than perfect.

"Get out," she told him.

"What, no kiss?" Jeff shrugged out of his jacket, draped it over the back of a kitchen chair and opened the refrigerator. "What's for lunch?"

She stood and clasped her thin silk robe snugly to her chest. He'd seen her in her robe thousands of times, but not since the divorce. It felt like an invasion of her privacy now. "There's a Taco Hut two blocks away."

"I wanted to let you know Kimberly's class was canceled and I can't take Lacey out tonight. I'll pick her up Saturday instead."

"That's what the phone is for."

"*And* I didn't think you would mind if I stopped by for a bite to eat, seeing as how I'm paying the mortgage."

"How stupid do I look?"

He glanced at her over the refrigerator door. "You don't really want me to answer that, do you?"

"You're here to gloat, admit it. Someone must have called to congratulate you by now. To let you know you've screwed me out of a job."

He pulled out a package of lunch meat, the mustard and a butter knife from the drawer, and put them on the counter. "You lost your job?" He flashed her that fake innocent look she could spot a mile away.

"Don't patronize me. Have you even thought about Lacey?"

"What about her?" He opened the pantry, searching for a loaf of bread. She slammed it shut and he yanked his hand away. "Hey! Watch the manicure."

"Haven't you noticed what this is doing to her? These mind games you're playing. Her grades have dropped, her appearance is atrocious. She's a mess."

"Maybe she'd be better off coming to live with me and Kimberly."

"*Better off?* Are you kidding? You've been a lousy father."

"Maybe you're a lousy mother. There is a nasty rumor circulating that you may not be a fit parent. What with your alcohol problem."

Her gut reaction was to snatch the butter knife off the counter and drive it repeatedly into his back. Then she considered the hassle it would be disposing of a two-hundred-pound corpse and changed her mind. Instead she put the knife back in the drawer and the lunch meat in the refrigerator. "Get out."

"Did I mention I won't be able to take Lacey out next week, either?" Jeff said. "I'm taking Kimberly to Hawaii for a few days."

He knew Sydney loved Hawaii. But if it meant never having to look at his arrogant face, she could live without their annual trip.

"We're going to the Virgin Islands next month," he added, and she clenched her teeth.

"What are you trying to do?" she asked. "Subdue her with jet lag?"

"Jealousy is so unattractive, Sydney."

She folded her arms across her chest. "I'm just curious to see how long it takes her to drain you and move on to her next victim."

His smug laugh echoed in her ears with the grating effect of nails on a chalkboard. "The only place she's draining me is in the bedroom. You can think about that while you're standing in the unemployment line."

Bastard. She should have used the butter knife when she had the chance.

"While you're here, the air-conditioning is acting up again," she told him and watched the smile disappear from his face. It frosted him that as part of the divorce settlement, not only did he have to buy her a house, but he was responsible for any maintenance and repairs as long as Lacey was a minor. One of the many benefits of having a shark for an attorney.

"I'll call someone next week."

"We can do this through our lawyers if you'd prefer."

Tight-lipped, he said, "I'll call today."

"Good. Now get the hell out of my house."

Lunch forgotten, Jeff grabbed his suit jacket and slung it over his shoulder and strode out the side door. He slammed it with such force her newly patched wall shook. She watched as the spackling came loose, fell away and landed with a splat on the floor.

LACEY SLIPPED DOWN THE HALL and into her room before her parents could see her. No way in a million years would she go live with her father and his bimbo.

Lacey hated *Kimberly* almost as much as she hated her father. The first and only time he'd taken them both out to dinner, Kimberly had looked at Lacey as if she were a bug she intended to squash. Her dad even had the nerve to suggest that his perfect little Kimberly could take her shopping for some decent clothes and teach her how to apply makeup correctly.

"Why, so I can look like a slut?" she had asked, and her father went ballistic. Now he only took her out on nights when the bimbo had class. She was learning French, or something lame like that. Lacey would run away from home and live in a Dumpster before she let some pasty-faced old judge tell her she had to go live with them.

She picked up the phone, dialing Shane's cell number.

"Yo," he answered, music blaring into her ear.

"Come get me," she whispered.

"Lacey? Is that you?" he yelled.

"Yes, it's me!" she hissed. "Turn down the music."

The music faded into the background. "Why are you whispering?"

"Come pick me up. I have to get out of here."

He hesitated. "But I just dropped you off, like, two minutes ago."

"I don't care! Come and get me, but park down at the corner. I'll meet you."

He let out a loud sigh. "Fine. I'll be right there."

She hung up and walked over to her bedroom door, peeking out into the hall. She could hear her mom in the kitchen, banging things around. She always did that when she was mad. And she'd been mad a lot lately.

Lacey crept back down the hall and out the front door, so her mom wouldn't hear her. Her father was long gone and when she reached the corner Shane was waiting.

"I thought you had to go home," he said as she climbed in.

"Not anymore." She used her cell to call her mom and tell her she would be late.

"Something came up at work and your dad can't make it tonight," her mom said.

Lacey knew it was a lie. She knew her father dumped her for the bimbo. *Again*. She had no clue why her mom always tried to protect him.

"I'll be home by ten," she said and hung up before her mom could say no.

She tossed the phone on the seat and turned on the radio, cranking up the volume. As long as the music was loud, she could forget about how messed up everything had become.

When her parents were still married and fighting constantly, she would sit in her room with the music turned up. She didn't want to hear the awful things they said to each other. She'd hoped the fighting would stop when they finally got divorced, but it had only gotten worse. Every time she saw her dad, he was meaner and meaner to her mom.

As Shane tore down the street, Lacey plucked a pack of cigarettes from his shirt pocket. He handed her a lighter and she lit them each one. She inhaled deeply, feeling the smoke burn her lungs.

Shane reached over and turned down the radio. "Okay, what did I do?"

She flicked her ashes out the open window. "What do you mean?"

"You only smoke when you're pissed off about something."

She brought her knees up to her chin and hugged her legs. "It's not you." The cigarette was starting to make her sick so she tossed it out the window. "My life sucks and it's all that bimbo's fault."

Shane huffed. "That's nothing. My dad brought home Bimbo Number Four last Saturday. I think he's getting married again."

It annoyed her that Shane always thought his problems were bigger. He didn't get it. His family was normal compared to hers. But he was cute, had a cool car and money to burn. And he didn't treat her like she was a freak. So what if he wasn't the best kisser in the world? Kissing was highly overrated as far as she was concerned. That was as far as she would let him go, anyway. No way was she going to take a chance and end up pregnant and married like her mom. She wasn't *ever* getting married.

"My mom lost her job today," Lacey told Shane, even though she was pretty sure he didn't care. "It's all my father's fault. I hate him." She turned to look out the window, squeezing her eyes shut. She wasn't going to cry. She never cried in front of anyone.

"So, what do you want to do now?" he asked.

"We've got finals to study for."

"Boring."

Typical Shane. He didn't take school seriously. Actually, there wasn't much he did take seriously. But he was right: studying was boring and she doubted she'd be able to concentrate anyway.

"Okay," she said, turning to him with a sly smile. "Let's do something fun instead. Something that will really piss my dad off."

"Great, let's do something fun."

She couldn't stop the bad stuff that was happening or change the past, but she could get back at her father for all the crap he'd put them through. And she knew just how to do it.

SYDNEY WOKE late the next morning, a blazing headache thrumming the inside of her skull. She shuffled to the kitchen, doing her best to ignore the damaged wall, and fished a can of coffee from the cupboard. She pried off the plastic lid and groaned. Empty.

Out of sheer desperation she put the kettle on to boil and dug out an ancient jar of instant decaffeinated shoved to the back on the uppermost shelf. A trace of caffeine was better than nothing. She spooned a clump of the gooey, congealed crystals into her cup, filled it with boiling water, and sipped, scrunching up her nose with distaste. It ranked right up there with the sludge left in the pot in the teachers' lounge at the end of the day.

"Why are you drinking instant coffee?" Lacey asked from behind her.

Startled, Sydney spun around, sloshing hot liquid down the front of her robe.

"Please don't sneak up on me like that!" She grabbed a sponge from the sink and dabbed up the stain. "Why aren't you at school?"

"Why are you drinking instant?" Lacey crossed her arms over her wrinkled blouse. Her hair, streaked green today, hung limply over her shoulders and looked like it could use a good washing.

Sydney dumped her coffee down the sink. "Because we ran out of the other kind."

"What am *I* supposed to drink?" she asked, as if the world revolved around her getting coffee in the morning.

"I'll stop at the market today." She dropped the jar in the recycling bin under the sink, and, turning back to her daughter, gasped. "Good God, what have you done to your face?"

"Isn't it cool?" Lacey reached up to press a finger to her slightly swollen, newly pierced eyebrow.

Breathe, Sydney. Don't kill her, just breathe. It was Lacey's way of taking control of her otherwise chaotic life. And it wasn't permanent, that was all that mattered. Although she couldn't help thinking tattoos would be next.

She tried to remain calm. "Honey, you already have ten holes in each ear. If you keep puncturing your head it's going to deflate."

Lacey rolled her eyes. "Ha-ha."

"Why aren't you in school?"

She touched her brow and cringed. "I have a headache."

Yeah, right. "Tough. Take two aspirin and get your butt to school. If you want to mutilate your body, you're going to have to live with the consequences."

"Fine," she grumbled. "I need a note for the office."

After Lacey left, Sydney showered and dressed, and because she'd forgotten to buy a gift yesterday, whipped up a quick chicken casserole to present to her new neighbor.

Call her manipulative, but if she was going to have to live next door to a cop, she might as well try to get on his good side.

Sydney stepped outside and cut across the grass to the house next door. She knocked and barely ten seconds passed before Deputy Valenzia appeared in the doorway. He hadn't shaved since yesterday, and the thick dark stubble made him look…dangerous. In her experience, most cops were.

He folded his arms across that impressively wide chest and said, "Don't tell me you hit it again."

She forced a smile and held out the casserole dish. "I brought you a housewarming gift."

He opened the door, stepping out onto the porch, and she instinctively took a step back. Holy cow, he was big. Tall and trim with just the right amount of muscle in all the right places.

Perfect.

He took the dish from her, their fingers barely brushing. There it was again, that annoying zing of awareness.

"I didn't introduce myself yesterday," he said, holding out a hand for her to shake. "Daniel Valenzia."

The absolute last thing she wanted to do was touch him, but she couldn't be rude, either.

"Sydney Harris." She slipped her hand into his and he clasped it firmly. Possessively.

It was the stupid badge he wore. That was the only reason she felt so nervous. It wasn't his rough palm against hers or the sexy grin that heated her blood. Or the fact that he seemed in no hurry to let go.

She pried her hand from his and gestured over her shoulder toward home. "Um, I should probably—" She was interrupted by the unmistakable howl of a crying baby. Deputy Valenzia had a *baby?*

No way.

"Shoot, she's awake." He yanked the door open. "Don't go anywhere. I'll be right back."

"But—"

"Give me two minutes," he called as he disappeared

into the house, then added in his cop voice, "Don't leave!"

She should have left right then, but curiosity got the best of her. Two more minutes wouldn't kill her, right?

She knew Deputy Valenzia wasn't married, so he must have been babysitting for a friend, although he didn't exactly strike her as the babysitting type. Not for an infant, anyhow.

Two minutes stretched into three and she peered inside, wondering if she should keep waiting or just leave. The baby was still wailing pitifully. Another two minutes passed and the screams increased in intensity, until the infant had worked itself into a frenzy of choking and gasping. It sounded as if the deputy needed some help, and if *he* didn't, that poor baby did. Sydney didn't typically walk uninvited into stranger's houses, especially strangers with the authority to throw her in jail, but she had to do *something*.

Her maternal instincts overwhelming her, she stepped inside. The house was smaller than hers, but cozy. A black leather sofa and matching love seat, glass-top coffee and end tables and a television on a mahogany credenza were the only furniture in the living room. Guy furniture. Dirty plates, cups, bowls and baby bottles littered every flat surface. The walls were freshly painted stark white, the hardwood floors newly polished. And it smelled like…baby powder.

She followed the screams down the hall past a small empty room, then a larger room with a mussed, king-size bed, chest of drawers and a floor covered in discarded laundry. Deputy Valenzia's bedroom, she surmised with a flutter of interest. She wondered how many women he'd taken to that bed… She probably didn't want to know. If the rumors were true, living right next door, she would see the evidence soon enough.

Feeling like a snoop, Sydney continued on to the bedroom at the end the hall and looked in. A white crib sat adjacent to a matching dresser and rocking chair, and against the far wall was a changing table. In the middle of it all Deputy Valenzia stood with the hysterical infant over his shoulder, patting her back, looking as if he might burst into tears, too.

It just might have been the sweetest thing she'd ever seen.

"Can I help?" she asked over the screams.

He didn't look angry that she'd let herself in. In fact, he seemed relieved to see her.

"She was up half the night. I don't think she likes the new house." He awkwardly shifted the baby to the opposite shoulder and patted her back. Sydney had never seen a man who moved with such natural ease look so uncoordinated holding a baby. It was unbelievably cute.

"Change is difficult for young children," she said, stepping tentatively into the room. "They're creatures of habit."

The baby whimpered against his shoulder, then lifted her head and wailed again—and Sydney's heart melted. The child's plump red cheeks were dotted with tears, her clear blue eyes wide and accusing.

"Oh, she's beautiful," Sydney breathed. "How old?"

"Five months."

She held out her arms. "Let me try."

"You have experience with babies?" he asked, extending a protective hand across the child's back.

"I worked in day care all through college, taught school for ten years and I have a daughter who suffered a severe case of colic," Sydney said. "Though I still say she's more trouble as a teenager."

"That's good enough for me." He thrust the squirming, noisy bundle into Sydney's arms. "This is April. She's all yours."

MILLS
BOON

www.millsandboon.co.uk

PLUS, by ordering online you will receive all these extra benefits:

- 🌹 Be the first to hear about exclusive offers in our eNewsletter

- 🌹 Try before you buy! You can now browse the first chapter of each of our books online

- 🌹 Order books from our huge back list at a discounted price

- 🌹 Join the M&B community and discuss your favourite books with other readers

CHAPTER THREE

"OH, SO YOU'RE April." Sydney held the baby up to get a good look at her. "I thought you were a puppy."

"A puppy?" Daniel asked.

"Yesterday you said April drooled on your cell phone so I assumed she was a dog."

"A puppy couldn't be much more destructive. She puts everything in her mouth."

He watched as his new neighbor laid the baby against her shoulder, rubbing her back. Sydney wasn't beautiful in the conventional sense, but there was something about her, something that appealed to him. The eyes that were a little too round, the slightly upturned nose that was too cute to belong to a mature woman, and the sprinkling of freckles across her cheeks that made her look twelve. Although, he was guessing she was probably only a few years younger than him.

She wasn't wearing much makeup, although she was attractive enough without it. Her hair was twisted up and fastened in a large clip. The loose wavy strands falling out from every direction gave her a natural, unspoiled appearance—bordering on wild and unruly. He tried to picture her prim and proper in the typical teacher wardrobe, but the only image he could conjure up was one of her sitting in a field of wildflowers, a chain of daisies around her head, holding her fingers up in a peace sign.

She cradled April against her bosom, which Daniel couldn't help but admire, and the baby instantly quieted. If he were nestled against her breasts he wouldn't be complaining, either.

Yeah, right, as if *that* would ever happen. As if his life wasn't complicated enough. He had a strict rule of never dating a single mom. Or a next-door neighbor. He tended to stay clear of divorcees, too.

"Her belly is tight," Sydney said.

Daniel's pulse skipped, his first thought being cysts or tumors or ruptured embolisms—proof he'd been watching too many hours of The Learning Channel all those late nights he'd spent pacing the floor, trying to get April to sleep. "Is that bad?"

"She probably has a gas bubble to work loose. Can I sit with her on the couch?"

"Sure." He led Sydney back to the living room. Gas he could deal with. He'd even grown accustomed to changing diapers, including the messier variety, when the stuff wouldn't stay *in* the diaper.

Sydney sat April on her lap facing Daniel and, supporting the baby's chest and neck, gently rocked her back and forth. Within seconds April stopped fidgeting and her plump little body relaxed. His new neighbor definitely had a way with babies. Why couldn't he find someone like this to babysit?

He'd received three calls that morning. Two were from college students and neither willing to work even close to the hours he needed. The other was from Margie at the station, with a message from his boss wondering when he would be back to work. If Daniel didn't find a sitter by Monday, it could mean his job.

He watched Sydney. She was talking softly to April, her voice soothing and patient.

"I guess she likes rocking like that," he said.

Sydney nodded. "It always worked for Lacey—my daughter. I just love little girls at this age. They're so sweet and innocent, then they get older and start piercing things and dyeing their hair."

"I saw her this morning. She's…colorful."

"And she came home with her eyebrow pierced last night. I just know the navel is next. When there's nothing left to pierce I'm sure she'll move on to tattoos."

He hoped he found April's family before he had to deal with anything like that. "You said you're a teacher. What grade?"

"Preschool."

"Sounds…demanding."

"It can be, but I love it. I couldn't imagine doing anything else."

"Where do you teach?"

Her smile wavered. "I'm sort of between jobs at the moment."

He wondered if she might be interested in babysitting for him until she found a new job. But as quickly as the idea formed, he dismissed it. Why would a teacher settle for a temporary babysitting gig? He could never match her salary.

April tensed suddenly, bucked in Sydney's lap and erupted like a volcano, spewing partially digested baby formula across the room. Daniel jumped out of the way but he was too slow. "Holy crap!"

"Projectile spit-up," Sydney said.

"I've never seen her do that before." He grabbed a burp cloth from the back of the couch and wiped curdled formula off his pant leg. "That must have been one heck of a gas bubble."

Daniel got on his hands and knees and cleaned up the mess. April was limp in Sydney's arms, her eyelids drooping. "She looks tired."

Sydney stood and gently raised April onto her shoulder. "Would you like me to lay her down in her crib?"

"That would be great."

Sydney carried April into the bedroom and placed her in the crib on her side, propping a blanket behind her back to hold her in place. April stirred for a moment, then curled her fist to her mouth and suckled in her sleep.

"I've never put her on her side before," Daniel whispered. "Will she sleep better?"

"Mine did. When she starts rolling over by herself you can put her on her stomach."

They stood together in silence, watching April sleep. Just an inch to the right and their forearms would touch, and for some reason the idea excited him. He glanced over at Sydney and she smiled, gazing up at him through a fringe of thick dark lashes. He hadn't noticed before, but her eyes were the same shade of blue as April's.

Maybe it was a sign.

It was a sign, all right. A sign that he needed to stay as far from this woman as humanly possible. Yes, she was hot, but she also had a kid, and she was the ex-wife of the most powerful man in town. He wasn't intimidated by the mayor and his lynch gang, but why invite drama to his life?

He gestured to the door and she followed him out into the hallway. "Thanks for your help."

"No problem. I take you don't have much experience with babies."

They walked to the living room. "Is my incompetence that obvious?"

She smiled, and it was somehow sweet and sexy at the same time. "You're babysitting?"

"Sort of. But there's a chance she could be with me awhile."

"Days?"

"Or months. It's tough to say at this point."

"Oh," she said, looking puzzled. "She's yours?"

"Not exactly. It's…complicated."

He could see that she was curious to know more, but to her credit, she didn't ask.

"I don't suppose you could recommend a babysitter?" he asked. "If I don't get back to work soon, I'm going to be out of a job."

She shook her head. "I haven't needed one in years." There was brief moment of awkward silence, then Sydney said, "Well, I should get home."

"Thanks again for your help. And for the casserole." He walked her to the door and pulled it open. "I'll bring your dish back later."

"No rush, and if April gives you any more trouble, just holler. I'll be home all day." She edged toward the door, glancing down the hall. "You could burp her in the middle of her feeding. That might settle her stomach and cut down on gas."

"I'll try that."

She took one step over the threshold. "And you could try soy formula. Some babies develop allergies to the regular kind. That could be why she's getting an upset tummy."

"Thanks, I'll remember that."

"Or you could—" She stopped, smiling sheepishly. "I'm sorry. You'll be fine. I'll see you later."

"Thanks, neighbor." He closed the door behind her and watched through the front window as she made her way across the lawn, her behind swaying beneath snug denim. And that hair. What was it about redheads that made him want to growl?

Abruptly, he turned away. No more leering at her, especially if he planned to talk her into working for him. Which he was seriously considering now, he realized. Temporarily, of course, until he found someone else and she found a job. He'd seen that sappy, lovesick look in her eyes when she'd held April. And he'd recognized her hesitancy before she left, as if he was totally unqualified to be alone with an infant. Which, let's face it, he probably was.

And his incompetence might be just the thing that would get her eating out of the palm of his hand.

As SHE UNLOADED GROCERIES from the van later that afternoon, Sydney glanced next door, wondering how Deputy Valenzia was doing with April. She was dying to know why he would be taking care of a baby that wasn't his. Men with his reputation didn't make it a habit of taking in stray infants. Especially if it might cost him his job.

She heard the roar of a car engine coming down the street and turned to see Shane's car pull up in front of the house. The engine rumbled and the bass from the stereo reverberated through the pavement beneath her feet.

No wonder Lacey never seemed to hear her; the kid was probably deaf.

Sydney wasn't crazy about Lacey dating someone several years older, but Shane seemed like a decent kid and he came from a good family. Besides, forbidding Lacey to see Shane—as Jeff had wanted to do—would only make him that much more appealing. Having had a thing for bad boys when she was younger, Sydney knew this for a fact. It was how she'd ended up in Northern California in the first place. She'd followed her boyfriend—for which her mother had never forgiven her. And as her mom had predicted, the relationship hadn't lasted.

But then Jeff had taken an interest in her. Fifteen years her senior, he was rich, sophisticated and powerful. And worse for her than any "bad boy" she could have ever chosen.

How was that for irony?

Lacey ambled up the driveway, her usual obstinate self. "I'm home on time today. Are you happy?"

"Good. You can help with these." She thrust the heaviest bag in her daughter's arms, listening with morbid satisfaction to her grumble all the way inside. Sydney grabbed the last two bags and was walking to the side door when she heard a bloodcurdling scream. She charged inside and nearly collided head-on with Fred McWilliams, Jeff's handyman.

"You scared me, Fred!" Sydney dropped the bags on the kitchen table. "What are you doing here?"

Lacey glared at him, her eyes reduced to slits. "I was putting away the groceries and he snuck up behind me."

He smiled sheepishly. "Sorry, ma'am, I didn't mean to scare her. Mr. Harris asked me to come by and see about the air conditioner."

Sydney held back her anger. Wasn't it just like Jeff to send someone out without warning her first? And she didn't appreciate him giving people her key. Well, it wasn't Fred's fault.

"I know Mr. Harris probably told you to come right in, but I'd like my key back."

"Sure, Mrs. Harris." With his bony shoulders stooped, he lumbered down the basement stairs.

"That guy gives me the creeps," Lacey said after his footsteps faded.

"He'll be gone soon," Sydney assured her.

"He's a weirdo."

"No, he's just a little slow."

Sydney was sure he was harmless, but deep down he gave her the creeps, too. The way he stared blankly from under his greasy brown hair with beady eyes. He had deep acne scars, and always reeked of strong body odor.

"By the way," Lacey said. "Did you know we have a *cop* living next door?"

"I know. I met him yesterday. He seems…nice."

Lacey raised her slightly swollen brow.

"Not all police are bad, honey."

"How do you know he doesn't work for Dad, and he moved in next door to spy on us?"

Because your father doesn't care enough to take the trouble, she wanted to say, but held her tongue. "He seems okay."

"Veronica thinks he's hot."

Veronica would be correct.

"For an old guy," she added.

He couldn't be more than forty, though she was guessing closer to thirty-five. Sydney's age. "Old?"

Lacey rolled her eyes. "You know what I mean." She rummaged through one of the grocery bags and pulled out a bag of corn chips. "What's for dinner?"

"Chicken casserole, and don't even think about ruining your appetite with those chips."

"Fine." Lacey dropped the bag on the table. "I'm gonna work on my tan."

Sydney put away the groceries and popped the casserole into the oven. Gathering the ingredients for a salad, she chopped lettuce, tomatoes and carrots, dumping them all in a bowl. Turning to get the salad dressing from the fridge, she nearly plowed into Fred. She let out a startled squeak.

How long had he been standing there? "I didn't hear you come up the stairs, Fred. What do you want?"

"Sorry, ma'am." He sniffed loudly and wiped his nose with the back of his hand. "I'm finished."

"Fine."

"You want that fixed, too?" He gestured to the hole in the wall she hadn't yet gotten around to repatching.

"No, thanks, I'll take care of that myself."

He didn't move.

"Is there anything else?"

His bushy dark brows knit together. "Mr. Harris said you'd pay me."

"Oh, did he?" Bastard. She folded her arms over her chest. "Well, you tell Mr. Harris it's not my responsibility."

He still didn't budge, so she walked over to the side door and opened it. "Goodbye, Fred."

He sidled through, but she didn't miss the look of contempt he shot her as he passed. Tough. Jeff knew darn well the maintenance on the house was his responsibility.

Flinging the door shut, Sydney turned to the fridge for a bottle of Italian dressing and grabbed the cucumber she found hidden behind the mayonnaise jar. She put the dressing on the counter and dropped the cuke on the cutting board.

As she assembled the salad, she glanced out the window to the backyard. Lacey was in her bikini, sunning herself on a lounge chair, headphones on, her head swaying to the music. Sydney couldn't remember ever feeling so carefree as a teenager.

When she was thirteen, her dad bailed on them after years of dealing with her mom's chronic bouts of depression. Her mom had been so devastated by his leaving that for months she had barely been able to function. It had been up to Sydney to take care of her. But when her mother still refused to get help after a couple of years, Sydney had started to rebel. Deep down, she thought she could shake some sense into her mother.

She started small. Things like staying out past her curfew, and hanging out with boys who were much older. When that didn't work, she graduated to smoking and causing trouble at school. She lost track of how many times she'd been suspended. Then, when she was seventeen, she'd been hauled in for underage drinking and possession of marijuana. When her mom didn't show up to bail her out, it was the last straw.

Her boyfriend at the time, a twenty-two-year-old with zero potential, had been talking for months about moving to California, and for her it was the ultimate rebellion. So, off she went. Their relationship lasted six months, but by then Sydney was eighteen and had a decent job working as a server in a local pub. That was where she met Jeff. He'd showered her with affection and attention—the two things she had always craved from her mother but had never received—and treated her like a princess. By the time she realized that he was arrogant, dishonest and overbearing, she was pregnant with Lacey and felt she had to marry him.

She stayed with him for their daughter's sake, despite his many affairs. But clearly that had done more harm than good. For her and Lacey.

Sometimes when she looked at Lacey, it was like looking in the mirror. Which was why she tried so hard to shelter her from the worst of it. She needed time to just…be a kid.

Lacey was now drumming her knees to the beat of the music and lip-syncing the words. Sydney smiled. Everything she'd worked for, the peace she fought for, was all for Lacey.

Sydney set the table and, as an afterthought, chopped an onion to go with the salad.

"Dinner ready?" Lacey asked from behind her, and Sydney jumped a mile, nearly chopping off a few fingers in the process.

"Please stop sneaking up on me," she said, glancing at her daughter, discreetly checking her bikini-clad body for new holes.

"Fred just left." Lacey plucked a cherry tomato from the bowl and popped it in her mouth. "He was watching me."

Sydney's brow furrowed. Hadn't Fred left a while ago? "What do you mean, watching you?"

"I mean, I opened my eyes and he was standing by the side of the house looking at me, then he walked away. He's a total creep."

"You know, I'm beginning to agree with you, Lacey. If you see him again, you let me know, and keep your distance."

"Like I'd want to be anywhere near him," she scoffed. "He's gross. When's dinner?"

"Ten minutes. I'll call you when it's ready."

Sydney finished dinner, keeping an eye out the kitchen window in case Fred returned. He had no business staring at Lacey. The idea made her uneasy. Maybe he wasn't as harmless as they had thought…and he'd forgotten to give her key back. Or maybe he hadn't forgotten. Maybe he'd kept it on purpose. And now he could get in whenever he felt like it.

First thing in the morning, she would call a locksmith and have every lock in the house changed. If Fred had the gall to stand there and leer at Lacey in broad daylight, who knew what he was capable of in the privacy of a house.

Later that evening, when Lacey went out to a movie with Shane, Sydney stood on the porch until the car was out of sight, and couldn't shake the feeling she was being watched.

You're imagining things, she assured herself. But as the sun began to set, casting long, eerie shadows, she began to think that waiting until morning to change the locks had been a bad idea. She pulled out the phone book, but every place that she called was either closed or couldn't come until the morning. She made an appointment for 9:00 a.m. then turned on every light in the house and locked all of the windows. She even hooked a chair under the doorknob in the living room—just in case.

God help me if there's a fire, she thought, hitching a second chair under the knob of the side door. She would just have to sit up and wait for Lacey, so she could let her in the house.

She jumped when the phone rang.

"My secretary told me you called," Jeff said, sounding annoyed.

"Fred came by today. I don't ever want to see him here again."

"Jesus, what's your problem now?"

"He scares Lacey."

"So?"

"What do you mean, *so?* She was lying out in a bikini and she said he was watching her. It makes her uncomfortable and it worries me. What do you really know about him?"

"He's a good handyman and he's cheap. If you don't like it, pay for the damned repairs yourself."

"You're willing to put our daughter's peace of mind, not to mention her safety, at risk to save a few dollars?"

"Lacey would say anything for attention. Get a clue."

Get a clue? Was he kidding? He was the clueless one.

"I'm tired of you using Lacey to manipulate me. Keep it up and I'll have to sic my lawyer on you. You're warping our daughter and I won't let you get away with it."

She heard a loud click and the phone went dead. "You stupid jerk."

She slammed the phone down and paced the kitchen floor, hating Jeff more than she'd ever hated another human being. And calling Jeff a human being was a serious stretch in itself. He was lower than human, lower than—

A flash of movement in her peripheral vision caught her attention and she spun toward the side door. She froze, her heart battering her rib cage. The curtains were open a fraction of an inch and she saw a glimmer of color under the side porch light.

Someone was outside.

Would Fred have the nerve to come right up to a lit doorway and force his way in? He couldn't be that demented. She slowly leaned forward, craning her neck to peek past the curtains, and nearly jumped out of her skin at the loud rap.

CHAPTER FOUR

IT WASN'T FUNNY, not at all, but Daniel couldn't seem to wipe the grin off of his face. Especially now that the color had returned to Sydney's face and her eyes had gone back to their normal size.

"I really am sorry," he said again. "I didn't mean to scare you. When I saw all of your lights on, I thought you wouldn't mind me stopping by."

"You don't have to apologize. I've been a little edgy today, that's all."

She tried to smile, but it didn't quite reach her eyes. Her mouth looked great anyway—lush and pink, full and pouty. And he reminded himself once again not to look at it. He had a job to do here, so to speak.

April fussed, so he readjusted her in his lap, and she lunged for the plastic key ring he'd placed just out of reach on the edge of the kitchen table. He'd discovered if she thought she wasn't supposed to have something, it made it that much more fun to play with.

Sydney reached for the baby and April squealed, her arms shooting forth at the invitation. *Good girl,* Daniel thought. She was making his job a lot easier.

"So, what's with the chair in front of the door?" he asked, nodding toward the living room. "I'm sure I don't have to tell you how unsafe that is."

"I got spooked. We had a sort of…incident today."

He frowned, wondering what her ex had done this time. Because he didn't doubt for a second that whatever it was, the mayor was probably responsible. "What sort of incident?"

She told him about the handyman, and the mayor's total lack of regard for his daughter's safety. Daniel wasn't surprised. In his line of work, he'd seen ex-husbands and wives do a lot worse to each other.

"What did you say the guy's name is?" he asked, pulling out his cell phone.

"Fred McWilliams."

"Age?"

She shrugged. "Mid-twenties, maybe."

He dialed the sheriff's office and Margie answered.

"Sheriff Montgomery's not in," she told him.

"I called to talk to you. I need a favor. Could you run a name for me?"

"Sure, honey. What is it?"

He gave her the information, and the McWilliams guy was in the system.

"He was collared last year for a drunk and disorderly, and he's got a DUI from three years ago. You want me to dig deeper?"

"Nope, that was all I needed. Thanks." He disconnected. "I don't think you have anything to worry about, Sydney. His only vice seems to be a tendency to drink, but he's never hurt anyone."

Sydney looked relieved. "I still wish the locksmith could have come tonight, but I'm not as worried."

"A trick I learned, if you can put a drop of super glue

in the key hole, it's impossible to get a key in. But only do it if you're sure the locksmith is coming, or you won't be able to leave the house."

"Thanks, Daniel. I really appreciate your help." April let out an earsplitting squeal and Sydney sat her on the table top in front of her. "So, what's the problem with you tonight, little girl?"

Daniel gave Sydney the baffled I'm-an-incompetent-moron look he'd been practicing. "She just won't go to sleep. I even started her on that formula you suggested."

"Is that true?" Sydney cooed, standing April in her lap. April screeched and bounced up and down on her chubby little legs.

"She sure does like you," he said.

"We girls have to stick together, don't we, April?" April let out another high-pitched squeal and latched on to a lock of Sydney's hair with a sticky fist. Sydney laughed and tugged it loose. "Did she sleep much for you today?"

"Most of the afternoon, but tonight she just fussed when I put her to bed." Actually, he hadn't tried all that hard to get her to sleep, but Sydney didn't have to know that part. She just had to think he didn't know what he was doing, which he didn't.

"You wouldn't want to go to bed at night, either, if you slept all day." She nuzzled April's nose with her own and the baby gurgled.

"I guess not." He just frowned and tried to look confused, scratching the stubble on his chin.

"Growing a beard?" she asked, glancing in his direction.

"Me?" He rubbed his rough cheek. "Nah, I just didn't feel like shaving today."

"Today?"

"Okay," he conceded. "This week."

"You might want to consider it."

"Growing a beard?"

"No, *shaving.*"

He sat back and folded his arms across his chest. "Why? You don't like hairy men?"

He could swear she blushed a little.

"I was thinking it probably feels like steel wool against April's skin." She tickled April's chin. "What do you think, honey? Does he need to shave off those icky whiskers?"

"You know, I never even thought of that." She did get really squirmy when he held her sometimes. Maybe he was hurting her and didn't know it. This parenting gig could be really complicated.

"Any luck finding a nanny today?" she asked.

He sat a bit straighter in his chair. "Why? Are you interested?"

She blinked rapidly. "N-no, of course not, I just…I was only curious."

Did she think he was angry that she'd asked? She was a tough one to figure out. One minute she was completely at ease, then bam, she wouldn't even look him in the eye. Maybe it was the badge, and her previous run-ins with the mayor's posse. Maybe she thought he was on her ex's payroll.

If he had any hope of persuading her to work for him, he was going to have to set the record straight.

"I make you nervous." he said.

"Why would you think that?" she asked, but she wouldn't meet his eye.

"Just a hunch. And considering your recent experiences with the local law, I can't say I blame you. But let me make myself clear. I think your ex is an ass."

She finally looked at him, but her eyes were wary. "I'd like to believe that."

He couldn't blame her for her apprehension. Which made the idea of tricking her into wanting to work for him feel downright sleazy.

"The truth is, I didn't come over here because I needed help with April. I just wanted you to think I was incompetent, so you might take pity on me and agree to be my nanny."

Her eyes widened. "You want *me* to be your nanny?"

"Only temporarily. I thought, since you're between jobs, it would be the ideal situation for us both. Until I either find someone permanent, or I locate April's family."

"Deputy Valenzia—"

"Daniel."

"*Daniel,* I'm sure you've heard the rumors—"

"I told you, your ex is an ass. I'm not inclined to believe anything he says."

"I appreciate that you trust me, but hiring me is tantamount to painting a target on your back."

"The mayor doesn't scare me. And like I said before,

if I don't find someone soon, I'm going to be out of a job. I'm desperate, Sydney."

She frowned, looking conflicted. "I don't know…"

"Don't make me beg."

"Can you give me a night to think about it?"

He nearly sighed with relief. That was a start. "Of course."

April pulled at the buttons on Sydney's shirt and let out a wail of frustration when they wouldn't come loose. Sydney cradled her against her chest, but she still squirmed and fussed. "I think she's getting tired."

"I should try feeding her and putting her down again." He stood and reached for April. "Thanks for your help."

"I didn't do much."

He glanced over at the chair in front of the door. "Have you got a pen and paper?"

"Sure." She got them from a kitchen drawer.

He wrote down his cell number. "Here's my number. If you get scared for any reason or just need to hear a friendly voice, give me a call. I'm usually up well past midnight."

She smiled. "Thank you."

"Don't hesitate to call. Anytime."

She walked him to the side door and pulled it open. "Good luck with April tonight."

"Thanks. And you try not to worry, okay? I'm right next door if you need me." He paused at the door and added, "I'll talk to you tomorrow?"

She nodded and smiled, and he had the strangest urge to lean in and press his lips to hers. Or maybe it wasn't strange. Maybe the fact that she was so different from the type of woman he was normally attracted to was what intrigued him. Or maybe it was just that she was attractive and available, and he'd been in a month-long dry spell. Maybe if the circumstances were different, he might indulge in a short fling.

But if Sydney did agree to work for him, she was off limits.

DANIEL ROLLED ONTO HIS BACK and stretched, slowly waking from the deepest sleep he'd had in weeks. The steady drum of a spring rain beating against the window registered through a groggy haze. Opening his eyes, he shifted up onto his elbow to read the display on the digital clock on the night table.

Eight forty-five.

Eight forty-five? He shot straight up in bed. He'd put April to bed at midnight. She should have been awake hours ago!

Frantically he kicked off the blankets. Something was wrong. She'd never slept more than a three- or four-hour stretch at night. A million different horrific images shot through his brain. He ran for the door, tripping over his tennis shoes and tumbling into the hall. He skidded to a stop outside April's door, fear growing in the pit of his stomach.

What would he find on the other side?

Poised with his hand on the knob, heart lodged in his throat, he heard a noise. A soft, playful babbling. A surge of relief coursed through him, and his legs threatened to buckle.

As quietly as he could manage, he eased the door open a crack, peeking into the dim room. April had rolled from her side to her stomach and turned one hundred and eighty degrees, scooting herself to the foot of the crib, grasping at the bumper pads, speaking in baby talk to the colorful images of farm animals. He wrestled with the urge to scoop her up out of the crib and hug her. She seemed so content playing, he hated to disturb her.

A grin spread across his face. She was a cute little runt, despite all the trouble she'd caused. And he felt guilty that he couldn't keep her, couldn't honor Reanne's wishes. The best he could do was find her real family. She would be better off with them.

The low rumble of thunder made the window above the crib vibrate and a brilliant flash of lightning lit the room. April turned her head and blinked several times—not frightened, just inquisitive—then she saw Daniel leaning in the doorway and squealed, kicking her little legs.

"G'morning, munchkin." He crossed the room and picked her up, lifting her high over his head until she giggled excitedly, then he drew her into his arms and hugged her tight. She was so soft and warm, so sweet. He'd always loved kids. He'd even been something of a surrogate father to his nephew, but never before had he felt this urge to nurture and protect.

"You scared Uncle Danny half to death," he told her. Uncle Danny. Somehow that just didn't sound right, but neither did plain old Danny or Daniel. *Daddy* definitely wasn't right, either. He hated to slap a label on their situation when he wasn't sure how long she would be around. He'd called Joe yesterday to check if there were any leads in finding April's family, but so far nothing. If her real father wanted her, assuming he even knew she existed, wouldn't he have come forward by now?

All Daniel could do for now was just wait and see.

SHE WAS GOING to do it.

It had taken her one long, sleepless night to make the decision, but now Sydney was sure. She was going to be April's nanny.

Temporarily.

Deputy Val—*Daniel*—needed her help. And now that she was out of a job, what else would she do with her time? She could overlook the fact that he was a cop because he hated Jeff and his cronies, and the fact that he trusted her despite the rumors earned him some pretty major brownie points. His sizzling good looks…okay, those might be a little harder to overlook. But knowing his reputation, he would never be interested in a woman with so much baggage anyway.

"It's the right thing to do," she rationalized.

She looked out the kitchen window and saw that his truck was in the driveway. The earlier heavy rain had eased off but it was still the kind of dreary, depressing drizzle that would likely last all day.

What the heck, it was only a couple hundred feet to his porch. A little rain wouldn't kill her. Opening the side door, she started out. She'd made it to the edge of her property when a bolt of lightning zigzagged across the sky and a simultaneous crack of thunder shook the ground beneath her feet. The sky opened up again and icy rain came down in a torrent. She ran the rest of the way to Daniel's porch, drenched to the skin by the time she made it under the overhang. She banged on his door and it swung open almost immediately.

"Jeez, what happened to you?" Daniel said, looking her over from head to toe.

"Can I come in?" she asked. "Before I drown?"

He held the door open, looking out. "It's really pouring out there."

"You think?" The minute she crossed the threshold into the air-conditioned room, she started to shiver.

"You don't have an umbrella?"

"When I left the house it was only sprinkling." She tried to rub warmth into her sodden arms. "Do you maybe have a towel I could use?"

"Of course, sorry."

He dashed to the kitchen, and while she waited a noise behind the sofa caught her attention. She craned her neck to see over the back where April lay in a playpen, swinging her hands at the play set hanging over her head. She batted a black-and-white-striped triangle and gurgled happily.

What was it about babies that made Sydney feel all mushy inside? Though it didn't used to be that way. She had always sworn she would never have kids. And after she got pregnant with Lacey, at first, she had been devastated. But the first time she heard Lacey's heartbeat in the doctor's office, she fell hopelessly in love.

Even though she was dripping on Daniel's floor,

Sydney tiptoed around the couch and peeked into the playpen.

April saw her and broke into a wide smile.

"Hi, sweetheart. Are you playing?"

April kicked her legs and squealed.

Suddenly Sydney was enveloped in something soft and warm.

"I had a load finishing up in the dryer," Daniel said, tucking the thick bath towel around her shoulders from behind. "It should warm you up." He dropped a smaller towel on the floor to soak up the puddle she'd made. "Take off your shoes."

She slipped out of them and stepped on to the towel. She should have stayed by the door. "Sorry about your floor."

Taking her by the shoulders and turning her to face him, he rubbed her arms through the towel. He still hadn't shaved, and his stubble was becoming a full-blown beard. "I don't care about the floor. I just didn't want you to slip and break your neck. I found out the hard way how slippery this hardwood can be. I was walking from the shower to the laundry room this morning and my feet flew right out from under me." He grimaced and rubbed his backside. "I'm still not sitting quite right."

She envisioned him with only a towel loosely fastened about his waist, his olive skin glistening and dewy.

Oh, boy. Definitely not the kind of thoughts she should be having. And that would be much easier if he stopped standing so close. And stopped *touching* her.

He stepped back and gestured to the couch. "Sit down."

She did, and he sat on the chair across from her. "So, did you get your locks changed this morning?"

"I did. I hardly slept at all last night. I was afraid that if I tried your glue trick something would happen and the locksmith wouldn't be able to make it for days."

"Tell me you at least moved the chair."

She looked down at her hands.

"Should I tell you about the bodies I've seen pulled out of burning buildings—"

"Ew, no! Please don't. I won't do it again."

There was genuine concern in his eyes. "I'll hold you to that."

She wondered what he would think of the chair she'd hooked under the side door, but figured it wasn't worth mentioning. "So, I've given your offer a lot of thought."

"And?" he said, looking anxious.

"And I'll do it."

He slumped with relief. "Thank God."

"However," she added, "I need to know what the situation is. Whose baby she is. If some woman shows up at the door saying April is hers, I need to know what to do."

"April's mother won't be showing up. She's dead."

CHAPTER FIVE

SYDNEY SUCKED IN a quiet breath. "How did she die?"

"Cancer," Daniel told her. "According to the social worker, she was diagnosed when she was pregnant. And knowing it could hurt the baby, she refused treatment until after April was born. But by then, I guess, it was too late."

"That's so sad. You were good friends with her?"

"That's the really strange thing. I hardly knew her. We had a brief affair. She wasn't in town long enough for me to get to know her very well. She was something of a drifter. No permanent home. She told me she grew up in the foster care system, so she probably didn't want April to end up there. I guess that's why she put my name on the birth certificate."

"You're sure you're not her father?"

"Not unless Reanne was pregnant for fifteen months."

"You mentioned trying to find April's family."

"I figure there has to be someone. At least, I'm hoping there is."

"You don't want to keep her?"

"What do I know about raising kids? I never even planned to have any." After watching his parents' marriage crash and burn, and seeing the way it affected his sisters, he'd decided never to marry. Sure, it could get lonely at times, but living in a tourist town, he never ran out of available women to date.

"It would be a huge responsibility for a single guy," she said.

"I don't exactly lead a lifestyle conducive to raising a kid. I'm a cop. Even though we don't get a lot of violent crimes in Prospect, it's still a dangerous line of work. If I were killed, what would happen to April then?"

"Foster care," Sydney said.

"Exactly. Which I'm assuming is what Reanne didn't want."

"Have you considered adoption?"

"If I can't find her biological family, that will be my only other option." Sydney looked troubled, so he asked, "You think I'm a bad person for giving her up?"

Her expression softened. "No, of course not. I was just thinking how tough it will be for her at first, being bounced around. But kids are resilient. And it's obvious you've taken good care of her. I take you didn't already have the baby furniture and toys and bottles. Or the house."

"I got most of it at second-hand shops. And I had been planning to move into a bigger place eventually, anyway. The one-room loft wasn't cutting it anymore. This just sped things up a bit."

"I'd say you've gone above the call of duty. She's lucky to have you."

"Well, I haven't done it all on my own. The first few weeks, my sisters helped a lot."

"How many do you have?"

"Five."

Sydney's eyes went wide. "*Five?* Wow. Older or younger?"

"Angie—Angelica—is my twin, and the other four— Abigail, Bethany, Delilah and Leah—are younger."

"That's a big family."

"Yeah, considering my parents never should have gotten married in the first place. I'm sure there must have been a time when they loved each other, but I never saw it."

"Divorced?"

"When I was seventeen."

"I was thirteen when my dad bailed on me and my mom."

"You're an only child?" he asked.

"I had a brother. He was four years younger than me, but he died when he was three months old from SIDS. My mom never really recovered. She was severely depressed for years. Still is, as far as I know. I think she blamed herself for his death."

April let out a warning shriek, one that usually meant she was about to start wailing. Daniel walked to the playpen and picked her up. Her diaper was wet. "I have to change her."

Sydney shot up from her seat. "Do you want me to do it?"

"I've got it. But why don't you come with me and I can show you where everything is."

"Sure," she said, following him to April's room.

While he wrestled April into a new diaper he gave

Sydney a quick rundown of where she could find things.

"Maybe I can help you organize," she said, eyeing the moving clutter that he hadn't yet found a place for.

"That would be a big help." He lifted April off the changing table and turned to Sydney. She stood in the doorway, the towel still draped over her shoulders, and... *hello.*

She must have been chilled, because he could see the outline of her nipples through her damp shirt. It was as if they were calling to him, silently begging him to notice.

He noticed. And God help him, he appreciated the view. His first thought was to ask if she'd ever been in a wet T-shirt contest. A clear indication that a month without female companionship was taking its toll. Maybe he could talk one of his sisters into watching April next Friday evening so he could go out. An evening at Moose Winooski's, the local brewery, was exactly what he needed to shake off the stress of a month in captivity.

With any luck, the P.I. would find someone to take April soon, and Daniel would have his life back.

He realized that he'd zoned out staring at Sydney's chest, and she must have noticed, too, because she pulled the towel down to cover herself.

"Did you want to hold her?" he asked.

She looked longingly at April, but said, "I shouldn't while I'm all wet."

"Maybe we should talk about money," he said.

"Money?" she asked, confused.

"I do plan to pay you to watch April."

"Oh, right. Sure."

"Let's go back to the family room." He carried April over to the playpen and laid her inside, hoping she would play a little while longer before lunch. Sydney sat on the couch, and he took a seat beside her. Maybe it was his imagination, but she seemed uneasy. Maybe she just didn't like talking finances.

"I'm not sure what the going rate for a nanny is, and I doubt I can even come close to matching your former salary—"

"Why don't you just pay me what you can afford?"

What if what he could afford was less than what she needed? Or maybe whatever he could pay was better than no pay at all. "I want to be fair. Why don't you give me a number. What you would expect for, say, a forty-hour week."

She though about it for a minute, then quoted a sum that even he considered ridiculously low. Not that he wouldn't love a great deal, but it wouldn't be right to take advantage of her. "Are you sure that's enough?"

"Let's just say that I'm not hurting for money."

He recalled hearing a rumor that she'd taken her ex to the cleaners in the divorce. It appeared as though it wasn't just a rumor after all.

"Besides," she added. "Think how convenient this will be for me. No morning commute, and if I have things to do at home, I can just bring her with me."

"True," he said, but it still seemed low to him. "You should know that occasionally I work the night shift."

"I don't have a problem with that. And maybe if I get a parking ticket…"

He grinned. "It would be nice if it disappeared?"

"Not that I would ever ask you to do anything unethical."

"You get a lot of tickets?"

"Over eight hundred dollars' worth in the past year."

He winced. That was blatant harassment. He didn't doubt the mayor's posse was responsible. And though fixing it for her could put him in hot water, it would be worth a minor scalding or two. "Consider it done."

"When do you need me to start?"

"Is Monday too soon?"

"Monday is fine." She paused and then asked, "So we have a deal?"

If she wanted to work for peanuts, who was he to tell her no? "Yeah, we have a deal."

He extended a hand to shake on it, and she hesitated before she slid her hand into his.

It was ice-cold. "Sydney, you're freezing," he said, rubbing her hand between both of his to warm it. "Why didn't you say something? I could have loaned you a sweatshirt."

She extracted her hand from his grasp and wound it with its mate in her lap, eyes lowered. "I-I'm fine."

There she went again, getting all nervous. Maybe it would just take time for her to trust him.

But what if it had nothing to do with the fact that he was law enforcement? What if she was nervous because she was attracted to him? Now that he considered it, she seemed to get edgy whenever he got close or touched her.

Testing the theory, he leaned casually against the cushion and rested his arm on the back of the couch behind her head. She tensed, and he smothered a wry smile.

Maybe she *was* attracted to him. Either that or she was uncomfortable with men in general. Or maybe she hadn't been with one in a while. Far as he could recall, she'd split with her ex at least a year ago, and he'd never seen her at any of the local singles hot spots since then. And since he'd moved in next door he hadn't noticed any men—besides her sleazebag ex—dropping by.

"Do your sisters live in Prospect?" she asked. Nervously, as though she felt the need to fill the silence.

He turned slightly, so that his knee was barely an inch from her thigh. "Angie, Beth and Dee live here. Abbi lives in Colorado and Leah is going to school in New York."

"And your parents?"

"My dad passed away three years ago. My mom lives in town. She works at the resort as an activities director."

He reached out and wound a damp ringlet of Sydney's hair around his index finger. "Would you like a towel for your hair?"

"No." She eased away from him, awkwardly smoothing her hair back down and tucking the ringlet behind her ear. "Thanks."

"Something wrong?" he asked.

"O-of course not."

"Are you sure? You seem awfully nervous."

"I'm fine."

"Are you?" He shifted so that his knee brushed her bare thigh and she jumped. "Call me crazy, Sydney, but I get the suspicion that you might be attracted to me."

SYDNEY BLINKED in rapid succession. "E-excuse me?"

"You're acting like you might be attracted to me," Daniel said again, even though she'd heard him perfectly fine the first time. "Are you?"

"What kind of question is that?" And why was he asking? And why were her cheeks suddenly on fire with embarrassment?

He couldn't actually be trying to seduce her, could he? Did he think that was part of the babysitting package? She had to admit, it would be one hell of a perk, but even if she was in the market for a fling, it would never be with a man like him. He was way out of her league. He oozed sex appeal, and for years Jeff had referred to her as the Ice Queen.

"I'm wondering if that's why you're so nervous around me."

"I just don't like cops."

"But you *know* I'm a good cop. If you didn't, you never would have agreed to watch April. And you only get nervous when I get close, or do something like this." His fingers brushed her earlobe.

"Stop that!" she said, batting his hand away.

He grinned, and if it hadn't been so damned adorable she probably would have decked him.

"I rest my case," he said, looking pleased with himself.

She hated that she was so skittish around men. It had just been so long since one had noticed her. And even longer since one had touched her. Not that she'd put herself in the position to be the object of anyone's interest. The one time she'd let her hair down and had fun, she'd been hauled off in handcuffs. Staying home just seemed safer.

"Even if I was attracted to you," she said, "I would *never* date a cop. Or someone I worked for. Or *anyone* nicknamed Deputy Casanova."

"And I would never date a single mom," he said. "Or a next-door neighbor."

Yet his impish grin said dating her was irrelevant, and he had something else entirely in mind.

Freedom.

Daniel watched as his mom backed out of the driveway and drove off, April strapped securely in the backseat. She had agreed to watch April not just for the evening, but overnight, and it was a night he didn't intend to spend alone.

He took the longest shower he'd had in a month, then shaved. He dressed in jeans, cowboy boots and a black PCSD—Prospect County Sheriff Department—T-shirt. He grabbed his keys from the kitchen counter and was heading out the side door when he noticed Sydney's dish sitting there. He'd forgotten to give it to her yesterday when she came by. And remembering her visit, the way she had jumped when he touched her, made him grin. She'd more or less admitted she was attracted to him. But, attracted to each other or not, they seemed to have an understanding that a relationship would be a bad idea.

He grabbed the dish and crossed the yard to Sydney's side door. He knocked, and it swung open a few seconds later. But it wasn't Sydney, it was her daughter.

"Hi, I'm Daniel from next door. Is your mom home?"

"Mom!" she called over her shoulder and held the door so Daniel could step inside. "The cop from next door is here!"

She looked as though she was probably a cute kid under the dark makeup and green hair. She had Sydney's wide blue eyes and upturned nose.

"You must be Lacey," he said.

"My mom said you hired her to be your nanny."

He couldn't tell if she thought that was a good thing or a bad thing. "Are you okay with that?"

"Sure. Considering my tool of a father got her fired from her job."

He smothered a grin. Apparently Lacey's opinion of her father wasn't much better than Sydney's.

"Don't call your father a *tool,* sweetheart," Sydney said, appearing in the kitchen doorway.

"Well, he is one," Lacey mumbled, then a car horn blared outside. "That's Veronica. Gotta go!"

She slipped past Daniel and out the back door, and Sydney called after her, "Have fun, honey! See you tomorrow!"

"Cute kid," Daniel said.

"Who obviously has issues with her father."

"I guess you can't exactly blame her." He held out

the dish to her. "I forgot to give this back. The casserole was good. Maybe I can get the recipe?"

She took the dish, eyeing him suspiciously. "You cook?"

"I'm thirty-six and single. It was learn to cook or live on fast food and frozen dinners."

For the first time since Sydney had walked into the room, Daniel really focused on her face and realized her eyes were a little swollen and red-rimmed, as if she'd been crying. Had she had a run-in with her ex? He felt his hackles rise. "What's wrong?"

His concern seemed to confuse her. "Why would you think that?"

"You look like you've been crying. Did your ex do something?"

She laughed. "No, nothing like that. I was watching a movie on Lifetime. Friday is usually movie night for me."

"But it's a gorgeous evening. You should get out. Have fun."

"The last time I did that, I was arrested. I feel safer staying home."

"Don't you miss seeing your friends?"

She shifted uncomfortably. "The truth is, I don't really have any. Jeff got them in the divorce."

Then they were even stupider than the mayor. And it bugged Daniel that Sydney was afraid to go out and have fun. She deserved better than that.

Before he could think what he was doing, he said, "Go get dressed."

She looked down at her T-shirt and shorts. "I am dressed."

"I mean, get *dressed,* I'm taking you out."

Her eyes widened, and she shook her head. "I told you, I don't date cops."

"It's not a date. It's just friends going out for a drink. And you *need* to get out."

"No, I don't."

"Trust me, you do." He took her by the shoulders, turned her in the direction of the kitchen door, and gave her a gentle shove. "Now go. And wear something... sexy."

She shot him a look over her shoulder.

"Trust me."

She reluctantly left the room, then he heard her bedroom door close. The reason, he figured, for her tendency to be nervous around him, was a complete lack of self-confidence. Which was totally unwarranted because she was a beautiful woman. Not to mention really nice. And if she was ever going to get her confidence back, she had to put herself out there. He knew a dozen guys on the force who would trip over each other to dance with her. If not because she was hot as hell, then out of curiosity because she was the ex of the biggest ass in a thirty-mile radius.

He took a seat at her kitchen table and waited, looking at his watch occasionally, hoping Sydney wasn't one of those women who took hours to get ready. Fifteen minutes passed before she appeared in the doorway.

"I'm ready."

He looked up and gave a low whistle. "Wow."

She'd dressed in form-fitting jeans that hugged all the right places, spike-heeled boots and a scoop-neck, sleeveless blouse made of some silky, layered fabric so transparent he could just make out the silhouette of her bra underneath. And the cleavage spilling out over the top…

Damn.

She'd put her hair up, leaving a few curls loose to frame her face and brush her neck. She'd applied only a little mascara and shiny lip gloss, but honestly, she didn't need more than that. She looked…breathtaking.

"Too much?" she asked, shifting nervously.

"Perfect," he said. She was going to have to beat men off with a stick. He got to his feet. "You ready?"

"I'm still not sure about this."

"You'll have a great time. Trust me."

She looked as if she might argue, then she grabbed her purse off the kitchen counter and said, "Let's go before I change my mind."

They crossed the lawn to his truck, and he opened the door for her.

"Buckle up," he said, as he climbed in the driver's seat.

She fidgeted beside him, as though any second she might throw the door open, jump out and make a run for it.

"Relax," he told her. "You're going to have fun."

He started the truck, backed out of the driveway, and headed in the direction of town. Thankfully it was only a few minutes' drive, so she didn't have much time to change her mind.

As they turned onto Main Street traffic grew thicker. The sidewalks were congested with tourists and locals. Though daytime activities kept most of the visitors up at the resort, town nightlife drew them down the mountain to the main strip. And because there was an antique car show this weekend, the city was exceptionally busy.

"I forgot to ask where we're going," she said

"Moose Winooski's."

She was dead silent, so he looked over at her and realized that most of the color had leached from her face. "What's wrong?"

"Jeff hangs out there."

"Sometimes. So what?"

"You don't think that will be...awkward?"

Probably not for the mayor, who seemed to think he owned the town. Which was exactly why she needed to go. "If he's there, ignore him. If he hassles you, I'll take care of it."

"He's not someone you want to piss off, Daniel."

"I told you before, I'm not afraid of him."

The brewery parking lot was already filled to capacity but they found a spot on a side street a block down. After he parked, Sydney reached for the door handle. "Don't touch that," he told her.

She yanked her hand back. "Why?"

He got out and walked around the truck and tugged her door open. "Because you deserve to be treated like a lady."

For the first time that night, she smiled. But as they walked down the street toward the entrance, the smile turned into a grimace.

"Don't be nervous," Daniel said.

"I'm not nervous. I'm *terrified*."

Her steps slowed, and since he figured there was a good possibility she might turn tail and run, he grabbed her hand. As they neared the building, they could hear a cover of a Tim McGraw song blaring from within, played by the local country western band that performed every Friday and Saturday night.

When they got to the door he pulled it open and had to practically shove her through. The bar was packed, as was the dance floor, and every table seemed to be occupied.

"Danny!" someone shouted, and he craned his neck to see Jon Montgomery, one of his fellow deputies, waving him over to the bar. He stood with a group of Daniel's friends. Keeping a tight grip on Sydney's hand he dragged her along with him, letting go only to shake hands with Jon.

"Where the hell you been?" Jon asked, and when he saw Sydney standing there, it was as if Daniel ceased to exist. "And who is this lovely woman?"

"This is a friend of mine, Sydney Harris," Daniel said. "Sydney, this is Jon."

Jon took Sydney's hand, but instead of shaking it, he kissed it instead. "A pleasure to meet you, Sydney Harris."

She flashed him a wobbly smile. "Hi."

Daniel heard someone call his name and turned to see his twin sister coming toward them.

"Hey, Angie," he said and reached out to give her

a hug. But Angie ignored him and went straight for Sydney.

"You must be Sydney," she said, pumping Sydney's hand. "It's so good to finally meet you."

Sydney looked a little confused.

"Sydney, this is my sister Angie," Daniel said.

Angie laughed. "I guess I could have introduced myself, huh? You're probably thinking, who is this crazy woman accosting me?"

"No, I figured it out," Sydney told her. "You look a lot alike."

"We favor our father. He was born in Argentina. Our mother is pure Irish. And she's dying to meet you, by the way. Maybe we could do lunch some day? Just the three of us? Of course, Beth and Dee will probably want to come, too. They're our younger sisters."

"Um, sure," Sydney said, seeming uncertain. Daniel didn't blame her; Angie did have the tendency to come on a little strong.

"Danny tells me you have a fifteen-year-old daughter. I have a seventeen-year-old son." She turned to Daniel. "Speaking of kids, where's April?"

"Mom has her for the night."

"Oh! Well, maybe I'll stop over there tomorrow morning so I can see her."

"I'm going to introduce Sydney around," Daniel told his sister, before she really got going.

"Of course," Angie said, shooing them away. "We'll talk later."

Daniel took Sydney by the shoulders and maneuvered her to the opposite end of the bar, saying under his breath, "So, is your head spinning?"

"A little. But I liked her."

Daniel introduced Sydney to his friends and everyone seemed eager to meet the mayor's ex. She was a little reserved at first, staying glued to his side, but after a while she started to relax. Eventually one of the women dragged her off to chat with a group of wives and girlfriends. And after a beer or two, she actually started to look as though she was having fun.

"So, is she the Sydney Harris I think she is?" Daniel's friend Russ, the only trustworthy mechanic in town, asked. "The mayor's ex?"

"Yep." Daniel took a swallow of his beer, watching as one of the local firefighters asked Sydney to dance, and she reluctantly followed him out onto the dance floor.

David Smith, a fellow deputy who was leaning on the bar to Daniel's left, asked, "And she's just a friend?"

"Yep."

"*Why?* She's *hot.*" That earned him a slug from his wife, Sammi.

"Watch it, pal," she warned, but she was grinning. She and David had started dating in high school, married a week after graduation and had been going strong ever since. Daniel wished all marriages could be so stable, but he knew they were the exception to the rule.

"I'll admit it was tempting," Daniel said. "But she's my next-door neighbor, she has a kid, and starting Monday she's going to be April's nanny."

"You know how pissed Harris would be if his ex was

dating a cop," Jon said. "Especially one who refuses to play by his rules."

"Speak of the devil," Sammi said, nodding to the door. "Look who just walked in."

CHAPTER SIX

DANIEL TURNED to see Jeff Harris come in, his girl-friend clinging to his arm, a member of his posse on either side. He watched with morbid curiosity as the mayor did a quick scan of the bar, then the dance floor, knowing the exact second he spotted Sydney. His brow lifted in surprise, then instantly lowered.

Oh, yeah, he wasn't happy. That gave Daniel way more satisfaction than it should have.

Daniel looked over at Sydney, but she seemed oblivious to the fact that her ex was there. And he hoped it stayed that way. She was actually having fun now. He didn't want Harris to spoil it.

A rookie cop—who had to be at least ten years younger than Sydney, cut in and the firefighter walked off dejectedly.

"I get the feeling he would be pissed no matter who she was dating. He seems to get off on making her miserable."

"Something's different with you," Sammi said. "Usually by now you've prowled the perimeter and chosen your conquest, but tonight you haven't left the bar."

She was right. Daniel had been so focused on Sydney that he hadn't made a single connection. He hadn't met a woman, townie or tourist he could take home tonight. It hadn't even crossed his mind until Sammi mentioned it.

But now wasn't the time. He had the feeling, by the way the mayor was watching Sydney, he was waiting for the best moment to make trouble for her.

"The way Daniel's been watching Sydney, I'd say *she's* his next conquest," Jon said.

"Just watching her back," Daniel told him. "She didn't want to come here, but I persuaded her. I told her she needed to get out."

"Well, she seems to be having a good time," Sammi said.

The song Sydney and the rookie were dancing to ended and he walked her to the bar to buy her a drink.

"Yeah, but the mayor is up to something," Daniel said. "I can feel it." And he wasn't going to leave her to fend for herself. She was still too vulnerable.

"So you're going to protect her?" Jon asked.

"That's what I do," Daniel said with a shrug. "Protect and serve."

"Don't you mean protect and *service?*" Sammi said, and the men laughed.

"Like I said, she's just a friend." But if she wasn't a single mom, wasn't his neighbor, wasn't his *friend,* he would seduce her in a heartbeat. He didn't think it would be difficult.

"So you wouldn't mind if I asked her out?" Jon said.

Daniel shrugged. "Nope."

"Aren't you a little young for her?" Sammi asked.

"She doesn't strike me as the cougar type." Jon gave her playful shove.

"So what do you think the mayor will do?" Jon asked.

"I'm not sure." But they didn't have to wait long to find out. The mayor's girlfriend excused herself to the ladies' room, and the second she was out of sight Harris was crossing the brewery, weaving through the crowd, heading for Sydney, who stood at the bar talking with one of the deputies' wives. Luckily Daniel was closer and reached her first.

"Let's dance," he said, linking an arm through hers.

She out let a surprised, "Oh!" as he half walked half dragged her to an open spot on the edge of the dance floor. A slower song was playing, so he tugged her close, and the way Sydney fell against him, unsteady on her spike heels, said the alcohol was going to her head. And instead of tensing the way she usually did when he touched her, she actually relaxed against him.

"Thank you for forcing me to come with you tonight," she said, smiling up at him. "I can't remember the last time I had so much fun."

Man, she had a sexy mouth. And he was seriously considering kissing her—just to see if she would let him—when he glanced past her and realized they were about to have company.

"Bogie at twelve o'clock," he said, nodding in the mayor's direction.

Sydney turned to look, cursing under her breath. But

then she gave her head a shake and said, "You know, to hell with him. I'm having too much fun to care."

"Sydney," the mayor hissed, stopping beside her and Daniel. "A word."

"No," Sydney said, sliding her arms up and around Daniel's neck.

The mayor's brow rose. *"Excuse me?"*

"She said no," Daniel told him.

Harris shot daggers with his eyes. "When you address me, *Deputy,* you address me as sir."

When hell froze over, maybe.

"What are you doing here, Sydney?" the mayor demanded.

"What does it look like I'm doing? Hanging out with friends."

"You don't have any friends." And it was clear he took a great deal of satisfaction in that assumption.

"You keep telling yourself that," Sydney said, leaning even closer into Daniel, until her breasts were nestled firmly against his chest.

Harris's eyes narrowed and he said, "Are you *drunk?*"

"Why do you sound so surprised? You're the one telling everybody what a lush I am. I'm just living up to my reputation." She looked up at Daniel and said, "Do you know the only times I ever drank while we were married? It was when Jeff wanted sex, and getting tipsy was the only way I could stand to have him touch me—"

"That's enough!" Harris thundered, grabbing Sydney's

arm and yanking hard. If Daniel hadn't been holding on to her she probably would have tumbled over.

Daniel was two seconds from decking the son of a bitch, when Harris's girlfriend appeared at his side, looking like a wounded doe, and said, "Jeffy, what are you doing?"

At that point people had stopped dancing and were watching, and maybe Harris realized that he'd just come off as the jealous ex-husband who was still pining for his wife, because he dropped Sydney's arm so swiftly she fell back into Daniel.

He gave Sydney one last furious glare and then stormed off, his girlfriend scurrying after him.

"Did he hurt you?" Daniel said, examining her arm.

"I'm okay," she said, looking a little rattled. "I guess I hit a nerve, huh?"

"You realize he just assaulted you. You should file a police report. You have a bar full of people who will corroborate." If Sydney had done the same to Harris, Daniel didn't doubt she would be cuffed by now. The bastard deserved a taste of his own medicine. He deserved to be humiliated.

"It's not worth it." She slid her arms back around his neck, pressed the length of her body against his. He realized that watching her stand up for herself had made him hot as hell.

He eased her into his arms, forcing himself to keep his hands north of her waist. When what he really wanted to do was cup her behind and grind himself against her.

Nope, not gonna happen. She was drunk, and he knew better. Fooling around with a woman who couldn't consent was a line even he wouldn't cross.

She gazed up at him with heavy-lidded eyes, a smile on her full, glossy mouth.

God, he wanted to kiss her.

"Is he watching?" she asked.

Daniel skimmed the crowd and saw Harris standing by the bar, eyes on Sydney, looking ready to spit nails. "He's watching. And he's pissed. You made an ass out of him."

"No, he did that to himself."

Good point.

She grinned up at him and said, "You want to give him something to be really pissed about?"

"What did you have in mind?"

She pulled his head down and brushed her lips across his.

Oh, man.

It was far from passionate, yet suddenly his pulse was racing. He'd kissed a lot of women, but he couldn't recall ever *feeling* it like this.

Sydney's eyes fluttered open and she gazed up at him, lips parted in surprise. Whatever it was he'd felt, apparently so had she.

Time seemed to stand still, the air between them so thick it was damn near impossible to draw in a full breath. Then she curled her fingers into the hair at the nape of his neck, her nails raking over his skin, and he almost groaned. Before he knew what he was doing, his lips slanted over hers and he captured her mouth. With not only her ex, but most of Daniel's friends watching, after he'd been so adamant about not dating Sydney.

Wrong, wrong, wrong. This was so wrong. He needed to stop this before it went any further. Before he couldn't stop.

He broke the kiss and pressed his forehead to hers. They were both breathing hard.

She gazed up at him, eyes glazed. "You want to get out of here?"

Shit.

Don't do it, Daniel. This is a bad idea.

But before he could stop himself, he was leading her to the door, walking so fast she could barely keep up with his longer strides. The only thing he could think about was getting her home and naked. He wouldn't allow himself to consider anything else. Like the inevitable consequences.

When they got to his truck he helped her in and then walked around. He'd scarcely made it into his seat before she was in his lap, straddling him, her lips crushed against his. He'd never been with a woman who kissed more passionately. Who tasted so sweet. She wound her arms around his neck, grinding her lower body against him. God, she was hot. But not only was this bordering on indecent, it was a logistical nightmare. There was a good reason he hadn't had sex in a car since he was a teenager.

"Not here," he said, lifting her from his lap and depositing her on the seat beside him. "Buckle up."

She snapped her seat belt in place. "Drive *fast*."

He drove the speed limit.

"Is what you told your ex true, or were you just trying to piss him off?" Daniel asked. "Did you really have to drink to be able to stand him touching you?"

"It's true."

He tried to imagine being with someone who physically repulsed him, and couldn't even fathom it. "If it was that bad, if you were so unhappy, why did you stay?"

"For Lacey. I didn't want her to grow up in a broken home."

So she had sacrificed her own happiness for her daughter's. "And how did that work out for you?"

Sydney let her head fall against the seat and sighed. "It was a disaster. I should have left him years ago."

He was probably asking too many questions, but he couldn't help himself. "Has there been anyone since him?"

She shook her head.

"So you haven't enjoyed sex in how long?"

"Well, even in the beginning it wasn't great. It wasn't awful, either. He was just always a...selfish lover, I guess. More concerned with his own pleasure than mine. So the last time I had really fantastic sex was probably... seventeen years ago."

That was just *wrong,* but it didn't surprise him. For Daniel, giving a woman pleasure was what turned him on, what fed his own pleasure. And Sydney was long overdue.

He stopped at a red light on the edge of town, reached over and hooked a hand behind Sydney's neck, leaned in and kissed her, quick and deep.

They lived only a few miles off the downtown strip, so it didn't take long to get there. And this time she didn't wait for him to open her door. She hopped out and landed unsteadily on the concrete driveway. Daniel told himself that it had more to do with her heels than her level of intoxication.

"My place," Sydney declared. "Lacey is sleeping at a friend's house. I want to be here if she calls."

A reminder of why he avoided single moms. Too much baggage. Tonight he would make an exception.

But what about tomorrow?

He shook away the thought and followed Sydney to her back door. She fumbled with her keys under the dim porch light, then dropped them when she tried to get the key in the lock.

Not drunk, just clumsy.

He grabbed the keys, found the right one and opened the door. They'd barely made it inside and her arms were around his neck, her lips locked on his. She started to drag him backward toward her bedroom, clawing his T-shirt free from the waist of his jeans. She stumbled and he had to catch her or she would have landed on her behind. She wasn't just a little tipsy. She was hammered.

He cursed silently. As much as she *seemed* to want him, her judgment was impaired.

He couldn't do this.

They got to her bedroom and she dragged him inside, shoving the door closed behind them. Because that's what moms did. They closed doors so kids didn't see things they shouldn't. Like their vulnerable mother getting it on with the bachelor next door.

Shit.

He *really* couldn't do this.

He took her by the arms, unwound them from around his neck. "Sydney, stop."

She looked up at him, brow wrinkled with confusion. "What's wrong?"

"We can't do this."

"What? *Why?*"

"Because you're drunk."

"So what?"

"You aren't thinking clearly. And there are at least a *dozen* other reasons this is a bad idea."

"But...I *want* to."

"I do, too, more than you will ever know. But I can't. I'm sorry."

Sydney looked absolutely crestfallen. And he cringed when, in the moonlight shining through her bedroom window, he could see the sheen of tears in her eyes. "But..."

"Take a second to consider what you're doing."

She looked up at him, then glanced around the room, as if she was wasn't quite sure how she had arrived there. Then the reality of what she had been about to do seemed to hit home.

"You're right," she said softly. "This would have been a mistake."

She lost her balance and had to sit on the edge of the mattress. "I guess I did have a lot to drink," she said, and it seemed to take extra concentration to form the words clearly. "I'm feeling a little woozy."

"Why don't you lie down."

She complied without question, crawling up the mattress to lay her head on the pillow.

"You want help with your boots?"

She nodded.

He gently tugged them off and set them by the closet where she wouldn't trip over them. "Anything else?" he asked, hoping she wouldn't ask him to help take her clothes off. Even he had limits. But she shook her head.

"I'm tired," she said, her eyes drifting closed.

Not ready to leave her just yet, he sat on the edge of the mattress beside her, smoothing back the loose tendrils of hair framing her face. She made a soft, contented sound.

"Thank you for taking me out tonight," she said drowsily. "I really did have a good time."

"We'll do it again."

"I'd like that."

He kept stroking her hair until she fell asleep, then he let himself out of her house, locking the door behind him, and went home. He walked in and switched on the light beside the couch. It was so quiet.

All he'd thought about for a month was getting a moment to himself, but now that he'd gotten it, he felt awfully...*alone*.

OH. MY. GOD. Her mom was doing it with the cop next door!

Lacey sat on her bed, unable to believe what she'd

heard last night, and listening for signs that her mom was waking up. For all she knew, *he* could still be in there. Last night, when she'd heard them come into the house and go straight to her mom's bedroom, Lacey had put her headphones on and blared her music. Whatever they were doing in there, she didn't want to hear it. And probably the only reason she'd heard *anything* was that her mom thought she was still at Veronica's house.

Lacey didn't know if she should be shocked or happy for her or totally grossed out. Moms were not supposed to have flings with next-door neighbors. At least not *her* mom. She'd never done a spontaneous thing in her life! Of course, if she was going to do it with anyone, why not a man as hot as Deputy Valenzia?

She thought of her father's little bimbo, who had the brain capacity of a fruit fly, and actually felt proud of her mom for picking someone like Deputy Valenzia. Maybe she deserved to have some fun after all the crap Lacey's father put her through. It was a bit gross and very weird. But maybe women her mom's age had needs just like men did, and it had probably been a really long time since her mom had sex.

Well, not anymore.

She wondered if this meant she would have a cop for a stepdad.

The phone rang and Lacey dug for the extension under a pile of clothes on her bedroom floor. "'Lo."

"Hi, angel, it's Daddy."

Lacey rolled her eyes. She hated it when he used the word *daddy,* as if she was still five. Like it would make her hate him any less. And she wasn't anyone's *angel*. "What's up?"

"Something came up and I won't be able to have you over today."

Boo hoo. Well, Lacey hadn't wanted to see him anyway. And she was sure that the "something" was the bimbo.

"Since you're out of school later this week, I thought I could come and pick you up Thursday and we'll spend the afternoon together. I'll take you shopping."

Wasn't that typical of her father, always trying to buy her off. Well, she didn't want anything from him.

"I can't," she said. "I'm going job hunting. I want to help Mom since her new job probably doesn't pay as much."

"What new job?"

No thanks to you, Lacey thought bitterly. "She's working for our next-door neighbor. Deputy Valenzia. She's his nanny."

"Since when?"

"She starts Monday."

There was a long pause, then he said, "Let me talk to her." His voice sounded funny, like he was really angry. Was it possible that he was mad that her mom was working again? Lacey knew he was the one who got her fired from her old job.

A sly smile curled her mouth. It was payback time. "You can't talk to her now, she's still in bed."

"It's after eleven!" he said, sounding appalled. "Wake her up."

No way. "I can't."

"Why?"

"Because she has…company."

"*Company?* Who?"

"Who is that on the phone?"

Lacey spun around to see her mother standing in the bedroom doorway in her robe, hair rumpled, last night's mascara smeared under her eyes.

"Is that your mother?" her dad barked. "Put her on *immediately.*"

"It's Dad," she said, holding out the phone. "He, uh, wants to talk to you."

Her mom rolled her eyes and took the phone. "What do you want, Jeff?"

Lacey could hear her dad shouting through the phone, and wondered if maybe this hadn't been such a hot idea after all.

Her mom's mouth fixed into a thin line, then she flashed Lacey a stern look. "She said I was doing *what?*"

Yeah, definitely a bad idea. Her mom looked pissed.

"Ice Queen? Yeah, sure, I'll pass on the information."

Lacey cringed. She'd heard her dad call her mom the Ice Queen more than a few times, and accuse her of being closed off emotionally. Her mom might not have been the most affectionate person in the world, but being married to Lacey's creep of a father, who would be? Lacey couldn't even remember the last time she saw her parents kiss, or even hug each other. In fact, she didn't know if she'd *ever* seen them do that.

"Frankly, Jeff, whether I am or not is none of your

damned business." There was more yelling and some distinct swearing, then her mom laughed. "Bad influence? Are you kidding me? This coming from Mr. I'm-cheating-on-my-wife-with-my-twenty-two-year-old-assistant?"

Whoa! Her mom really must have been mad to blurt that out. Lacey knew about her dad's affair with the bimbo—and the ones before that—but her mom had never said a word about it in front of her.

There was another pause, then she said, "And explain to me exactly *how* this is different?"

Apparently her dad had every intention of doing just that, because Lacey heard more swearing and yelling. Then her mom did something she'd never done before. Right in the middle of his rant, she slammed down the phone.

"The man's ego knows no bounds," she grumbled, rubbing her temples as if she had a headache. Of course, listening to Lacey's dad shout would give anyone a headache.

The phone started ringing again almost immediately. "Do not answer that," her mom warned.

The machine picked up on the fourth ring and Lacey could hear her dad shouting from the other room. Her mom turned to her, and Lacey waited for the explosion.

Instead, she said calmly, "Why did you tell your father I'm having an affair with Daniel?"

"That's not what I said."

"No, but you implied it."

"Well, you are, aren't you?" Lacey said defensively. "Why not tell Dad?"

Her mom sat on the edge of her bed beside her, shoving a pile of unfolded laundry to make room. "First off, no, I am *not* having an affair with Daniel. And even if I was, that would be my private business."

Lacey wasn't used to talking about this kind of stuff with her mom. Usually she would just say something snotty and walk away. But for some reason, she knew it would be wrong to do that this time. She'd been a real pain lately and her mom had been putting up with it for the most part, but Lacey could tell her patience was wearing thin.

"I heard you guys come in last night. I'm not stupid. I know something was going on in there."

"I thought you were staying at Veronica's."

"I had a headache, so I came home." She twisted the ring on her thumb. "It's okay. I was kind of grossed out at first, but I'm not upset or anything. I think you *should* start dating."

Her mom sighed. "What you heard last night was Daniel helping me in because I had too much to drink. Then he left."

"Oh."

"I appreciate that you're okay with me dating, honey, but if I do, it won't be our next-door neighbor. Or a man I'm working for."

"He's really hot."

She sighed. "Yeah, he is. I'm just not ready to date anyone yet."

Her mom slipped an arm around her and Lacey rested

her head against her shoulder, like she had when she was little. It was nice. Sometimes she wished she was little again. Things had been so much easier then. Her parents hadn't hated each other as much. And her mom hadn't been so sad all the time. Maybe if she started dating she'd be happy again.

"From now on, let's keep my personal business personal, okay?"

Lacey nodded. "Sorry."

"You should get ready. Your dad will be here soon."

"No, he won't. He canceled again."

Her mom squeezed her shoulder. "Oh, honey, I'm sorry."

"I'm not. I didn't want to see him anyway. I hate him."

"He's made lots of mistakes, but he's still your father. He deserves your respect."

"You always told me that to earn respect you have to give it. Well, he doesn't respect *me*. All he does is make fun of the way I look."

"He's just…"

"An opinionated, egotistical jackass?"

Her mom tried to hide a smile. "But he's here."

She knew her mom was referring to her own dad, who took off when her mom was only thirteen. Lacey had never even met her grandparents. Her grandma supposedly had mental issues, and her mom hadn't seen her since she left Michigan. Lacey couldn't imagine going that long without seeing her parents. Even if her dad was a tool.

"I have an idea," her mom said. "Since neither of us has plans, why don't we go to the lake? The water will still be a bit cold, but we can work on our tans. We could pack a picnic lunch."

Normally Lacey would consider going to the lake with her mom pretty lame, but she had the feeling her mom needed the company. "Sure. That sounds like fun."

"You could invite Veronica if you'd like."

Lacey shrugged. "That's okay. It can just be us this time."

"By the way, I'm sorry I said that about your father. About him cheating."

"It's not like I didn't already know, Mom. Everyone knew."

"I know."

"And just so you know, if you change your mind and want to date Deputy Valenzia—want to date anyone—it's really okay with me. I want you to be happy."

"Thanks, honey. I love you."

For some stupid reason, tears brimmed in Lacey's eyes. "I love you, too, Mom."

CHAPTER SEVEN

SYDNEY WISHED she was one of those lucky people who blacked out after drinking too much. Because then she wouldn't remember, in precise detail, the way she'd thrown herself at Daniel last night.

What the hell had she been thinking?

Simple, she hadn't been. She'd had so much fun, and so much to drink, she obviously hadn't been thinking straight. For the first time in…well, she couldn't even remember how long, she'd felt *alive*. And attractive. And when she'd kissed Daniel it had honestly only been to make Jeff mad, which, she now realized—now that she was sober—had been incredibly childish. But once she'd started kissing him, she didn't want to stop. And obviously, neither did he. She was just relieved he'd had the good sense to apply the brakes before they went too far.

And what had possessed her to bring him home? The fact that Lacey had heard anything filled her with shame. As if the kid wasn't confused enough already. If she and Daniel were in a committed relationship, that might be different. But Lacey needed stability in her life, and she wouldn't get that thinking her mom was having one-night stands with men she hardly knew.

Sydney glanced over at her daughter in the passenger

seat, her headphones on, eyes closed, her nose pink from the sun. She'd been stunned when Lacey agreed to go to the lake, and even more surprised when she hadn't insisted on bringing a friend. And though Sydney had pretty much spent the entire afternoon sleeping off a killer hangover, it had been nice to spend the day together, just the two of them. They didn't do that nearly often enough anymore.

Jeff had called while they were at the lake to say that he'd rearranged his schedule and he would be picking Lacey up in half an hour, and he'd been furious when Sydney told him it was too late. What the hell did he expect, that after he had repeatedly canceled their plans, Lacey would drop everything on a moment's notice to see him? That she would sit around waiting for him to acknowledge her?

Sydney had sworn to herself the day Lacey was born that she would always be there for her daughter, would always protect and support her. She never wanted Lacey to know what it was like to feel abandoned or ignored. Though now she wondered if everyone would have been happier if she had never married Jeff. Not only had it done Lacey no good to see her parents so unhappy, but Sydney had wasted years of her life with a man she didn't love.

But it wasn't too late to start over. Until last night at the bar she had forgotten what it was like to feel attractive, to feel *wanted*. And knowing that Lacey was okay with it made Sydney wonder if it was finally time to put herself out there. To consider a relationship with a man.

Any man but Daniel, that is.

Speaking of Daniel, Sydney thought, she was going to have to stop at his place and apologize for last night. For the way she threw herself at him. Not that he'd seemed to mind, not at first anyway.

As if she wasn't uncomfortable enough around him. Now every time she looked at him, she was going to remember how it felt to be pressed against him, the taste of his lips, the spicy scent of his skin. And she would always wonder what it would have been like if he hadn't said no.

When they pulled into the driveway, the sun was just beginning to set, and as soon as the van stopped Lacey opened her eyes.

"Home already?" she said, yawning.

Sydney handed her the keys. "Unlock the door. I'll get the stuff from the back."

She got out and walked around to the rear of the van, but before she could grab the beach bag, Lacey called to her.

"Mom, did you forget to shut the back door when we left?"

She circled around to find Lacey standing by the back door, looking worried. "No, why?"

Lacey pointed. "It's not closed anymore."

She was right; the door was standing ajar. Had Sydney forgotten to pull it shut? She'd had her arms full when she'd left. Was it possible that she just hadn't pulled hard enough? It did tend to stick.

Lacey reached for the knob and Sydney said, "Wait!"

It certainly wasn't worth taking a chance. If someone had broken in, they could still be there.

"Come with me," she said, waving Lacey over.

"Where?"

"Next door."

Amazingly, Lacey didn't argue.

They crossed the yard to Daniel's house and Sydney knocked on the front door. He opened it, April on his hip, looking surprised to see them there. And her worry must have shown, because immediately he frowned and asked, "What's wrong?"

"We just got back from a day at the lake and the back door is open. I *think* I closed it when we left, but I thought, just in case…"

"You did the right thing." Daniel held the door open. "Come in."

As soon as they were inside he handed April to her. Without a word, he disappeared into his bedroom and emerged a second later holding a gun. Lacey's eyes went wide, and Sydney's heart stalled.

"Stay here with the baby," he said.

"What are you going to do?" Sydney asked.

"Make sure no one is in your house."

"Shouldn't we call the police?"

He looked at her funny. "I *am* the police."

"I know, but shouldn't you call for backup or something?"

"Don't worry, okay? Just stay here with April."

He stepped outside and Sydney watched out the front window as he crossed the yard to her house, gun at his side, until the van blocked her view.

"She's cute," Lacey said, gesturing to April. "Can I hold her?"

"Sure, honey." She handed April over. The baby tangled her fingers in Lacey's hair.

Sydney turned to keep looking for Daniel. She hoped that if someone had been in her house, they were gone now. Or maybe she just hadn't shut the door all the way. Maybe she was making a big deal out of nothing.

"I've never seen a gun that close before," Lacey said, sounding a bit awestruck.

"Me, neither, honey."

"It was weird."

Actually, it was kind of…sexy. If she could set aside the worry that Daniel might be in danger. Maybe she should have just called 911 instead of dragging him into this.

Sydney paced anxiously by the window. Nearly fifteen minutes passed before he reappeared, the gun tucked into the waist of his jeans.

She met him at the front door. "Well?"

"No sign of forced entry or an intruder."

"So I overreacted and bothered you for nothing."

"It's better to be safe than sorry."

She still felt stupid. She'd just been so paranoid since the "Fred" incident.

"Can I go in the house now?" Lacey asked.

"Sure, honey." She took April from her. After Lacey was gone, she told Daniel, "I'm really sorry about this."

"Don't be."

"I feel like I'm taking advantage of you. Just because

you're a cop, it doesn't mean I have the right to come running to you whenever I have a problem."

"It's okay, Sydney. I honestly don't mind."

In her experience, that was the kind of thing people said, but didn't actually mean, but he seemed sincere. He was so *nice* to her. She wasn't used to that. With Jeff everything had been about what *he* needed or wanted.

She couldn't help but feel she should be waiting for the other shoe to fall. For Daniel to show his true colors. After all, she'd known him less than a week. The guy was bound to have flaws. Jeff had seemed nice at first, too.

Or maybe she should consider the possibility that Daniel was exactly who he appeared to be.

She handed April to him and said, "I should get home."

"I was just about to put her down for the night then I thought I'd sit on the porch and have a beer. Care to join me?"

She really should get home. After last night, maybe it wasn't such a good idea to be alone with him.

"I should get home," she repeated.

"You have plans?"

"No, but…"

"So you would rather sit home alone than have a beer with me?"

No, she would much rather be with him, and maybe that was the problem. But she didn't want to hurt his feelings, or seem ungrateful for his help.

"A beer sounds good. Although, we might be more comfortable on my deck. I have a patio set and citronella torches for mosquitoes. You can bring the baby monitor so you could hear April."

"Sounds much more luxurious than my porch. I'll put her to bed then meet you out back."

At least at her own house Lacey would be there, eliminating the opportunity for hanky-panky. Never in her life had she entertained the idea that her teenage daughter would be her chaperone.

While Daniel got April settled, Sydney crossed the lawn to her house. She decided to leave their beach gear in the van for now, and went to her bedroom to change, since she was still wearing her bikini under her shorts and tank. She considered taking a quick shower to wash away the sunblock and beach grime, but she didn't want to keep Daniel waiting. It wasn't as if he would be getting close enough to tell, anyway.

She changed into a soft cotton sundress, readjusted her ponytail and smoothed on some lip gloss.

Not great, she thought, checking her reflection, but passable.

She stopped by Lacey's room to tell her she would be in the yard, and found her sound asleep in bed. Lying in the sun all day must have wore her out. Not to mention that she may not have slept well, thinking her mom was in the next room with the neighbor.

She closed Lacey's door behind her. So much for a chaperone.

It was already dark as she went out to the deck. Daniel was already there, leaning against the railing, holding two beers. He'd lit the torches and they shed dim light across his profile. He was looking out over her yard, and when he heard her he turned and smiled. "I thought maybe you changed your mind."

"Sorry, I had to change."

He twisted the tops off both beers and handed one to her. She took a long swallow and leaned on the railing beside him. The night was clear and the moon hung full and unusually bright in the eastern sky. "Pretty night."

"Yeah. Glad I'm not on duty, though."

"Why?"

"Full moon. Brings all the nuts out."

She couldn't tell if he was serious or teasing her. "I thought that was an old wives' tale."

"Nope. People really do act weird during a full moon."

Maybe that explained her behavior last night. The moon made her do it.

"So, should we set a limit for you?" he asked. "Now that I know what happens when you drink too much."

Suddenly Sydney's cheeks were on fire. She'd been hoping they could just forget about last night. She should have known Daniel wouldn't let her off that easy. He had an aggravating habit of liking to talk about things, and a predilection toward brutal honesty.

Her philosophy was far less complicated. Why talk when it was so much easier to sweep issues under the rug?

But she could feel his gaze boring through her. She picked at the label on her beer, so she wouldn't have to look at him. "I'm *really* sorry about that."

"If you'll recall, I wasn't complaining."

"No, but it was wrong to throw myself at you. And in front of all your friends. I can't even imagine what they must think."

He took a swig of his beer. "That I'm a lucky guy."

"They think we're…?"

"Wouldn't you?"

She cringed. "I'm sorry."

"I think Jon wanted to ask you out."

"Deputy Montgomery? Seriously?"

He nodded. "He thought you were hot."

"What is he, twelve?"

"Mid-twenties, I think."

She swallowed a mouthful of beer. "I guess I should probably thank you."

"For…?"

She kept her eyes on her bottle. "Stopping things before they went too far. Not taking advantage of me. I'm not normally that…aggressive. It's just, well, it's been a long time. Since I've…you know…"

"Had sex?"

She nodded, her cheeks on fire again. He was probably used to talking about this sort of thing. He oozed sexuality from every pore, and she was the ice queen. But the things he could probably do to make her melt…

"Had I been sober, that never would have happened," she said.

"Are you saying that you weren't turned on by me specifically? I was just…convenient?"

She could tell by his grin that he was teasing her again, and she couldn't resist playing along. "Pretty much."

His grin turned sly, and his eyes smoldered like hot coals.

Uh-oh.

"Are you sure about that?" he asked, setting his beer on the railing and sliding closer.

Oh, no, what had she done? "P-pretty sure."

"So if I did this…" He took her beer from her and set it next to his, then he held her hand in his much larger one, palm up, and with his other hand, gently traced a finger down the center of her palm.

Oh, dear God.

This time her flush had nothing to do with embarrassment.

"Anything?" he asked.

"Nothing," she lied, hoping he didn't hear the waver in her voice, and also hoping he *did*. Whatever it took to keep him doing exactly what he was doing. Because as petrified as she felt, and as wrong as this was, she *liked* it. She liked his teasing grin and the heat in his eyes. She wanted to touch him, feel his hard muscle, run her fingers through his hair. But what if he was only playing with her? What if he didn't really want her?

She felt paralyzed by indecision.

"So why is your heart pounding?" He reached up and caressed the pulse point at the base of her throat, which only made it beat faster. She tried to think of some clever comeback, but her mind had gone blank.

"No comment?" he asked.

She opened her mouth to say something, anything, but then he stroked her throat with the backs of his fingers and a sigh slipped out instead. His eyes locked on hers and she went limp all over.

"You don't have the slightest clue how beautiful you are, do you?" he asked. "What did he do to make you so unsure of yourself?"

It was what he hadn't done.

Sure, at first Jeff had been amazing. He'd showered her with gifts and affection. He'd made her feel that she was the most important thing in his entire world. But it hadn't lasted. She wanted to believe that Daniel would be different, but experience had taught her otherwise.

"You're going to make me prove it, aren't you?" he asked, but the heat in his eyes told her he didn't mind in the least.

Oh, please do, she thought, even though she was terrified. But Daniel was leaning in to kiss her, and she could feel herself being drawn closer, like a moth to a flame.

His lips hardly brushed hers, teasingly, and before she knew what she was doing her arms were around his neck, pulling him down.

It had to be the full moon, she rationalized, but then he deepened the kiss, and she stopped thinking altogether. She could only feel. The sensual rhythm of his tongue, the strength of his arms as they pressed her against his body, his beard stubble scratching her chin. Good Lord, did the man know how to kiss.

His hands slid slowly down her back to cup her behind, and when he held her tightly, there was no doubt that he wanted her just as much as she wanted him.

But was it really Daniel she wanted, or the idea of

Daniel? Someone who would treat her well, be nice to her. Maybe she wasn't ready to be with *anyone* yet. Especially when she knew this was an impossible, dead-end relationship.

What was she *doing?*

She broke the kiss and pushed gently at his chest.

"We need to stop doing that," she said.

"Why?"

"Because I don't date cops, and you don't date single moms."

"Who said anything about dating?" he asked with a wicked grin.

"Daniel, I'm serious."

"So am I."

She shot him a look, and when he realized she meant it, he sobered. "Why?"

She untangled herself from his arms and backed away. "Because I can't do this. Not with you."

"You can't tell me you're not attracted to me."

"That doesn't mean it's a good idea. When it comes to relationships, we want very different things."

"You want a commitment?"

Yes, and it was obvious by the edge to his tone, he didn't. "I wasted fifteen years in a lousy relationship. I have a chance to start over now, and this time I refuse to compromise." She took his hand. "The past few days have been great. You've been a wonderful friend. I don't want to lose that."

He squeezed her hand. "You won't. And I didn't mean to pressure you into anything."

"How could you have known, with all the mixed

signals I've been sending out? Maybe *I* didn't even know."

"But you do now."

And it was because of him. He forced her to take a good hard look at her life. The way she had been wasting it. She'd been happier this past week, felt more like *herself,* than she had in years.

"Well, the message is clear this time," he told her. "From now on, we'll just be friends."

He actually sounded disappointed, which made her feel good and rotten at the same time. What woman didn't enjoy being wanted? And she wanted him, more than she had ever wanted a man before. She knew that sex with Daniel would be nothing short of thrilling.

But she wasn't in it for the sex. At least, not entirely. She wanted someone kind and gentle and responsible. And safe. A man who was interested in going the long haul, and maybe having another baby. She wanted a real relationship.

Daniel wanted none of those things.

"This isn't the beer talking, is it?" he asked.

"Not this time." Maybe the beer made it easier to say the words, but the feelings were genuine.

So why did she feel so darned unsure of herself?

CHAPTER EIGHT

LACEY WAS crazy nervous.

She stood outside the door of AAA Landscape, the company Daniel's sister Angie owned, wondering if she was wasting her time. According to her mom, Angie was looking to hire a few high school kids for the summer. But would she be willing to take on someone with zero job experience? She would just have to hope that Angie took pity on her and gave her a chance. Her only other option was a summer job at the resort, which would mean having to rely on her mom for rides, or at a fast-food restaurant, which would totally suck.

But she couldn't get any job if she didn't at least try. She pulled open the door and stepped inside. She figured she'd find an entire staff, but there was only one woman sitting at a desk doing something on a computer.

At the sound of the door opening, the woman looked up and Lacey knew she had to be Daniel's sister. She was dark like Daniel and really pretty. She had long, glossy black hair pulled back in a ponytail that hung halfway down her back.

She smiled. "Hi, there, can I help you?"

"Hi," Lacey said. "My mom is Sydney, your brother's nanny, and she said that you said you were hiring."

"You're Lacey!" she said, rising to shake her hand.

Her grip was so firm it actually hurt a bit. "Your mom said she would send you by. I thought maybe she forgot, or you found a job somewhere else."

"Well, school just let out yesterday, and before that I had finals to study for."

"Right! Of course. Your mom did mention that." She shook her head and laughed. "I'd forget my head if it wasn't attached. Come on in and grab a seat. I'll get you an application."

Lacey sat down while Angie rifled through a file cabinet. She seemed a little flighty, but super nice. She found what she was looking for and shoved the drawer closed with her hip. She handed the application to Lacey and gave her a pen.

"I don't have much experience," Lacey said, toying with the ring in her brow—the stupid thing still hurt like hell. "Just some babysitting. Is that okay?"

"Sure." Angie propped her feet up on the desk. "We all have to start somewhere. Don't even worry about that part. I just need your personal info and your social security number."

Did that mean Angie was actually considering hiring her?

As Lacey was filling out the form, the door opened behind her, and a deep voice said, "Hey, Mom, we're leaving to do the strip mall."

Lacey turned, her eyes traveling way, way, *way* up to the face of the guy standing behind her, and for a second she could swear her heart actually stopped beating. This was Angie's *kid?* Her mom had mentioned that Angie had a seventeen-year-old son, but for some reason, Lacey had pictured a scrawny, nerdy kid. There was nothing nerdy about this guy.

He was *totally smoking hot.*

"Jordan, this is Lacey," Angie said. "Her mom is April's nanny."

"Hey," he said, barely even glancing at her. He looked a lot like his mom. And Daniel, too, and he was just as big. Definitely a jock. And though she didn't usually go for the athletic type, she would make an exception. If she didn't already have a boyfriend, that is.

Jordan took off his baseball cap and swabbed his sweaty forehead with the hem of his T-shirt, exposing a totally ripped and tanned stomach.

Shane? Shane who?

Lacey realized that she was practically drooling and forced herself to look away.

"I got a call from the Petersons," Angie told Jordan. "They're throwing an engagement party for their son and they want to totally revamp their yard by next week."

"Seriously?" Jordan said, sounding exasperated.

"Yeah, and they're paying handsomely, so try to see how many people you can talk into working overtime. Tell them they'll get time and a half."

"I'll see what I can do." He turned, his heavy work boots thudding on the linoleum floor, and Lacey resisted the urge to check out his ass. She doubted it would be anything but perfect.

"How are you doing with that application?" Angie asked.

"Um, done, I think."

Angie took the application and scanned it quickly. "Ever plant flowers or shrubs, do any landscaping?"

"I've helped my mom with the garden and she makes me cut the lawn."

"You free this week, starting tomorrow?"

She nodded. "Sure."

"Awesome! I'll have Jordan pick you up on his way to the Petersons in the morning."

"Does that mean I'm hired?"

Angie laughed. "Of course you're hired. The job starts at minimum wage."

"Okay." Minimum wage was better than no wage.

"Do you own a pair of work boots?"

"I have hiking boots."

"That'll do. And wear jeans. It's supposed to be close to ninety degrees tomorrow so bring lots of water."

"Okay. Cool." Lacey rose from her chair. "I better go. My boyfriend is waiting for me outside."

"Don't forget, 7:00 a.m."

"I won't. Thanks, Angie!"

Out in the parking lot Shane was lying on the hood of his Camaro smoking a cigarette, a pair of sunglasses shading his eyes. As she made her way to the car, she saw a man across the street and immediately recognized him as her dad's creepy handyman. That was weird. She could have sworn she saw him outside the school two days ago when classes let out.

He didn't look her way, or act as if he knew she was there, so she wrote it off as a coincidence.

"It's about time," Shane said as she approached, rolling to his feet. "How long does it take to fill out one stupid application?"

"It's not stupid," she snapped, her excitement instantly overshadowed by a wave of prickly irritation. He still didn't take any of this job stuff seriously. "They hired me. I start tomorrow."

Shane ground his cigarette into the pavement with his running shoe and opened the driver's side door. "What am I supposed to do while you're working?"

Like I care, she thought, getting in the car. He was being such a jerk, maybe she didn't want to see him anymore. Maybe it was time to find a new boyfriend. One who treated her with respect.

One who was tall, dark and *hot.*

Shane started the car and peeled out of the parking lot. Lacey grabbed the edge of the seat to keep from tumbling over.

"I still don't get why you need a job."

"I told you a million times, I want a car."

"So ask your dad to buy you one."

She snapped her seat belt into place as he rounded another sharp turn at excessive speed. "I don't want anything from him. I'll earn it myself."

He shrugged. "Hey, whatever. Just don't expect me to sit around waiting."

"Is that a threat?"

Shane didn't understand. His parents practically trampled over each other to buy him everything he asked for. At first she had thought it was pretty cool dating a guy with the hottest car and money to burn, but he didn't have any ambition.

Not that she was in the market for a marriage-material type of guy. But sometimes she got so bored with Shane she wanted to scream. He treated her as if she didn't have a brain half the time—and seemed to like it that way!

Lacey thought about seeing Jordan in the morning, and got a squishy feeling in her stomach.

"Lacey!"

"Huh?" She turned to Shane.

"I asked if you want to go to your house. It's too hot to be outside."

She shrugged. "Yeah, sure. Whatever."

"Are you dense or something? I called your name three times and you didn't even hear me."

It was amazing how much he sounded like her dad just then. But she didn't care.

"Sorry." She turned her head and looked out the window, unable to suppress a smile. "Just thinking about my new job."

DANIEL PULLED HIS CRUISER into the AAA Landscape lot next to the shiny new BMW parked there. He didn't have to run the plate to know who it belonged to.

He was still holding out the hope that the guy was a passing phase. That Angie had learned her lesson with her ex-husband, Richard. Although Daniel seriously doubted it. He'd spent the better part of his adolescence and his entire adult life keeping his twin out of trouble. Guiding her away from stupid decisions.

Lately it had been a full-time job.

He got out of the cruiser and pushed through the door

into the building. Angie was sitting at her desk and Jason Parkman, her "boyfriend," sat perched on the edge of the desk in golf attire, leering at her bare legs.

Daniel was instantly on alert. Jason was too...*perfect*. His clothes were never wrinkled, his shoes never scuffed, and Daniel often wondered if he cut his prematurely salt-and-pepper hair on a weekly basis because it was always the exact same length. Even worse, the man was perpetually nice—nice to the point of being irritating. And though he never flaunted it, Daniel knew he came from a wealthy family, just like Richard.

Richard had been a nice guy, too, and possessed that same air of casual sophistication. He'd once told Daniel he fell in love with Angie's quirky personality and admired her spunk and free spirit. But he'd had a dark side no one knew about. At least Angie had gotten a pretty fantastic kid out of the deal. And since Jordan only saw his dad a couple of times a year, Daniel had been the only consistent male role model he'd had.

As Daniel came through the door Angie looked up and flashed him a nervous smile. "Hey, Danny."

"Hello, Daniel." Jason slid off the desk, extending a hand to shake. Daniel gripped it firmly.

"Jason," he said, being polite for Angie's sake.

"How is Sydney today?" Angie asked with that teasing look he'd grown accustomed to this past week, since he was getting it from everyone, despite how many times he insisted he and Sydney were just friends.

"You wanted to see me?" he asked his sister.

"That's my cue to leave," Jason said, leaning over to kiss Angie, making Daniel glower behind his sunglasses.

He could have the decency not to do that when Daniel was around.

"Bye, sweetie," she said, watching him leave with a sappy, lovesick expression that made Daniel want to vomit. The man had her completely snowed.

"Bye, Daniel. See you next weekend."

"Don't even say it," Angie said after he was gone.

"I didn't say a word."

"Yeah, but you want to. I just don't get why you don't like Jason. *Everyone* else likes him. Even Abbi, and she hates *all* men!"

Which was why it sucked being the only man left in a family full of gullible women.

"I've been seeing him for six months. When are you going to accept that he and I are serious? I love him."

He would never accept that, because this relationship wasn't going to last. "He said he would see me next weekend. What did he mean?"

Angie took a deep breath and blew it out. "Okay, now I don't want you to get mad—"

Daniel groaned and rolled his eyes. When she started a conversation that way, he knew it would be bad. "What did you do?"

"Just listen," Angie pleaded. "I probably told you that Jason has a house on the coast, off the cove in Stillwater."

"Yes, you've told me."

"Well, he's invited the family to come stay for the weekend."

"The *whole* family?"

"Mom can't come because she has to work, but Beth

and Dee will be there. And Jordan, of course. And I said you would come, too."

"Angie—"

"Danny, *please*. It would mean so much to me. And I know you won't believe it, but it will mean a lot to Jason, too. He loves me, and he knows how unhappy it makes me that you disapprove. He wants to give you a chance to get to know him."

She got up from her chair and grabbed his hands. "Please, Danny? You know you owe me. Big-time."

He hated it when she played the guilt card. She *had* been an enormous help when April had been dumped in his lap. He hadn't had a clue what he needed to buy or what to feed her. Angie had saved his behind. And April's.

"Pretty please," she said. "Do this for me and I swear I'll never ask another favor from you ever again."

Well, they both knew that was crap. But this weekend obviously meant a lot to her. And maybe if he did go, it would be an opportunity to somehow to drive a wedge between her and Jason.

"How long would we be gone? Because if you recall I've taken an awful lot of time off work lately."

"We would drive there Friday evening after work and come back Sunday afternoon."

"When?"

"A week from this Friday." She steepled her hands under her chin. *"Please."*

Daniel cursed under his breath. He knew he was going to regret this… "Fine, I'll go."

She squealed and threw her arms around his neck.

"Thank you so much! You're the best brother in the world!"

"All right, all right," he said, disentangling himself.

"This is going to be so much fun! Dee is going to bring Jake and Beth is bringing Louis."

"So everyone is bringing a date but me?"

Her smile evaporated. "Um, yeah. I guess so. I hadn't really thought about that."

Wonderful. So everyone would pair off and he'd be left with April and Jordan? Sounded like a blast.

"You can bring someone, too."

"Who? I haven't been on a date in over a month. I'm not seeing anyone."

"Hey, why don't you ask Sydney?"

"Sydney and I are *not* dating," he snapped. And it had been hard as hell keeping his hands to himself the past few days. He didn't know why but he found her... fascinating. The way she looked, the way she moved. The scent of her skin. He couldn't stop thinking about touching her. And it was obvious she wanted him, too.

And a commitment.

What was it with women? After suffering through such a rotten marriage, why would she want to do that to herself again?

"Ask her anyway, as a friend. She can bring Lacey. That will give Jordan someone his own age to hang around with. And Sydney can help you with April."

That actually wasn't a bad idea. But would she agree? Maybe if he made it part of the job, and offered to pay her.

"Why aren't you dating her, by the way?" Angie asked. "I've seen the way you look at her."

"How do I look at her?"

"Like she's a nasturtium, and you're a bee looking to do some pollinating."

"Nice," he said, shaking his head, unable to suppress a laugh.

"And you two were going at it pretty hot and heavy on the dance floor Friday night."

"I'm not dating her because she just wants to be friends."

"That's never stopped you before."

"Yeah, well, this is different." He could see Angie was waiting for him to elaborate. "She wants a real relationship."

She gasped. "Oh, horrors! A *real* relationship?"

"I don't want to hurt her."

"Again, that's never stopped you before."

"Sydney is different. I…I like her. She deserves better than someone like me."

"If you like her that much, have you considered the possibility that you might be ready to have a real relationship?" He glared at her, so she shrugged and said, "Or not."

"I'm happy being single. Indefinitely."

"And childless?"

The way she said it made Daniel feel like an ogre, when he was only doing what was best for April. "April will be better off with her real family. With two people to raise her. I can't give her what she needs."

"How's the search going?"

Not well, unfortunately. "The P.I. called yesterday and said that he may have tracked down a cousin of

Reanne's in Utah. But to know for sure, he has to actually go there, and that will cost more than I can afford right now."

"I would think that if Reanne had wanted this cousin to have April, she would have made sure that happened."

"I want to exhaust all possibilities before I resort to adoption."

Angie's tight-lipped silence said she didn't approve. Nor did his mom, or his other sisters. But if they were asked to take in a virtual stranger's baby, he'd bet they'd react the exact same way.

And he wasn't going to rehash his motivations all over again, because Angie wouldn't listen anyway. "I have to go."

"Let me know what Sydney says so I can tell Jason."

She had better hope that Sydney agreed to go, and if she didn't, Daniel was able to find someone else who would. Because he'd be damned if he was going by himself.

"I SAID *stop!*" Lacey shoved Shane as hard as she could and watched him roll off the couch and land with a thud on the den floor. He'd gone too far this time—*way* too far.

He scrambled to his feet. "What's the matter with you?"

She glared at him as she refastened her shorts. "What's the matter with *me?* Are you dense? I asked you to stop about five times."

He looked confused. "Every girl says stop. That doesn't mean she actually *wants* you to stop."

Was he serious? "I actually wanted you to stop!"

"Why?" He was completely mystified. He honestly couldn't believe she didn't want him groping her. "What's the big deal?"

She picked one of his tennis shoes up off the floor and threw it at him, nailing his right arm.

"OW! Lacey!" The other shoe went flying and connected with his left leg. "Lacey, stop it! What is your problem?"

"We are so done," she said.

Disbelief played across his face. "You're *breaking up* with me?"

"I'm breaking up with you."

Shane pulled back his shoulders and puffed out his chest, which wasn't all that impressive considering how skinny he was. It made Lacey think of the way Jordan's tank top strained over all that muscle.

She should want her boyfriend to kiss and touch her, but when Shane did, she just felt…uncomfortable. And the whole time he was kissing her today, she was thinking about Jordan.

"I could name a dozen other girls who would come running if I snapped my fingers," he sneered.

She picked up his shoes and shoved them at him. "Then start snapping."

"You bitch," he snarled, and for a second he looked as if he might hit her. She'd seen her dad look at her mom that way before. He'd never actually hit her, but there were times when she thought he'd probably come close.

So Lacey did what her mom would do. Instead of backing away, she stood her ground, looking Shane right in the eye.

If he'd been considering violence, he changed his mind. He grabbed his shoes and stormed down the hall toward the front door. "You'll regret this."

"I seriously doubt that," she mumbled, following him. When he was out the door she shut it behind him, fell against it, and exhaled. Thank God that was over. Maybe she should have felt bad or guilty for wounding his pride, but all she felt was relieved. For weeks she'd been unhappy with Shane, but she hadn't let herself admit it. Maybe she'd thought that a jerk of a boyfriend was better than no boyfriend at all.

Until she met Jordan. Until his voice sent chills up her arms, and she looked into his deep, dark eyes and felt all tingly inside. Of course, Jordan didn't know she existed, but that was about to change. She would make him notice her.

She was good at that.

Lacey heard the side door open and had this sudden vision of Shane sneaking back in to beg her forgiveness. Then she heard her mom calling her.

"In here," she answered.

Her mom appeared in the living room doorway holding April who was gnawing on a teething ring, drooling all over the place. "I just saw Shane leave and he looked upset. Did you guys have a fight?"

"We broke up." She walked over to her mother and

took April from her. April bounced excitedly, reaching for her hair and yanking it.

"Oh, sweetheart, I'm sorry." Sydney folded Lacey in her arms until they were all bunched up in a three-way hug. Both she and April smelled like soap and baby powder.

"Actually, I'm fine. It was my decision." She backed away and noticed her mother's shirt was drenched. "Jeez, Mom, you're all wet."

"Huh?" Sydney looked down at her shirt. "Oh, I was giving April a bath. It's like trying to wrestle an octopus. I came home to change. Why did you break up with Shane? He seemed nice."

"Let's just say he has hearing problem."

Her mom frowned. "What do you mean?"

"He doesn't listen when I say *no*."

Her brows rose. "Oh. Well, good for you, then."

"Besides, he was pissed about me getting a job and he would have given me a hard time about it."

"You went to see Angie today?" She gestured for Lacey to follow her to the bedroom.

"I filled out an application."

Her mom handed April over then she stripped down to her underwear, tossing the wet clothes into the hamper. "And?"

Lacey sat on the bed with April, who promptly tried to climb out of her arms. "She hired me."

"Oh, honey, congratulations! When do you start?"

"Tomorrow. Early."

"Do you need a ride?"

"They're picking me up."

Sydney nodded, then turned to her closet. She chose a loose-fitting blue sundress and pulled it over her head.

"Why are you wearing that?" Lacey asked.

"Because it's comfortable."

"But you have a really nice figure. You should show it off."

Her mom gave her a look. "This coming from the girl who wears jeans three sizes too big?"

"Because I *don't* have a figure."

"And who am I showing it off for?"

Lacey shrugged. "No one in particular."

"I'm babysitting, not looking for men."

Well, with Daniel around she didn't have to look far. She had to know that he was gorgeous, and even Lacey could see that he liked her. What possible reason could she have *not* to date him? It would be kind of cool to have a cop for a stepdad.

"Just so you know, Daniel's working the afternoon shift tonight so I won't be home until after eleven," her mom said.

She shrugged. "Whatever. I'm probably going to bed early anyway."

"I just didn't want you to worry."

No, she didn't want Lacey to think she was over there playing tonsil hockey. "You know, I really like Daniel. And I can tell he likes you. *A lot.*"

Her mom shot her a stern look. *"Lacey!"*

"What? He *does*."

"We're just friends."

"Do you make out on the dance floor at Moose Winooski's with *all* your friends?"

Her mom's cheeks turned bright pink. "Who told you that?"

So it was true. "This is a small town, Mom. People talk."

"Despite what we did or did not do at Moose Winooski's, Daniel and I are just friends. End of story."

"Well, Veronica said he looks like he would be a good kisser."

"He's a little old for Veronica."

"Ew! Gross, Mom. She didn't say *she* wanted to kiss him. She was just…speaking hypothetically."

Which reminded her, she had to call Veronica and tell her she'd dumped Shane. Veronica would be happy, since she thought Shane was a narcissistic tool.

"I should get going." Her mom took April from her. "You know where I am if you need me."

Lacey got up and followed her to the side door. "Mom?"

Her mom stopped and turned. "Yeah, honey."

"I don't mean to nag about you and Daniel. I just…I want you to be happy. You deserve it."

Her mom smiled. "Thank you, sweetie. And I want you to know how proud I am of you for standing up for yourself with Shane. For not letting him pressure you into something you're not ready for. There will be other guys. Guys who treat you with the respect you deserve."

"I know." In fact, she was hoping she'd met one already.

CHAPTER NINE

SYDNEY STEPPED OUT the side door and started across the lawn, thinking that, for all the grief Lacey gave her sometimes, she was one hell of a sweet kid. Then she saw that Daniel's police cruiser parked in front of his house and sighed.

Not again.

This was the second time he'd been by today. He'd been by twice yesterday, too. In fact, he'd been by the house at least twice *every* day that week. As if he was keeping tabs on her or something. He'd said he trusted her, but now she wasn't so sure.

Monday he'd had been gone only two hours when he came back home, claiming to have forgotten a form he needed to give his boss. She'd believed him, and even bought his excuse when he showed up again later that afternoon to "grab a soda since I was in the neighborhood." Tuesday, he'd supposedly forgotten his wallet when she was almost positive she'd seen him take it with him in the morning. Then he'd stopped by around one "for a bite to eat." But he'd mostly just played with April, and had barely touched the pizza Sydney had reheated for him.

Yesterday morning, he said he'd spilled coffee on his pants and needed to change them, and though there *was* a stain, she suspected he'd done it on purpose to have an excuse. Then, yesterday afternoon, she'd taken April grocery shopping and he had appeared in the parking lot as she was loading the van. He said he happened to be driving by and saw her, but she had the feeling he'd actually followed her there.

Maybe, being a cop, he just naturally mistrusted people. But it was beginning to get on her nerves.

Even so, it didn't stop the warm, wistful feeling she got every time he walked through the door. It didn't stop her from constantly second-guessing herself, and questioning her decision to keep their relationship platonic.

Every one of her instincts was telling her that even though Daniel said he didn't want to settle down, *their* relationship would be different somehow. But she was also sure lots of women had thought that. Right up until the minute he broke their hearts.

What if she fell in love with him and ended up brokenhearted like all the rest?

And what if she didn't? What if she was different? What if he fell in love with her, too?

Was it worth taking a chance? Worth the risk of being hurt?

What she needed was a sign. She needed proof that he was capable of changing.

She opened the front door and stepped into Daniel's house. He stood in the kitchen, cell phone to his ear. She sighed softly, like she did whenever she saw him, imagining what it would be like to wrap her arms around his neck and kiss him hello.

When he saw her he snapped the phone shut and said, "Hey, where were you?"

"Next door. I had to change my clothes. I gave April a bath and she got me all wet."

He walked over and took April from her. "Hey, munchkin!"

April squealed happily as he gave her a big smacking kiss on the cheek. He may not have been ready for the responsibility of a child, but April was sure ready for him. She adored him. It broke Sydney's heart to think of her being shuffled off to strangers. Especially when Daniel was such a good dad. To see them together, no one would guess he was anything but a loving, devoted father.

"I gave her a bath this morning," Daniel said.

"I know, but she had rice cereal for dinner, and by the time we were finished she was wearing most of it."

"How's it going with the solid foods?"

"Good. But it's getting hard feeding her in her bouncy seat. She tries to crawl out. You're going to have to consider getting her a high chair. I'm sure you could find a cheap one at the resale shop in town."

"It's a lot to ask, but if I gave you the cash, do you think you could pick one up for me?"

It wasn't a lot to ask, considering Sydney would be the one who benefited the most.

"Sure. I'll go tomorrow." She moved to the kitchen to wash the dirty dishes and bottles. "What are you doing here?"

"I had a few minutes and I wanted to talk to you."

She tensed. In her experience, when someone said

they wanted to "talk" to her, it was never good news. Maybe he was finally going to tell her why he'd been checking up on her.

"Did I do something wrong?" she asked.

The question seemed to surprise him. "Of course not. Why would you think that?"

She shrugged, scrubbing the inside of a bottle with a soapy brush.

"I need to ask you a favor. And you are under no obligation to say yes."

"What kind of favor?"

"Angie has this boyfriend, Jason—"

"She told me about him. He sounds really nice."

"Yeah, well, he's invited our family to his place on the coast for the weekend. Dee and Beth are both going, and I said I would, too, and I thought maybe I could talk you and Lacey into going with us. I could really use your help with April. I'll pay you, of course."

Sydney rinsed the bottles and set them in the drain board. "Why would you pay me to come when your sisters are going to be there to help you? You said they adore April."

Daniel shifted, looking uneasy. There was definitely something he wasn't telling her.

"Is there another reason you want me to go?" she asked.

He took a deep breath and blew it out. "The thing is, Dee and Beth are both bringing their boyfriends. And Angie will have Jason."

Leaving Daniel the odd man out. A position she was willing to bet he rarely found himself in.

That made much more sense.

"When?"

"A week from tomorrow. We would leave after work and come back Sunday evening. I guess Jason's place is right on the water. And he has a boat."

"It sounds like fun. I'd love to go."

His brows rose. "Seriously?"

"Sure. Lacey and I could use a vacation. And you don't have to pay me."

"Sydney, you have no idea how much I appreciate this. And don't worry about Lacey being bored because my nephew, Jordan, will be there."

"I'm sure she'll have fun. And if you want, we can take my van and car pool. You and me and Angie and the kids."

"That would be great. You have no idea how much I appreciate this."

For some stupid reason, the fact that she'd made him happy made her feel good.

"Well, I'd better get back on the road," Daniel said, handing April over to her, seeming almost reluctant to let her go, to leave her alone with Sydney.

Ugh.

So much for those warm, fuzzy feelings. And though she hadn't intended to confront him, the words just spilled out. "Is there a reason you don't trust me?"

He looked genuinely perplexed. "What are you talking about? Why would you think I don't trust you?"

She set April in her playpen and gave her a toy to amuse herself with. "You stop by home every day. You follow me to the grocery store. What am I supposed to think?"

"Sydney, if I didn't trust you, I never would have asked you to watch April."

"Then why do you keep checking up on me?"

"I'm not checking up on you. I just…" He let his words trail off, and dragged a hand across his afternoon stubble.

"You just *what?*"

"It's stupid," he said.

"What?"

"For weeks I was with April 24/7. Now that I'm back to work…" He shrugged, as if he wasn't sure what he wanted to say.

But Sydney knew, and her heart climbed up and lodged in her throat. How had she not seen it before? "You miss her, don't you?"

"Maybe. A little," he admitted, looking so adorably confused she could have hugged him.

There was no maybe. For all his talk about not being ready to be a father, April had gotten under his skin. He cared about her. And if he couldn't go more than a few hours without seeing her, how would he cope if someone took her away for good?

He couldn't. Maybe he didn't know it yet, but April was *his*. He wouldn't be giving her up, no matter what he said. Sydney was sure of it.

Could this be the sign she'd been looking for?

She wasn't certain how it happened, but one second Daniel was standing several feet away, and the next her arms were around him. And oh, it felt wonderful. Her eyes closed as she laid her cheek against his chest. She flattened her hands across his wide, strong back, breathing him in, wishing she could crawl inside his skin to get closer.

"Whoa," he said, sliding his arms almost tentatively around her. "What's this for?"

"Because I wanted to," she said. "And because you looked like you needed it."

"If you had any idea how tough it's been not touching you this week, you wouldn't be getting this close to me."

His words thrilled and terrified her. And made it all too clear that this was exactly what she wanted. It just felt right. Besides, where was the fun in playing it safe? Hadn't she been doing that long enough?

"Or maybe you get some sort of warped thrill torturing me," he said. "In which case I might just have to retaliate."

"Maybe I *want* you to retaliate."

There was a pause, as if he was trying to decide if she was serious. "Maybe, or you do?"

"I definitely do."

"You said you want a commitment. I can't give you that. I don't do forever."

"I think what I really want right now is to have some fun. To feel like I'm getting on with my life." It wasn't completely true, but she knew it was what he needed to hear.

Another pause. "You're sure?"

She gazed up at him, into the inky depths of his eyes. "Why don't you kiss me and find out?"

This time there was no hesitation. He cradled the back of her head in his palm, making her tingle, and brushed a tender kiss across her lips. It was nice, but she could feel him holding back and couldn't blame him. She'd been playing emotional ping-pong for days. But even if she tried to resist him now, she couldn't. She wanted this too much.

She wrapped her arms around his neck, pulled his head down and kissed him deeply, so there would be no question in his mind what she wanted. The message was received loud and clear. Daniel moaned and pulled her against him, taking command of the kiss, and though he was clearly calling the shots now, she felt a thrilling sense of power.

He kissed away her doubts and her inhibitions, until Sydney felt herself going limp with need. And she *liked* it. She wanted *more*. But she had to pace herself.

She broke the kiss, bracing her palms against his chest, so breathless she felt light-headed. "Wow."

"Yeah. And for the record, changing your mind again is no longer an option."

"I won't. But I need to take this slow, Daniel."

"I can do slow." He pressed his forehead to hers. "It might kill me, but I can do it."

She smiled. She couldn't deny that it was a thrill to know he wanted her so much, it was going to be a struggle for him to keep control.

Daniel glanced up at the clock and cursed softly. "I'm on duty. I really have to go. What are you doing tonight around eleven-fifteen? You don't have to rush home for anything, do you?"

Lacey had mentioned going to bed early, so really, there was no reason Sydney had to be at home. "Nothing comes to mind."

"Maybe we could spend some quality time together?"

"We could do that."

"Then it's a date." He gave her one last deep, mind-numbing kiss, said goodbye to April and headed out the door.

This would be their first date. And despite the fact that they couldn't actually go anywhere, she had the distinct impression it would be a memorable one.

LACEY PACED in front of the living room window, her eyes fixed on the driveway.

"You're going to wear a hole through the carpet," her mom said from the kitchen doorway. She was still in her robe, drinking her first cup of coffee. And she looked exhausted, which Lacey was guessing had a lot to do with whatever was happening at Daniel's until 1:30 a.m.

Just a friend, huh?

"Are you nervous about your new job?" she asked.

"A little," Lacey said. Although it wasn't the work so much as the guy who was supposed to be picking her up.

"I'm sure you'll do just fine," her mom assured her.

A horn blared outside and Lacey's head swung back to the window in time to see a truck pulling into the driveway. She strained to see who was in the driver's seat. His face was concealed in shadow, but she could tell the person was male, and large.

"Sounds like your ride is here." Her mom stepped up beside her and looked out the window. The horn blared again. "You'd better go."

"See you later," she said, darting out the door and over to the truck. She grabbed the handle and flung the door open.

"Hi," a cheerful voice said. "You must be Lacey."

The guy's light brown hair was shoulder-length and he was really cute. But he wasn't Jordan.

"The one and only," she said, trying to disguise the disappointment in her voice as she hopped up on the seat. The interior of the truck was dusty, the carpet was filthy with clumps of dirt, and a pair of heavy work gloves lay on the seat between them.

"I'm Mike," he said, waiting for her to buckle her seat belt before he backed out of the driveway. "Did you know elephants are the only animal that can't jump?"

She blinked. "What?"

"It's true. Every other mammal can jump, but not the elephant."

"No kidding."

"Did you also know you can lead a cow upstairs, but not down?"

Lacey shook her head. "Nope, didn't know that, either."

"Most people don't." Mike glanced her way. "Is your hair always green?"

"Sometimes it's purple."

"Cool." He looked genuinely impressed, and he was

so cheerful, Lacey couldn't help but like him. Even if he wasn't Jordan.

"Did you know a duck's quack doesn't echo but no one knows why?"

She couldn't resist a smile. "You're just full of animal trivia, aren't you?"

"Not just animals. My brain is bursting with useless facts. It's a gift. Everyone on the crew calls me the Professor."

"Really? Who else is on the crew?"

Mike, the Professor, told her the names of all the crew members, which she couldn't help notice were almost all male, but he didn't mention Jordan.

"I met someone in the office yesterday—I think his name was Jordan," she hedged.

"He's Angie's kid. She puts him on whichever crew needs extra workers."

Mike chattered nonstop while he drove, soothing Lacey's frayed nerves. It was hard to be jittery around someone who kept her smiling constantly. But as they pulled up to the house where they were scheduled to work, and she saw Jordan leaning against another truck drinking bottled water, her heart went berserk again.

What was wrong with her? She'd liked guys before and never felt this weirded out.

"Jordan, I've got your new recruit," Mike called as they headed toward him. "Her name is Lacey."

Keep your cool, Lacey reminded herself. *Don't let him know you're interested.*

"Hi," she said in the detached, I-couldn't-care-less-what-you-think-of-me tone she used when she didn't want people to know what she was thinking. Jordan stared at her, his eyes slowly taking everything in from the top of her head down to her feet, until she felt naked. He was *huge*—at least a foot taller than her and twice as wide.

"We met yesterday," she added to break the monotonous silence, and still he stared at her. It wasn't a good stare, either. This blank stare said she was invisible and not even worth his time. A stab of anger suddenly replaced her nervousness.

"What's your problem?" she heard herself say.

"Do you have sunblock?" he asked, and she was so surprised he'd spoken, she lost her voice for a second.

"S-sunblock?" she stammered.

Jordan walked to the passenger door of the truck he'd been leaning on and reached in the open window, grabbing a small bottle off the seat. He tossed it to her. It was a tube of sunblock.

"Put it on, then meet me in the back." He walked away and she watched him, seeing several other workers already laying bricks at the side of the house. She turned to say something to Mike but he was unloading supplies from the truck they'd arrived in. He probably hadn't heard their conversation. If she could classify what they'd just had as a conversation.

"Hey," Mike said, coming up behind her with an armful of tools and a flat of petunias. "Did you know thirty-eight percent of America is wilderness, but Africa is only twenty-eight percent wilderness?"

"No, Mike, I didn't," she said, tossing the sunblock back through the truck window. She would rather cover herself in battery acid than use Jordan's sunblock. She also had the sinking feeling this was going to be the longest day of her life.

CHAPTER TEN

Unfortunately Daniel and Sydney's date never happened.

There was a huge fight at one of the less reputable bars in town and Daniel was held up at work until after 1:00 a.m. By the time he got home they were both too exhausted to do anything more than get ready for bed.

Sydney was disappointed, but it wasn't as if they didn't have the next night, and the next.

Though she hadn't fallen asleep until after 2:00 a.m., Sydney woke early the next morning to see Lacey off on her first day of her first official job. After she showered and dressed, she dumped the ingredients for spaghetti sauce in the slow cooker and set it to simmer. At eight, she locked up behind her and crossed the lawn to Daniel's house. Usually he unlocked the door in the morning so she could come in and take care of April while he got ready for work, but today it was locked. Figuring he'd probably forgotten, Sydney used her key and let herself in. She expected to smell coffee brewing, and hear the shower, but the house was dead quiet. Had he forgotten to set his alarm?

She cracked open his bedroom door and peered inside. Daniel was still in bed, snoring softly. If he didn't get up soon he was going to be late.

She slipped into the room and sat on the edge of the mattress. She wasn't sure what he was wearing under the sheet, but from the waist up he was naked. And *beautiful*. His chest was wide and muscular and sprinkled with dark hair, his stomach flat and defined. She considered taking a quick peek under the covers. She even reached for the edge of the sheet, but it seemed wrong to take advantage of him while he was sleeping.

She gently shook his shoulder instead. "Daniel, wake up."

He snapped awake instantly—no doubt a cop thing—looking up at her with bleary eyes, then glanced over at the clock. "Hey, what are you doing here? Is something wrong?"

"I came to watch April. I thought you had to be to work by nine."

He rubbed a hand over his face. "I thought I told you, I switched with Dave again. I'm working the afternoon shift. I'm sorry."

"Oh, that's okay."

"I would get up and make coffee, but April woke up at four and didn't go back down until almost six. I'm beat."

"Go back to sleep."

She stood, but Daniel grabbed her wrist. "You don't have to go."

"I should let you sleep."

"Why don't you slide in with me?" He pulled back the sheet and scooted over to make room for her. She was a little disappointed to see that he was wearing cotton pajama bottoms. But climbing into his bed? She wasn't sure if that was such a hot idea.

"Maybe I shouldn't."

"Nothing is going to happen." He patted the bed next to him. "Come on," he coaxed. "I like to cuddle."

What woman in her right mind could resist a sexy man who wanted to cuddle?

She climbed in beside him. He tucked her against him, spooning her so that her back was against his chest, his skin still warm from sleep.

Oh, this was *nice*.

It had been a long time since she'd snuggled in bed with a man. It was something she hadn't even realized she'd missed until now.

She must have been really exhausted because she fell right back to sleep. When she opened her eyes again Daniel was sitting on the edge of the bed, pressing soft, teasing kisses to her bare shoulder. He smelled like soap and toothpaste, and his hair was wet. He was dressed in jeans and nothing else.

"Wake up, sleepyhead," he said.

She stretched and yawned. "What time is it?"

"Eight forty-five. I guess you were tired. You passed out cold the minute you laid down."

"Why are you up?"

"I couldn't get back to sleep, so I got up and showered. And made coffee. I thought I could make us breakfast."

"Is April awake?"

He shook his head. "When she's up in the middle of the night she usually sleeps in late. She probably won't be up for another hour and a half at least." He leaned down, pressed a very soft kiss to her lips and then whispered against them, "Why? Did you have something other than breakfast in mind?"

He had no idea how tempting that was, considering how disappointed she'd been last night. But she wasn't sure how she felt about their first date taking place in his bed.

But he was kissing her lips and jaw, working his way over to nibble her ear. And she could feel herself melting.

"We're supposed to be taking this slow," she reminded him.

"We are," he said, kissing the curve of her neck. "We won't go any further than you want. Say the word and I'll stop."

In that case, maybe it wouldn't hurt to fool around a *little* bit. She beckoned him closer with a crook of her finger. He climbed in beside her with a grin.

For a while all they did was kiss, and kissing him was so nice, it was enough. He touched her face and rubbed her back, combed his fingers through her hair—nothing overtly sexual. But that didn't stop her from getting crazy turned on. After a while she was the one who was having trouble keeping her hands to herself. And she began to wonder if her plan was an unrealistic one.

She'd forgotten it was supposed to feel like this. So... *good*. For years, sex had been a duty. Something to tolerate, not enjoy. And then there had just been...nothing. No wonder her libido was slamming into overdrive. It hadn't been out to play in a *long* time. And Daniel wasn't doing enough playing.

"Hold on." She sat up to pull her shirt over her head, tossed it on the floor, then settled back down beside him.

He was grinning. "You trying to tell me something?"

"Maybe we don't have to go *quite* that slow." Although, with her past experience, she couldn't help but fear that she was destined to disappoint him. What did she know about pleasing a man? Near the end of her and Jeff's physical relationship, she hadn't done a whole lot more than just…lie there. And wait for it to be over. There had been a time when she enjoyed sex, but that was many years ago. She was sure, with practice, it would come back to her.

Daniel kissed her neck, her shoulder, then she felt him pulling her bra strap down and tensed.

He stopped and looked down at her. "Too much?"

Too much, too little. "I'm just a bit out of practice. I don't want to…disappoint you."

"Sydney, that isn't even a possibility. Besides, all you have to do right now is let me make you feel good."

Make her feel good? But what about him?

He slid the lace cup down, exposing her breast, and pressed an openmouthed kiss to her nipple.

She moaned and dug her fingers through his hair.

He bared the other breast and took it in his mouth, sucking hard, and for the life of her she could no longer recall why she thought going slow was a good idea. All she could process in her hormone-drenched brain was

that she wanted *more*. She wanted to touch him. Feel
him. But when she tried he intercepted her hands.

"Just you," he said.

He leaned over and pressed a kiss to the uppermost
part of her stomach, then another just below it, then
another, gradually working his way down.

He reached the waistband of her shorts, tracing a path
across her stomach with his tongue, from one side all the
way to the other. Sydney was so turned on, her thoughts
were murky and unfocused, and the ache between her
thighs was becoming unbearable. Daniel was going too
fast, and not fast enough. And all she wanted was for
him to touch her.

Expecting him to kiss his way back up to her breasts,
she gasped when he pressed his mouth to the inside of
her right thigh instead. The sensation was so foreign and
erotic—and *good*—she gasped, jerking involuntarily.

He pulled back and looked up, as if he thought he
might have gone too far. "Too much?"

Yes, but not in the way he thought. It was so good
she felt completely out of control. And she *liked* it. If he
stopped now she honestly didn't think she could stand
it. "Don't stop."

He unfastened her shorts and sat up to tug them
down. She lifted her hips to help him.

She expected him to lie back down beside her, but
instead he lowered his head and kissed her again. This
time higher, using his tongue to tease the crease where
her body met her thigh.

She moaned and arched, her thighs falling open. Her
wanton behavior should have embarrassed her, but she

was walking the fine line between arousal and bliss, a place she hadn't ventured anywhere near in longer than she cared to remember. Daniel pressed her thighs even farther apart. The he pulled her panties aside and dipped his head.

The reaction was instantaneous. She cried out as pleasure wrenched through her. So perfect she wanted to sob, and laugh, and cry.

When she couldn't take any more, she pushed at his head, pulling her legs closed, saying breathlessly, "Too much."

Daniel grumbled a protest, trying to gently pry her legs apart. "Let me do it again."

"I can't."

"Yes, you can. One more time."

She shook her head. "Too sensitive."

She wasn't used to this. Her body had been ignored for so long, she needed to take her time. Besides, what about his pleasure? He must have expected something in return.

He started kissing his way back up her body, every touch of his lips causing a thrilling little aftershock. He settled beside her, but when she reached for the fly of his jeans, he stopped her.

"Don't," he said.

"Why?"

"I meant what I said. Right now all I want is to make you feel good."

SYDNEY LOOKED AT HIM as though he'd just beamed down from the mother ship. "But…what about you?"

Was he turned on? Hell, yes. And though his own body ached for release, he could wait. He *wanted* to wait. She needed to know that her pleasure was his top priority right now. That not all men were selfish when it came to sex. And making her see that was the only satisfaction he needed right now.

"Don't worry about me," he said.

"But—"

He smothered her words with a kiss. And for a while that was all he did. Kiss her and stroke her skin. Well, that and redirect her roaming hands as they strayed closer to his crotch. He finally got fed up and clasped her wrists together, pinning them to the mattress above her head.

She opened her mouth to complain, so he kissed her again, slow and deep. Not so easy to talk with his tongue in her mouth, was it?

She made a sound of protest and pushed against his hands, and if he'd thought for a second she wasn't enjoying it he wouldn't have hesitated to let go. But her struggle lacked conviction. In fact, being restrained seemed to fuel her arousal. After only a few minutes of kissing and touching her, he had her writhing and whimpering again. But this time he was going to make it last.

He slid his hand inside her panties to tease her, but the instant he touched her warm, dewy flesh, she shattered again. She arched against his hand, riding it out, until she moaned and crushed her legs together, gasping, "Please, no more."

She may have wanted to take things slowly, but her

body seemed not to grasp the concept. She was making this way too easy.

Sydney rolled on her side and curled against him, pressing her forehead to his chest, her breath coming in shallow bursts. "That felt…so good."

He reached around her back and flicked open the clasp on her bra. "You say that like we're finished."

"I am," she said, but she didn't stop him as he slid off her bra.

"I don't think so." He tossed her bra over his shoulder, then reached down to tug off her panties.

"I really can't," she insisted, lifting her hips so he could ease them down. For someone so adamantly against this, she was being awfully helpful. And he didn't doubt for a minute that he could talk her into making love. The weird thing was, he didn't want to.

No, it wasn't that he didn't want to. God knows he did. And if she had been any other woman he wouldn't have hesitated. But this was different. *Sydney* was different.

And maybe he was a little different now, too.

"You can," he said, kissing her before she could argue, determined to prove her wrong.

As many times as possible.

LACEY KNELT on the hard ground and planted flowers until her kneecaps felt like exploding. Then someone tossed her a pair of leather gloves and she was told to unload bricks and pass them to the bricklayers. This seemed to go on for hours, until her arms ached and her back had all but seized up from the bending and stretching. To top it all off she was soaked with sweat and felt like a boiled lobster.

When the crew stopped for lunch at one o'clock, she sat in the shade with the burger and soda Mike had bought her—since she forgot to bring money—and prayed someone would hit her in the head with a shovel and put her out of her misery.

Unaware of her silent suffering, Mike cheerfully informed her the original color of Coke was green.

Becky, the only other girl there, sat next to Lacey, showing off her various tattoos and piercings. A few in places Lacey would have preferred not to see. And despite looking like she could kick anyone's butt—even Jordan's—she was friendly.

Jordan's attitude hadn't changed all morning. He laughed and joked with everyone else and practically ignored Lacey. When he did speak to her, it was in that same cold, intolerant tone, and every now and then he would bark out an order or two.

When lunch was over she gathered up her garbage and limped to the trashcan. Turning back around, she ran face first into Jordan's chest.

"Watch where you're going," she snapped, but before she could back away he grabbed her arm and inspected it.

His brow furrowed and he shook his head slightly. "I gave you sunblock."

She ripped her arm out of his grip. "Who are you, the sunblock police?"

"I'll get the Professor to drive you home."

What? "I'm not going home."

"You're a mess. You're limping, sunburned and exhausted. Just admit you can't hack it and leave." He started to walk away.

Forgetting her various aches and pains, she stomped after him. "Is that what this is about? You're so chauvinistic you don't think a woman can do the job?"

Jordan just kept walking so she reached for his arm. The effect was like a static charge she felt all over. His skin was hot and slick with sweat, the muscles underneath hard as a rock.

Whoa.

He stopped and looked at the hand on his arm and then back down at her face, but the motion seemed to take an hour, as if the world were running in slow motion. She yanked her hand away and stuffed it into the back pocket of her jeans. "I'm fine. I can do the work."

He studied her for another eternity, and Lacey became aware that everyone else had abandoned what they were doing and turned to look at them. All the while Jordan kept those intense eyes glued to her face.

"Professor," he called suddenly and she jumped at the sound of his voice. "Take her to the truck, make her put sunblock on, then give her something easy to do."

He was letting her win this time, but not without humiliating her in front of everyone first. But she wouldn't let him or anyone else see how embarrassed she was. She lifted her chin, smiled up at Mike and said loudly. "If you're lucky, I'll let you do my back."

She hoped Jordan would hear, but he was halfway across the yard by that time.

Lacey spent the remainder of the afternoon picking up garbage, pulling weeds and gathering tools, with Jordan spouting occasional orders at her.

He wasn't rude or mean, just indifferent, and she had no defense against that. If she was rude, she'd seem childish. If she tried to evoke any reaction at all, good or bad, she'd seem desperate for his attention. No matter what she did she came out looking like an idiot, but for some reason she couldn't just sit back and be ignored.

By that evening she was relieved to be getting away from him. She couldn't imagine going through this day after day.

"Did you know an ostrich's eye is bigger than its brain?" Mike asked as they strolled to the truck. "And the longest recorded flight of a chicken is fourteen seconds."

"Professor!" Jordan called, jogging up next to them. "I need you to run to the office and drop off the equipment." He hitched his thumb in Lacey's direction. "I'll drive her home."

"Sure thing," Mike said, giving Lacey a sympathetic smile and a wink.

When they were alone, Lacey turned to Jordan. "I have a name, you know."

"Well, *Lacey,* unless you're walking, get in the truck."

She was so furious she probably *would* have walked if it hadn't been over five miles to her house. But with no other choice she got into Jordan's truck and sulked. He climbed in next to her and started the engine. "Buckle your seat belt."

"Make me."

He gave her one of those blank looks. "The truck doesn't move until your seat belt is on."

"I've got all the time in the world," she said, crossing her arms over her chest.

Jordan let out a quiet sigh and shook his head so subtly she almost didn't see him do it. Then he shocked her by leaning across the her and fastening the seat belt for her. In the few seconds he was stretched across her she could smell a hint of aftershave and the strong scent of a guy who'd worked in the sun all day. And she liked it. As a matter of fact, she liked it a *lot*. She wondered what he would do if she reached up and touched the soft jet-black curls peeking out from under the ball cap he wore. But as fast as he had pinned her, he straightened in his seat.

"Undo that and I'll put you over my knee," he warned tonelessly, putting the truck in gear and pulling away from the curb.

"Do you hate all females, or is it just me?" she asked.

"Who says I hate you?"

"Is *resent* a better word?"

"So, you assume I'm a woman hater?"

"It was just a question. Why do you care what I think, anyway?"

She saw his knuckles whiten as he gripped the steering wheel, and he didn't answer. Though she tried two more times to engage him in an argument, he fell back into that controlled indifference. He was infuriating— and fascinating. And as much as she wanted to hate him, he was getting under her skin and she couldn't figure out why.

When Jordan pulled up in her driveway, Shane's car was parked across the street. Shane was sitting on the hood waiting for her.

"Shoot." She instinctively sank lower in her seat. He'd texted her about fifty times that morning. She hadn't responded, so he started calling and leaving messages when she wouldn't pick up. It had gotten so annoying she'd had to shut off her phone.

Jordan looked at Shane then over at Lacey hunched low in her seat. "Problem?" he asked.

"I broke up with him and now he's stalking me."

"Is that the moron who was sitting in the parking lot the other morning?" he asked and Lacey nodded. "Figures you'd date someone like that."

"I told you, I broke up with him. He won't leave me alone."

"Well, then, you should be happy. You seem to like drawing attention to yourself."

"Screw you, Jordan." Shoving the door open with her shoulder, she stormed toward the house. Shane was behind her in a flash.

"Hey, Lace, stop. I want to talk to you."

He put his hand on her arm and she shrugged it off. "Not now, Shane, I'm tired."

"I just wanted to tell you, I'm sorry for whatever I did and if having a job is that important to you, I guess it's okay with me."

"Wow, that's awfully generous of you."

He grabbed her arm again, stopping her. "Lacey,

come on. You can quit playing hard to get. I said I was sorry."

"Hey, pal, you want leave my girlfriend alone?"

She heard Jordan's deep voice behind her, and like that day in the office, the sound made her tingle. She and Shane both turned to see Jordan walking casually toward them, and for once that look of indifference was aimed at someone other than her.

"Who is this guy?" Shane asked, backing up a step. Jordan outweighed him by about fifty pounds—all of it muscle.

"You heard him, he's my new boyfriend," Lacey said, following Jordan's lead, trying not to stiffen when he slipped a sweaty arm around her shoulder and tugged her against his side. But she liked the feel of his arm there. She liked it so much she started to get that squishy feeling again.

"I have to go drop off the equipment but I'll stop by later," Jordan said, then stunned her by lowering his head and pressing his lips against hers. It wasn't a passionate kiss, but his lips were warm and soft, and she felt it *everywhere*. In places she never knew she was supposed to feel a kiss.

Kissing Shane was never like this.

When Jordan finally pulled away she was so dizzy she had to cling to him to keep from falling over. Shane hadn't hung around to watch, he was already halfway to his car.

"Thanks," she said, smiling up at Jordan, and was met by his usual cold, impersonal stare. As quickly as the grateful feelings enveloped her, they were gone.

"We're even," he said, then turned and strode toward the truck.

Humiliated, she held back a sudden well of tears. Foolishly, for that brief moment, she'd thought he liked her at least a little, but she had obviously been mistaken.

She was just about to turn toward the house when movement by the side of the house across the street caught her eye. She looked over just in time to see someone dart into the backyard.

Stupid nosy neighbors. They always looked at her like she was a freak. Not that she gave a damn what they thought of her. She didn't care what *anyone* thought of her.

And if she never spoke to that creep Jordan again it would be too soon.

CHAPTER ELEVEN

WHEN SYDNEY'S CELL PHONE rang later that evening and she saw an unfamiliar number, she almost didn't answer it, but Lacey had gone out with friends, so she picked up just in case.

"Hey, Sydney, it's Angie. Daniel's sister."

Angie was not someone she could easily forget. "If you're trying to reach Daniel, he's on duty."

"No, I called to talk to you."

"Oh." April grabbed the phone, so Sydney laid her in the playpen. "Is there a problem with Lacey."

"Oh, no, not at all! She's a supersweet kid."

Supersweet? "We are talking about my daughter. Lacey Harris? About five-three, blondish-green hair."

Angie laughed. "I really like her, and Jordan told me she's a hard worker."

"I'm glad to hear that."

"The reason I called was to tell you how happy I am that you're coming to Jason's. I know we'll have a blast. Even though Daniel doesn't like him."

"He doesn't?" Daniel was so easygoing, Sydney couldn't imagine him disliking anyone. Except maybe Jeff, but he deserved it.

"He thinks Jason is too much like my ex-husband,

Richard. But other than having money, they have nothing in common. Danny's just really protective of me."

The fact the he was so devoted to his family was a good sign. Not that Sydney was thinking in terms of a permanent relationship yet. At least, she was trying not to. But it was tough not to fall head over heels in love with the guy.

"I know you and Danny are just friends, and I respect that, so I'll only say this once. I think you would make a pretty awesome couple."

She wanted to tell Angie that they were kind of a couple now, but she wasn't sure what Daniel wanted his family to know, if maybe he wanted to keep their relationship quiet. Or if he thought they even *had* a real relationship. Maybe to him it was just a fling. Just sex. Although if that were true, wouldn't he have tried to actually *have* sex with her?

She certainly didn't want to push him, but this was something they needed to talk about. Just so she knew what to tell people if they asked.

"You're awfully quiet all of a sudden," Angie said. "Am I making you uncomfortable? I mean, for all I know you might not have those kinds of feelings for him. I'm sorry if I overstepped my bounds. I tend to get really nosy when it comes to Danny's relationships."

"I'm not uncomfortable. And as for my relationship with Daniel, it's…"

"Complicated?"

"Yeah."

"Well, as I'm sure you've probably figured out, Danny is a little commitment shy. But I always thought that would change when the right woman came along. And I don't mean to say that I think that's you. Or that it isn't you. I mean, unless you *want* it to be you. And if not, you know, just ignore me." Angie paused for a second then laughed. "I should shut up now."

"I understand what you're saying." Sydney had the feeling Angie was hoping she would either confirm or deny a relationship, but she didn't feel it was her place. And how could she when even she didn't know what was going on?

After she hung up with Angie, Sydney looked up local secondhand kids' stores, then she strapped April into her car seat in the van and they went in search of a high chair. She found a really nice, cheap one at the third store they tried. It was so cheap, she had enough money left over to get April a few toys, too.

When they got back to Daniel's house his patrol car was parked in the driveway and he was sitting on the porch drinking a soda. But this time instead of feeling defensive, Sydney knew he was probably on break, and there to see April for a few minutes.

She parked in her driveway and hopped out of the van.

"I'm not here to check up on you," Daniel called from his porch. But she already knew that.

"You want to help me?" she called back, walking around to open the back of the van.

He crossed the lawn, looking so good that, if they hadn't been in plain view of the entire neighborhood, she might have thrown her arms around his neck and kissed him. Then he stunned her when he hooked an arm around her, tugged her against him and proceeded to kiss her senseless. He tasted sweet, like the soda he'd been drinking.

"Hi," he said, smiling down at her. She couldn't see his eyes behind his mirrored glasses, but she was sure they were as lust-glazed as her own.

"Hi. What was that for?"

He shrugged. "Do I need a reason?"

Absolutely not, and he obviously didn't care who saw.

"I see you found a high chair," he said.

"You want to carry it inside while I get April?"

He grabbed the chair from the back of the van and carried it into his house, but when he tried to set it up, he became hopelessly confused.

"Here, let me show you." Sydney unfastened April from her car seat and handed her to Daniel. The baby went straight for his glasses, so he took them off and set them on the coffee table. Sydney showed him how to unfold and fold the high chair, how to raise and lower the height of the seat, how to remove the tray and hook it back on, and how to recline the seat for smaller babies who weren't quite sitting up yet.

"These things have changed a lot since my sisters were little," he said. "I don't recall them being so… complicated."

"I got a great deal. I want to scrub it down really well before I put her in it. Since you can't be too careful. And I had a few dollars left over, so I got her some toys, too."

"Thanks. I've been meaning to pick some up."

"It's no problem."

"I don't suppose…" He paused.

"What?"

"Well, I never anticipated having her this long, and she's been growing like a weed. All the clothes I got her are getting small."

She had noticed that. "You want me to get her some new clothes?"

"Only if you don't mind. Shopping was never part of the job description."

"I don't mind at all. I probably have a better idea of what she needs anyway. And I know where all the good sales are. Unless you'd prefer I buy resale."

He shrugged. "Whatever is easiest for you."

"Maybe we'll run out tomorrow after her nap." In fact, April seemed ready for bed now. Her lids were heavy and she kept laying her head on Daniel's shoulder and snuggling against his neck. Sydney was a little surprised she hadn't fallen asleep in the van.

"You want me to lay her down?" Daniel asked.

She was going to tell him no, that she could do it, but she had the feeling he really wanted to. "Sure."

She followed him down the hall and stood in the doorway as Daniel hugged and kissed April, then laid her in her crib.

"Good night, munchkin," he said, stroking her hair back from her face. Sydney watched, feeling the tiniest bit choked up. She was still convinced that, despite what he said, Daniel would never be able to give April up.

He closed the door on his way out and they walked back to the family room. "Before I forget, how would you feel about going out on a real date tomorrow? Since I covered for Dave, he and Sammi offered to watch April for the evening. I thought we could go to Moose Winooski's."

"That sounds like fun."

"However," he said, tugging her into his arms, "I feel compelled to warn you that the only man you'll be dancing with this time is me."

That was perfectly fine with her. He was the only man she wanted to dance with. "I suppose."

"It's possible the mayor might be there," he warned.

"He's in Hawaii with the bimbo." Although she almost wished he would be there, so he could see how happy she was. She'd had an unpleasant conversation on Tuesday when her lawyer sent his lawyer a bill for the locksmith. Jeff had called her from Hawaii, in the middle of his vacation, ranting about how she'd had no right to have any work done on the house without first getting his permission. Which they both knew was ridiculous. She reminded him that if his creepy handyman hadn't had a key, she wouldn't have needed to change the locks.

He launched into a tirade about Sydney's "boyfriend" and how she was losing sight of what was important, and that he was going to sue her for full custody, which again, they both knew was a load of crap. The fact that she sat quietly listening to his tirade, not reacting to his threats, seemed to infuriate him even more. After a bit more name-calling, he'd finally slammed the phone down. Her lawyer called a couple of hours later saying that they'd received a check for the bill. Which was what Jeff should have done in the first place.

Sydney didn't know why he expended so darned much energy antagonizing her. He had his bimbo girlfriend. Wasn't it time they both moved on? Although the truth was, he didn't annoy her nearly as much as he used to. She just…didn't care anymore.

"This is going to sound strange, but I feel kind of sorry for her," Daniel said.

"For who?"

"The bimbo. The way she follows him around like a puppy."

"You know what's really sick? I used to be just like her. But that's a story for another time. You have to get back to work."

He looked at his watch. "Yeah, I do. Can you stick around for a while tonight?"

She couldn't suppress a smile. "I'm sure we can arrange something."

He pressed a soft, lingering kiss to her lips. "I was thinking we could pick up where we left off this morning. If you think you're ready for that," he said.

Oh, she was *so* ready. The taking-things-slow plan had been a really dumb idea. She grinned and rose up on her toes to kiss him. "I'll see you at eleven-fifteen."

WHEN DANIEL LET HIMSELF into the house that night after work, Sydney was stretched out on the couch with the television on, April sprawled on her chest asleep. And when she looked up at him and smiled, he was struck with the oddest sense of…*peace*. He used to prefer coming home to an empty house, but he was getting used to having her and April there.

Although, in her formfitting tank top and cutoff shorts, with her hair pulled back in a ponytail, she looked a bit like a teenage babysitter. Which made him a degenerate for the thoughts he was having. But despite how she looked, he knew for a fact that Sydney was all woman.

She switched off the television and said, "Hi. How was work?"

"Busy. Bar fights, domestic disturbance calls, kids cutting loose. Typical Friday night stuff." He leaned over and kissed her, then April. "Couldn't she sleep?"

"I started her on applesauce tonight and it upset her tummy. But I think she's ready for bed now." She rose from the couch, cradling April close.

"I have to go change. You want me to lay her down?"

"Would you?"

"Sure. Why don't you grab us a couple of beers?"

"That sounds really good. It's been a long night."

He carried April to her room and set her gently in her crib, but she was sleeping so soundly a bomb could have gone off outside and she probably wouldn't have budged. He changed into jogging pants and a muscle shirt, shaking his head when he saw that Sydney made his bed again and the dirty clothes from his bedroom floor had been washed and folded. He'd told her repeatedly that she didn't have to clean his house and she especially didn't have to do his laundry. Or April's, for that matter. Yet every day he came home to a spotless house and clean laundry. It was as if she couldn't help herself.

Which was why he wasn't surprised to find her in the kitchen washing dishes.

"I'll do those tomorrow," he said.

"It'll just take a second." She never left his kitchen anything but immaculate. She gestured with her elbow to the beer on the counter by the fridge. "That's yours."

He grabbed it and took a long swallow. "Anything exciting happen after I left? Besides the tummy ache."

"Not really."

Sydney was totally focused on scrubbing baby bottles and not looking at him. She seemed…distant. Which Daniel was learning meant there was something on her mind. Growing up in a household with five sisters had trained him to be attuned to the subtleties of female emotions. Which he was sure had a lot to do with his past success with the opposite sex. "Something bothering you?"

She shook her head. "No."

And women accused men of not being open with their feelings. He stepped behind her and wrapped his arms around her waist, tugging her against his chest. "Come on, tell me."

She grabbed a dish towel and dried her hands. "It's nothing."

He turned her so she was facing him. "Talk to me, Syd."

"Angie called me today."

"Oh, God."

She laughed. "It was nothing bad. She just wanted to

tell me she was excited that I was coming on the trip. And she made it really clear that she thought we would be a good couple."

"That sounds like Angie."

"Well, I wasn't sure what to tell her. If I should even tell her anything at all."

"Why wouldn't you?"

"I wasn't sure if anyone was supposed to know."

"Is there a reason people *shouldn't* know? Are you worried how it will affect Lacey?"

"No, not at all. Lacey actually gave me permission to date you."

He shrugged. "So what's the problem?"

"Is that what we're doing?"

Daniel was beginning to understand what she was getting at, although for the life of him he didn't know why she wouldn't just ask him. "So what you're saying is, you want to know if we're dating, and if it's okay to tell people."

Sydney bit her lip and nodded.

"Yes, and yes. We're definitely dating, and I see no reason to deny it to anyone. Besides, after what happened at the bar last week, no one would believe me anyway."

"I know I probably seem very naive, but I haven't dated since I was eighteen. I've forgotten the rules, I guess."

"Well, you're lucky, then. Because I know them all." He grinned and tugged her in the direction of the living room. "And right now, the rules say it's time to make out on the couch."

CHAPTER TWELVE

DANIEL HADN'T BEEN KIDDING. He didn't let her dance with anyone but him at Moose Winooski's Saturday night. Not that she wanted to, and no one would have dared ask, with his arm looped around her waist all evening. It felt nice, since it had been an awfully long time since anyone had *wanted* to put their arm there.

She had been a little worried that people would treat her differently this time. Maybe last time they were simply being polite, but she was accepted just as easily as if they had known her for years. She felt as if she fit in. When she was married to Jeff, she'd always had the feeling she was an imposter, someone playing a role. Now she felt comfortable being herself. And the fact that she had been married to Jeff, and ceremoniously dumped him, made her something of a legend.

The more she talked with people, the more she began to realize just how many people didn't like him—and that a lot of people who seemed to like him, actually couldn't stand him. It had just been politics.

Their so-called friends hadn't been true friends at all. Their affection had been a political smokescreen, as she'd discovered after the divorce. What Sydney felt with Daniel's friends was genuine.

But what she found truly remarkable was the

acceptance she received from Daniel's family. They had been at the bar a couple of hours when Bethany and Delilah came in. They both had the same dark, striking features as Daniel and Angie. Apparently Angie had been singing her praises, and they were both eager to meet the new woman in their brother's life.

When Daniel moved down the bar to talk to Jon, Dee slid onto the empty bar stool beside Sydney. "So, Angie tells me you used to be married to the mayor."

"Yep."

Dee drained her glass and gestured the bartender for another drink. "He's an ass."

Sydney had been hearing that a lot lately. "Tell me about it."

"I probably shouldn't mention this, but he hit on me once, a couple of years ago."

Maybe that should have bothered her, but knowing Jeff hit on a woman, when there were so many others that he'd slept with, seemed insignificant. Sydney honestly didn't care any longer. "I'm sure he hit on a lot of women."

"I politely declined, and when I turned to walk away he grabbed my ass and made a disparaging comment about my heritage."

Dee smiled, as if the memory was a satisfying one. "I called him a fascist pig and threw my drink in his face."

Sydney laughed. She couldn't even count how many times she'd had that exact same impulse; she'd just never had the guts to follow through. "I wish I could have been there to see it."

"Not one of my finer moments. But it felt good. Danny wanted me to press charges. I figured wearing my scotch was humiliating enough."

Sydney had felt the same way when Jeff had grabbed her on the dance floor last week. He was his own worst enemy, and one of these days his temper was going to get him in trouble.

"Now, Danny," Dee said, nodding in his direction, "he's a good guy."

"I know." She glanced over at him and got a little shiver of excitement and attraction. And contentment. Everything in her said this was right. That Daniel was the man for her. Forever.

He must have sense her watching because he looked over and winked.

The bartender set a drink in front of Dee and she took a sip. "He must really like you."

"Why is that?"

"Because he's breaking all his dating rules to be with you. You're divorced and you have a kid."

"And I live next door."

"Exactly. And he tends to date women who are slightly…younger. Not that I'm saying you're old. It's just really nice to see him in a mature relationship for a change. He's hardworking, responsible and financially stable, but emotionally he's got Peter Pan syndrome."

"What do you mean?" Sydney hadn't seen any sign of that.

"He doesn't want to grow up. But I think having April around has forced him to reevaluate his life." She shrugged and said, "Like I'm one to talk. My longest relationship lasted less than six months. Our parents' marriage was so lousy I think we're all emotionally stunted to a degree. Except Angie. I swear she's made of Teflon. Things hit the surface and slide off."

Sydney felt an arm loop around her shoulder and turned to see Daniel.

"Care to dance?" he asked, pressing a kiss to her bare shoulder. Slow dancing with Daniel was like a form of foreplay. Lots of bumping and touching and kissing.

She slid down off the stool. "Love to."

He looked at his sister and frowned. "How many is that, Dee?"

She dug her keys out of her back pocket and handed them to him. "They're all yours, Deputy."

"We can drive you home later."

"That's okay. I'll catch a ride with Beth."

"Let me know if you change your mind." He took Sydney's hand and led her to the dance floor, tugging her close. "I thought you might need saving."

"What do you mean?"

"Dee has a tendency to get...*dark* when she drinks. And sometimes she says things she shouldn't."

"Like how my ex came on to her, and she threw a drink in his face."

Daniel shook his head and sighed. "Yeah, like that."

"It didn't come as a big shock. And it explains why you dislike him so much."

"I dislike him for a lot of reasons."

His sister Beth and her boyfriend, Louis, sidled up next to them.

"You take Dee's keys?" Beth asked Daniel.

"Yeah. What's her deal tonight, anyway?"

"Jake bailed on her. She thinks he's seeing someone else. He's her on-again off-again boyfriend," she told Sydney. "And it sounds like they're going to be off-again soon."

"Swell," Daniel muttered.

"Are you dragging her out of here or am I?"

"I told Dave and Sammi I'd be home by midnight." He glanced at his watch. "And it's eleven-thirty now."

Sydney could hardly believe it was so late already. The night had flown by.

Beth held out her hand and Daniel dropped Dee's keys onto her palm.

"Good luck," he said, and Beth rolled her eyes.

"Nice to have met you," she told Sydney. "We'll chat next weekend and I'll tell you some really embarrassing stuff about my brother."

"Goodbye," Daniel said, giving her a playful shove. When they were gone he told Sydney, "Sometimes I wish I had brothers."

"You guys are obviously very close."

"Things weren't easy when we were kids. We had to watch out for each other."

"Your parents' marriage was that bad, huh?"

"Both my parents had pretty volatile tempers. Occasionally the fights would get physical."

"Your dad was abusive?"

"It wasn't just my dad. My mom liked to throw things. One time, when I was in high school, they were fighting about something—probably money—and she threw a crystal vase at him. He wound up with a concussion and six stitches in the back of his head. My mom refused to drive him to the hospital, so I had to. He told the doctor in the E.R. that the vase had fallen from a high shelf and hit him. They separated a couple weeks later."

When he had said his parents' marriage was bad, she never realized *how* bad. Her parents' problems seemed mild in comparison.

"Did they ever hit you and your sisters?" she asked.

"My mom had an old breadboard she used for spanking us. My dad used the belt. But when I got older, he would just crack me in the mouth with the back of his hand."

"I couldn't imagine Lacey doing anything so horrible that I would be compelled to hit her. And for all Jeff's faults, he never so much as spanked Lacey. And he never raised hand to me." Physical violence wasn't in his nature. He'd been more of an emotional abuser. And a pathological liar.

"It stopped after the divorce," Daniel said. "It was as if they brought out the worst in each other. I figured we'd all learned from their mistakes. Then Angie married Richard."

"You didn't like him?"

"At first I did. We all did. They both seemed really happy, but then Angie started to change. My sisters kept telling me that something was wrong. I guess I didn't want to see it. I was friends with Rich. I couldn't believe that he could be mistreating her. And when I asked him about it he said that Angie was just having a hard time adjusting to being married. He basically blamed it on her, and I bought it. Then she showed up at my door one day with a split lip and a black eye. She was pregnant with Jordan at the time. Turns out the bastard had been knocking her around almost since the honeymoon."

The idea that someone would treat a woman as sweet as Angie that way made Sydney sick to her stomach.

"The thing I find the most ironic is that when my dad found out he flipped. He teamed up with a couple of his buddies from work and they paid Richard a visit. By the time they were done, he looked a hell of a lot worse than Angie did. And suffice it to say, he never laid a hand on her again. It's just common sense. If you're going to abuse your wife, don't marry the daughter of a cop."

"Your dad was a cop?"

"I never told you that?"

She shook her head. This Richard person must not have been very smart.

"Maybe Rich figured, since our parents got into it, it would be acceptable. He learned the hard way that wasn't the case."

"So Angie got a divorce after that?"

"Not right away. They separated and went to counseling for a few months. But he was offered a job in Washington state that he wanted to take, and there was no way Angie would leave her family, so they called it quits. The divorce was official when Jordan was six months old."

"And I thought it was bad that my parents ignored me."

He was quiet for a minute. Then he said, "You know what I just realized?"

"Hmm?"

"Besides my family, and a few close friends, I've never talked to anyone about this."

The idea that he trusted her enough to confide in her made her heart skip a beat. That had to mean something, right? She laid her head on his chest and hugged him hard.

"What's this for?" he asked.

"Because I—" She stopped herself when she realized the words that had almost spilled out of her mouth.

Because I love you.

Whoa.

Did she? Did she really love him, or was she just enormously infatuated? Was it possible to fall in love with someone in two weeks?

Daniel tipped her chin up to look at her. "Syd?"

"Just…because."

He must have seen through her, but she didn't give him a chance to question it. She slid her hands up his chest and behind his neck, and kissed him. The kind of kiss that she hoped would make him forget whatever it was he'd been about to say.

The low growl as he wound his fingers into her hair told her it was working. And she got so into it, she nearly forgot they were in a public place. When they broke apart, they were both a little breathless.

"You're getting me all frisky," he said.

"I want you frisky."

He grinned. "Lacey is sleeping over at Veronica's?"

"Yep."

"So you don't have to rush home?"

"Nope." She didn't have to be home at all. She'd told Lacey to call her cell if she needed anything, or if she decided to come home for any reason.

He flashed her a steamy smile. "Want to go to my place and make out?"

"Yes." Last night had been so...*fun.* It was almost like being a teenager again. Passionate necking and petting over the clothes. Although some skin-to-skin action would be nice, too. Why did he think she'd worn a skirt tonight?

"Maybe we should go soon. Just in case there's traffic or something."

"We probably should," he agreed, leaning down to nibble her earlobe. Then he cupped her behind and her legs went weak. "In fact, I think we should go right now."

No ONE HAD EVER kissed Sydney as passionately, as *thoroughly,* as Daniel did. She couldn't get enough of his mouth. The feel of it and the taste of it.

She straddled him on the couch, knowing that as wonderful as kissing him was, this time it wasn't going to be enough. She was ready for more.

She wasn't just ready. She *needed* it. Maybe taking things slow had been a good idea two days ago, but everything was different now. Sometime over the past week and a half, she had stopped being afraid.

Daniel, on the other hand, didn't seem to be in a hurry. He was still holding back from taking that next step, so she took it for him.

She pulled her top up over her head and dropped it on the floor, and the rumbling sound Daniel made in his chest said he wasn't going to stop her. He wrapped his hands around her sides, running them upward, over her rib cage to hold her breasts, using his thumbs to tease her through the lace cups. She moaned and closed her eyes, convinced that every time he touched her it felt better and better.

"Your breasts are so beautiful," he said. He kissed the swell of one, then the other, and though it was pure bliss, it wasn't enough. She reached behind her to unfasten her bra, then tossed it on the floor.

"Even better," he said. He seemed content to just look for a while, but she wanted to be touched. She hooked a hand behind his neck and pulled him to her breast, and just before he took her nipple in his mouth, she could swear he mumbled something in Spanish, but it was drowned out by the sound of her own moans.

"Did you just speak Spanish?"

"Yes," he said, kissing his way to her other breast. She moaned and arched as he took that one in his mouth, too.

"What did you say?"

He gazed up at her and grinned. "You don't want to know."

"Yes, I do."

"It was a curse word. And not a very nice one."

"Can you say anything else?"

"A few words," he said, doing amazing things to her with his mouth. "Mostly I just know how to swear."

"Do you know how to say that you want to make love?"

"No, but…" He trailed off as the meaning of her question sank in, and his gaze shot up to hers. "Do you mean…?"

"Yes, I do. I want to make love."

"Are you sure?"

"I don't think I've ever been so sure of anything in my life." All of her apprehension, all of her fears, were just gone, as if they'd never even been there.

And her certainty must have shown in her face, because he didn't question her. "Bedroom?" he asked, but she shook her head.

"Here, like this." She fisted his shirt and tugged it over his head, but when she tried to get at his fly, her skirt got in the way.

"Take it off," he said, lifting her off his lap, and in the time it took to yank her skirt and panties down, his jeans and boxers were on the floor. And he was… perfect. Beautiful all over.

He sat up and tugged her closer, leaning in to press a kiss to her stomach, then another. He started working his way down, and when his tongue darted out to taste her, her legs nearly buckled. It felt so good, she didn't want him to stop, but she was so close already. This time when it happened, she wanted him inside her.

She pushed him back against the cushions and climbed over him, straddling his legs, trembling with anticipation. She centered herself over him and sank slowly down, taking him in. He gasped and dug his fingers into her hips. She rose up and sank back down.

Again and again. And it was so perfect she wanted to weep. This was how it was supposed to feel. This was what making love was supposed to be. And she did love him. She could feel it deep in her soul.

"Syd…" Daniel rasped. She wrapped her arms around his neck, feeling her muscles begin to tighten. Daniel cursed again, in English this time, and for some reason that pushed her over the edge. Pleasure gripped her like a vise, fast and hard, and when he groaned and rocked against her, she knew she'd taken him over with her.

She went limp against him and Daniel dropped his head on her shoulder, breathing hard.

"Tell me we didn't just have unprotected sex."

She sat back to look at him. "Of course not. I'm on the pill."

He blew out a relieved breath and let his head fall back against the cushions. "Thank God."

"I guess I should have mentioned that earlier."

"Yeah, because I think I just lost ten years off my life. I figured since you weren't sexually active, there was no reason for you to be on it."

"I take them to regulate my cycle."

"Good to know. And in case you're wondering, I got tested recently. I'm disease-free."

Which she should have considered before they made love. She'd just been so…swept away. She wasn't normally so irresponsible. In fact, Jeff's promiscuity was what had motivated her decision to stop sleeping with him.

"I hope I didn't ruin it for you," she said.

"Oh, no, not at all," he said. "I was so turned on

watching you that it took me a minute to realize I'd even forgotten. And for the record, I usually last longer than forty-five seconds."

"You know what's really cool?" she asked him.

"What?"

"You get to spend all night proving it to me."

CHAPTER THIRTEEN

"WHAT THE HECK are you doing?" Sydney asked Lacey, who was sitting on her bed sulking instead of packing. "We're leaving in less than an hour."

"I won't go," she said, folding her arms defiantly.

"It's only two days and we could both use a vacation."

"I'll stay home by myself," Lacey insisted. "I'm old enough."

"Nice try. You're coming with us, unless of course you want to stay with your dad and the bim...Kimberly."

Lacey narrowed her eyes. "I'd rather poke my eyes out with a fork."

"Then I guess you're coming with us."

Lacey got up and stomped her foot, something she hadn't done since she was six. "I want to stay here!"

"And people in Hell want ice water. Be ready, *or else*."

"This sucks," Lacey shouted after her as Sydney returned to her bedroom to pack the last of her things. She had no idea why Lacey was so against going to Jason's. Especially since Angie's son, Jordan, would be there. What teenage girl wouldn't want to hang out at the ocean on the beach for two days sunning herself with a cute boy?

And Sydney had seen him. He was really cute.

At Lacey's age, Sydney would have been thrilled. Of course, growing up in Michigan, they didn't exactly have access to the ocean. Lots of lakes, though. Not that her mother had ever taken her to one. Maybe when she was little, when her father was still around. She honestly didn't remember. It was the reason she had always tried to do those sorts of things with Lacey. Why she figured Lacey would enjoy this trip.

So much for *that* brilliant plan.

April was in her bouncy seat on Sydney's bedroom floor and she squealed happily when Sydney walked back in. "At least you're happy to see me," she mumbled, opening her lingerie drawer. She paused when she realized her silk camisole wasn't there.

"Lacey!" she called and Lacey stuck her head in the bedroom door a second later, scowling. "What."

"Did you borrow my white silk camisole?"

"No."

"Have you seen it anywhere? Did it maybe get mixed in with your clothes?"

She huffed. "*No.* You probably left it at Daniel's house."

Sydney shot her daughter a warning look.

"*What?* I'm just sayin'."

Even if she'd been trying to hide their relationship from Lacey, they had blown that when she'd walked in on them kissing in the kitchen the other day. Sydney thought she might be upset, but all Lacey did was say, "Ew, Mom, get a room," and go back to her bedroom.

The truth is, it was a small miracle that Lacey hadn't

seen anything earlier. Ever since Saturday night when she and Daniel had made love, Sydney hadn't been able to keep her hands off him. It was embarrassing, really, how completely under his spell she had slipped. Maybe it was hormonal, or her body was making up for lost time, but she couldn't seem to get enough of him. They made love in the evenings after April went to bed, and she'd started coming over an hour early in the mornings, after Lacey went to work, waking Daniel in some very creative ways. She'd even started scheduling April's nap when she knew he would be on break and stopping by the house. It was amazing what they could accomplish in fifteen minutes when properly motivated.

She'd begun to worry that she might wear the poor guy out, but so far he hadn't complained. The fact that she'd been so nervous about not being able to please him now seemed utterly ridiculous.

And while she had spent a lot of time naked at Daniel's house, she always wore her undergarments home.

"I did not leave it at Daniel's," she told Lacey.

Lacey shrugged. *"Whatever,"* she said on her way to her room. She was back a few minutes later, the camisole in her hand, looking a little less cocky. "I guess it did get stuck in my laundry."

When Sydney was finished packing she carried her suitcase and April to the kitchen. She heard raised voices out the side door and looked out. Daniel and Angie were standing in the driveway, by the rear of Sydney's van, arguing.

"This is not my fault!" Angie was saying.

"Well, if they don't have to go, I shouldn't have to go," Daniel said.

"Come on, Danny. Don't be like that."

Uh-oh. Maybe she'd just strong-armed Lacey into packing for no reason.

Leaving April securely in her seat, Sydney stepped outside. Daniel and his sister appeared to be at a stand-off, and Angie was obviously on the verge of tears.

"Sydney," Angie said, clearly relieved to see her. "Would you please talk some sense into him?"

"What's going on?" she asked.

"He's being a jerk, that's what!"

Daniel turned to her. "Dee's boyfriend dumped her. So she isn't going. And now Beth isn't going because she doesn't want to leave Dee alone. And the *only* reason I agreed to go is because *they* were going."

And Sydney could see he was pretty dead set against going. He was going to need some serious incentive.

"Angie, could you excuse us a minute?" Sydney said, and gestured Daniel into the house. When they were inside she said, "Why don't you want to go?"

"Look, it's no secret that I don't like Jason. I didn't want to go on this trip, but Angie guilted me into it. She made it sound like some big family thing because Beth and Dee were going to be there. But if they don't have to go, I don't think I should have to, either."

"It obviously means a lot to Angie."

"She'll get over it."

"You don't care that you're hurting her feelings? She's almost in tears. She doesn't strike me as the type to cry unless she's really upset."

Daniel frowned and folded his arms across his chest.

"You can make an exception, just this once."

"Once? I'm *constantly* humoring her."

Sydney doubted that. "Then do it for me," she said, unfolding his arms and stepping into them, pressing against him in a way that she knew would drive him crazy. "Think how much fun we could have."

His arms closed around her and something warm and sexy sparked in his eyes. "What did you have in mind?"

"I think we could get creative. And fewer people there means more time alone."

She could see she was getting to him. "Keep talking."

"I've really been looking forward to this," she said, rising up on her toes to give his lips a soft nibble. "Pretty please?"

"Ugh, gross." Lacey said from behind them. Sydney turned to see her standing in the kitchen doorway, her stuffed duffel bag on the floor beside her. "So, are we going or not?"

She had obviously heard at least part of the discussion. Sydney looked up at Daniel. "Are we going?"

He sighed and shook his head, as if he couldn't believe what he was about to say. "Yes, we're going."

"Dude," Lacey said, shaking her head sadly, "you are so whipped."

"Go put your duffel in the van," Sydney told her. "And strap April into her car seat."

Lacey plucked April out of her bouncy seat and headed outside.

"She's right," Daniel said. "You owe me big-time."

It was a debt she looked forward to paying in full.

ANGIE LEANED FORWARD and whispered to Sydney from the middle bench seat where she sat with April. "What's with those two?"

Sydney looked to the back of the van, where Lacey sat hunched into the corner next to the window, her black lipstick intensifying the scowl she'd been wearing since they left, iPod blaring. Jordan occupied the opposite end, the brim of his baseball cap pulled down over his eyes, arms folded over his chest, his music equally loud.

"I don't know," she whispered back, although she doubted they could hear her. They probably wouldn't hear a nuclear explosion. "Do they not like each other?"

Angie shrugged. "I have no idea. They work together every day and Jordan hasn't mentioned them not getting along. Of course, Jordan doesn't say much about anything. He had a girlfriend for three months before I heard a word about it."

"Of course they like each other," Daniel said from the driver's seat, not even bothering to lower his voice. "That's why they're acting like they don't. I don't even have kids and I know that."

"Maybe if they were twelve," Sydney said.

"She's right," Angie told him. "Kids their age should've grown out of that."

Daniel shrugged. "Whatever you say."

Angie gave his shoulder a playful shove. "Trust us on this. We're mothers, we know our kids."

They passed the sign marking their arrival to Stillwater.

"Where to now?" Daniel asked.

"Follow this road through the city," Angie said. "Jason's place is south of town."

Daniel drove through the congested streets of what looked like a trendy tourist town, until they reached the cove. Though it was nearly eight o'clock, people still occupied a long expanse of white, sandy, private beach. An assortment of canoes and sailboats dotted the clear blue water. The only thing bluer than the water was the pallet of cloudless sky. They couldn't have asked for a more perfect day to begin their vacation.

Reaching the end of town, they followed the road south, driving parallel to the shoreline for several minutes then turned off on a narrow residential road.

"It's the last house on the right," Angie said. They passed several mid-size homes and a row of luxury condos, but when Sydney saw the sprawling white, Cape Cod-style home set off by itself at the end of the road, her jaw nearly landed in her lap.

"This is a *vacation* home?" Sydney asked.

"I know. Isn't it beautiful? It belongs to Jason's parents. It's been in their family since before Jason was born."

"How big is it?"

"Thirty-five hundred square feet. Six bedrooms, three baths. And what I love is that they don't have a single television in the house."

Daniel glanced in the rearview mirror at the kids. "That should go over really well."

He pulled up the long dirt drive and around to the front of the house, pulling up in front of a porch that spanned the entire length of the house. Beyond the house the landscape dipped to a wide strip of private beach with a breathtaking view of the entire cove.

The door opened and a tall, slender man, who Sydney assumed was Jason, stepped out on the porch. Angie's eyes lit up and she hopped out of the van. Jason's smile said he was just as happy to see her. They met at the bottom of the porch steps and Angie launched herself in his arms. They were clearly crazy about each other, which didn't seem to go over well with Daniel, if the scowl he wore was any indication. Sydney hoped he would at least be civilized.

"I'll get April," he grumbled, and Sydney got out to stretch her legs, breathing in the salty ocean air.

Jordan and Lacey climbed out as Angie and Jason walked over to the van.

"Hey, Jason," Jordan said, speaking for the first time since they'd left the house. Jason greeted him with some complicated handshake and Jordan actually smiled. "Not bad."

"Told you I would get it," Jason said.

"Sydney, this is Jason," Angie said, practically glowing she looked so happy.

"Sydney," he said with a warm smile, reaching out to shake her hand. "It's wonderful to finally meet you."

He was very attractive, but older than Sydney expected, or maybe it was the salt-and-pepper hair aging him. "You, too. You have a beautiful home."

"And this is Lacey," Angie told him.

If Jason was shocked by her appearance, he didn't let it show. "Hi, Lacey. Nice to meet you. I have twin daughters who are right around your age. Fifteen, right?"

Lacey nodded. "Are they here?"

"Unfortunately not. They live in Los Angeles with their mom. We'll have to all get together some time when they're visiting."

Lacey nodded. "Cool."

Daniel emerged from the van holding April.

"Hey, Daniel," Jason said.

Daniel politely shook his hand, but there was obvious tension between them.

"And this must be April," Jason said, taking her sticky fist and shaking it, too, which made her gurgle excitedly in Daniel's arms. "She's a cutie. It seems like yesterday mine were this small."

He seemed so nice, Sydney couldn't help wondering what Daniel didn't like about him. It was clear from in the way Jason looked at Angie that he adored her.

"I wasn't sure if anyone would be hungry so I took some hot dogs out," Jason said. "I thought we could build a bonfire."

Sydney hadn't roasted hotdogs over a fire since summer camp when she was eight.

"That sounds like fun," Angie said, smiling up at him.

"Can I help with the bags?" he asked Daniel.

"Sure," Daniel said, handing April to Sydney.

Angie looped one arm through Sydney's and the other through Lacey's, who surprisingly didn't object. "Come on, I'll give you guys a tour of the house."

Though it was enormous, the house had a distinctly cozy and lived-in feel. Decorated in a mishmash of furniture styles from a dozen different eras, it possessed a slightly jumbled but appealing quality. Comfortable, yet functional. Just what she would expect from a summer home.

"This is really nice," Sydney told her.

"I'll show you where you'll be sleeping," Angie said leading them up a slightly creaky staircase to the second level.

"Only the master on the main floor has its own bath, so everyone up here will have to share." She gestured into a bedroom the was distinctly feminine and told Lacey, "This will be your room. It's where the girls usually stay. Sydney, you and Daniel have the bedroom at the end of the hall."

Her and Daniel? "Daniel and I are sharing a room?"

Angie blinked. "Yeah, I thought…"

They were sleeping together? Yeah, but not with her daughter down the hall.

Lacey, however, seemed to know exactly what was going on. "Mom, it's okay," she said. "I don't care if you guys share a room."

"Lacey—"

"You think I don't know what goes on at Daniel's house every night?"

Naively, she had hoped not. If her own mother had

shared a room with a man after the divorce, Sydney would have been horrified. Of course, her mom hadn't been stable enough to date. Most days, she didn't even get out of bed.

But Sydney didn't want Lacey to feel she had to accept it if it made her uncomfortable. "Honey, are you positive it's okay? Because I won't be upset if it's not."

"It's totally cool," Lacey said. "I'm gonna go down and grab my bag."

"I'm really sorry about that," Angie said when she was back downstairs. "I wasn't thinking."

"It's okay."

"She's a great kid."

Sydney smiled. "She definitely has her moments."

Angie showed her to the room she and Daniel would be sharing. It was small but cozy, with antique furniture and French doors that led to a balcony overlooking the ocean. There was even an old portable crib with a mobile set up in the corner for April.

"This is beautiful," Sydney told her. She laid April in the crib and the baby squealed excitedly when she saw the mobile, kicking her legs, before rolling over onto her belly and pushing herself up on her arms.

"Hey! Look at that," Angie said.

"She started doing that last week. You should have seen how excited Daniel was the first time he saw her. You would have thought she was the first baby in history to roll over by herself."

Angie crouched down beside the crib. "He seems to love her. It's hard to imagine that he could give her up at this point."

"I know." But as far as Sydney knew he was still looking for April's family. What she really hoped was that someday she and Lacey and Daniel and April could be a family. But she knew it would be a long time before he was ready for that. She could wait. This time, she was determined not to rush things.

"So what did you think of Jason?" Angie asked, pulling herself to her feet.

"He seems really nice. And it's obvious he's crazy about you."

"I've been divorced for seventeen years and Jason is the first man I've ever seriously considered spending the rest of my life with. The truth is, I've always been kind of a jerk magnet. And Danny knows that. But Jason is different. He's…*amazing*. I just wish Danny could see it."

"I'm sure he will once he gets to know him."

"I hope this weekend wasn't a bad idea. Oh, by the way." She gave Sydney a quick, firm hug. "Thank you for talking him into coming. I don't know what you had to promise him as leverage, but I hope it isn't too much of a hardship."

Sydney couldn't fight the smile curling her lips. "Oh, it won't be."

Angie laughed. "Why do I get the feeling that if I'd put you in separate rooms, you would have wound up together anyway?"

"What's this about separate rooms?" Daniel asked, appearing in the doorway with their luggage.

"I was just saying," Angie started, then she looked

from Daniel to Sydney and shook her head. "Never mind. I'm going to go find Jason."

When she was gone Daniel set the bags on the floor by the closet and said, "So, we're sharing a room?"

"If that's okay."

"You know it's okay with me, but how will Lacey feel about it?"

She loved that he cared enough to worry about her daughter's feelings. "She says she's fine with it."

"Good." A sly smile lifted the corners of his mouth as he shut the bedroom door. "I've been looking forward to spending the night with you again."

"Me, too." They'd only spent the night together that one time, but it had been so nice sleeping curled up against him and waking in his arms.

He started toward her, giving her the look he usually had just before their clothes started flying. "So, what do you want to do?"

She stopped him with a hand on his chest. "I think we're supposed to be downstairs for a bonfire."

He sighed and flopped down on the bed, which made a loud creak. "No way," he said, bouncing a few times. The bed groaned under his weight. "Is this a cruel joke?"

"It is a little loud. I'm sure we can figure something out."

There was a soft knock at the door and Daniel got up to open it. Lacey stood on the other side, looking wary, as if she was afraid she might see something gross. "Angie said to tell you to come downstairs. They're starting the fire. And she said bring a sweater because it gets chilly after dark."

"Tell her we'll be right down. I just have to change April," Sydney said.

Lacey left and Sydney scooped April out of the playpen and laid her on the bed to change her.

"By the way," Daniel said, "when we were bringing the bags in I asked Jordan what the deal was with him and Lacey."

"What did he say?"

"He shrugged and said, 'Nothing.'"

"So they *don't* like each other."

"No, that means they *do*."

She frowned. "That makes no sense."

"It makes perfect sense."

"And you're the relationship expert?"

He just smiled. "You'll see."

SYDNEY WAS *SO* GONNA GET IT when Daniel got her upstairs.

They'd spend the last hour and a half cuddled up together on a lounge chair under a blanket by the fire, and she'd had a severe case of wandering hands. Every time he'd let his guard down one would be trailing up his thigh or sneaking under his sweatshirt. He sat there in a constant state of semiarousal, counting the minutes until they could be alone. If he'd thought to bring his handcuffs, he could have resolved the issue by locking her to the chair. Which evoked some very interesting scenarios, making the problem worse.

By eleven-thirty Daniel was in agony. He made a production out of yawning and said, "I'm beat."

"It is getting late," Angie said. "Maybe we should call it a night."

Sydney couldn't get off his lap fast enough. She must have been as eager to go upstairs as he was, but like him, she probably hadn't wanted to be rude.

"I'll go put April to bed," Sydney said, and lifted April from her bouncy seat, where she'd been sleeping soundly since ten.

Daniel hung back to help douse the fire, then he, Jordan and Jason carried the chairs back up to the porch, while Lacey and Angie brought in the hot chocolate cups and sticky marshmallow skewers.

When everything was cleaned up, and all the doors locked, he said good-night and headed upstairs. The bedroom door was closed, so he knocked softly.

"Come in," she said in a loud whisper. He opened the door to find the room dark and Sydney already in bed. He reached to turn on a lamp but she whispered, "Don't. You might wake her. She's restless."

He closed the door as quietly as possible and tiptoed to the side of the bed. "Are you naked under there?"

She smiled and lifted up the covers. Oh, yeah.

He shed his clothes and climbed in beside her, wincing as the bed creaked under his weight. "Man, that's loud."

"Then we'll just have to do something that doesn't require a lot of movement," Sydney said with a smile that said she already had something in mind. She carefully sat up, trying to make the least noise possible, and threw a leg over him, straddling his thighs. He was about to ask how she thought this would be a quieter alternative, but then she kissed him. His mouth, his chin, the side of his neck. Then she started working her way lower. Down his chest, then his stomach, until it was clear where she was going with this.

She circled her hand around his erection, leaning over, and he felt the heat her breath…then April started to cry.

He cursed.

"I'll try propping her bottle up," Sydney said, crawling off the bed and walking to the crib, trying to get April to settle down, while he lay there in agony. After a minute April quieted, and Sydney crept back to the bed, but the second she leaned on the mattress, and it creaked, the baby jolted awake again.

Sydney sighed and sagged in defeat. "Why do I get the feeling she's not going to let us have any fun."

"She's in a strange place, in an unfamiliar bed. I guess we should have expected this." Daniel grabbed his boxers from the floor and pulled them on. April wasn't in full-blown hysterics yet, but if he let it go that far she would wake the whole house. "Give her to me."

Sydney lifted the baby out of the crib and handed her to Daniel.

"Hey, munchkin," he said, stretching out on his side and laying her down beside him, with her back to his chest and she calmed right down. He had the feeling he would be pretty much stuck like this for the rest of the night.

Sydney slipped into a pair of panties and a T-shirt and

climbed into bed, lying on her side facing him. "Maybe tomorrow?"

He reached over and took her hand. "I'm sure we can work something out."

"Besides, it's not like we didn't already make love this morning."

"Twice." And every day for the past week. Maybe they were getting spoiled.

"I had a lot of fun tonight," she said.

"Groping me?"

She smiled. "That, too. But I meant in general. Just hanging out with Angie and Jason. He's a great guy."

"Hmm."

"I don't understand why you don't like him. You should at least try for Angie's sake. She's crazy about him."

"I don't trust him. He's *too* nice. Just like Richard. If you could have seen how messed up she was—"

"That was a *long* time ago. And the fact that she hasn't had a serious relationship since the divorce is a pretty good sign that she's not going to fall for just anyone."

Sydney had a point, but every one of Daniel's instincts was telling him that he needed to protect his sister. So that was what he planned to do.

CHAPTER FOURTEEN

THOUGH LACEY HAD PLANNED to have a terrible time all weekend to spite her mom, and she was still kinda pissed that she'd been forced here in the first place, it really hadn't been that bad. Mostly because Jordan was doing everything he could to avoid her.

It had been like that at work lately, too. He would bark occasional orders, but otherwise he ignored her, and she ignored him right back. She could hardly believe that she'd thought she liked him. He was the biggest jerk she had ever met. Even worse than Shane.

Everyone got up late Saturday morning, and after a huge breakfast of eggs, bacon and homemade waffles, the adults got dressed and went for a tour around the cove on Jason's boat. Lacey stayed at the house to babysit April and was relieved when Jordan took off jogging down the beach. She didn't like the idea of being stuck alone with him.

She played with April on a blanket in the sand for a while, then gave her a bottle and put her down for a nap. It was weird, but she had half expected to see creepy Fred out there. It seemed as though he was hanging around everywhere she went, spreading his creepiness. When she was picking up trash off the strip mall grass the other day before the mowers went through, she'd seen him hanging out in front of the pub across the street. And when she and Veronica went to get ice cream the other night, he was in line behind them.

He never said anything to her, or even looked at her. She was sure it was just a coincidence, but still it gave her the creeps.

Since she hadn't taken one that morning, she grabbed a quick shower while April was asleep. Thinking she was still alone in the house, she dried off and wrapped herself in a towel, grabbed her dirty clothes and started down the hall to her room...running face-first into Jordan, who was standing just outside the door.

He was shirtless and sweaty. And so gorgeous she had to remind herself again how much she didn't like him.

"Took you long enough," he said.

She glared up at him, clutching the towel to her chest. "Has anyone ever told you you're a Neanderthal?"

He looked down at her and without warning a lop-sided grin spread across his face. It was the first time he'd ever smiled at her, and for a second it actually took her breath away.

He reached out and touched a damp lock of her hair. She had to fight not to flinch. "It's not green anymore."

"It's a gel—it washed out."

His eyes wandered across her face, in the same slow, precise way he did everything, and she started to feel nervous.

"What are you looking at?"

"You're pretty without all of that garbage on your face."

Garbage on her face? She suddenly remembered who she was talking to and shoved him away. "You're a jerk."

He let out a surprised laugh. "I compliment you and you call me a jerk?"

"I'm pretty without the *garbage* on my face. You call *that* a compliment? You don't even like me. You're just messing with my head again."

"Again? When did I ever mess with your head?"

"When you helped me get rid of Shane. You made me believe you liked me."

His brow lifted, and she realized how that had sounded.

Good going, Lacey. She'd just let him know he'd gotten to her, that she *wanted* him to like her. She tried to push past him but he stepped in front of her.

"Why does it matter if I like you or not?"

"It doesn't. Now get out of my way." She tried to get past him again, but he wrapped a large sweaty hand around her forearm. He wasn't even kissing her this time, and she was getting those funny feelings again. *All* over.

"I don't understand why you do this," he said.

"Do what?"

"This." Jordan reached up his other hand and brushed his finger over the ring piercing her brow. Every inch of her tingled with awareness. "The piercings, the dark makeup. And why do you change your hair weird colors?

Why do you do all of this…*garbage* when you look so pretty without it?"

He thought she was pretty? She hated that the idea made her heart beat faster. Why did she care what he thought? He was a creep.

"To be different," she said.

"Why do you want to be different?"

At first she thought he was being a jerk again, but when she looked into his eyes she could see he genuinely didn't understand. And for some reason that made her uncomfortable. She lowered her gaze and shrugged. "I don't know, I just do."

"There has to be a reason." He let go of her arm and lifted her chin until their eyes met. His expression was so intense she almost couldn't stand it. She wasn't used to anyone looking at her that way, as if he could see right through her. People stared all the time, but they never really *saw* her. And that was exactly the way she liked it. They hit the surface and bounced off.

"I guess I want people to notice me."

Jordan's mouth curled up in a grin that made her stomach plummet. "Trust me, people would notice you anyway."

He ran his thumb over her bottom lip and her heart started slam dancing with her ribs.

She turned her head. "Don't do that."

"Why? I like your lip. It always sticks out, like you're pouting."

She caught her lip in her teeth. "I should go check on April."

"Already did. She's asleep." He dipped his head,

so their mouths were almost touching. She could feel his breath, feel the heat radiating from his body like a furnace.

"Are you going to kiss me?" she asked, but the words came out all soft and breathy.

"Do you always ask first?"

"I don't like surprises."

"Maybe I will. But you have to promise me something first."

Lacey's heart was beating so hard and fast she felt light-headed. "What?"

"No more weird hair color or crazy makeup."

All those warm, trembly feelings fizzled away. Just when she thought he was a nice guy, he had to go and *ruin* it.

"Drop dead," she said, shoving him away. "If you can't accept me for who really I am, I would rather remove my own skin with a vegetable peeler than kiss you."

Jordan shook his head, giving her that blank look again. God, she *hated* that.

"As soon as you figure out who that is, you let me know." With that, he walked past her into the bathroom, and shut the door behind him. She hated to admit it, but the words stung.

When April began to cry several minutes later, Lacey was still standing there.

SOMETHING WAS UP.

Jason and Angie disappeared into the master suite for about an hour that afternoon. At the time, Sydney figured they were doing what any couple would do when locked in a bedroom—what she wished she and Daniel could do—but when they emerged to make dinner, something was off. Angie seemed nervous. Jason kept looking at her and smiling, and Angie kept looking from Daniel to Jordan, then back to Jason, as if she was waiting for something. Or waiting for the right time to say something.

And Sydney had the sneaking suspicion that whatever it was, Angie was pretty sure Daniel and Jordan weren't going to like it. Which made Sydney nervous. They'd had a good time so far. She hated to see it ruined.

After dinner, everyone pitched in and helped clean up, and when they were finished, Angie said, "Why don't we all sit on the porch. Jason and I have something we need to talk to you about."

Daniel shot a look Sydney's way, as if he thought she knew what was going on, and she shrugged. Everyone seemed puzzled as they walked out onto the porch.

It was a gorgeous evening. The sun was just beginning to set over the water, reflecting the reddish-orange streaks that spread across the darkening sky.

Sydney and Daniel sat on the swing with April while Jordan and Lacey took chairs on opposite sides of the porch. Angie and Jason leaned against the railing with their backs to the sunset. He took her hand and gave it a squeeze.

Angie cut right to the chase. "Jason and I are getting married."

Sydney felt Daniel tense beside her.

"That's great," Jordan said, looking genuinely happy

for his mom. "But I thought you were going to wait until next year."

"We were," Angie said.

"So why don't you?" Daniel asked, in a tone that made his sister flinch.

"Because," Jason said, "Angie and I are having a baby."

"Wow," Jordan said, looking stunned. "I didn't know you were planning on having kids."

"We weren't," Angie said, glancing at her brother. "This was a big surprise. But now that the shock has worn off, we're both excited."

"When did you find out?" Jordan asked.

"I took the test before dinner. Two tests, actually, just to be sure."

"Excuse me," Daniel mumbled, pushing off the swing with such force Sydney jerked forward and almost lost her grip on April. He walked into the house, letting the screen door bang shut behind him.

Angie's face fell, and any trace of joy and excitement disappeared. Though Sydney could tell he was trying to hide it, Jason was clearly angry. "Do you want me to talk to him?" he asked.

Angie shook her head, looking miserable. "It will only make things worse. I guess it was too much to expect him to be happy for me."

Jordan got up, and gave his mom a kiss on the cheek and a big hug. "*I'm* happy for you."

"So am I," Sydney said, and Lacey added, "Me, too."

Angie smiled and wiped away the tear that had

escaped down her cheek. "Thanks, everyone. That really means a lot to me."

"I'm going to go talk to Daniel," Sydney said, rising from the swing. Someone had to tell him what a jerk he was being. And maybe Angie thought Sydney might be able to reason with him because she didn't try to stop her.

She passed April to Lacey, then went inside to look for him. But he wasn't on the main floor. He wasn't in the bedroom, either. She checked the entire house, but there was no sign of him anywhere. He must have slipped out the back and gone for a walk. And since she had no idea which direction he had taken, she couldn't go after him.

All she could do was wait.

THE WAY JORDAN HUGGED and kissed his mom…well, that was really sweet. Maybe he wasn't as big a jerk as Lacey had thought.

After everyone else went inside, he walked down to the beach by himself. Lacey gave him a few minutes, then followed him. He was sitting in the sand, close to the shore, looking out over the water.

She sat down beside him, propping her arms on her raised knees, wondering if he might tell her to get lost. He glanced over at her, but didn't say anything.

"That was awesome," she said. "The way you hugged your mom."

He shrugged, as if it was no big deal. "She looked like she needed it."

"Daniel was acting like a tool."

"Yeah. He's just really protective of her because of my dad."

"He didn't like your dad, either?"

"I guess he used to, until he found out that my dad was beating the crap out of her."

Lacey sucked in a surprised breath. She never would have guessed that someone like Angie would let anyone hit her. And she couldn't understand why someone would want to. And she was even more astonished that Jordan had told her.

"Did you ever see him do it?" she asked.

"No, they got divorced when I was a baby. I found out about it when I was ten, when he went to jail for doing the same thing to his second wife. I was supposed to visit him in Washington for two weeks during summer vacation. My mom felt I had the right to know why I couldn't go."

"How long was he in jail?"

"Just a couple of months. But all his visitation rights were revoked. He had to go to therapy for a long time before they would let me see him again. And then he had to come to California. I wasn't allowed to go back to Washington until I was fifteen."

"My dad cheated on my mom," Lacey said. She didn't mean to. It just sort of came out.

"Is that why they got divorced?"

She nodded. "And I think she knew about it for a long time before she left him. Everyone did. It was humiliating."

"Parents do really stupid things sometimes."

They were quiet for a minute, then she said, "Can I ask you a question?"

"I guess."

"Why were you such a jerk to me at work?"

"When you came to the office that first day I figured you were a spoiled private school girl," he said, then a smile tipped up the side of his mouth. "Yet, as much as I didn't like you, I was somehow strangely attracted to you."

She smiled. "Me, too."

"Yeah. I figured as much."

"You know, you were right. This isn't really me. All this *garbage*. I only do it to piss my dad off."

"Yeah, I figured that, too."

"It was worth it for a while, knowing how much he hated it. Honestly, now I'm just getting sick of it. But I know if I go back to the way I looked before, he'll be really happy, and I don't want to give him the satisfaction."

"Maybe it's time to stop worrying about what *he* wants, and do what *you* want."

He was right.

Lacey reached up and unhooked her brow ring, pulled it out and flung it at the water. Moonlight glinted off its surface then it disappeared beneath the surface.

"Better?" he asked.

Better, but not enough. She pushed herself up onto her feet, kicked off her flip-flops, and walked to the edge of water. She paused for a second, then stepped into the surf, clothes and all, and waded out a ways. Then she took a deep breath and dove under. She swam a few feet, washing the gel from her hair. When she broke the surface and scrubbed her hands over her face, the salty sea water stung her eyes. But it was a good sting.

She walked back to the shore, where Jordan stood watching her. Her clothes were wet and heavy and she was freezing, but she felt a million times better.

"How's that?" she asked, smiling up at him.

Jordan didn't say a word. He just smiled, wrapped his arms around her and kissed her.

AFTER SEEING the hurt look on Angie's face as he stormed off the porch, Daniel knew immediately that he was being an ass. But he couldn't seem to make himself go back and apologize. Not until he'd had a chance to think things through. Which was what he had been doing for the past couple of hours as he paced up and down the shore.

And as he walked, he began to realize that he'd been so worried Angie would get hurt again and so suspicious of Jason's motives that he'd been blind to fact that the only person hurting her now was him.

The truth was, Jason had never said or done anything to suggest he wasn't genuinely devoted to Angie. Daniel had tried and convicted the guy before he ever had a chance. Guilty until proven innocent.

And Daniel had to wonder if part of the reason he didn't like Jason was simple jealousy. Daniel had been Angie's protector for a long time, and though he complained, maybe he wasn't ready to pass the torch.

Maybe the thought of losing her to Jason permanently was too much to take on the heels of the news he'd gotten from the P.I. yesterday. The investigator had a good lead on a cousin of Reanne's and needed the okay to fly out to Utah to look into it. A month ago, Daniel wouldn't have hesitated to write him out a check. He didn't want to keep April. And even if he did, he couldn't give her what she needed—two parents and a stable home.

None of that was part of Daniel's plan. He didn't want to be permanently tied down to anyone. Yet when he tried to imagine Sydney and April not being there to greet him when he got home from work, when he thought of Sydney not crawling into bed with him every morning before he started his day, he felt so...empty.

He tried to tell himself that it was habit. He'd seen so much of her lately, he'd probably gotten used to her being around. Meaning he could just as easily get un-used to her, too. At some point he was going to have to back off. Maybe if he let the relationship run its natural course, he wouldn't have to worry about anyone's heart breaking. Maybe they could end this as friends.

But what if it wasn't so easy to let go this time? Which would he regret more? Making a commitment to Sydney, or walking away from her for good?

The house was dark when he got back, and though he wouldn't have blamed Angie and Jason if they'd locked him out, the door was open. He climbed the stairs, careful not to wake anyone, and crept into the bedroom. Sydney was curled up on her side, April tucked against her. He'd been a real jerk to dump April on her like that, knowing she would feel obligated to take care of her. Proof that he would be a lousy father.

He undressed and got into bed as gently as possible, but the horrendous squeaking woke Sydney.

"Hey, you're back," she whispered sleepily. "I was worried."

He lay facing her. "I needed some time alone to think. I'm sorry I stomped off like that. I acted like a complete ass."

"Yeah, you did."

Her candid response made him smile. He liked that she didn't let him get away with anything.

He touched her cheek, smoothed a stray curl behind her ear. "I'm going to talk to them and make this right. If they ever speak to me again, that is."

"All Angie wants is for you to be happy for her."

"I am. Or at least, I'm trying to be."

"The fact that she loves Jason doesn't mean she loves you any less."

God, was he that transparent? "I know."

"Have you ever heard why Jason and his wife got divorced?"

"Angie never mentioned it." Probably because she knew he wouldn't listen. And didn't care.

"She left him for someone else. He said he was blind-sided. He didn't even have a clue she was having an affair, but it had been going on for over a year. He was devastated."

"Well, he won't have to worry about that with Angie. He'll never find a woman more devoted."

"Why do you think he loves her so much? He told me that she taught him to trust again."

Jason was always so confident and put-together, it

never occurred to Daniel that he might be just as vulnerable as Angie. That he had a lot to lose, too. And maybe Jason wasn't the only one with trust issues. When Angie married Richard, Daniel had welcomed him into the family without question. He had been like the brother Daniel never had. Daniel had trusted him to take care of Angie, and Richard had betrayed that trust in the worst way. He hoped he could learn to trust Jason.

He was about to tell Sydney that, but when he looked over, he realized she'd gone back to sleep.

DANIEL MANAGED to get a few hours of restless sleep, but he woke at five, guilt gnawing his insides. He rolled out of bed and dressed as quietly as he could and headed downstairs, surprised to smell coffee. It seemed he wasn't the only one who couldn't sleep.

There was no one in the kitchen, but the front door was open. He poured himself a cup of coffee and stepped out on the porch. Jason sat in one of the chairs, in his robe. He looked up as the storm door creaked open.

"You're awake early," Jason said. "I hope it's because you feel like a piece of crap for what you did to your sister."

Ouch. That was the first time Jason had been anything but perfectly polite to Daniel, even though Daniel had at times been less that warm and friendly. Apparently there was a limit to what Jason would take, and Daniel had found it.

"I do."

"You know," Jason said, looking out over the water, "I don't really give a damn what you think about me,

Daniel. You can be a jerk to me if that's what you want. I don't care. But you hurt the woman I love and that is not acceptable. And if you do it again…" He met Daniel's eye. "Badge or no badge, I *will* take you down."

Daniel didn't doubt that for a second. And it confirmed to him that Jason would never hurt Angie. It was time for Daniel to let her go.

"If it'll make you feel better, take a swing at me now. God knows I've earned it."

"Don't think I'm not tempted. You really hurt her. But Angie would have my head, because no matter how much of an ass you've been, she still loves you."

"It won't happen again."

Jason looked up at Daniel. Really studied him, then said, "I believe you."

He was cutting Daniel a hell of a lot more slack than Daniel had ever cut him.

"I also want to say congratulations. About the baby."

Jason smiled. "Thanks."

"I guess it must have really come as a shock."

"More for Angie than me. I always wanted more kids. And who knows, with twins running in both our families, we might even get two."

The thought of Angie juggling a career and newborn twins made Daniel smile.

"Hey," Jason said suddenly. "Do you fish?"

"Not since I was a kid."

"We should go."

"Now?"

"Why not?"

Fishing with Jason? Weirder things had happened. "Sure, I'll go fishing."

"Great. Why don't you go wake Jordan up. Meet me down at the boat in fifteen minutes."

"Sure." Daniel went upstairs to Jordan's room. He had just lifted his hand to knock, when across the hall Lacey's door creaked open and he caught a shirtless Jordan red-handed.

Jordan went beet-red when he saw Daniel standing there.

So much for them not liking each other.

"This isn't what it looks like," Jordan said.

Through the open door Daniel could see Lacey, still sleeping under the covers. What the hell was he supposed to say at a time like this?

"You want to go fishing?" he asked.

For a second Jordan looked confused, as if maybe it was a trick question. "Uh, sure."

"Jason said to meet him at the boat in fifteen minutes."

Now he looked downright baffled. "You're going fishing with *Jason?*"

"Yep."

"Did I miss something?"

Daniel just smiled. "Get ready."

Daniel peeked in on Sydney and April, who were both sound asleep, and grabbed his shoes and socks. Jordan was waiting for him by the door when he got downstairs.

"You ready?" Daniel asked.

"Uh, yeah," Jordan said, but hesitated. "Uncle Danny, you're not gonna tell my mom about me being in Lacey's room, are you?"

"Should I?"

"No! We were just talking."

"That's funny, the last time I *just talked* to a woman, I remember leaving my shirt on."

Jordan grinned sheepishly. "Okay, maybe that's not *all* we did."

"Be careful."

"I will."

"I don't know if you talk to your dad about stuff like this."

"Considering the circumstances, I don't talk to him about much of anything. But my mom has been drilling me on the virtues of safe sex since I was thirteen."

That sounded like Angie.

"Besides," he added, "Lacey wants to wait until she's married."

Daniel was genuinely surprised. He didn't think kids these days held out in the face of peer pressure. Of course, Lacey did seem to march to the beat of her own drummer. "And how do you feel about that?" he asked Jordan.

"I think it's kinda cool. And it's not about sex, anyway. I mean, I really like her that way, but I also like just being with her. Talking and stuff. She gets me. You know what I mean?"

He nodded. He knew exactly what Jordan meant. And he was proud of him. In a way, he wished he had a son he could talk to. Give advice to. Daniel used to be a pretty integral part of his nephew's life, but with Jason in the picture now, Jordan might not need him as much.

And that was okay, because it was obvious that Jordan liked and respected Jason.

He heard Jason start the boat. "We should probably go, before he leaves without us."

Jordan followed him down to the dock and onto the boat. Jason, wearing a John Deere cap and a pair of dark sunglasses, sat waiting in the captain's chair, a cigar clenched between his teeth. "Welcome aboard. Grab a chair."

They sat down and Jordan looked from Daniel to Jason. "So, are you guys, like, bonding?"

"I don't know." Daniel turned to Jason. "Are we?"

Jason shrugged as he started the motor. "Sure. Why not?"

"I think you have to hug," Jordan said.

Daniel's brow furrowed and he looked at Jason. "We don't have to hug, do we?"

Jason laughed. "Hell, no. We just have to catch fish."

CHAPTER FIFTEEN

SYDNEY PACED in front of the kitchen window, watching the cove for any sign of Jason's boat. "Do you think they're okay? They've been gone a long time."

Angie fed April the last few bites from a jar of mixed fruit. "If you're worried about Daniel, I'm sure Jason won't hurt him too badly. Of course, if you need to dispose of a body, the ocean is a pretty good place."

"That's not funny," Sydney said. Jason had been furious last night. Not that she thought he would actually hurt Daniel. At least, she hoped he wouldn't.

Angie blew out an exasperated breath. "Oh, hell, I can't stay mad at him. He's a doofus, but I love him to death. He has a good heart."

"'Morning," Lacey said shuffling into the kitchen. "Is there any coffee left?"

Sydney turned in her direction to reply and stopped dead, her mouth nearly falling open.

Gone were the colorful streaks in her hair, and the obnoxious makeup. Sydney had almost forgotten that Lacey's eyes were large and round like her own, not dark slashes in her face. She'd taken the ring out of her brow and had only two small stud earrings in each ear.

Sydney wanted to tell Lacey how great she looked, but she was afraid she might jinx it.

"There a little left in the pot," Angie said, her eyes also fixed on Lacey.

"What are you two staring at?" Lacey asked, obviously enjoying the shock value.

"Did you do something different with your hair?" Angie asked casually, pouring Lacey the last of the coffee.

Lacey took the cup and spooned sugar into it. "You guys are weird. Has anyone seen Jordan?"

"In his room asleep." Angie pointed her spoon at Sydney. "Hey, you think maybe they got lost in the Bermuda Triangle?"

Lacey rolled her eyes—her big, beautiful eyes. "The triangle is in the Atlantic Ocean between Miami, Bermuda and Puerto Rico. And Jordan isn't in his room."

Angie frowned. "He's not?"

As if on cue, Sydney heard the sound of a boat engine.

Angie looked out the window. "They're back. And Jordan is with them."

Sydney moved next to Angie and peered out. Jordan was tying the boat to the dock. Jason hopped out next, then Daniel—in one piece, thank God. As a matter of fact, they all looked…happy?

"Is it my imagination or are they smiling?" Sydney asked.

The three men walked up the beach to the porch. Jason was first through the door.

"Good morning, ladies." He tipped his baseball cap at Sydney and Lacey, and kissed Angie.

She wrinkled her nose and frowned. "Have you been *smoking?*"

Daniel and Jordan followed him inside.

"Where have you been?" Sydney asked.

"We went fishing," Daniel said.

Hearing his voice, April squealed and banged the high chair tray until he came over and dropped a kiss on the top of her rumpled head. "G'morning, munchkin."

"If you went fishing, where are the fish?" Angie asked.

"We didn't catch any," Jordan said. "We mostly just talked about sports. It was a male bonding thing."

Male bonding? Last night Jason and Daniel had wanted to hurt each other.

Angie looked from her brother to her fiancé. "So, you two are good now?"

Daniel looked at Jason. They both shrugged and Jason said. "Yeah, we're good."

"Oh, and by the way," Daniel said, walking over to Angie. He pulled her into his arms and hugged her hard. "I'm sorry."

She kissed his cheek. "You know I can't stay mad at you."

Sydney glanced over at Lacey and realized she was gazing up at Jordan with the biggest doe eyes Sydney had even seen, and Jordan was smiling back at her.

Huh?

When had they stopped wanting to zap each other off of the planet?

Jordan gestured toward the door and Lacey, without

taking her eyes off of him, said, "Mom, we're going for a walk."

Jordan took her hand and they stepped onto the porch. Eyes wide, Angie asked, "What the hell was that? I thought they hated each other."

"Who called it?" Daniel said, sounding proud of himself.

"Called what?" Jason asked.

"He thought that they were pretending they didn't like each other, because they actually *did* like each other," Angie said.

"Hell, I knew that," Jason said, and Angie gave him a playful shove.

"Who wants breakfast?" she said.

Sydney and Angie made everyone a pancake breakfast. Afterward the kids went down to the beach for a swim, while the adults lounged on the porch, drank iced coffee and chatted. It was a perfect day. Sunny and warm with a gentle breeze blowing off the ocean. Sydney wished they could stay another night, but everyone had to work Monday, so around four they packed up the van and piled in. This time Lacey and Jordan sat cuddled together in the corner, and every now and then out of the corner of her eye, Sydney saw them sneak a kiss.

"Is that not the sweetest thing you've ever seen?" Angie leaned forward to whisper.

"They do make a cute couple," Sydney whispered back.

Daniel, looking puzzled, asked, "When did her hair stop being green?"

When they got home Angie gave Sydney a big hug and said, "Thanks for coming with us. I loved having you there."

"I had a great time."

"We're going to do a girls' night out soon. Me and you and my sisters. Dinner and a movie."

Sydney tried to recall the last time she'd been out with the girls, but found she couldn't remember. "Sounds like fun."

Lacey and Jordan said a long, lingering goodbye, as if they wouldn't be seeing each other for a month, when in reality they would be reunited the next morning at work. And not five minutes after she finished unpacking, Lacey was calling him on her cell phone.

Sydney unpacked, and was on her way out the door to Daniel's when the home phone started to ring. When she saw Jeff's number she almost didn't answer it, but she saw on the caller ID that he'd called several times while they were gone, so this must be important.

The first words out of his mouth when she picked up were, "Where the hell have you been?"

Normally that would have annoyed the hell out of her, but Sydney had had such a fun weekend, nothing could spoil her good mood.

"We went away for the weekend," she told him.

"Without telling me? With *my* daughter," he snapped.

"Yes."

Her calm disposition seemed to infuriate him. "Where did you go?"

"Away with friends," she said.

"Friends? You mean your *boyfriend*."

"He was there."

"And you think that's an appropriate atmosphere for our daughter?"

"Yes, I do."

Her answer must have stunned him, because it took him a full ten seconds to respond. "I'm disappointed in you, Sydney. And you leave me no choice. I'm calling my lawyer in the morning and I'm going to file for sole custody."

As if she hadn't heard that tired old threat a dozen times before. "You go ahead and do that."

"You don't think I will?"

"Frankly, I don't care either way."

"Oh, I see. Now that you have a boyfriend, you don't want your daughter around?"

"Lacey is almost sixteen, Jeff. Do you honestly think a judge is going to change the custody order without talking to her first? And what do you suppose she'll say? That she'd love to go live with her dad and his girlfriend, the one he was screwing while he was still married to her mother? I'm sure she won't tell the judge what a horrible, humiliating experience it was to have the whole town know her family's business. So you go ahead and file for full custody."

"You're turning her against me," he said.

"No, you've done that all by yourself. Now, I have to go. I've got a date with my boyfriend." A boyfriend who cared about her feelings and treated her a damn sight better than Jeff ever had. And because of that, because of his decency, in the short time she had known Daniel, she'd come to care more about him, come to love him more, than she'd ever loved Jeff.

She was tempted to tell Jeff that, but he wasn't even worth the breath she'd have to expend. She hung up instead.

THE NEXT SIX WEEKS were more wonderful, more *perfect,* than Sydney could have ever hoped for. So wonderful and perfect, in fact, that she couldn't help wondering when the other shoe was going to drop. And when it finally did, it wasn't just one shoe. It felt like an entire closetful.

Her period was late.

She was sure it was fluke. She hadn't had a late period in four years, since she started taking birth control pills. And the fact that she was *on* the pill should have made getting pregnant impossible. Right?

But her period should have started on Tuesday, and now it was Friday and she hadn't so much as had a cramp. She didn't honestly think she could be pregnant, but she decided that taking a test, and seeing the negative result, would give her the reassurance she needed.

And if it wasn't negative? There was no point in even considering that, because it wasn't a possibility.

Daniel was working the afternoon shift, so after he left for work she packed April in the van and they took a trip to the store. She needed groceries anyway, so why not kill two birds, right? There were a dozen different brands of test, so she chose the most expensive, thinking it would be the most reliable, and grabbed a second, just in case the first was defective.

Back at her house, Sydney set April in her ExerSaucer, then carried in the groceries and put them away. She felt weird taking the test at Daniel's house. With her luck he would stop by and catch her in the act. Which would undoubtedly freak him out, even if it did turn out negative.

So she dragged the ExerSaucer into the hallway outside the bathroom, so she could keep an eye on April, then she sat on the edge of the toilet and read the directions thoroughly. Twice. Then, following them to the letter, she took the test.

Even though she was sure she wasn't pregnant, the next three minutes were among the longest of her life. *Pregnant* or *not pregnant*. She watched the seconds tick by, and when the three minutes were up she took a deep breath and turned it over.

Oh, shit.

Pregnant.

No, that couldn't be right. She was on the pill. There was no way she could be pregnant. She grabbed the second test and ripped open the plastic.

This time the three minutes took an *eternity*. She picked up the test with a trembling hand.

Shit.

Another positive.

No. This could *not* be happening. Then she had a thought. Maybe being on the pill could cause a false positive. Didn't it make a woman's body think it was pregnant?

That made perfect sense.

She heard the front door open, and Lacey called out.

Sydney grabbed the test wands and stuck them back in the box, which she then shoved into the cabinet under the sink.

"Why are you in this bathroom?" Lacey asked from the doorway.

"Straightening up," she lied, pulling herself to her feet. "Why are you home so early?"

"Early? It's almost six." She nodded to Sydney's shorts and tank. "Is that what you're wearing?"

"Wearing?"

"To the movie. Angie said she would be here at six-thirty to get pick you up."

Oh, hell. She had completely forgotten she and Angie were having a girls' night out and Lacey and Jordan were watching April. Dinner and a movie was the last thing she wanted to do right now. But she couldn't cancel on such short notice.

"I need to get in the shower," Lacey said. "I'm all sweaty from work."

"Sure, of course," Sydney said, stepping out into the hall, hoping Lacey wouldn't look under the sink.

"Are you okay?" Lacey asked. "You seem…nervous."

"No, I'm just…it's been a busy day."

"Okay, well, I'll be out in a few minutes."

It was too late to call the doctor's office, so Sydney grabbed April, went into the den and booted up the computer. She did an internet search on "birth control pills" and "false positive pregnancy tests." The more she read, the lower her heart sank. According to every source, there was nothing in birth control pills that could cause a false positive.

Meaning the odds were pretty good that she was pregnant.

She erased the search history and, feeling oddly numb, forced herself to go to her room and change, wondering how she was going to tell Daniel. How would he react? He already had one baby that he hadn't planned for. And she knew he didn't want to get married. Not yet, anyway. She honestly believed that they would be a family eventually, but after only a couple of months? She didn't think Daniel was even close to being ready for such a permanent commitment.

Sydney didn't need more time to know that she would be happy spending the rest of her life with him. And although it came as a shock, she wanted this baby. She loved Daniel. And though he had never said it, there was a chance he loved her, too.

And really, there was no reason she had to tell him right away. Maybe first she should try to get a feel for his state of mind. Hint around about the future and see how he reacted. And if he reacted badly? If he didn't want her or the baby? She couldn't fool herself into thinking that wasn't a possibility. At least this time it was *his* baby. Though given the circumstances, she wasn't sure how much of a consolation that would be.

"ARE YOU *sure* YOU'RE OKAY?" Angie asked as they were driving home from the movie theater.

"I'm fine," Sydney assured her, for about the fifteenth time since dinner. She was trying to act as if everything was normal, but it was tough. All Angie talked about during the meal was her pregnancy, and the small wedding she and Jason were planning for next month. Sydney had only managed to choke down a few bites of her pasta, and all through the film her mind kept wandering. She imagined a dozen different scenarios of what Daniel's reaction would be when she broke the news, and the next thing she knew the credits were rolling.

"So what did you think of the movie?" Angie asked.

"It was really good," Sydney said, even though she couldn't recall more than a few minutes of the story.

"Wasn't it hilarious when Jane pushed Devon off the dock into the water?"

She nodded, forcing a smile. "Yeah, it was funny."

Angie glanced over at her. "That never happened, and the characters names were Joan and Dennis."

Busted. "I guess I was a little distracted."

"Did you and Danny have a fight? Did he do something stupid? Because if he did, I'll totally kick his ass for you."

"He hasn't done anything. In fact, he's been wonderful. Other than arguing about where we're going for dinner, we never fight. It's almost too good." That meant something, right?

"There's no such thing as too good. And I'm glad to hear it, because you're the best thing that's ever happened to him."

Sydney just hoped Daniel felt the same way. But if he wasn't ready to get married yet, that was okay. There was no reason she and Daniel couldn't just live together, and raise April and the baby. They could be a family without being married.

"Daniel hasn't mentioned finding April's family lately. Has the P.I. had any news?"

"No. It was all pretty much a dead end. There was a cousin, but she was in rehab. Needless to say, she was in no condition to take a baby. He's looking into adoption now."

"He's not seriously going to give her up? He can't."

"Well, he got information from a couple of different agencies, and they all told him they could place April with no problem. That was almost a month ago and he hasn't made any arrangements. He hasn't said he's keeping her, but he also hasn't said he isn't."

"What the hell is this?" Angie said. Sydney followed her gaze out the windshield. The street was dark, but up ahead, in front of either her or Daniel's house, several police cars sat with their lights flashing.

Her heart dropped. Her first thought was April. Could she have choked or gotten hurt somehow? She was into everything now that she was crawling.

"Where are the kids?" Angie asked.

"Daniel's house."

As they got closer it was clear that the cars were parked in front of Sydney's house, and she could see Lacey and Jordan standing on Daniel's porch. And Lacey was holding April.

"Look," Sydney said, pointing them out. "They're fine."

"Thank God," Angie said, parking across the street from Daniel's house. They got out and Sydney could see that there was someone in the back of one of the patrol cars.

What the heck was going on?

"Sydney!"

She turned and saw Daniel, still in uniform, walking toward them from the side door.

"What's going on?" she asked him.

"Mom!" Lacey said, jogging up to her, April bouncing happily in her arms. Jordan was right behind her. "You are not going to believe what happened!"

"First, is everyone okay?" Angie asked, taking April from Lacey, looking her over thoroughly.

"Everyone is fine," Daniel assured her.

"Fred, Dad's gross handyman, was here again," Lacey said. "He grabbed me. But it's okay because Jordan punched his lights out."

Sydney's heart stalled. "What happened?"

"We were at Daniel's watching TV and we decided we wanted to watch the X-Men movie, so I came home to get it. I was unlocking the door and someone grabbed my arm. Then suddenly Jordan was there and he punched him."

"I was watching out the window," Jordan said. "It was dark, but I thought I saw someone sneaking around the house. I got there just as he grabbed her."

"And you punched him?" Angie said.

Jordan shrugged. "What else could I do?"

"He knocked him out cold with one punch," Daniel said, sounding proud of his nephew. Sydney was just relieved he'd been there to watch over her daughter.

"I think he's been following me around," Lacey said.

Sydney frowned. "What do you mean?"

"It seems like I've been seeing him everywhere lately."

"Why didn't you say something?"

"He never looks at me or talks to me, so I just figured it was a coincidence. I guess not. I told you he was a creep."

And Jeff thought Fred was harmless. She hoped he felt rotten when he learned what happened. Although, knowing Jeff, he would find a way to blame it on someone else. But Sydney was glad she listened to her instincts and changed the locks.

Jon Montgomery walked up to them.

"Hey, Angie. Hey, Syd," he said before turning to Daniel. "We're finished here. I'm going to take him in."

"I'll meet you there in a few minutes," Daniel said, then told Sydney and Angie, "Let's go inside."

They went over to Sydney's side door and gathered in the living room. Lacey must have gone in at some point because the lights were on.

"So, what happened after Jordan knocked this guy out?" Angie asked, sitting in an armchair with April. Lacey and Jordan sat on the couch.

"Jordan called me and I came right over," Daniel said. "Fred was just starting to come around when I pulled up."

"If you'll excuse me," Angie said, handing April to Lacey. "I don't want to miss anything, but I have a baby on my bladder. If I don't use your bathroom I'm going to wet myself."

"Go," Daniel said, waving her away.

"I want a restraining order against him," Sydney said. "I don't want him anywhere near my daughter."

"I think that's a good idea," Daniel said. "And I think an assault charge will stick if Lacey files a formal report."

"Does she have to do that tonight?"

"It can wait a day or two. Jon took her statement."

"And if we get a restraining order and Fred still bothers her?"

"California has pretty stiff anti-stalking laws. We'll keep him away from Lacey."

"We have a problem," Angie said coming back into the room. Everyone turned to look at her.

"What now?" Daniel asked.

"Look what I found on the bathroom counter." She was holding the pregnancy test box in one hand, and the wands in the other. "They're both positive."

How had they gotten on the bathroom counter?

"I'm sorry, Mom," Lacey said, looking mortified, her cheeks bright red. "I wanted to talk to you about it. That's why I left them out. I didn't think anyone else would see them."

"Jordan, I taught you better than this." Angie said, and the poor kid went white.

He stared at Lacey, then at his mom and said, "B-but, we haven't even had sex."

Well, that was good to know, although Sydney would have preferred not to find out quite like this.

"Angie, Lacey isn't pregnant," she said.

Clearly confused, Angie said, "But she said she put them there."

"I hid them under the sink, she found them and took them out."

"Syd?" Daniel said, now as pale as Jordan. There was no doubt *he* knew exactly what was going on.

This was not the way she'd intended to handle this.

Angie slapped a hand over her mouth. "Oh, my God, Sydney, I am so sorry. I thought…if I had known—"

"It's okay," Sydney said. But considering Daniel's shell-shocked expression, things were far from okay.

He was surprised. That's all. She just needed to give him a minute, to let it soak in. He would be fine after that.

"Lacey, Jordan," Angie said, setting the tests and boxes on the coffee table, "Why don't we go next door and put April to bed."

"Mom?" Lacey said, looking wary.

"Go ahead, honey. We'll talk later."

When they were gone Daniel reached out and picked up one of the tests, as if he had to see for himself.

He stared at it for a second, shaking his head, then he looked up at her and said, "What the hell, Sydney? How did this happen?"

"I don't know."

"You said you were on the pill."

"I was. I *am*."

"Did you miss a day? Forget to take it?"

She shook her head. "Never."

"Then how the *hell* did this happen?"

He was definitely not okay with this. He was nowhere near *okay*.

"I told you, I don't know how it happened. It just… did."

"I don't want kids."

"I know."

"You said all you wanted was *fun*."

"I remember what I said."

"What am I supposed to do now? Huh? *Marry* you? I don't want to marry *anyone*."

"Then you'll be happy to hear that I don't want to marry you, either." Why would she want to marry someone who didn't want her? Sydney had lived through that hell already. Definitely not a mistake she cared to repeat.

"I should have known this was too good to be true," he said. "I should have known there would be a catch."

"You say that like I did this on purpose."

"Did you?"

If he'd struck her, if he'd slapped her across the face, it couldn't have stung more. If Daniel thought that she was capable of something that underhanded and deceitful, he obviously didn't know her at all. And he sure wasn't the man she'd thought he was.

"Please leave," she said.

Those words, barely louder than a whisper, seemed to surprise him. He blinked, then opened his mouth as if he was about to say something, then closed it again. Then he did what she asked and left.

Feeling as if her legs might give out, Sydney sat on the couch. There was a pain in her chest, in her heart, so sharp and all-encompassing she found it difficult to breathe.

It was over. Just like that.

She heard a soft knock on the side door, and felt a glimmer of hope that maybe Daniel had come back. Maybe he wanted to at least say he was sorry. But it was Angie.

"Hey, you okay?"

"No. Not really."

"Sydney, I am so sorry. I never even considered that those might be yours."

"It's okay, Angie." If she had told him tonight, or next month, or three months from now, his reaction would have been the same. He didn't want a baby. And he didn't want a wife.

"He was upset?"

"You could say that."

"He was just surprised. You guys are going to be okay."

"No, we won't." The way Sydney felt right now, she would never be okay again.

CHAPTER SIXTEEN

WHEN DANIEL pulled into his driveway an hour later, Angie's car was still parked across the street. Sydney's house was dark.

He shut the engine off and sat there for a minute, not looking forward to going inside and having to hear about what a shit he'd been. He was already clear on that fact.

What he didn't understand was Sydney's reaction. Why didn't she tell him he was being a jerk? Why did she just stand there and let him push her away? Why didn't she...*fight?*

He looked at his front window and sighed. Might as well get this over with.

He crossed the lawn to the front door and let himself in. Angie was on the couch with her feet propped on the coffee table, watching TV. When he stepped inside she switched it off.

"April just had a bottle and she's out. The kids left pizza in the fridge." She grabbed her purse and fished out her keys, then stood. "I'll see you later."

She started to walk toward the door.

Wait, that was *it?* "You're not going to lecture me on what a bastard I am?"

She stopped and turned. "I think everyone is pretty clear about that."

Touché.

Angie stood there, obviously unwilling to divulge anything without making him ask for it. "Did you talk to Sydney?"

"Yes."

"What did she say?"

His sister folded her arms. "Not much. I did most of the talking."

"Was she mad?"

"No. I don't know what you said to her, but it worked."

"What do you mean?"

"You've pushed her away. She is...*done*."

"Done with what?"

"*You,* Danny." Angie shook her head, eyes filled not with anger or disappointment, but with pity. "You're alone again. But that's the way you like it. Right?"

With that she turned and walked out. What the hell was with everyone tonight? Why wasn't she calling him names and telling him what a huge mistake he'd made?

And he didn't believe Sydney would really write him off. He was the father of her child, for God's sake. Yeah, he'd overreacted. And insinuating that she'd done it on purpose was definitely not one of his finer moments. He obviously hadn't meant it. And she was entitled to be furious with him, but she would cool off and they would talk about this and figure something out.

And the only reason he'd reacted the way he had

was that as soon as he'd figured out the tests were hers and not Lacey's, he'd imagined him and Sydney, with Lacey, April and the baby, together as a family. And how happy they could be. And it had scared the living shit out of him. That had *never* been part of the plan. But now, somehow, it just…made sense. He was used to having her around. He *liked* having her around.

Which was probably why he was so determined to make her think he didn't.

Which he knew made no sense at all. But old habits were hard to break. He wasn't accustomed to letting people in. Or keeping them around.

Sydney was going to have to understand that it would take time. If they were going to make this work, they would have to take things slowly. Maybe they could live together for a while, and if that worked, then they could talk about getting married.

Maybe.

Since Daniel knew Sydney wouldn't come to him, he swallowed his pride the following morning and went to her. He owed her that much. But the second she answered the door, he could see what Angie meant. She didn't smile, didn't frown, she didn't look angry or upset. Her face wasn't red and puffy, as if she'd been crying.

She didn't betray any emotion at all, and it made him nervous.

"Can we talk?" he asked.

"There's nothing more to say. You were pretty clear about your feelings last night."

Yeah, he deserved that, although he didn't think she

was trying to hurt him or make him feel guilty. "Please, just for a minute."

She moved aside so he could step in.

"April is taking a nap," he said, even though she hadn't asked. He tapped the monitor receiver that was clipped to his belt. "I'll hear her if she wakes up."

No smile, no shrug. She just stared up at him, that nothingness in her eyes.

"I wanted to say that last night, I reacted…badly."

She didn't confirm or deny it, didn't say anything at all.

"The thing is, I'm really sorry for the way I behaved. When I insinuated that you did it on purpose, I didn't mean it."

Nothing. No reaction. She could have had the decency to swear at him, or tell him to take his apology and shove it.

He started to get a very bad feeling.

"Sydney, would you please say something?"

"What would you like me to say?"

"Something. Anything. You could acknowledge that I'm talking to you."

"I hear you."

"But you have no comment?"

"I'm not sure what you expect me to say."

"I want to make this work, Sydney."

She frowned. Finally some sign that she wasn't an empty shell. "Why?"

"Because…I do."

"But *why?*"

Daniel didn't know how to answer that. He knew

exactly *why,* but couldn't put it into words. "Because...
we're supposed to be together."

"Supposed to be together?"

"Yes."

"You and me."

"Yes."

"The man who was in my living room last night, I
don't even know who he was. And I have no idea what
you wanted me to do. Scream at you? Throw things?
Maybe that worked for your parents, but that isn't
me."

That hurt. Badly. All his life he had wanted to be
anything but like his parents. But he had been a jerk
last night. Instead of trying to talk it through he'd overreacted and he'd expected her to play along.

That was the last time it would ever happen. "The
man in your living room last night was not me."

"You know what they say. If it looks like a giraffe,
and walks like a giraffe..."

Through the monitor, he heard April start to cry.

"You should go get her," she said.

"Come with me. We'll talk."

"There's really nothing left to say."

"Sydney, please."

She held the door open. "Goodbye."

Daniel had a million things he wanted to say to her,
if he could make her listen. And if there *was* a way, he
sure as hell didn't know how. She had obviously made
up her mind.

Angie had been right. Sydney was *done.*

And he'd been home five minutes before he realized

that leaving, not staying and fighting, was without a doubt one of his stupidest moves yet. And suddenly he knew exactly what he wanted to say.

What he should have said a long time ago.

DANIEL SERIOUSLY did not know when to quit.

Sydney thought she'd made herself pretty darned clear. And it had taken every ounce of strength she possessed not to break down, not to throw herself into his arms and tell him she loved him. But what would be the point? He wanted her now because he knew he couldn't have her anymore. Or maybe it was the same overdeveloped sense of responsibility that had motivated him to take April in. He felt compelled to do right by his child.

Whatever the reason, he was back at her door an hour later. This time carrying April. And this time he didn't ask if they could talk, or wait for her to step aside. He simply waltzed right in.

And for a second she just stood there, unsure of what to do. He was obviously having trouble with the whole breaking-up concept.

He walked through the kitchen and disappeared into the living room. She was about to follow him, when he returned carrying the ExerSaucer. He set it by the kitchen table and put April in it. "Talking may now commence," he said.

Who said she wanted to talk? Hadn't she already said that she was done talking?

"Should I start?" he asked, almost...cheerfully.

There was something very different about him. He

wasn't the repentant, remorseful man he'd been an hour ago. The one who didn't have a clue what he wanted or why. Only that he wanted *something.*

This guy *knew,* and it was making her uneasy. He'd blown it. He didn't deserve a second chance.

Sydney turned her back to him, leaning on the counter and looking out the window. "I don't want to talk to you."

"Is this what you did to Jeff? You froze him out? Is that what your mom did to you?"

She spun around.

He shrugged. "Hey, if you get to play the family dysfunction card, so do I."

She hated that he was right. That was exactly what her mother used to do. When she couldn't cope, she shut down. And yes, Sydney had probably done the same thing to Jeff. But her mother had an excuse. She was clinically depressed.

Sydney was fairly well-balanced, all things considered.

Daniel took a step toward her and she took one back, colliding with the edge of the counter. And she had that peculiar feeling again, like the first time he'd been in her kitchen. He was too…big. He was gobbling up all the air in the room.

"This isn't going to work, Daniel. I can't be with someone who freaks out every time things get a little stressful."

"And I can't be with someone who shuts down every time I freak out."

Uh, hadn't he just proved her point?

"And right now you're thinking that I just proved your point."

She blinked.

He took another step toward her. "But you're wrong." He paused, and when she didn't speak he said, "This is the part when you ask me *why*."

Okay, she would play along. "Why?"

"Because we're supposed to be together."

He took yet another step toward her, too close now. *Way* too close. She couldn't think straight.

"Ask me why," he said.

Like an obedient child, she asked, "Why?"

He propped his hands on the edge of the counter on either side of her, leaning in. "Because I love you. Because I want to marry you, have babies with you and spend the rest of my life with you."

Wow. For weeks she'd wanted to hear those words from him, but she never imagined him saying them with such feeling, with so much naked emotion in his eyes.

He wasn't telling her what he thought she wanted to hear. He meant every word.

He leaned in farther and kissed her so softly, so sweetly, that she felt herself melt. There was no way she could stay mad at him now. "In case you weren't sure," he whispered, pressing his forehead to hers, "this is the part where you tell me you love me, too."

"I do. I love you, Daniel." She closed her eyes and smiled. After keeping it bottled up inside for so long, it felt good to finally say the words. "I've wanted to say that for a really long time."

He pulled back a little so he could look at her, reached

up and touched her cheek. "I'm not going to lie to you. The idea of forever still scares me. But the idea of losing you? That *terrifies* me."

"And April?"

He looked over at the baby, bouncing in her seat, babbling at the toys, and smiled. "She managed to turn my entire life upside down. But I couldn't love her more if she were my own flesh and blood. She's my daughter. Although she figured that out a long time before I did."

Sydney wrapped her arms around him. "I never really believed you would give her up."

"Deep down I don't think I did, either. And I'll bet she's going to be an *awesome* big sister."

She smiled against his chest and hugged him tighter.

"I'm really sorry, Sydney, for the way I acted. I seem to have this knack for ruining what should be happy, tender moments."

"I actually never expected you to be happy about it. I hoped, but I didn't expect."

"Are you saying that I exceeded your expectations?"

She laughed. "I guess that's one way to look at it."

He lifted her chin, so he could look at her. "I'm happy now. I've been happy ever since you backed into my car and I made you nervous as hell. I knew there was something special about you."

"I'm happy, too." In fact, Sydney hadn't known it was possible to be this happy. She hugged him tight again, unable to let go just yet, and glanced over at the wall beside the door. That ridiculous hole was still there. She'd gotten so used to it, she barely noticed anymore. But she was glad it was there. It had become a symbol, a reminder that not so long ago her life had reached an all-time low, and here she was now, the happiest she'd ever been.

Funny how that worked. And she wouldn't have it any other way.

* * * * *

You're Invited to a *Double* Baby Shower!
For: Sydney Valenzia & Baby Boys (yes, two!)
Angelica Parkman & Baby Boy and Girl
Time: 2:00 p.m.
Given by: The very proud (and slightly over-whelmed) Grandmother and Aunts.

Bring your favorite dish to pass and plan on having a lot of fun!